under the influence

noelle crooks

under the influence

a novel

GALLERY BOOKS

New York   London   Toronto   Sydney   New Delhi

G

Gallery Books
An Imprint of Simon & Schuster, Inc.
1230 Avenue of the Americas
New York, NY 10020

First Gallery Books hardcover edition August 2023

GALLERY BOOKS and colophon are registered trademarks of Simon & Schuster, Inc.

For information about special discounts for bulk purchases, please contact Simon & Schuster Special Sales at 1-866-506-1949 or business@simonandschuster.com.

The Simon & Schuster Speakers Bureau can bring authors to your live event. For more information or to book an event, contact the Simon & Schuster Speakers Bureau at 1-866-248-3049 or visit our website at www.simonspeakers.com.

Interior design by Davina Mock-Maniscalco

Manufactured in the United States of America

10 9 8 7 6 5 4 3 2 1

Library of Congress Cataloging-in-Publication Data

Names: Crooks, Noelle, author.
Title: Under the influence : a novel / Noelle Crooks.
Description: First Gallery Books hardcover edition. | New York : Gallery Books, 2023.
Identifiers: LCCN 2023003690 (print) | LCCN 2023003691 (ebook) |
   ISBN 9781668004944 (hardcover) | ISBN 9781668004951 (trade paperback) |
   ISBN 9781668004968 (ebook)
Subjects: LCSH: Young women—Fiction. | LCGFT: Novels.
Classification: LCC PS3603.R66545 U53 2023 (print) | LCC PS3603.R66545 (ebook) |
   DDC 813.6—dc23/eng/20230308
LC record available at https://lccn.loc.gov/2023003690
LC ebook record available at https://lccn.loc.gov/2023003691

ISBN 978-1-6680-0494-4
ISBN 978-1-6680-0496-8 (ebook)

To everyone who has always believed in me.
But more important, to everyone who didn't.
(Yep, it's that kind of book.)

under the influence

1

Girl's Gotta Eat!

Girl, are you tired of everyone telling you what you can and can't do? Are you so over the patriarchy and middle-aged white dudes mansplaining how things work in the "real world"? Ever wish that people who talked so much about the real world actually lived in it so people like you and me could succeed?

I'm talking money, girl, like the money you need to pay your bills and your rent and to buy those cute outfits that you deserve to be wearing. Real money, not my-parents-are-rich-so-I-can-take-an-internship-and-still-make-it money, but I'm-gonna-earn-my-way-to-the-top-'cause-I-got-hustle-for-days-and-what-I-lack-in-connections-I-make-up-for-with-ambition kind of money. Money you earned and deserve, fair and square.

We all gotta eat, girl, but we don't have to eat sh*t, if you know what I mean. So if you're more interested in getting sh*t done than taking it—and if you want to join a diverse community of like-minded badass babes who know that the world is better when we let everyone have a seat at the table—then this is the *job for you. But we don't like to call this a job. It's more of a calling, an answer to the warrior woman who lives inside of you, the one who is willing to break barriers and shatter glass ceilings!*

We're manifesting a new Visionary Support Strategist to be the right hand to our superstar founder. As the newest team member, you'll be learning from the best and crushing the rest. From daily tasks to innovative asks, our fast-paced environment will give you countless opportunities to shine. So, if this sounds like something you'd be interested in, what are you waiting for, girl? Join us at The Greenhouse!

"You're not serious," Harper said, looking up from the screen at her roommate, Poppy, who was refilling their glasses of rosé and smiling.

"I'm totally serious, and you have to admit it's kind of dead-on about all the things you've been bitching about."

"I haven't been bitching," Harper said, stung, because yes, she had been bitching. If Harper were honest, it was the only thing she had been successful at for the last three months.

She accepted her refill and sat back on her end of the couch facing Poppy, their legs outstretched toward each other. They always sat like this, with Poppy's legs, which went on for days, hanging over the armrest on either side of Harper. In the middle, on the blanket draped over their knees, they propped up the ever-present bowl of popcorn that they picked at when reading magazines, books, their iPads, or, like tonight, job listings on a laptop they passed back and forth between them.

"I can't say I blame you for being fed up, and by the sound of this ad, you're not alone. And while I don't love being called out for being wealthy enough to work for free, it *is* true, so . . ."

"You work hard, Poppy; I've never seen anyone work as hard as you do. Besides, I'm grateful to your parents for letting me live here for so little. I wouldn't be able to live in Manhattan on a freelancer's salary if it weren't for them." It still nearly killed Harper to pay her share of the rent each month, cobbled together from the cater-waiter jobs she did on the weekends and the college essays she edited and overcharged for. After a series of bad luck that had seen Harper lose her job at a literary agency after it folded and then an entry-level job at a small publishing house when it was gobbled up in a merger, she still hadn't been able to find a steady paying gig. She hadn't expected it to be so hard to find another job where she would be overworked and underpaid—New York was full of them. But at twenty-seven, when there were younger competitors who were willing to work more and get paid less, Harper's road seemed to be leading nowhere.

"My parents are fine with what you pay. Besides, they've had this place forever. They got it when my dad was doing his residency, and I'm sure they paid nothing for it back in the day."

It was true that the large, boxy two-bedroom apartment in a prewar doorman building on the Upper East Side had been acquired for a fraction of what it was worth now, but even that fraction was the kind of money that Harper had never known. Like everyone else who had only experienced New York City through movies or books, Harper Cruz had arrived in Manhattan looking to find the kind of real estate steal that characters in television shows always mentioned when justifying their giant apartments in prime neighborhoods—the ones they were supposedly house-sitting or that had been passed down to them or were miraculously rent-controlled.

Harper had chosen to believe that she was going to be lucky too, because Manhattan Harper's life was going to be far more glamorous than Poughkeepsie Harper's life. But she soon realized the only apartment she could afford was the one in New Jersey she ended up sharing with a cat-loving schoolteacher named Norma. The commute into the city was brutal.

If life were a movie, a handsome, wealthy man would have bumped into our young, fish-out-of-water protagonist on the subway, asking her: *Hey, what's with all the hives on your face?* She'd tell him it turned out that she was allergic to her roommate's cats, but she couldn't leave now because she'd given her first and last months' rent, which was really all the money she had left. She'd assure him that the two-hour commute wasn't all that bad because it gave her time to read in the mornings. She could just take an antihistamine every day, even though that made her drowsy. And he'd look at her like he was charmed by her weird logic, swollen face, and puffy eyes, and say something like, *You know, my roommate is moving out, and if you wanted, you could take his room. You'd only have to pay the maintenance fee on the apartment, 'cause my rich parents aren't looking to make money on the place. They just want me to have someone who is stable and nice and normal to live with, no strings attached, no funny stuff . . . So what do you say, Hives?* And of course, our heroine would say *yes!* and we would all feel butterflies in our stomachs because clearly, sparks are going to fly between these two, and we cannot wait to see it all unfold!

In real life, that handsome young stranger had been Poppy, Harper's gorgeous coworker at the now-defunct literary agency they met at. Standing just shy of six foot two, Poppy was the type of beauty that required no makeup and looked like a long-lost Hadid sister. The departing roommate, who was actually a model, spent all her time partying and always ended up bringing the party home, so anyone compared to her looked pretty great to Poppy's parents. And instead of a romance, a friendship flourished because it turned out that Poppy was even nicer than she was beautiful. So it all worked out in the end . . . at least until Harper lost her job twice and discovered just how hard it was to get another one. Whether she liked it or not, Harper had entered the beggars-can't-be-choosers phase of her job hunt.

"I don't know," Harper said, reading the ad again. "*Girl? Badass babe?* Can you imagine Gretchen calling us that?"

"I can't imagine Gretchen remembering our names, which is why she called us *Lady* all the time," Poppy said, adding chili-lime salt to her palmful of popcorn. "Come to think of it, I don't think she remembered anyone's names, not even her authors, which is probably why her literary agency folded."

"Hey, *Lady*, I need you to do something for me," Harper said, imitating her former boss. "I'm not sure which is worse—lady or girl?"

"Lady," Poppy said, rolling her eyes.

"You're just saying that to make me feel better. I told you, you don't have to feel bad about your promotion. You deserve it. You're a great editor." Harper meant it, although she would be lying if she didn't admit that part of her found it hard to watch Poppy's obstacle-free ascent to associate editor at a major publishing house. Having financial security meant that Poppy didn't have to take on extra work after hours to make ends meet. She was free to attend as many literary events and network with her well-connected parents' even more well-connected friends as much as she wanted, without ever worrying about her credit card being rejected at lunches or cocktails. "If there's anyone I want to see killing it out there, it's you and not some—"

"Other rich girl who can afford to work fourteen-hour days for fifty thousand a year?" Poppy said, knocking Harper's shoulder with her foot.

"Exactly. Those other girls suck." Harper said it to make her roommate laugh, and it worked.

Even though Poppy was privileged, she did her best to make the most of it by volunteering what little time she had at the nearest library, where she ran adult literacy programs and handled preschool story time the third Tuesday of every month. She was passionate about the work she did, but nothing was going to change the fact that Poppy didn't actually *have* to work for a living. And if things went the way Poppy's parents expected them to, starting with her marrying her doctor-boyfriend, Charles, and moving back to Connecticut to raise a family, she might actually stop working one day. But unlike Poppy, Harper *needed* to make money . . . *like the money you need to pay your bills and your rent and to buy those cute outfits that you deserve to be wearing.*

Harper took another look at the ad, which was obnoxious but catchy. She had to admit: it did feel like it was speaking directly to her.

"I don't even know what this job is for," she said, scanning the listing for more details.

"It's *not* for a small press in Poughkeepsie," Poppy said, tilting her head and looking Harper in the eye.

A job as an editor at the *Poughkeepsie Press,* the town's tiny literary magazine, had just opened, and Harper's parents weren't exactly subtle about wanting her to apply for it. She knew they were only trying to help, especially since they were no longer going to be able to support her financially anymore, but the thought of moving back home still made her want to die a little. It was bad enough she had to ask for help after she lost both jobs, hoping she'd be able to find something else quickly. But now that she knew her parents' business was struggling, that was no longer an option. And if she wanted to avoid moving back home, she would have to change her situation—fast.

"Point taken," Harper said.

Poppy reached for the laptop. "*Visionary Support Strategist.* You have to admit, that sounds way cooler than *Entry Level Editorial Assistant.*"

Harper had to admit that it did.

"And what does it pay?" Harper asked. She'd missed it the first time.

"*Better than average, with perks,*" Poppy said, reading aloud. "And, wait for it, a housing allowance *because living in the city ain't cheap*."

"You're kidding."

"I'm not!" Poppy said. "You should apply! What do you have to lose?"

"I don't know . . ."

"Look, I attached your résumé. You can always hit send. If you get contacted, do the interview, and if it's not for you, you don't have to take it. I can float you for another month, it's no big deal." She reached over and patted Harper's hand. "Now, I'm going to call Charles and have him get us some more wine and some food on his way over. And don't worry, I've got this," she said, getting up to call her incredibly nice boyfriend.

Soon he would arrive with food and drinks and flowers and probably even something for Harper, because he was thoughtful that way, but after that would soon follow another night of Harper being forced to listen to Poppy and Charles having loud sex through their bedrooms' thin shared wall, and getting a crick in her neck from the noise-canceling headphones she would have to wear if she wanted to get any sleep.

In the morning, they'd invite her to breakfast after they went jogging because she had no plans, and offer to pay because she had no money, and she'd decline and go to Central Park instead with her everything bagel with cream cheese. She'd sit on the same sad bench she used to share with Dylan, her high school boyfriend turned college boyfriend turned ex, who dumped her after they graduated from NYU because he didn't love New York City the way she did and wanted to move back home. He liked his small-town life and his small-town dreams. Apparently, he also liked wasting her time.

Harper had waited for that moment when he would come back to tell her he had made a mistake—a real-life rom-com—but he never did. Then she waited for someone else to take his place, but that didn't happen either. Then she'd vowed that she'd show them all, *them* being an umbrella category that would go beyond her ex and the guys she went on terrible dates with to include employers and coworkers of all kinds by *becoming* a giant success. But instead, here she was, a little tipsy, a lot broke, and desperate to turn things around.

Harper exhaled loudly, polished off her glass of wine, and pulled the laptop close. The words *what are you waiting for* shone up at her, demanding an answer. Realizing she didn't have one, she hit send.

2

#Girlbosses

Welcome to the team, girl!
You got this! Hit me back for
meeting deets!

Harper checked the time on her phone—7:30 a.m., too early to be getting texts on a Sunday morning, especially when they contained this many exclamation points. She rubbed the sleep out of her eyes and tried to bend her ear to her shoulder. She had indeed fallen asleep with her headphones on again. It had been a busy night for Poppy and Charles. She was just about to text back *Who is this?* when her screen lit up again.

FYI-Bella here, by the way,
Charlotte Green's Support Superstar
at The Greenhouse. We're so excited
to meet you! We're wheels up at
9:30 am, so text me back ASAP.

Wheels up? Welcome to the team? There must be some kind of mistake. Harper had only submitted her résumé the night before. She was about to go back to bed when Poppy appeared in her doorway, already in her Alo Yoga running gear, holding up her phone.

"Someone named Bella is on the phone for you. She said she's been trying to reach you all morning about the job and hasn't heard back."

"All morning?" Harper whispered incredulously. "She just texted me. Why is she calling you? And how did she get your number?"

"I'm one of your references, remember?" Poppy passed her the phone, looking excited.

"Hi, this is Harper Cruz."

"Oh, Harper, thank God, I thought something happened to you when I didn't hear back."

"You only texted me a few minutes ago," Harper said, stunned.

"I know, right? Anything could've happened in that time. You could've fallen in the shower, been mugged, or choked on a bagel. Hashtag New York problems! Anyway, I'm just glad you're okay. So now, more importantly, *loved* your application, *loved* your references, *loved* your Insta and Facebook profiles, though they are a bit sparse . . ."

"Wait, you checked my . . ."

"Totally jelly that you have a rad pad in Manhattan, but it'll still be there when you get back."

"Get back from where?"

"We'll be at your place in thirty minutes. I thought you could meet Charlotte on the way to the airport, do your interview, then have some one-on-one time. If all goes well, you can get a flight out to Nashville tonight and get settled, and tomorrow we can hit the ground running!" Bella's cheerful voice rang in Harper's ears.

"Wait, hold up—*Nashville*?" Harper asked. She didn't remember the ad saying anything about Nashville.

"You'll love it."

"I don't even know what my responsibilities are, or what the starting salary is."

Harper looked up to see Poppy, who was giving her a reassuring thumbs-up.

Bella was quiet on the other end of the phone for a moment and then spoke, her voice serious. "Look, I know it seems fast, but when Charlotte knows, she knows, and out of all the applications, she picked yours personally. She's a one-woman empire with three bestselling books, a series of webinars, sold-out conferences, and more meaningful collaborations than anyone else I know. So when she says she knows, people listen. I listen. *You* should listen. But if working for a powerhouse for a starting salary of a hundred and twenty thousand dollars at a company that believes women crush it literally every damn day isn't for you, then tell me now. But we had fifteen hundred applicants apply to our job posting and it was only up for an hour, and to be honest, I'd really rather not go through all of them."

"Wow, I don't know what to say."

"Take a second. Think about it," Bella said. "I'll call you back." She hung up the phone, and in answer to the look of curiosity on Poppy's face, Harper blurted out, "Fifteen hundred applicants, Charlotte Green picked me personally, one hundred and twenty k—" But before she could say anything else, the phone was ringing. Clearly, when Bella said to take a second, she meant literally.

Harper looked up at Poppy, who looked at Charles as he joined her in the doorway, having overheard the whole thing from the living room. He gave Harper a big encouraging smile, then leaned in and kissed Poppy on the neck. He whispered something in her ear, making her blush. Unwittingly, Harper reached her hand to her own neck and wondered when the last time was that someone had kissed her that tenderly. For a brief time, Harper had really believed that all her dreams were going to come true—but now it felt like she had nothing. Everything good that she had was thanks to Poppy, and how much longer could this living situation possibly last? Charles was always sleeping over, and Harper wouldn't be surprised if Poppy got engaged by the spring, and then what did she expect them to do? Let her stay living with them forever? Adopt her?

She picked up the phone. Bella's voice bursting with energy on the other end of the line. "So what do you say, girl—are you ready to crush this interview?"

It was nice to be wanted for a change, it was nice to hear yes, and 120k was more than triple what she would've made if she'd been promoted before the publishing company ended. Not to mention that every penny would go a lot further in Nashville. She could pay Poppy back, she could make her student loan payments on time, she could stop being a burden to her parents, she could find a new calling . . . A little voice inside her said, *Slow down, you don't even know who this Charlotte Green is. You took a long time making New York work, spent years doing it, don't rush into anything.* But the idea of starting her twenty-seventh year with a brand-new job and an exciting new place to live was a hell of a lot more appealing than going home to Poughkeepsie and telling her parents she was still unemployed and broke, or having Poppy and Charles take her somewhere nice and try to cheer her up with stories that the best was yet to come. Maybe the best had just arrived with this insane job offer? Maybe this time it really was her time. At this point, she had nothing left to lose.

She made eye contact with Poppy and smiled, giving her a thumbs-up. Poppy clapped her hands together in excitement.

"You know what, *girl*?" she said. "I am ready to crush that interview!"

While Harper ran around getting ready, Poppy sat on the edge of Harper's bed, scrolling the internet for information about Charlotte and shouting it out.

"She's big," Poppy said, her eyes scanning the screen. "She has almost two million followers, three bestselling books, and a series of self-help webinars."

"Really? So why do I know nothing about her?" Harper asked,

coming over to look at Poppy's phone. There was a photo of Charlotte holding up a green smoothie in a perfectly clean, all-white kitchen—#drinkyourGREENS—and another of the Green family on a boat for the Fourth of July, all of them wearing coordinating red, white, and blue stripes—#ProudToBeAnAmerican; #ProudToBeAGreen—and Charlotte at some influencer summit in Aspen—#girlbosses.

"I don't know. How many self-help influencer gurus do you follow?"

"Follow? None," Harper replied. Ask her about her favorite authors or the best book of the year, and she could tell you. But when it came to social media, Harper had about as much knowledge as cat-loving Norma.

"I've heard of her," Charles said, bringing them coffee. "She's this tiny little powerhouse with long blond hair, married to this giant New England Ken doll. And she always wears these green Vans—it's her trademark. She used to wear black stilettos all the time, but then she changed it up to stand out from all the other heel-wearing influencers."

"*Why* do you know all of this?" Poppy asked, slightly horrified.

"Because my aunt Minnie loves her."

"Aunt Minnie, the one who lives in Texas with the boozy book club?"

"Red, white, and true," Charles said. He handed Harper a mug. "They only do romance novels about true love and inspirational nonfiction books. And they drink red and white wine. A *lot* of it."

"Okay . . ." Harper said, trying to keep up.

"Anyway, the last time I visited her, Charlotte was all she would talk about. Quotes her all the time! *Give yourself the Greenlight. Stop saying no and start saying go.* Charlotte's big on self-transformation, and my aunt credits her with transforming her from being a sad housewife to a rich divorcée—and inspiring her to wear more comfortable shoes."

"Okay, well, I'm happy for your aunt Minnie, but I should probably do a bit more research," Harper said, sipping her coffee.

"You don't have much time for research; she'll be here soon," Poppy said. "But look, you're smart, you're hardworking, and if you can work for Gretchen, you can work for anyone. There's a reason she picked you out of all those other applicants, so don't worry. You'll figure it out as you go, *girl*!"

"*Girl*, you know I will!" Harper said, hoping that if she said it like she meant it, it could be true.

3

Flying High

Charlotte Green rolled up to Harper's apartment building exactly twenty-nine minutes later. Charlotte was always early, Bella had told Harper via text, except when she was late, which didn't really count because it meant that she had a really good reason or was putting out some fire or dealing with something so important that it couldn't wait. But because she was always early for her people her people always needed to be early for her.

"Cute outfit," Charlotte said, giving Harper the once-over and nodding approvingly after Harper had settled into the back seat of the Lincoln Navigator. Charlotte was so tiny that her green Vans barely touched the floor. She twirled one of her strategically waved strands of long blond hair and tucked it behind an ear that was studded with a series of small diamonds and pearls. Pursing her glossy lips, she narrowed her eyes and took Harper in.

"*Super* cute," she emphasized, then adjusted her oversize soft tan cashmere sweater wrap and brushed an imaginary piece of lint off her jeans.

Harper had done the best she could in the time she had. She'd sprayed her hair with dry shampoo, pulled it back into a messy bun, slapped on some tinted moisturizer and mascara, and gave herself bright red lips and gold hoop earrings. She'd put on a black jumpsuit, white VEJA sneakers, and her tortoiseshell glasses.

"Thank you," Harper said, trying to figure out why Charlotte was being so fidgety. But then she caught a look in Bella's giant dark brown eyes, a look of pleading. Bella tilted her head toward Charlotte, her mouth silently saying, *Compliment her.* Oh.

"I love your sweater," Harper blurted out. "That color is amazing on you."

Harper had never before complimented a boss on their appearance, never mind one she'd never met before. It was a weird thing to do, but she could feel the energy shift in the car the moment she did, Charlotte brightening and Bella's whole face relaxing.

"Thank you. It's part of my upcoming collaboration with Target," Charlotte said with a happy sigh. "The ones in the store won't be cashmere because *hashtag price point*, but they'll have the same great color and feel. It's like wrapping yourself up in a great big hug, or better yet, it's like getting a great big hug from *me*. No, it's like . . ." She pursed her mouth and furrowed her brow, looking at Bella.

"It's like a . . . *community* hug?" Bella offered, tossing her long black hair over her shoulder.

Charlotte shook her head and turned to Harper, her blue eyes wide, waiting.

"It's like . . . a *group hug* because we're all in this together, *girl*?" she said, not exactly sure how to play this particular game.

"Yes, love that. That's it. Write that down, Bella. I love how we just jammed on that, how you took what *I* came up with and used it as inspiration to build on."

"Well, you make it easy because you always have the best ideas, so there's just so much to work with," Bella said, fawning.

"It's true, I do give you a lot. It's just who I am," Charlotte replied. She placed her hand on Harper's and squeezed it. "I'm a really generous boss. My team is the best because I handpick them myself, and because we work so closely together, they get a chance to grow from my mentorship and realize their full potential. We're like a family, minus the screaming kids. Child labor and all."

"Right," Harper said, slowly.

"Although I sure wouldn't mind sending my little buggers off to work once in a while, the spoiled brats."

Before Harper could say anything, Charlotte laughed and slapped her arm. "I'm kidding! I love my kids, all five of them."

"Six," Bella corrected.

"Right— I mean the five that I gave birth to. The one step-kid's easy to forget because he lives with his mom in Connecticut and hates my guts. The point is, I'm a family person, and not only do I treat every one of my employees like family, I make it my mission to give them as many opportunities as I can to help them be the best they can be. Not every boss is like that, but I'm not like any other boss. I *really* care." Charlotte tapped her fist to her heart. She closed her eyes and started to rock back and forth, pumping herself up, her face full of emotion. She put her finger in the air and moved it in a circle, the way people did on film sets to say that the cameras were rolling. Bella pulled out her phone to film whatever impromptu inspirational speech was about to happen, her face mirroring the emotion on Charlotte's. Harper, having no idea what was happening, leaned back in her seat and watched in surprise.

Charlotte spoke directly to the camera. "When people ask me why I care so much, I tell them it's because I've been there. I know what it's like to have to build your life from scratch because I've done it."

"By yourself . . ." Bella whispered.

"By myself. I had no one to rely on but me. I didn't get any hand-outs . . ."

"No, you didn't," Bella said.

"But I sure heard no a lot."

"All the time."

"But I took those nos and turned them into yeses."

"Because that's what you do," Bella said.

"Because that's what I do," Charlotte repeated. "And that's what I want you to do too, my Greenhouse Fam, because I care about you. I'm a highly empathetic person, which means that sometimes I care about you so much that it hurts. But it's worth it, because *you're* worth it," she exclaimed, blinking back real tears as she preached to the camera. "That's right. Every single one of you is worth it. And if I can do this, you can too. I got your back, *girl,* just like you have mine, and together we're going to *crush it. See you in Nashville!*"

She smiled and took a deep breath, nodding her head knowingly for a moment. Then she signaled *Cut* and Bella pressed stop.

"That was amazing!" Bella shouted, high-fiving Charlotte.

Charlotte looked at Harper, who was quickly trying to rearrange the look of shock and horror on her face into something more closely resembling appreciation and awe. "Wow," she said slowly, "that was . . . amazing. I mean, I don't even know what to say."

Saying "that was absolutely insane" certainly wasn't going to help her chances of landing this job.

"It's just what I do. We get a lot of my best stuff on the fly, you know, real from-the-heart stuff, because that's what my fans identify with. I'm real like them, although not exactly like them, obviously." She gestured to the car, her enamel Chanel watch and large diamond wedding ring shining brightly as she did. "But you know what I mean."

"Sure, you're inspirational and aspirational all rolled into one," Harper said, treading carefully.

"I told you," Charlotte said to Bella, "even if she's never heard of me, she'll pick it up quickly."

"I've heard of you," Harper said, hoping she wouldn't have to be more specific. Telling Charlotte that she heard she was a hit with middle-aged Texan women who liked to get their drink on wasn't exactly going to cut it.

Charlotte turned to Harper, her eyes narrowed and her face serious.

"No, you haven't, not really. And I know that because I wasn't in any of your hashtags on Instagram and Twitter, neither of my books were in your Goodreads queue, and you once tweeted that the only influencer you knew was the kind that put you in bed with a fever of one hundred and two degrees for three days."

"I was joking," Harper said, turning red. "It was a joke about the flu. In*flu*encer? Get it?" From the outer edges of her brain, she pulled Corrine James's name into focus and, in an effort to impress Charlotte, trotted it out. "And actually, I've met an influencer. Corrine James. She was an author my boss worked with. She came in to talk about women in the workplace and—"

Harper was just about to say that Corrine's talk had taught her a lot when she caught Bella's panicked expression. She shook her head and ran her finger back and forth across her throat, signaling for Harper to cut it.

"If you really knew anything about me, you'd know that C.J. and I can't stand each other. She's a privileged snob who cares more about Wall Street than Main Street, and she treats her business like a corporation instead of a community. Maybe that's because she never had to pay her own way, unlike those of us who had student loans and had to work two jobs to put ourselves through college, am I right?" Charlotte said, flicking her hair over her shoulder and leveling a stare at Harper.

"Totally, that's why I knew I wanted to work for you, you get it," Harper lied, hoping to turn things around.

Charlotte smiled, her sunny disposition returning. "Anyways, what I'm saying is, it doesn't matter. If I wanted a sycophant, I could be offering this job to the other fourteen hundred and ninety-nine people who applied for it. But I want a fresh perspective, a new set of eyes, and a more cosmopolitan take on things."

"Okay . . ."

"And we really believe in diversity at The Greenhouse, so I think you'll feel really at home there," Charlotte said, nodding sincerely. "Just ask Bella."

"I'm not sure I know what you mean," Harper said.

"Well, because Bella's half Asian, and you're half Filipino. You are half Filipino, right? That's what Bella said. Isn't that what you said, Bella?"

"Well, I just thought because your last name is Cruz . . . and I did some looking, not that it matters," Bella said quickly.

"Uh yeah, my mom's Filipino, and my dad's family is all from Pennsylvania. Cruz is my mom's maiden name and my middle name, but I use it professionally . . ." Harper said, not sure where this was going.

"Love that. Feminism," Charlotte said. "And just so you know, I have so much respect for immigrants like your mom, and Bella's family. They have the best work ethic—am I right?"

"I guess," Harper said, feeling uncomfortable.

"My point is, I believe in embracing everyone at The Greenhouse. I don't care if you're gay, straight, Black, white, Asian, or all of the above. My creative director, Oliver, is gay and Indian, and he's also one of my best friends. And let me tell you, we raised a lot of eyebrows when we were growing up in Georgia, but we said fuck you if you had a problem with it. Sorry, I cuss sometimes. Do you cuss?"

Harper's head was spinning, unsure whether she should find Charlotte's speech on diversity alarming or reassuring.

"Sometimes, I guess . . ."

"You're shocked; I shocked you. I'm just trying to keep it real. So forgive me if I went about that differently from what you might be used to here in New York. I'm sure there's some politically correct HR-approved method to have that conversation, but I'm a Georgia Peach, and in Georgia, we believe you can be sweet *and* a straight shooter, like sweet tea spiked with whiskey. Is that okay with you?" Charlotte leaned forward.

"As long as we're only shooting metaphorically," Harper said, laughing nervously.

"Thatta girl," Charlotte replied, smiling. "You're funny too. I got that from your writing. I liked the piece you did that went viral. The one about interns with a side hustle that explained how they were *really* able to live on those small salaries? So many dog walkers and babysitters. I could totally relate. I had three jobs when I started out. Hustle was how I got where I am. It's also why I believe in paying people properly." She leaned back against her seat and smiled.

"You are *so* generous," Bella agreed.

"I am, and I believe in rewarding talent. You're a good writer, Harper. Maybe you could even write for me one day."

"But I thought *I* was in charge of your social," Bella said, looking at Charlotte, her eyes wide.

"You are, but I'm talking *real* writing, Bella. Harper's been to college . . ."

"I've been to college," Bella said.

"I know that, but you didn't go to *NYU*, not that I'm judging. I mean, look at me—I went to little ol' Georgia University, and I'm a huge freaking success. Tri Delta sister, top of my class . . . but I don't like to brag about it, of course. It makes people feel intimidated, and that's not me."

"Of course not," Bella agreed.

Harper, struggling to keep up, just nodded and smiled.

"Anyway, we've got lots to do before then. I just want us all to be open to doing whatever is best for The Greenhouse, okay?"

"Absolutely," Bella said, looking down.

"Oh my God, wipe that sad look off your face, Bells. You know you're like my doppelganger-sister-from-another-mother work wife, right?" She reached forward and squeezed Bella's arm, a huge smile on her face.

"I know, I'm being stupid," Bella said, twisting her fingers through her long dark hair.

"So stupid," Charlotte said, laughing.

"You're right," Bella replied, shaking her head. "I'm sorry; that's my baggage about my worth, not yours. Of course, whatever is best for Team Green is best for all of us."

"Good," Charlotte said. She looked at Harper. "Do you have any questions?"

Harper had nothing but questions, but she didn't know where to begin, so she shook her head instead and tried to push down that little voice inside her that said, *Run.*

They pulled up to the airport curb, and Bella handed Harper a large mint-green folder that read WELCOME TO THE GREENHOUSE! "Everything you need to know about getting started is in there: company mission statement and vision, job responsibilities, a one-year contract—"

"You haven't signed a contract yet?" Charlotte asked Harper, as if it was her fault.

"What? No, I just did the interview."

"Oh sure, but that was only a formality, or you wouldn't be here. I don't have time to waste on interviews. But you gotta sign that first before we give you anything else. I mean, this is all insider team stuff. We can't have it out there on social—not like you're even *on* social—but you know."

"Right, okay . . ."

"You can sign it now." She checked her watch. "But hurry, because I can't miss this flight." She signaled for the driver to get her bags from the trunk.

Harper pulled out the contract and scanned it as quickly as she could. The salary was right, her job title of Visionary Support Strategist was listed correctly, but it was a lot to read so quickly, and she could feel her heart beating faster as both Bella and Charlotte stared at her and the driver stood waiting with the luggage on the curb. Her mind was swimming as she turned the page quickly. Someone honked at the car. "Just a minute!" the driver called. Charlotte sighed loudly, and Harper put down the pen.

"Look, this is a great opportunity, I know, but it's just all happening so fast. I think I need time, and . . ."

Charlotte motioned for Bella to leave the car, and as soon as they were alone, she turned to Harper, her eyes sincere and her voice kind. "You're freaking out. I get it. Change is scary. Taking a leap is scary. Trusting your gut is fucking *scary*, but it's what every great woman has ever done—charged into the unknown boldly, said yes now, and then figured out how to do it later. It's what I've always done, and it's gotten me to where I am at The Greenhouse, but you have to feel good about joining us because although it's a shit ton of fun, it's also a shit ton of work. If you think for even one second that your life is working better for you now than it could be working for me, then I want you to know that I understand, no hard feelings, and I sincerely wish you the very best." She reached over and gave Harper a big hug. She got out of the car, walking ahead as Bella lingered on the curb. Then she paused and turned around. "I won't land for another few hours. Think about it while I'm in the air, and then let me know by touchdown. The decision is yours. But I hope I'll see you tomorrow in Nashville."

Harper stared after Charlotte, her mind reeling. Charlotte was right—she was freaking out. She took a deep breath to center herself. It wasn't what Charlotte had said that had thrown her off guard, but the way she'd said it. No one in publishing would ever give an interview like this, but then again, no one in publishing had ever given her the opportunity to run before she could walk. All this time Harper had been hoping to catch a break, hoping that someone would take a chance on her, and here was Charlotte doing just that. The question was whether Harper was brave enough to take it.

4

Greener Pastures

Harper went straight from her interview with Charlotte to Penn Station to catch the train to Poughkeepsie to see her parents as promised, even though the timing couldn't have been worse. It had been almost two months since she had seen them, which was why, when her mother texted to say that she was baking her favorite cookies for her already-twice postponed visit, she knew she couldn't cancel again. But all she really wanted to do was go back to her apartment and discuss everything with Poppy. She only had a few hours to make a decision and she was desperate to talk it out.

The last time Harper had been up to Poughkeepsie to see her parents had been for a Fourth of July celebration they were hosting at the inn they'd owned and operated ever since Harper was born. In an effort to boost the family business that had been on a steady decline as hip boutique hotels and Airbnbs popped up, they'd hosted a big backyard cookout with a fireworks display as part of their "stay two nights, get one free" promotion. Looking back, Harper wasn't sure what she'd been expecting, but watching her parents run around catering to guests wasn't it. In previous years there had been staff on hand, but staff for the long weekend had been hard to come by, her parents said, so they decided to just do the work themselves. Still, it was an impossible undertaking for only two people, so Harper had rolled up her sleeves and jumped in. It was only at the end of the weekend that her exhausted parents finally admitted that the staff shortage was because of a shortage of funds and, as much as they wanted to, they couldn't keep helping Harper financially. Shame and embarrassment had caused Harper to keep making excuses about why she couldn't come back home for a visit since then, but now she had an actual job offer on the table.

"Harper!" her mom, Eva, said the moment she opened the door to the little wood and stone house Harper had grown up in. Although Eva was small in stature, she had a larger-than-life personality. She wiped her hands on her apron before wrapping Harper in a hug and pulling her in tight. She had bits of flour in her hair and on her face and smelled like sweet powdered milk. Harper knew she must have been making polvoron, the Filipino version of shortbread that all her non-Filipino friends called milk candies. They were a specialty of her mother's, and she often made them with whatever was in season—pumpkin spice at Thanksgiving, finely crushed candy canes at Christmas. They were a favorite of Harper's and everyone who tried them.

"You're just in time. Tell me what you think of this new flavor," Eva said, leading her daughter into the kitchen. "I used freeze-dried strawberries. Apparently, Christian's fiancée, Janice, loves all things strawberry, so I'm sending these to San Francisco for their engagement party."

Christian was Harper's lone male cousin, the baby of the family, and, with the exception of Harper, the last to get married.

"Wow, they're really doing it." Harper said. Part of her couldn't believe he was finally settling down, while the other part was annoyed that the spotlight about a love life—or lack thereof—was now going to be entirely on her.

"They better be. I've been working around the clock on these," her mom said, removing a row of cookies from a cooling rack onto two small plates.

"You're not needed at the Inn?" Harper asked, trying to suss out if business had gotten any better.

"Oh, it's not that busy right now. You know, end of summer." Eva fixed them two cups of coffee.

"Isn't that when you're usually busy—last getaway of the summer and all that?"

"It's different now; everybody wants all the bells and whistles. Did you know that the Hilltop Inn is putting in a swimming pool? I mean, we've got the Hudson River right over there," her mom said, pointing out the window. "And Landing Point started a brewery on-site and does tastings. What happened to going for a beautiful hike, having a great meal, and ending the night with a good book?"

"I guess people want to get as much for their money as they can?" Harper said, treading lightly. She took a seat at the kitchen table that faced the backyard and had a view of the Inn at the other end of the property. She felt sorry for her parents, who had spent their whole lives making the Inn as warm and welcoming as possible. But without the renovations and new offerings it needed—neither of which her parents could afford—it had become a bit worn and tired over the years.

"I know," her mom said, taking a seat. "But big changes cost money, and I just don't know if it's worth it. Your dad and I aren't getting any younger." She picked up a cookie and took a bite.

"Speak for yourself," Harper's dad, Dan, called, coming in the back door. "I've never felt better." He flexed his biceps, making them both laugh.

Harper jumped up and gave her dad a hug and caught the scent of freshly mowed grass.

"You're mowing the lawn now too?"

"Yup. I decided if anyone is going to get paid twenty dollars an hour to cut grass, it's going to be me," he said, washing his hands at the sink before drying them on a tea towel and joining them at the table. "Which reminds me, you're late with my paycheck," he joked to Harper's mom.

"Get in line," Eva said, passing him the plate of cookies.

Harper often wondered how her parents had gotten together in the first place. Her mom was bubbly and talkative, while her dad was a man of a few well-chosen words with a dry sense of humor. They'd attended the same high school in Pennsylvania, but it had taken Dan until their senior year to ask her mom out. They'd been partnered up to work a spring fundraiser together, and, as her dad told it, her mom persuaded everyone who came up to their corn dog stand to buy two, as it was for a good cause. She didn't stop talking the entire time they were together.

It wasn't until her dad walked her mom to her car at the end of the day that she turned to him and said, "You know, you haven't told me one thing about yourself." To which he turned to her and said, "I've been trying all day, but you never gave me a chance."

Harper used to blush at this next part, where her dad took a step closer to her mom and said that he had never met anyone who talked so much in his whole life who he could still listen to all day. Apparently, that shut Harper's mom up, and then before she could say anything else, he asked her out. The rest was history.

"So now, what's your big news? Your mom said you had something to tell us," her dad said, picking up a cookie.

"Well, I've been offered a job," Harper said.

"In publishing? That's fantastic!" Her mom reached across the table and squeezed her hand. "I knew you'd find something if you didn't give up."

"No, not in publishing exactly," Harper said, making sure to keep her voice light and a smile on her face. Harper's parents had sacrificed a lot to make sure she could go to school in New York and pursue her dream career, and she hadn't realized until now how leaving to be an influencer's assistant would sound.

"What's the job, then?" her father asked, raising his bushy eyebrows.

"Well, it's in social media, as a visionary support strategist for a well-known influencer named Charlotte Green."

The look on her parents' faces told Harper she could have been speaking gibberish for how little that meant to them, which, to be fair, was about as much as it meant to her until a day ago.

"Does her vision strategy include influential books?" Eva asked, trying to connect the dots.

"Yes. She's a very successful self-help author, and I'd be working for her as kind of an executive assistant."

"What does she influence people to do?" her dad asked.

"Live their best life, connect to the warrior women inside them—it's really all about empowering women," Harper said. "She has a huge following on Instagram, and her main headquarters is in Nashville."

"Uh-huh," her dad said, reaching for a second cookie. "Is it a good offer?"

This was Harper's opening, and she dove in. "It's a great offer—more than three times what I was making, a rent subsidy, and the chance for growth in the company. Charlotte personally picked me out of everyone that applied, and she loves that I have a fresh perspective, went to a great school, and worked in publishing. She does a lot of writing and has published three bestselling books, and if things go well—which they will—I could even write for her."

"Oh well, that's good. I like the idea of you getting back to your writing—you were always so good at it," her dad said.

"You should've started with that, honey. What kind of writing? Does she have a magazine?"

"She didn't say exactly . . . but she said she really liked my writing, so you know . . ." Harper trailed off, suddenly aware of how little she really knew about the role of visionary support strategist.

Harper watched her parents exchange looks in that way of theirs that told her they were biting their tongues. "It's the best offer I've had," Harper said quietly.

"Better than working at the *Poughkeepsie Press*?" her mother said, sitting back in her chair and crossing her arms in front of her. "That job is actually in publishing, and even though they won't pay as much, they're very supportive of local writers if you wanted to try your hand at that again. And under your own name."

Harper hated that her parents were tiptoeing around the fact that she had given up on her writing dreams after a series of false starts. Harper had spent the first year after graduation freelancing by day and working on a novel by night. But without bites on the book or any cushion to fall back on if she didn't get enough writing gigs each month, she was forced to admit that what she really needed was a paycheck. If she couldn't write, she could help other writers get their stories out into the world by working in publishing, and that could be just as rewarding—or so she told herself.

"Mom, we've been through this. I need to make real money, and Charlotte's offering me a lot of money." Harper paused, embarrassed to tell her struggling parents just how much.

"Enough to cover health insurance?" Eva asked sheepishly.

Harper's parents had kept her on their health insurance for as long as they could, but after she turned twenty-six she was off the family plan, and she knew how much it pained them not to be able to help her.

"More than enough. I'll be able to pay off a big chunk of my student loans and could even help you and Dad if you—"

Harper's mom cut her off. "That's very generous, sweetheart, but you need to start saving for your own future."

Harper took a deep breath. "It's a great offer. It's not what I envisioned myself doing, but I don't know how I could pass it up."

"We just don't want you to rush into anything. Do you really know what you're getting into?"

"What choice do I have? I can't live with Poppy forever, and I need a job."

"You could always live here and work at the Inn," her mother said. "Figure things out if you don't want the job at the *Poughkeepsie Press*. A lot of people your age move to the city and then decide it's not for them. Look at Dylan. I saw him at the Food Stop the other day, and he said he's very happy here. He's even working at his father's insurance firm."

Harper took a deep breath. There were so many land mines in what her mother had just said that she needed to tread carefully. Ever since her ex-boyfriend, Dylan, decided to return to Poughkeepsie, his stock had risen in her mother's eyes. It wasn't even that her mother liked Dylan so much as she liked that he had moved back and had now apparently joined the family business. Harper's parents had never pressured her to abandon her dreams and help them run the Inn, but as soon as those dreams seemed intent on abandoning Harper, she had felt a shift in their attitude.

"Dylan also decided that *I* wasn't for him, remember?" Harper said.

"Yeah, the guy's clearly an idiot," Harper's dad said, winking at her.

"Thanks, Dad."

"I just mean that he's happy here," Eva said, "and if you wanted to move back, you could always stay here rent-free—"

"I couldn't do that," Harper said.

"Well, you could work at the Inn in exchange—"

"Eva," Harper's dad said, placing his hand on her mother's. "If Harper wants to try something new, this is the time to do it, before she has any obligations or responsibilities. We should support that." He looked at her mother in a way that made Harper wonder what he wasn't saying.

"Of course. Of course if it's what you really want, then you should go for it. Just think about it. You don't have to decide right away." Just then, Harper's phone buzzed with a message.

Things are moving fast. I need to know if you're in or not ASAP.

"Actually, this is Charlotte's assistant right now, so I'm pretty sure I

do," Harper said to her mom with a wave of the phone. She typed back,
I was just talking it over with my parents.

Bella's response came almost immediately.

Your parents—love that. Family is everything. Bet they're proud of you.
Tell them Charlotte's offering you a 30k signing bonus if you say yes now.

Harper's jaw dropped and she stared at her screen. One hundred
fifty thousand dollars was more than three years' salary at her old jobs.

You in or out?

Harper looked at her parents and saw the worry on their faces. It was
a look she'd seen more and more over the last six months, and she was
eager to replace it with something else. A job she knew nothing about in
a city she'd never been to that paid a small fortune was still better than a
life she did know—unemployed and living at home with her parents in
the small town she'd vowed to leave. She took a deep breath, and then
paraphrasing Charlotte, she said, "Sometimes you just have to charge into
the unknown boldly, say yes now, and then figure out how to do it later."

She took a deep breath and typed back, YES!

Seeing Green Monthly Newsletter:

September

September has always felt like back to school. Colored pencils, scented markers, marbled notebooks . . . Who doesn't love that? A new outfit and finding the best table in the cafeteria and the coolest kids to hang out with? Not so much. Remember all that shit? Worrying whether you'll be popular, picked as prom queen, voted class valedictorian, or most likely to succeed? All that worrying about things that aren't actually important, when all that really matters is the learning and the growing. It's what I tell my kids, and I mean it. They go back to school, and I go back to schooling myself on all the things that I want to be and get done. Just because you're not in a classroom doesn't mean you're not learning. We're all students in the school of life, and personally, I want to be the biggest nerd at that school—who doesn't? There's no graduating from real-life school, no letters at the end of your name, no fancy alma mater to talk about years later. This is the real world, and in the real world, the most successful are the ones who say yes to learning more and being more and doing more every damn day. If we're not learning and growing, we're dying. So shake off summer, roll up your sleeves, and get ready to learn who you really are and what you can really do. Get ready for personal growth, and get ready for our Greenlight Inner Growth Academy 30-day workshop that will reignite the student within. Let's do this!

xo Charlotte

5

Welcome to Nashville!

Harper looked for the sign bearing her name in the sea of cowboy hats that floated at the bottom of the escalator and yawned. It was hard to believe that just twenty-four hours earlier, she'd awoken to a phone call from Bella. In the brief time that had passed since she'd accepted the job with Charlotte, she'd said goodbye to her parents, packed up her life in New York City, and had a tear-ridden final movie night with Poppy where they recited nearly every line of their favorite movie, *He's Just Not That Into You*. Somewhere in the crowd below her was supposed to be Aaron, Harper's ride. She adjusted her grip on her suitcase and wiped her sweaty palm on her pants, regretting for the hundredth time since landing that she had worn jeans and boots. Although wearing boots and a cowboy hat didn't seem to be a problem for anyone else around her, neither apparently did the heat. It felt like the middle of summer, only more humid, and Harper couldn't wait to get to her new apartment to shower and change. She couldn't believe how fast everything had happened, which was probably for the best because it meant that Harper had had little time to second-guess her decision. It also meant she had

had little time to properly research all things Charlotte Green, which was why, instead of sleeping on the plane, she had fallen down the rabbit hole of her new boss's perfectly curated life. Ten-dollar airplane Wi-Fi had never been more worth it.

Charlotte Green's Instagram life could be compartmentalized into three distinct categories: family, marriage, and work. The family pictures were a color-coordinated display of vacation shots, joy-filled family gatherings, and quiet snuggly moments reading books with her children, watching sunsets, and building sandcastles on the beach. They were the kind of pictures used for holiday cards or as backdrops for inspirational memes. All the photos included hashtags like #grateful, #familyiseverything, #blessed.

Similarly, posts highlighting Charlotte's marriage to her husband, Ryan, alternated between super-romantic dates and doing mundane tasks together, like building a bookshelf for the many copies of Charlotte's bestselling books. For these pictures, Charlotte liked to use the hashtags #keepingtheromancealive and #keepingitreal.

And then there were the pictures of Charlotte's work life. Those were the ones meant to show what Charlotte's life was like behind the scenes and how hard she worked—so hard, harder than everyone else. But even these seemed carefully staged. There were pictures of Charlotte mostly makeup-free and wearing sweats, her blond hair pulled back in a messy ponytail as she sat in a comfy chair working away on her laptop late at night. These photos favored the hashtags #upatthecrackofdawn, #burningthemidnightoil, #neverquit, #awomansworkisneverdone. No matter what the photo, though, one thing was clear: Charlotte Green was a force, a brand with a capital B.

As she reached the bottom of the escalator, Harper spotted a man about her age wearing a white T-shirt, blue jeans, and yup, cowboy boots, holding a sign that read HARPER CRUZ!

"Hi, I'm Harper! You must be Aaron," Harper said, walking over and extending her damp hand. He grimaced slightly as he shook it. "Sorry,

I wasn't expecting this heat. I'm overdressed. Everyone is gearing up for fall in New York."

"Everyone is gearing up for fall here too," Aaron replied, cracking a smile and taking her suitcase from her.

"Right, of course. I just meant that I'm dressed for New York weather, not Nashville weather."

"Got it," he said over his shoulder, already leading the way through the crowds. Harper quickened her pace, struggling to keep up. "Well, don't worry. Charlotte keeps The Greenhouse nice and crisp; you'll be fine." He led them outside, and the humidity hit her smack in the face.

"Actually, I was hoping to go to my apartment first, to shower and change, before making my way over to the office—if that's all right?"

"It isn't," he said, leading her toward a pickup truck that was parked in a designated pickup zone. He lifted her suitcase, revealing a line of tattoos that ran the length of the underside of his arm.

"Excuse me?" Harper asked, her mind whirling. He opened the passenger-side door for her, and she got in.

"It's just that Charlotte likes everyone to get to work before she does," he said, hopping into the driver's seat and starting the car. "Bella told me to bring you straight over."

Harper checked her watch. "But it's only seven thirty. I thought we didn't start work for another hour."

"Officially you're right. Unofficially, we need to get there soon." He snuck a look at her as he brushed his hair from his face and pulled out of the parking lot. "Tell you what, we've got a couple of minutes: Why don't we hit a drive-through and grab coffee and breakfast, so you can eat on the way over?"

"That'd be great. How long have you been working for Charlotte?"

"Almost two years. I'm her audio-visual guy, and I'm also the airport taxi driver. I live close by," he said, answering the look on Harper's face.

"You don't live at the—"

"Green Suites? Nope. I've got my own place and my own deal. I get to come and go as long as I'm also willing to jump in and run errands. The Green Suites are just for the Green Team, and although the twenty-minute walk to work is definitely a perk, I prefer a little more distance."

"Green Team?"

"Charlotte's employees?" He shook his head and smiled at Harper. "Everything's branded. You'll get used to it."

"As long as *we're* not actually branded," Harper said, nodding at Aaron's tattoos.

"No, that's all my doing. Although who knows?" Aaron said, smirking.

"Look, this all happened really fast," Harper said, turning in her seat to face him, "so maybe you could tell me—" But Aaron had already turned on the music and was singing along to a country music station. Before she could say anything else, her phone buzzed with a text from Bella. Welcome to Nashville! See you soon!

Thirty minutes, one breakfast sandwich, and a giant latte later, Harper was starting to feel a tad more human. As they pulled into the parking lot of The Greenhouse, Harper noted that it was neither green nor a house, but it was still impressive. A beautiful single-story brick building, The Greenhouse—as noted in large neon-green letters above the front door—was located in a converted factory in an area of downtown called the Gulch, which was home to a string of cute bars and restaurants. As Harper entered the courtyard that was strung with café lights and dotted with small white metal tables and folding chairs, she admired the building's oversize windows and allowed herself to get excited at the possibility that she might have an actual office with natural light, a luxury she had yet to experience back in New York.

"Well, here we are," Aaron said, "your new home away from home."

"Except I won't be living here," Harper said.

"Not technically," Aaron replied grimly as he lifted her suitcase up over green lettering that was stenciled on the ground. GOOD THINGS ARE GROWING INSIDE! He carried her suitcase up the three steps to the entrance and opened it for her.

"If I didn't know any better, I'd think you were trying to scare me," Harper said.

"If you scared easily, you wouldn't have moved hundreds of miles from home to take a job for a woman you obviously don't know much about. And I mean that as a compliment, by the way."

His comment caught Harper off guard, which was why she didn't see the woman with a small cardboard box barreling right into her.

"Shit," the woman said, getting knocked on her ass and taking Harper down with her. She stood up and began to pick up the things that had scattered across the floor.

"Mandy, are you okay?" Aaron asked, stepping in to help her.

Harper picked herself up and dusted off her pants. "I'm so sorry, I didn't see you."

The young woman looked remarkably like Charlotte. She even had the same hairstyle and green Vans. As she stood up, Harper could see that she'd been crying.

Mandy looked at Harper's suitcase and nodded slowly. "That was fast."

"Mandy, let me help you out," a handsome bald Indian man said, sweeping in.

"I think you've helped enough, Oliver," Mandy said, regaining her composure.

A tall woman with a blunt-cut bob, who looked to be about Harper's age, appeared at Mandy's side. She gave Harper a once-over and sighed. "I've got this." She took Mandy by the arm and helped her down the steps.

Harper turned back to find the others staring at her, until the man broke the silence. "I'm so sorry you had to see that. I'm Oliver—The Greenhouse creative director and COO. Welcome," he said, shaking her hand. He was breathtakingly handsome and resembled an Indian Mark Consuelos. With his charcoal trousers, form-fitting tan blazer, and perfectly folded pocket square, he could have been the sixth member of *Queer Eye*. "Why don't we go find Bella, and she can give you the tour." Oliver swept Harper inside. They had gone just five steps when Bella came rushing forward.

"Harper, I'm so glad you made it!" Bella said, pulling her into a quick hug. "Here, let me show you around." She grabbed Harper's suitcase and tucked it into a closet off one side of the hallway. "Well, this is where the magic happens," she said, extending her arms wide.

Harper took in the wide-open concept space, which had polished concrete floors and high ceilings. In front of them were three distinct clusters of workstations in varying shades of green, all of which lined up vertically next to a large green shag carpet. Each long table had five or six employees typing away on their laptops.

"So this side is where the Green Team works, in the middle is the Green Garden, and on the other side of the garden is where Charlotte and Oliver have their offices. The conference room is there too."

"Oh, I didn't realize they're the only ones with actual offices."

"Well there's a small office tucked into the back next to the hydration station where Cynthia from accounting works. She's a hoot, but she's not really part of a team," Bella said, waving to an attractive middle-aged Black woman opening the office door. She then pointed to the table at the end of the space. "Over there near the back is the Create Team. They're responsible for creating all our products: journals, notebooks, stationery, pens, prints, candles, that sort of thing. Some of it's sold in stores, and some of it, like our Growth Planners, is only available online on our website. That way we're out in front of the consumer, but also bringing people back to the source," Bella said, as if Harper surely knew all of this already.

"Growth Planners?" Harper asked.

"Yeah, they're new. There are all these great prompts to help you envision the future you want. As a part of your morning routine, you're supposed to write your desires down and then spend the rest of the day focusing your thoughts on making them grow into a reality."

"Right, sure, makes sense," Harper said, smiling at some of the people who looked up at her and waved. Harper was a little surprised that they just looked like regular office workers, wearing various levels of business casual. She hadn't expected everyone to be as glamorous as Charlotte and Bella, but the contrast was noticeable. She followed Bella as they made their way to the middle of the space.

"And this station we call Community, because that's what it's dedicated to building. Everyone on this team works on things like our Inspire conference, brand partnerships, speaking tours, and online courses. This is where Tiffany works; you saw her on your way in," Bella said. Harper recalled the woman with the bob. This team was noticeably more fashionable than the other group, and Harper wondered if there was some kind of correlation.

"Right, and who was that woman that was—" Harper started, but Bella wasn't done.

"And this is us—directly across from Charlotte's office." Bella leaned in close to Harper and whispered, "It's where the coolest people work, obvi."

Ah, so there is *some sort of employee hierarchy*, thought Harper, looking at the table set just for two.

"You and I have the smallest station because we're *core*. We're on the Connect Team, handling all of Charlotte's and The Greenhouse's internal and external media. That includes her book tours, speaking events, funny videos, her 'Love, Charlotte' email blasts, newsletter, Instagram reels, that kind of thing."

It sounded like a lot to Harper, who was starting to sweat just thinking about the workload. "And it's just the *two* of us?"

"No, Charlotte helps. Oliver too, and Tiffany—she supports two teams right now." She lowered her voice. "We're Charlotte's most important team. It's why our workstation is positioned right across from her office. That way she can always see us and we can always see her." Bella pointed to a glass-walled office on the other side of the garden that had Charlotte's name engraved on the door. Oliver's was emblazoned on the door next to hers.

"Oh wow, it's all so . . ." *Public*, Harper wanted to say. At least she had a cubicle to hide in at her old job.

"Connected," Bella said proudly. "Growth has no walls here. And finally, this is the garden, where we all gather." Bella stood on the large green shag carpet that divided the workstations on one side and the glass-walled offices of Charlotte and Oliver on the other.

"Okay," Harper said. Giant colored beanbags—she guessed they were supposed to represent flowers—circled a lone stool made from a tree stump. "Is this even comfortable?" she asked, starting to sit.

"You can't sit there! That's the Tower of Power."

"Oh, sorry." Not even wanting to ask what that meant, she got up quickly, noticing a giant neon sign at the far end of the office that read: SUCCESS NEVER SLEEPS! "Wow," Harper said, nodding at the sign.

"I know, it's inspiring, isn't it?" Bella said, following Harper's gaze. "It's, like, our mantra, although we get others daily on the Vine."

"The Vine?" Harper asked, following Bella back to their workstation. She sat down at her seat and grabbed the laptop in front of her.

"It's our company Slack. It's where we all communicate and where Charlotte posts the day's objectives. The welcome letter should be there too; you'll want to read that before she gets here. Oh, and there's a personal intake form that you need to fill out and get back to me. The form is in that folder." She pointed to the shiny green folder below Harper's laptop, and then sat down across from her and logged on.

Harper adjusted her chair height, took off her blazer, and immediately put it back on. Aaron was right; it was freezing. She reached into her pocket and pulled out her lip balm and placed it on her side of the workstation. Picking up the folder, she noticed a small coffee ring underneath that was still warm to the touch. Had this desk belonged to the newly departed Mandy? She was just about to ask Bella why Mandy was let go when Bella stood and snapped her fingers. "Read the letter. She'll be here soon."

"Right, okay," Harper said, opening the folder and getting all the tech info she needed to log on and access her email. She opened her laptop, signed in, and read the letter.

Hi! If you're reading this, you're new, and I just wanted to take a moment to say welcome! I'm Charlotte Green, founder and Chief Badass of The Greenhouse! I'm so happy that you are joining this amazing community of greenspirational warriors who, like you, were hand-selected to create this community of like-minded badass babes committed to making a difference! What we do matters, but how we do it matters just as much. So before you dive in, please take a moment to read our company values, because this Greenhouse is all windows, all transparent, all the time.

Growth. WHEN WE EACH GROW, WE ALL BLOSSOM.

We have a growth mindset. If we're not growing, we're dying. We're a say-yes-now-figure-out-how-later kind of place. We don't just say "yes" to constructive criticism. We say "HELL YES" to change!!

Reach. OUR TEAM REACHES FOR MORE.

We're a tribe that knows it's not just about climbing the ladder. It's about BUILDING the ladder! We boss up at every level and don't stop till we're at the top. We don't step forward into growth—we LEAP into the best version of ourselves. Because either you run the day or the day runs YOU!

Energy. ENERGY IS OUR CURRENCY.

It doesn't matter where you're from or what you look like. We're a diverse team that believes HOW you show up matters! Our crew influences the energy of every freaking room we walk into because we're rooted in the truth that when you're fired up on all cylinders, there's NOTHING you can't do!

Enthusiasm. WE PROTECT OUR POSITIVITY.

Making dreams happen every day requires relentless positivity. You've got to let go of all the BS that weighs you down if you're truly ready to SOAR. Our core belief is that when you focus on the good, the good gets better.

Nimble. THIS TEAM MAKES IT HAPPEN.

We don't knock on the door of success. We knock DOWN the door! We're vibrating higher and buzzing around even the toughest challenges. We're the grind-all-day hustlers who don't get distracted because we know Sprint Season means winning season.

Harper had just gotten to the last section of the letter when Bella jumped up out of her chair, holding her phone to her ear. "Finally! She's in a mood today, Aaron. She's been texting me all morning," she whispered into the phone. "We need something feisty—she's one minute away. Work your DJ magic." She turned her attention to Harper and gasped. "Oh my gosh, Harper, put that away," she said, staring at Harper's desk.

"Put what away? My lip balm?" Harper asked, incredulous as to how a tiny tube of gloss could cause a problem.

"Yes. You can't have stuff scattered all over your desk like that. No personal belongings—no photos or plants or decorations. Didn't you read your folder?"

"No, I just finished the welcome letter," Harper said, rifling through the folder for the handout on desk regulations.

"You can't read it now! She'll be here any second and—"

The rest of Bella's sentence was cut off by the sound of Katy Perry's

"Firework" blaring through the sound system. Everybody jumped to their feet.

"Get up," Bella said, coming around to Harper's desk and Harper jolted up out of her seat. She opened a hidden drawer and swept the lip gloss and folder inside. "Let's dance!" she said, manically moving her body to the music, her face a mask of forced cheer.

Harper stood glued to the spot, shocked at how quickly everyone had just switched from work mode to party mode. She stared at Bella and the other members of the Green Team who were rocking out like they were at a wedding and had taken one too many trips to the open bar.

From across the room, she saw Aaron deejaying at his laptop and checking the door as Charlotte, dressed in a white blazer, graphic tee, light wash jeans, and trademark green Vans came in, clapping her hands above her head and singing along to the music as it reached an ear-shattering decibel. Having only ever seen Charlotte sitting down, Harper wasn't prepared for how short she was—she couldn't have been more than five feet tall. But what she lacked in height she made up for in energy.

Punching her fists in the air, with her bouncy blond blowout swaying in time to the music, she sent a current through the room that was infectious. As Charlotte pointed to people, they stepped forward and danced even harder. Harper looked for any signs of annoyance or embarrassment on the faces of her new colleagues but didn't see any. It was something her jaded New York spirit found hard to believe, but people were practically glowing.

Charlotte stood still in place and smiled wide before bending her knees and drumrolling her hands on her thighs. Within a moment everyone had joined her in whispering, *Let's Go Green Team Let's Go,* over and over again, their voices gradually getting louder and louder until they erupted into a cheer. Harper stared, her eyes wide at the sight of her new coworkers jumping in the air and shaking their hands like pom-poms.

"Come, everyone, let's gather around," she called, motioning them over to the green shag carpet. She held her hand out to Oliver, who helped her onto the Tower of Power. "As you know," she said, clasping her hands together, "I've had to do some pruning lately, and I know how upsetting that can be. But not every seed we plant grows into a flower. Sometimes, even if they look like flowers, they are actually weeds. And no matter how much we tend to and nurture them, their roots will still travel underground and rob the soil of nutrients the other plants need. Slowly they'll twist themselves around the other flowers in an effort to get closer to the sun. If you don't act decisively—some might even say ruthlessly—to rip those weeds out, your whole garden will die before you know it. I don't want that to happen to this garden."

All around Harper, people were nodding and looking solemn. Harper looked to Bella, whose whole face was flush, and there were tears in her eyes. It was a lot of garden analogy, but Harper was dying to ask Bella what had led up to this. Charlotte stepped down from the stump and started to walk around the circle slowly.

"We want this garden to flourish. Right?"

"Right!" everyone answered as one, Harper a beat too late, realizing that she was supposed to be joining the chorus.

"We want this garden to grow, right?"

"Right!"

"I think we could all use a little love shower right about now. Some good mojo to wash away the bad," Charlotte said, her face full of sincerity. "Bella, can you give us a little love?"

Bella quickly stepped forward and, pulling out her phone, began scrolling as everyone waited. "I just need a second . . . uh . . . here we are . . . *Charlotte Green is my hero. A teacher, inspiration, and friend all in one. Even though we've never met, I feel like she's always in my corner. I don't know where I'd be without her.* Annie from San Diego."

Charlotte nodded slowly and looked around the room. "I am. I am in her corner." She looked back at Bella expectantly.

"*Charlotte Green isn't just an influencer—she's a visionary. A badass babe, kicking ass and taking names.* Diana from Denver."

"Truth, Diana," Charlotte said, her voice a little louder as she stepped back onto the Tower of Power.

"*Following Charlotte's thirty days to a better me did more for me than ten years of therapy ever did. I'm brighter, bolder, and betting on myself. I've gone Green, and I'm not going back!* Amy from Texas."

"That's it, Amy from Texas," Charlotte practically bellowed. "That's what I'm talking about. Change is hard, but change is good. Change is *growth*. There is no going back; there is only going forward. Forward is the future and today is the beginning. And on that note, let me introduce the newest member of the Green Team, who is just *beginning* her journey at The Greenhouse—Harper Cruz."

Bella nudged Harper into the center of the carpet, where Charlotte took both her hands and looked up into her eyes. "Harper, we're so glad you're here, and we can't wait to watch you grow." Harper smiled tentatively as the room applauded and then came to an abrupt stop as Charlotte once again lifted her hands in the air like pom-poms. With that, everyone dispersed and went back to their workstations.

Harper stood awkwardly in the middle of the room, slightly shell-shocked and unsure of what to do next. That's when Charlotte called out, "Bella, Harper, in my office." Bella was already five steps ahead as Harper followed, dazed and bewildered, wondering what exactly she had gotten herself into.

6

Three Minutes of Fame

"It's only three minutes," Bella said tentatively. "I'm not sure we can get all of that across in that amount of time, especially on such short notice."

Charlotte had gathered Oliver, Bella, Aaron, and Tiffany in her office to share the news that *Nashville Starz* and its host, Reed Phillips, was going to be doing a three-minute segment on Charlotte and The Greenhouse.

"Short notice? It's not until *tomorrow*."

"Right, of course," Bella stammered.

"And *only* three minutes?" Charlotte said, standing and placing her elbows on the desk. "That's like six commercials or two lengths of an Olympic-sized swimming pool. Have you ever sat through six commercials or held your breath for *only* three minutes?"

Harper could practically feel Bella holding her breath. She looked over at Oliver, who leaned back in his chair and laced his fingers behind his smooth bald head, his dark eyes darting back and forth between the two women.

"I just meant—" Bella said.

"Oliver, have you?" Charlotte asked, turning to face him.

"I think Liam's mother's speech was three minutes long at our wedding, and I held my breath through that," he said, making Charlotte laugh and cutting through the tension.

"It's a long time, right?" Charlotte said.

"An eternity," Oliver replied. "Bella, three minutes is more than enough time to show off the new space, show off Charlotte, and make the big announcement."

"What big announcement?" Harper asked. It was the first time she had spoken up, and everyone turned to face her. So far, no one had even told her why she was there.

"Well, I'd like to save it for tomorrow so we can catch everyone's reaction in real time, but let's just say that I've found us a sponsor for our Inspire conference," Charlotte said, tossing her hair behind her shoulder and smirking.

"You did?" Tiffany asked, sounding surprised.

"I did."

Harper was doing her best to keep up. She knew from Charlotte's Instagram that the conference was Charlotte's big event of the year. Women from all over the country came together for a weekend of inspirational talks, workshops, and community bonding all meant to *Greenlight their lives!*

"Um, as your event maestro, shouldn't I have known about this?" Tiffany asked, her brow furrowing.

"You know now. But not a word. I know how hard C.J. was pursuing them for her stupid conference. She's going to be pissed."

"You don't mean—" Tiffany hesitated, her eyes wide.

"Don't say it," Charlotte demanded. "I want it to be a surprise, and I don't want word getting out. The last thing we need is to give her time to swoop in and change their minds. Got it?" She raised her eyebrows at Bella and Tiffany.

"Of course," they answered, taken aback.

"Good. Now, as for the segment, I thought we could start with me meditating in my office before we show Reed Phillips our regular morning routine."

"Meditating?" Bella asked, incredulous.

Judging by the looks on everyone's faces, Harper guessed that meditating wasn't something Charlotte normally did.

"Yeah, you'll come and get me when we're done. Aaron, I want you filming them filming me."

"You got it," Aaron said.

"I'll need some crystals and candles, but I want our logo on everything, so make sure that you print up our stickers. And a yoga mat! A good one—high-end, green—and one of those things you sit on, those, you know . . ."

"Cushions?" Harper asked.

"Yes, but the meditation kind," Charlotte said. "Oh, and an orchid, a white one. It should feel very peaceful in my office. And I'll want some outfit options for the segment, casual but cool. And get my hairdresser to come in tomorrow."

"Will they be filming you at the house? Should I have Ryan and the kids get haircuts for the segment too?" Bella asked.

"No, we won't be able to squeeze them in. Another time."

Charlotte turned to stare at Harper and tilted her head. "You must have a great memory."

"Excuse me?" Harper said, confused.

"To not have to write any of that down?" She crossed her arms in front of her body.

"Oh! You want *me* to do all that?" Harper said. "I didn't realize that I—"

"Well, who else, Harper? *You're* my visionary support strategist, and right now, I need you to support my vision for a kick-ass profile on *Nashville Starz!*" Charlotte held up her hand to high-five Harper.

"Right," Harper said, trying without success to remember where in her job description it said anything about running Charlotte's errands.

"I think someone's a little jet-lagged," Tiffany commented.

"No," said Harper quickly. "I just thought that I was going to be working on messaging and branding, that kind of thing."

"And you will be, don't worry. We all wear a lot of hats around here. And right now, the hat I need you to wear is my personal assistant hat, so you can get me some clothes and things to decorate my office. Do you think you can do that?" Charlotte asked.

Before Harper could answer, Oliver cleared his throat, catching Charlotte's eye. Harper was aware there was some kind of silent exchange between them, and the next time Charlotte spoke, her voice was soft and sincere.

"Harper, I don't want to assume anything. So I need to ask if you are okay with wearing a lot of hats. The last thing any of us wants is another morning glory in the garden."

"Morning glory?" Harper asked.

"A weed that pretends to be a flower. Someone that says one thing but feels another? I can't have that."

Out of the corner of her eye, Harper saw Bella and Tiffany stiffen. "I need to keep it real around here—you know what I'm saying? We're all in this together; my success is your success. And I can't succeed without your help, whether that's getting my dog groomed or writing a speech for me. All good?"

Harper knew it wasn't a real question, but she answered anyway. "Absolutely!"

"Thatta girl. Thanks, everyone! Bella, make sure you give Harper everything she needs," she said, waving them all away.

"C.J. is going to lose it," Tiffany whispered under her breath to Bella as they were walking out the door.

"Tiffany, hang back, I need to talk to you," Charlotte called out, stopping Tiffany in her tracks.

Harper caught the look of concern on Bella's face as Tiffany, with her back to Charlotte, rolled her eyes.

"Oh, and Bella—shut the door behind you," Charlotte said.

———————

An hour later, with the back seat of the car full, Harper backed Charlotte's enormous BMW out of the parking lot and followed the GPS directions to Charlotte's house. Luckily, Charlotte's three favorite stores had all been on the same strip, and Harper was able to dart from one to the other in the two hours she had to shop, drop everything off at the Green residence, and get back to the office. She ran through the items she'd purchased for what felt like the millionth time: the outfits, crystals, cushion, orchid. She just hoped that the salespeople who knew Charlotte better than she did had guided her correctly in selecting everything. Bella had given Harper the rundown on Charlotte's tastes, which—between Bella's details and her own Instagram deep dive—Harper had already summarized in her mind as Malibu meets the Magnolia Network. A little boho with a blazer, taking it from the office to the patio. Lots of dainty little necklaces, gold accessories, and fringed kimono jackets over motivational T-shirts that said things like, "You've Got This!" and "Yes, you can, Mama!" Harper's own wardrobe may have stuck to dark jeans, Chelsea boots, and trendy jackets, but she had watched enough reality TV with Poppy to know that Charlotte's aesthetic was the same as a host on a hip home-renovation show.

Right on cue, a call came in from Bella. Harper took the call on speaker and slowed to a crawl.

"Hey girl, how's it going? Just wanted to make sure you got everything."

"All good. Holy shit, these houses on Charlotte's street are insane," Harper said, gawking at the mansions. Harper didn't see houses like this in Manhattan. In New York, everyone was in an apartment or condo or, if they were really loaded, had a narrow brownstone to themselves. These houses had tennis courts and swimming pools and perfectly landscaped gardens with fountains out front.

"I know, right? They're worth millions," Bella said.

Millions. In New York, someone could spend millions on a two-bedroom apartment. Harper had no idea what these houses went for, but there was no doubt she'd be checking Zillow the moment she could. Just how much further could her dollar go in Nashville? Was it possible that she could actually afford to buy a place here? *Focus, Harper, don't get ahead of yourself*, she thought. It was only her first day, and she still hadn't seen where she'd be living for the next year. Although the idea that it could be one-tenth as nice as what she was looking at excited her.

"Charlotte's house is the one at the end with the big circular driveway. It's the nicest, of course, no surprise there. She has such great taste," Bella said, ending their call.

That she does, thought Harper, pulling in. The two-story, white-brick house had black-paned windows that took up most of the main floor, and they were framed by a row of manicured boxwoods. Two huge stone urns with yellow and white honeysuckle sat on either side of the entrance. Harper walked past a stone fountain to the double-wide glossy green doors, her arms loaded with shopping bags and cradling the orchid in her hands. She buzzed the intercom on her left with her hip and waited.

"Hello? Who are you?" a man's voice asked.

"Hi, I'm Harper. Charlotte's new visionary support strategist? She asked me to drop off some things."

"Hang on," the voice said before calling out, "Annette? Annette?" Silence. Then, "Shit, she's gone to get the kids for lunch. Okay, I can't come to the door right now—my hands are full—but I'll buzz you in. Just come straight through to the backyard."

"Okay. I'm new, so I might need some help finding—" The buzzer cut Harper off, and when she managed to open the door and enter the house, she was immediately greeted by two small white Westies that ran into her so enthusiastically that she lost her balance and Charlotte's orchid went flying from her hands. "Shit!" Harper dropped the bags and rushed to scoop the spilled soil back into the pot, relieved that the plant and its pot were still in one piece. "No, no, don't eat it, please," she said, as the dogs scattered dirt everywhere before running off. She picked up the plant and tried to wipe up the mess. It was no use; she'd need a broom and dustpan. Hopefully she could clean up the dirt before the man—Charlotte's husband?—noticed.

She wandered down the hallway, hoping to find a kitchen, but couldn't help but gawk at the gorgeous living room on her right. It was two stories high with a vaulted beamed ceiling that supported an oversize beaded chandelier that must've been at least three feet wide. Beneath it, a deep-green velvet sofa faced two large white armchairs with ottomans and bronze side tables. Harper ran her hand along the back of the couch, admiring the black-and-white portraits of the Green family hanging above the fireplace opposite it. On either side of the mantel were gold étagères that showcased a carefully curated collection of objects and vases, and nestled between two gold *G* bookends were the books Charlotte had written: *Going Green: Say No to Processed Foods and Yes to Eating Clean; Green with Envy: Turning Marital Jealousies into Hot Date Nights*; and *Greenspirations: Daily Doses of Wisdom for Warrior Women.* Harper slid her finger along the spines of each book, carefully pulling them out. The words *National Bestseller* stared back at her on all three covers. Damn.

Out of the corner of her eye, she saw the dogs run by her and remembered that she was supposed to be getting a broom. Harper put the books back and wandered down the hallway to the back of the house to find a giant eat-in kitchen with white marble counters. A wooden dining table sat in the corner with an upholstered bench on one side and rattan chairs with mint-colored cushions on the other.

Harper had only ever seen kitchens like this in *Architectural Digest.* Not even Poppy's parents, who had just renovated their Upper East Side apartment, had a kitchen like this. It probably cost more than the house Harper grew up in. Just how much money did an influencer make?

She grabbed a broom and a handful of paper towels and cleaned up her mess, accidentally getting soil on herself in the process. Looking for a bathroom to fix herself up, she found one to her right and jumped at the sound of Charlotte's voice coming from the speakers as she stepped inside.

Hey you, while you're here take a moment. A moment for yourself, a moment to reflect. When you look in that mirror, see yourself as you really are.

Harper did as Charlotte's voice instructed. What she saw was a woman with puffy eyes who'd had very little sleep with a big patch of dirt on the bottom of her shirt. She grabbed a handful of soap and turned on the tap to scrub the spot clean.

You're beautiful. You're strong. You are everything you need to be. Now go out there and show the world just how amazing you are.

Harper squeezed out the bottom of her shirt and exited the bathroom, nearly tripping over one of the Westies as they dropped a ball on her foot. She picked up the ball and watched as the dog ran back through his doggy door and out into the garden. Shit. The man who let her in was probably wondering what was taking her so long. She took a deep breath and headed outside.

"Wow," Harper said under her breath as she passed through the sliding glass doors. She admired the shale-bottom swimming pool, surrounded by black-and-white-striped cabanas and white-cushioned chaises with green towels folded at the edge. Girl really stuck to her color scheme.

"Goddamn it!" Harper heard a man shout, and she turned toward the sound of a crash that was coming from a guesthouse at the back of the garden. Tentatively, she walked over and poked her head into the open door to find Charlotte's husband, whom she recognized from Charlotte's Instagram, lifting a fallen microphone stand. He was surrounded by open boxes.

"Fuck. You didn't hear me swear," he said, standing to his full height, which had to be at least six five. "You must be Harper. Ryan." He extended his hand toward her.

"Nice to meet you," Harper said, shaking hands.

"Did you get lost on your way out or something?"

"No, I just dropped an orchid and was cleaning up the mess— or rather, trying," Harper said, self-consciously trying to hide the patch of wet fabric on her shirt.

"Relax, I'm just kidding. No need to tell me; everything you did is on camera. Charlotte's got the whole place wired."

Suddenly Harper was glad she hadn't done more snooping. "It's important to have good security," she offered.

"Or get good behind-the-scenes footage for all our fans," Ryan said with a laugh. "Let me guess—Cooper and Casper greeted you at the door and you nearly went flying."

"Yes." Harper was trying not to stare at the golden pompadour that sprouted from the top of Ryan's head. With his bright white veneers and perfectly toned muscles, he looked like a real-life Ken doll. He was so stereotypically handsome it was almost goofy, and Harper struggled not to laugh.

"They're little shits, completely untrainable. But the kids fucking love them. You got a dog?" Ryan asked, moving some papers off a couch and offering Harper a seat.

"No, I just moved here from New York this morning."

"You got kids?" he asked, folding himself into a massage chair and turning it on.

"No kids, no pets," Harper replied.

"Good—you won't have time for either. With Mandy gone and the big conference coming up, you're going to have to hit the ground running. But I bet you're used to that coming from the Big Apple." He reached into his pocket, pulled out a vape pen, and took a hit. "The Big Apple, whoever came up with that? Why not Empire City or Tiny Jungle, you know?"

"I don't know," Harper said, trying to wrap her head around the fact that this was actually Charlotte's husband.

"Don't worry," he said, noticing her staring at the vape. "It's not pot; this isn't New York. It's just nicotine, Starburst flavored. You can't get it anymore; they had to take it off the market because it was too tempting for kids. It's a shame—they were great clients. Not to mention their product is fucking delicious."

"You're in marketing?" Harper asked.

"I'm the CEO of a branding firm—or rather, *was* the CEO. I left to help Charlotte get The Greenhouse off the ground. And then, three years and three bestselling books later, I thought it was time to spread my own wings. Well, it's been two fucking years since I worked at The Greenhouse and everyone still thinks of me as *Mister Charlotte Green*. But that's all about to change, I've got a new thing." He held out the vape pen. "You want a drag?"

"No thanks. I don't smoke." Harper coughed. The smoke was already making her nauseous.

"Me either, if anyone asks." Ryan took another long hit. "Anyways, as I was saying, I've got a solo project now, no more joint ventures with anyone. I tried a few of those and none of them really sparked joy. But I thought about it, and I figured if everyone thinks of me as 'The Mister,' why not be *The* Mister, you know?" He held out his arms wide. "So I'm going to be launching *Mister Class*. It's like Master Class, only better, because I'm the host and all my guests will be successful, overlooked men like me. We'll be teaching other men our trade secrets for success. It's an untapped market. No one cares about us these days."

"White men?" Harper asked, trying to keep a straight face.

"Not *just* white. That wouldn't be cool."

"Of course not," Harper said, wondering just exactly what Ryan's criteria for cool was.

"Anyway, I thought I'd announce it on *Nashville Starz* tomorrow.

But I don't want to be accused of stealing Charlotte's thunder, so don't mention anything to her, okay?"

No, not okay, Harper wanted to say. She didn't like the idea of being a secret keeper for her boss's husband. Especially when she hadn't even clocked in a day's worth of work yet. "Well, I'll let you get to it," she said, suddenly eager to leave. "I left the bags for Charlotte in the hallway."

"Right. I guess I better get moving too if I want them to film in here." Ryan stood up and started tidying his office.

"Oh, they're not coming by the house," Harper said, standing to go. "Charlotte said they couldn't squeeze it in."

"Oh. Good to know." Ryan's face fell even as he tried to sound non-chalant. For a moment he looked lost in thought, but then he perked right back up and continued talking with a huge smile on his face. "Really great to meet you, Harper—and thanks." He gave her a short nod.

Harper made her way back to the car and paused for a moment, taking in the view of Charlotte's picture-perfect house. From the monogrammed beach towels, clean-cut husband, and bestselling novels, it was obvious that each detail of Charlotte's life was curated flawlessly. It was as if Harper had walked straight into one of Charlotte's Instagram posts. To the outside eye, it was *hashtag perfect*.

But, as Harper was quickly learning, appearances could be deceiving.

7

Home Suite Home

It was late by the time Harper finally got to her apartment at the Green Suites, a low-rise glass and brick building with twenty units that was an easy twenty-minute walk to work. With Bella leading the way, she stumbled out of the elevator onto the third floor to her new place at the end of the hall. Up since three in the morning, it was all she could do to keep her eyes open.

"I'm sorry I can't show you around tonight. This building is actually really cute, and it has a great pool and games room," Bella said. "But with *Nashville Starz* coming tomorrow, there's still a lot to do, and I know Charlotte will want to go over everything."

"Again?" Harper asked, wondering how there was anything left to go over. They'd worked through lunch, and it was now way past dinner. What else was there to discuss?

"Charlotte's a perfectionist; it's one of her best qualities. I don't think she'll need anything from you, but leave your phone on just in case. Oh, and we'll be starting early tomorrow."

"Today wasn't early?" Harper asked.

"No, today was a normal day—we normally start at seven thirty," Bella said, sounding surprised.

"Okay, I'm confused. I thought our workday started at eight. But when Aaron picked me up at seven thirty he said we had to go to the office right away, because Charlotte likes everyone to get there before she does, so I thought *that* was early. Now you're saying I should get to work even *earlier* tomorrow?"

"Oh, I get it. Yeah, *technically* we all work eight to five, but the truth is we just work as long as it takes to get the job done, you know? This isn't a regular job with regular hours; it's so much more—in all ways."

More is right, thought Harper, her head spinning.

"Don't worry, you get used to it." Bella dropped Harper's keys on the table. "I hope it's okay, but I put a few things in the fridge after the cleaners left. I can show you where to get groceries tomorrow."

"Thanks," Harper said, her stomach rumbling.

"You definitely got one of the nicer apartments. I left some things from the former tenant, like the plants and those cute rugs and cushions. It didn't seem right to throw them out. You might as well enjoy them. I'll let you get settled, but if you need anything, just text. Oh, and don't forget to *reach*."

"Reach?" Harper asked.

"You know, from 'GREEN'? The core values outlined in your welcome letter?"

"Oh, the acrostic," Harper said.

"Right. R is for reach, and that includes reaching out on social." Bella said it as if Harper should know this already. "Charlotte would expect you to post something about your first day."

"*Reach*—got it."

After Bella left, Harper opened the fridge and was grateful to find coffee, milk, bread, peanut butter, berries, and even a bottle of wine. It was everything she'd need for dinner and breakfast tomorrow. Bella was a lifesaver. She poured herself a large glass of wine and made herself a peanut butter sandwich, and then surveyed her new place. So this was going to be her new home for the next year. A place without roommates, if you didn't count the other nineteen Greenhouse employees who lived in the building. In that way, it was more like a dorm, although Harper had never had a dorm as nice as this. The Greens had bought two floors of preconstruction units to rent to employees, who were effectively paying off their mortgage with the housing allowance they were given as part of their salaries. They were welcome to live elsewhere, but Bella told Charlotte that the rent the Greens charged was way under market value, which made the Green Suites pretty irresistible. Every month the housing allowance would be deducted from Harper's check, before she even got it. No references, no first and last months' rent, no security deposit—it was a no-brainer.

Harper took in her new home. There was no way her fifteen-hundred-dollar-a-month housing allowance would get her anything as nice as this in New York, especially without a roommate. Exposed brick walls, a brand-new kitchen with a breakfast bar and high stools, an open-concept living room with a leather couch on one side and a TV on the other—it was perfect. She even had sliding glass doors that opened onto a small balcony, and, just down the hall, a bedroom big enough for a queen-size bed. Even a double had been a tight squeeze in her old place. Harper wasn't sure what she'd been expecting—maybe something clean and sparse like the office headquarters. But clearly, the no-personalization rule that applied to desks at The Greenhouse didn't apply here. The last tenant had painted the walls a soft gray and had left a pale pink faux fur rug in the middle of the living room, which was sitting beneath a giant paper lantern. There was a matching throw on the couch, which perfectly complemented the framed art prints hanging around the space. It was prettier than Harper had hoped, and she was excited to show it to Poppy. She pulled out her phone and snapped a series of pictures to send and then stopped. *Reach.* She should get that over with first. She checked Charlotte's Instagram to see how she tagged her photos and noted the bio in the profile. Wifey to @Mr.RyanGreen, Mama to 5 Teeny Greenies and Stepmama to 1 Big Greenie, Mogul to my #GirlBosses.

Curious, she checked Ryan's Instagram next. There must've been hundreds of photos of the two of them, dating all the way back to the beginning of Charlotte's account. Harper loved looking at the fashion evolution and changing hairstyles, but what was even more interesting was how the pictures showed the power shift in their relationship. Early pictures showed Charlotte as a doting wife glued to Ryan's side as she stared up at him, adoringly, while later photos showed her slightly ahead of him, standing tall and looking forward while he stared at her. It was as if Charlotte had gone from being Ryan's plus one to the other way around over the years.

Unlike the Greens, Harper wasn't nearly as comfortable posting pictures of herself, so she took a picture of the Nashville skyline, #NewView, and posted it for her 260 followers, remembering to tag @TheGreenhouse. Her account was private, so the picture couldn't be reposted, but at least Charlotte would know she was taking her new job seriously.

She then sent pics of her place to her mom and dad and Poppy— New Digs—and then another just to Poppy of her glass of wine and sandwich—Dinner.

Haha came back Poppy's reply. New city, same Harper. Cute place! How was day one?

Too tired to tell

Ok. Get some sleep.

Success Never Sleeps!

What?

Charlotte's mantra.

WOW. Poppy texted a scared-face emoji.

Harper followed up with a laughing-crying emoji. Talk soon. She ended her text with a heart and got one back.

Outside it was already dark, and the city lit up the sky with brightly colored lights from the restaurants and bars that lined the strip below.

Harper closed her eyes and listened: no sirens, no honking horns . . . just the faint sound of music coming from someone's balcony. It was hard to believe it, but she was *here*. She wasn't sure what to make of her first day except that she had gotten through it. She hoped that after the *Nashville Starz* segment was taped and things calmed down, she'd have a better understanding of what exactly her role at The Greenhouse would be. But now wasn't the time to jump to conclusions or make assumptions about her new job. She was beyond tired and needed a good night's sleep.

She exhaled deeply, finished her wine and sandwich, and put her plate in the sink. Unzipping her suitcase, she grabbed her toiletry kit. She'd unpack the rest of her things after her shower. Stripping down in the middle of her living room, she was relieved to be out of her poorly chosen clothes at last and shuffled to the bathroom, gasping as she turned on the light. There on the mirror was a Post-it Note that read, *Good luck—you're going to need it.* Harper's whole body went cold as she looked at the note. It felt like a warning, but for what? Who would leave this for her, and why? She didn't know, but one thing was certain: she wasn't about to fall asleep anytime soon.

8

Dance Like EVERYONE Is Watching

"I want it to look natural, like I did it myself. Only better, obviously," Charlotte said as her hairdresser lifted her hair off her forehead with a big round brush and smoothed out the frizzy curls that Harper, who was already used to Charlotte's perfectly tamed waves, had no idea existed. Charlotte was sitting in the conference room that had temporarily been transformed into a makeup and wardrobe trailer. Fully made up, she appeared glowing and rested, which, based on the number of messages Harper had woken up to on the Vine, couldn't have been further from the truth. Harper had stared at her phone in disbelief as the messages started coming in. They began at four in the morning, a stream-of-consciousness musing on the day ahead that started out full of inspiration then slowly became more agitated as the hour ticked on and Charlotte's frustration with being the only person awake in her company grew. At five o'clock, just as Charlotte was asking why everyone was sleeping in on such an important day, Bella messaged back to reassure Charlotte that she had barely slept a wink. She was so excited and was just getting ready to head to the office. That had set off a series of messages from other employees logging on and wishing each other good morning. Then Charlotte had shared her official Greenspiration for the day—Turn up your light and let yourself glow—and set off another wave of notifications.

If there was one thing Harper had learned from the last two jobs she had, it was how important it was to set expectations. Buy your coworker a morning coffee once and they'll always expect one; agree to pick up your boss's dry cleaning because it's on your way and they'll think they can ask you to do it every time. Bella had said that no one was expected to be on the Slack until work started, so Harper had made a conscious choice not to chime in until after she got into the office. She could still get another hour of sleep if she tried, so she'd put her phone on silent and went back to bed.

"I didn't know she had curly hair," Harper whispered to Bella, whose bloodshot eyes told Harper that she hadn't slept much. Harper wondered if Charlotte looked the same way under her layers of concealer.

"It's why she keeps it so cold in here. If she sweats, it frizzes *a lot*," Bella said. She made sure that no one was listening and then leaned in closer to Harper and whispered in her ear, "Perimenopause."

"Right, makes sense. At least it's that gorgeous blond color," Harper said, pulling her wrap tighter.

"Well, *not exactly* . . ." Bella hesitated. "It's naturally a mousy brown. She flies to L.A. to spend a fortune on highlights. Don't tell anyone." She was deadly serious.

"I won't," Harper reassured, unrolling the sleeves of her button-down to keep her arms warm. Maybe her New York City fall wardrobe would be fine after all. "Did you need me to organize the clothes into looks or anything?" Everything Harper had bought Charlotte was hanging on a clothing rack off to one side, and Harper was relieved to see that she had indeed bought enough options.

"No, that's okay. Charlotte's going with what she's wearing. You remembered to keep the receipts, right? So you can return everything?"

"What? I don't understand—did I pick out the wrong things?"

"Oh no, she hasn't even looked at them," Bella said matter-of-factly.

Charlotte stood and took in her appearance in the full-length mirror that had been set against the wall. She was wearing slim joggers, a matching cropped zip-up hoodie, and a fresh pair of white and green Adidas sneakers.

"But why would she ask me to get all that stuff if she's not even going to look at it?"

"She likes to have options, and we need to be ready for that. But at the end of the day, she follows her gut, and her gut is *always right*. And that's not just any yoga wear, trust me," Bella said with a knowing smile.

"Harper, you're here!" Charlotte said, finally noticing. She waved her over. "I was worried that maybe you'd overslept."

"What? No, I was here at seven, just like you said."

"Oh good." Charlotte touched Harper's arm affectionately. "Walk with me." She checked her makeup in the mirror and, clearly liking what she was seeing, walked with Harper to her office, where Oliver was putting the finishing touches on its transformation into a meditation room. To the left of the desk was a pale green yoga mat on the floor, with a white meditation cushion at one end and a collection of crystals in a gold tray at the other. An electrician had installed a dimmer overnight, and the whole room glowed.

"It's just," Charlotte said, adjusting the cushion, "that I didn't see your Post-it Note this morning, so I thought you'd slept in."

"My Post-it Note?" Harper asked Charlotte.

"Your daily intention? After I send out the Greenspiration for the day, everyone writes it down on a sticky note and then shares a picture on the Vine and on their socials of where they've placed it in their home. You're supposed to put another Post-it with your personal daily intention next to it."

Harper thought of the Post-it she had seen the night before on her bathroom mirror. Whoever posted that clearly had a different intention in mind for Harper. "I have to take a picture and share it?"

"You don't *have* to. Only if you *want* to. But why wouldn't you? Sharing is a part of our culture here, and it's how we get to know you and what you're working on. That way we can support you."

"What if your intention is something private?" Harper asked, trying to keep her voice light. The idea of essentially public journaling making her uncomfortable.

Charlotte took Harper's hands in hers and turned her body toward the door slightly.

"Just remember, Harper, no one can read a closed book. But when we open ourselves up, our story can reach others, help us to make connections and form community. It's community that supports and inspires us. None of us gets where we are alone. You don't ever have to go it alone again, Harper. You're part of The Greenhouse, and we're excited to see you grow." Charlotte picked up a pen and a Post-it Note and passed them to Harper, who stared at Charlotte wide-eyed. "Do you want to share your intention for the day with all of our followers?" she asked.

It was then that Harper noticed that Oliver had left the room so Aaron could film their interaction.

Harper stood awkwardly for a moment, but then took a deep breath and wrote, *Dance Like Everyone Is Watching*. Harper knew that the expression was actually "dance like no one is watching," but Charlotte cared what other people thought. Other people watched her every move on Instagram, other people were going to be taking a look inside The Greenhouse, and other people were constantly judging her, so it was important to Charlotte that the only judgment she received was positive. Everyone *was* watching, which meant that everyone was going to be watching Harper too. Her Greenspiration also covered two of the company's core values—energy and enthusiasm. She hoped that Charlotte got all that.

"Yes!" Charlotte said, placing her hands on either side of Harper's arms and giving her a squeeze as Aaron zoomed in on the Post-it. "Yes," she repeated, nodding enthusiastically until Harper joined in.

"And *cut*!" Bella called, rushing in. "That was amazing."

"We can use this for our own behind-the-scenes feature. Or maybe we can show it to Reed, in case he needs something for his B-roll," Charlotte said.

"I love it." Bella pulled out her Greenhouse Inspiring Ideas notebook and scratched something off her list.

"I didn't realize we were going to be filming," Harper said, running her hands through her hair self-consciously.

"You have to be ready for everything and anything at all times. Everything we do, we do it to share. Open book, Harper, open book." Charlotte flashed her a wide grin.

"Open book," Harper repeated, making a mental note that if she was going to have to be one, she'd better be careful what she shared. She needed to reveal enough to satisfy Charlotte's desires for transparency while still protecting her privacy. Maybe her book could be *open*, with a lowercase *o*.

"And remember, I want Reed to see everyone working in their Growth Planners, so make sure Tiffany hands them out," Charlotte said, pointing to a large cardboard box on the floor. She placed her hands in prayer above her heart. "Namaste." She waved Harper out.

The room was practically vibrating by the time Charlotte gathered everyone in the garden to make her announcement in front of Reed Philips and the crew of *Nashville Stars*. Everything and everyone had been *extra* during filming. Extra invested in writing in their Growth Planners, extra focused on work, extra attentive in conversations, extra sincere, and extra joyful. It didn't strike Harper as being fake, but it didn't feel particularly authentic either. The presence of the camera had made everybody hyperaware of themselves and it had given Harper gas, probably because she kept holding her breath due to nerves.

From what she could tell, everything had gone off so far without a hitch. Reed had greeted Charlotte just as she came out of lotus position during her "morning meditation," then they'd done the company dance-off followed by Charlotte checking in with members of her Green Team. Finally, *Nashville Starz* shot the big-ideas brainstorm between Charlotte and Bella in the conference room to discuss the upcoming In-spire conference. It was amazing to watch Charlotte in action—the way she talked to Reed as if they were old friends, the enthusiastic sincerity in her voice, and her insistence that she was just trying to do her small part to make the world a better place for everyone. If the Charlotte that Harper had met during her car ride interview had been persuasive, this Charlotte had her own force field that made her impossibly magnetic. She was like a movie star or celebrity, capable of increasing the wattage of her personality in relation to the size of her audience. And there was no doubt that the audience tuning in to *Nashville Starz* would be her largest yet.

"And now, the big announcement you've all been waiting for," Char-lotte said to the group now standing in a circle in the garden. Before she could say anything else, Bella picked up the tree stump and brought it over to Charlotte.

"What's this?" Charlotte asked as she nervously checked over her shoulder.

"The Tower of Power, for the announcement," Bella said with a big smile.

"Tower of Power?" Charlotte sounded confused, as if she hadn't heard the term before, and shook her head. "I don't think so; we're *all* powerful here, Bella." She motioned for her to take it away.

As soon as the director of *Nashville Starz* called action, Reed Phillips walked over to Charlotte. "So this is the *garden*?" He chuckled, looking around. "When you said we were gathering in the garden, I was expecting a real one," he said, laughing.

Charlotte's smile faltered for just a moment before she regained her composure and locked eyes with Reed. "We create our own realities every day, Reed. And there is nothing more real than the bright minds and big hearts gathered here. This is where we come together to share and grow every day. It's inspiring. It's just like *Nashville Starz* always says, if you can dream it, you can make it happen."

There was no way that Reed Phillips could argue with that. "Well, I for one am *inspired*. And I understand that you have a big announcement to make?"

"I'm so glad to hear it, Reed, and yes, I do." Charlotte took a deep breath and turned to look just to the right of the camera. "As you all know, our little Inspire conference continues to grow each year thanks to our incredibly passionate community who believes in us as much as we believe in them." She placed her hands on her heart and tilted her head to the side. "And this year is going to be better than ever thanks to our first-ever sponsor . . ." Here, Charlotte unzipped her sweatshirt, letting it drop to her waist, and slowly turned her back to the camera so they could read what was printed in bright green letters on the back of her T-shirt: SERENE X GREEN.

"Serene? The yoga wear company? Wow, that's huge," Reed said.

"It is! We're their first-ever collaboration. Not only am I a longtime fan of all their products, but we share a vision of empowering people everywhere to be their best selves. It just goes to show: whether you're a billion-dollar company or a scrappy little passion project like us, we're all connected." Charlotte stretched her arms out to take hold of the hands of the people on either side of her, who immediately followed suit until everyone in the circle was holding hands and beaming at their fearless leader.

Just then, Ryan and the kids came running in. Charlotte's four-year-old twins Willow and Wyatt raced up to her, their blond curls flying as they wrapped her in a huge hug. Following close behind were ten-year-old Maddie, eight-year-old Henry, six-year-old Jagger, and Ryan bringing up the rear. He held two bags of take-out lunch.

"Well, this is a surprise! I'm sorry, Reed, I had no idea they were coming!" Charlotte said, looking genuinely taken aback.

"No, no, this is great, keep rolling," Reed said to his crew. "The whole family is here!"

"Sure is!" Charlotte said as her kids turned to face Reed and angled their bodies just so toward the camera. It was obvious they were used to being filmed. Off camera, Harper could see Bella waving her arms and frantically mouthing something to Charlotte.

"I mean, almost the whole family. My stepson Jameson's missing; he's in high school," Charlotte said quickly.

Maddie flipped her hair over her shoulder and smiled. "Mama we brought you lunch!"

"You did?" Charlotte said, looking at Ryan as he made his way over. He was wearing a navy bomber jacket over a white T-shirt, with khakis and white sneakers. With a fresh haircut and new tan, he looked like he had just stepped out of a Ralph Lauren catalog. "Surprise!" Ryan flashed his Chicklet-toothed grin.

"Sure is, but what's the occasion?" Charlotte asked Ryan, her eyes wide.

"Oh, honey, you've just been working so hard that the kids wanted to surprise you and have lunch with you," Ryan cooed, kissing his wife on the cheek.

"Well, I *am* surprised, that's for sure," Charlotte replied, and Harper thought she could detect a hint of annoyance in her voice.

"Geez, I wish someone would bring me lunch sometime," Reed said, chuckling.

"Well, you're welcome to join us," Ryan said.

"It seems like your family is big enough." Reed chuckled and slapped Ryan on the back.

"Don't say that! We're hoping for one more, right, honey?" Ryan wrapped his arm around Charlotte and pulled her close.

For a split second, Charlotte's face hardened, and then she playfully slapped Ryan on the chest. "You can hope, but unless you're the one getting pregnant, I think we should count our blessings at six."

"I swear, if I could get pregnant, I would," Ryan said, smiling wide.

"What a guy." Reed affectionately punched Ryan in the arm.

"He's the best. Really, I couldn't work as hard as I do without his support and devotion. Not every working mom has it this good, and I know that, trust me," Charlotte said, angling herself toward the still-rolling camera.

"Aw, that's sweet. I love that," Reed said, pointing his finger back and forth between Charlotte and her husband. "It's kind of a role reversal in some ways, I guess, but it looks like you're both good with it."

"Well, actually, we support each other," said Ryan. "You see, right now, I'm—"

"Trying to get your wife to eat lunch, I get it. I get it." Charlotte laughed loudly, nudging her children ever so slightly so that they joined in, and soon Ryan and Reed were laughing too.

"And *cut*!" the director yelled.

"That was great!" Reed exclaimed. "I love that spontaneity. Love that we get to see Mogul Charlotte and Mom Charlotte all in one."

"Mogul Mom," Charlotte joked as Oliver thanked everyone and sent them back to their desks.

Ryan tried to get Reed's attention. "Are you sure you don't have another sixty seconds to fill? I'd love to tell you about my new *Mister*—"

"Reed, we need to get one more exterior shot of you before we wrap," an assistant said, coming up to him.

"Right, of course," he said, tightening his tie. "Sorry, Ryan, no time, but this is great. We got everything we needed, including an appearance by husband of the year. Charlotte, we'll be in touch in case we need anything else. Otherwise, my assistant will reach out to your people with the air date and answer any questions you might have."

"Sounds great. Let me walk you out," Charlotte said, taking Reed's arm and leading him away.

"Fuck," Ryan muttered under his breath, as he was left alone in the garden. He turned and caught Harper watching before she could turn away. "Did you say anything to Charlotte?"

"About what?"

"About announcing my *Mister Class*."

"No," Harper said, aware that Oliver was watching and coming their way.

"Fuck." Ryan shook his head.

"Ryan, why don't you come have lunch with the kids in the conference room? Charlotte should be back any moment," Oliver said.

"I don't need you to babysit me, Oliver." Ryan stood tall and folded his arms across his chest.

Harper watched as Charlotte came back in and started applauding her Green Team.

"That was wonderful, everyone. You did yourselves proud, and you did *us* proud," she said, joining Ryan in the middle of the garden and hooking arms. "We always say there is no 'I' in 'team,' but there are two Es in 'Green,' and we know that *each* and *every* one of you plays an important part in what we do here. So thank you for all that you do. Truly, thank you," she said, looking directly at Harper. "Harper, why don't you join us for lunch?"

It wasn't a request so much as an order. Harper wasn't sure what she was really being thanked for, but something told her it wasn't good.

9

A Seat at the Green Table

"Harper, can you please get the kids set up?" Charlotte asked, seating Wyatt and Willow next to one another at one end of the conference table. She reached into the cabinet that ran the length of the wall where the supplies were kept and pulled out a couple of fruit pouches for the twins, and box of crayons and a pad of paper for Jagger. "Maddie and Henry, no iPad until after lunch. You can read or help Jagger with his drawing." They rolled their eyes and put their devices on the table.

"Sure," Harper answered, taking out containers of sandwiches and fries and salads, along with straws and napkins that the group of kids grabbed from her.

"Hey, can I talk to you for a second?" Charlotte asked Ryan. He was sitting in the chair farthest away from his kids, scrolling on his phone.

"Five bucks if you hit Jagger between the eyes," Henry whispered as his mom looked away. He tore off a corner of the napkin and rolled it between his fingers before popping it in his mouth. Catching the twins looking at him, he held his finger up to his lips for them to be quiet.

"Ten," Maddie said, copying him.

Harper looked at Jagger, who was drawing circles with his crayons.
"Guys, I don't really think you should—"

"Nobody asked you," Henry said.

"Who are you, anyway? What happened to Jenny?" Maddie asked.

"You mean Mandy," Henry said, before spitting a ball that missed
his brother by two inches and stuck against the wall. The twins started
laughing. "Jenny was the one before Mandy."

"I don't know. I'm new," Harper said.

"Obviously." Maddie snorted as she continued to shred napkins.

"What was that all about? Showing up here and surprising me?"
Charlotte asked Ryan, ignoring her children's antics. "I thought we agreed
we would meet back at the house."

"Really? That's strange, because Harper told me that *Nashville Starz*
wasn't coming by the house because you couldn't *squeeze it in*," Ryan
said, grabbing his own drink. "Figured I'd make things easier for you."

Charlotte paused for a nanosecond before answering, and Harper's
whole body stiffened. "They weren't, but then I convinced them otherwise.
Why would I tell you and the kids to be ready after lunch if they weren't
going to swing by?"

Harper could feel Charlotte's eyes on her and busied herself with
handing out the food to the kids. She watched as Maddie deconstructed
her entire sandwich, while Henry devoured his and then reached over
to take half of Jaggers. *Animals,* thought Harper. She snuck a look at
Charlotte and tried to recall if there had been anything in the Vine chat
or in their morning meeting about *Nashville Starz* going to the Greens'
home, but came up with nothing. And she hated that it now felt like she
was keeping a secret from both Charlotte and Ryan.

"You did? Well, I, uh, thought this was better—more spontaneous,
more on brand," Ryan said defensively.

"You're right, it was. Reed loved it—*I* loved it. Except for that crack
about having another kid."

"Would that be so bad?" Ryan asked.

"You just want me at home," Charlotte said. Her voice was unnaturally high and sweet, and it made Harper tense. Maybe it was just because their children were present, but Harper couldn't believe this was how two married people actually argued. Everything she'd heard and read about the Greens painted them as the perfect couple. Date nights to keep the love alive, pillow fights to stay young at heart, and cooking together to stay together. "Date Nights, Pillow Fights, and Tasty Bites" was actually a chapter in *Green with Envy*.

"Can you blame me? You heard Reed talking about our 'role reversal,' " he muttered under his breath. "It's emasculating. Besides, I thought it could be my turn for a change. You're not the only one with big plans."

"Oh, you mean your *Mister Class?* Well, it's too bad your surprise visit meant that he didn't get to see the house and your studio. That *is* what you wanted, right? To give him a tour and talk about your *big plans?*"

"Well, if the opportunity came up, I thought it wouldn't hurt to tease it," Ryan said. He shifted in his seat as Charlotte sat on the edge of it and took Ryan's hands in her own.

"Of course, I get that. And believe me, babe, I would've loved for Reed to have seen your setup, but at the end of the day, it's only a three-minute segment. That's not a lot of time."

Not a lot of time—that wasn't what she told Bella when she said the same thing. Harper was so busy eavesdropping that she hadn't noticed a spitball flying her way, and in her haste to avoid it, she accidentally knocked over her drink and sent its contents spilling all over the table toward Jagger.

"My drawing! You ruined my drawing!" Jagger wailed.

"Shit, shit, shit!" Harper said, grabbing a handful of paper towels to clean up the mess.

"Language!" Charlotte and Ryan snapped at the same time.

"Oh my gosh, I'm so sorry. I didn't mean to swear," Harper stammered, turning bright red as the kids laughed.

"Harper's got a potty mouth! Put a dollar in the jar!" the kids chanted.

"Put three," Maddie said. "She said it three times."

"Shit, shit, shit," Willow and Wyatt chanted as they banged their hands on the table.

"Willow! Wyatt!" Charlotte shrieked, and shook her head. "Now, kids," she lowered her voice, "I'm sure Harper didn't mean to swear. Why don't we let her have this one mistake? That's what we would want, right? A second chance?"

"And if she does it again?" Henry asked.

"Oh, well, then she'll have to pay," Charlotte said, laughing.

"I'm really sorry," Harper said, balling up the wet paper towels and putting them in the trash can. "It just slipped out."

"Must've. Well, let's make sure we don't have any more slips." Charlotte walked over to each of her children and kissed them on the head as they pushed their empty take-out containers aside. "Would you look at the time? You should get back to school," she said, heading to the door.

"Wait, where are you going?" Ryan asked.

"Back to work, babe. I've got an afternoon full of meetings. We can't all take the day off."

"I'm not taking the day off," he said, clenching his jaw.

"No, of course not." She gently tilted her head. "I meant taking the day off from *here*. Look, it was your idea to leave The Greenhouse and find your own thing, and I respect that. Now I need *you* to respect that with you gone, I need to work more than ever."

"Well, when will you be home?" Ryan questioned, standing up and stuffing his hands in his pockets.

"I don't know. Why?"

"It's Annette's day off, and I was hoping—"

"You'll figure it out," she said quickly, and stood on her tiptoes to kiss Ryan on the cheek. "Love you, Greeners!" she called out to her kids. She motioned for Harper to join her. The moment they stepped out of the conference room, Charlotte turned to Harper. "In my office."

Once they were inside, Charlotte shut the door and walked straight to the rack of clothes at the back of the room. Slowly, she took the items off their hangers and handed them to Harper. "Have you ever been married, Harper?"

"Married? No."

"Lived with someone?" Charlotte asked, admiring one outfit and then passing it to Harper.

"A boyfriend once, but that was a few years ago, in college," Harper replied.

"And? What happened?" Charlotte pried, passing her an empty shopping bag.

"Well, it turned out that we wanted different things," Harper said, slowly folding a beautiful cashmere wrap and placing it in the bag. She wasn't sure where this was going, but she was painfully aware that Charlotte was suddenly in no rush to get to those meetings she had told Ryan about.

"Like kids?" Charlotte pressed. "Because I know what a big decision that is, although sometimes, it's not yours to make."

Harper stopped what she was doing and looked at Charlotte.

"Oh no, not me. All my kids were planned, right down to their astrological signs. No, I meant my stepson, Jameson. Ryan and his first wife, Annabelle, had just graduated college when she got pregnant— she was ready for marriage and kids, he wasn't, and then he met me. Timing is everything."

"Well, timing wasn't the reason we split. And for the record, I love kids. Just not now."

"So career then," Charlotte said, passing a dress and a shirt to Harper.

"Yeah, and where we lived. He wanted to go back to Poughkeepsie, where we're both from, and I wanted to stay in Manhattan."

"And be a big-city girl with a big-city life." It wasn't a question, and Harper felt her cheeks get hot.

"Kind of. I mean, I was trying to make it as a writer, and when I realized how hard that was, I decided to work in publishing—and that's where publishing happens," Harper said lamely.

"It happens in other places too. I'm sure there's some small press in Poughkeepsie that would've been happy to have you." Charlotte took the last of the items and dumped them into Harper's arms.

"Actually, there is, but I just wanted—"

"More. You wanted more because you're *ambitious*, and that's a good thing, but it can make relationships difficult. Ambition can scare someone off or make them feel like they don't measure up—I'm guessing that was your ex-boyfriend's problem. He probably accused you of changing from the Harper he first met. I'd bet he probably muttered how you don't make him *feel* like a man. It happens; they feel threatened and worry that you're going to steal their spotlight, even if you're the reason their light is shining in the first place. You know what I mean?"

"I think so."

"Ryan wants his own spotlight," Charlotte said. She moved close to Harper and spoke in a clear whisper. "And if he gets it, that's less light on us, and do you know what happens to a garden that doesn't get enough light?"

"It dies?"

"It *dies*," Charlotte repeated, staring at Harper. "Now, that doesn't mean I'm not supportive of other people's ambitions. I'm all about lifting others up and encouraging them to live their dreams. I wouldn't be here without Ryan devoting so much time to supporting me. Especially during the early days, I had nothing but dollars and dreams. But now, it's even more essential that the business stays a success, or else nobody wins. So while you may wonder why I didn't tell him that *Nashville Starz* wasn't going to be coming by the house, the truth is that I am really just trying to make sure we stay on message, and right now, that message has to be all about the Serene sponsorship and the Inspire conference. It might sound harsh, but sometimes loving someone means doing what's best for them, even if they might not know it at the time."

"I understand," Harper said, trying to keep eye contact with an unblinking Charlotte. But she couldn't help but feel that Charlotte's decision not to tell Ryan the truth was more about spite and less about helping him. If she really wanted to help, she could've just made a comment about how amazing it was that he found the time to bring her lunch when he was so busy developing a new project. "I wasn't trying to cause problems by telling him that *Nashville Starz* wasn't filming at the house, honestly."

"No problem, it's all good," she said, throwing her hands in the air. She stopped and walked around to take a seat at her desk. She opened its top drawer, pulled out her keys, and tossed them to Harper, who just managed to catch them. "Take those clothes back and be ready to brainstorm in an hour." She lifted the receiver of the phone that was on her desk.

"Got it!" Harper said, realizing as she walked out of the office with the bags full of clothing that she had no idea what she was supposed to be brainstorming about.

10

Inner Circle Only

"I'm sorry," Harper said, making sure she had heard correctly. "But you want *me* to find up-and-coming designers and do what?" They'd been at it for over an hour already. From what Harper could gather, Charlotte had pitched the idea of a clothing design collaboration with Serene despite the fact that she had no designs, let alone a designer. The news had come as a surprise to all of them, especially Oliver, who seemed to be under the impression that Serene was just going to sponsor the event and sell their merchandise at the Inspire conference. It was Charlotte who had sold them on a yoga wear collaboration, promising a fresh limited-time-only capsule collection that she herself would curate. Apparently, Ryan wasn't the only one who liked to go rogue.

"Get inspired," Charlotte said, as if she were stating the obvious. "There is so much talent out there just waiting to be discovered. I'm thinking about someone new and unknown. Someone with a fresh take on things that we've never heard of. They don't even have to be from America. You know, come to think of it, it might be better if they aren't."

Harper looked to Bella, Oliver, and Tiffany, hoping one of them would jump in with suggestions, but they were all ignoring her gaze. She pressed on.

"Inspiration, right, I get that. But, um, then *what*, exactly? Should I reach out and ask them if they are interested in designing for us?" Harper asked, writing the words *design inspiration* in her notebook and circling it.

Charlotte looked over at Oliver, who leaned forward.

"No, I wouldn't reach out to them and say that." He looked to Charlotte.

"You don't need to reach out to them. You just need to use their designs as a template for our inspiration."

"But won't we still need an actual designer to make the clothes?"

"No, Serene can handle the logistics of that. We're just going to create the looks," Charlotte said.

"Okay, but if we don't have a designer and are just using other people's designs to um, inspire our *looks*, isn't that just copying?" Harper asked.

Harper could practically hear everyone holding their breath.

"Who said anything about copying? I'm talking about inspiration. You know, inspiration is the sincerest form of flattery, Harper," Charlotte said, standing up and coming over.

The saying was actually "imitation is the sincerest form of flattery," but Harper wasn't about to correct her boss. Charlotte placed her hand on the back of Harper's chair and leaned over her.

"By the time these designs get to our followers, Serene will have put their mark all over them. We just need to give them something to work with, that's all. It's just research we're doing, curating source material."

"Right, okay, but just so I'm clear, you want me to collect designs and bring them to you?"

Charlotte sat on the desk so that she was facing Harper and looking her in the eye.

"Maybe it would help if you think of it like a book. It starts out as the author's idea, but then eventually their agent gets involved and an editor, and everyone pitches in to make it great until it's ready to be published. By then, it's not really just the author's anymore, is it?"

"I know what you mean, but it's a little different because the original idea was the author's . . ."

"And the original idea for this collaboration with Serene was mine, so you don't have to worry about that." Charlotte placed her hand on Harper's and gave it a little squeeze. "I love your integrity, Harper, because at the end of the day, that's all any of us have."

Harper opened her mouth to speak, but before anything came out, Bella placed her foot on top of Harper's and pressed down hard, making Harper bite her lip.

"So true," Bella said. "And you know, I was thinking we should have Harper write about the design process for social. A 'Behind the Seams' feature for our 'Love, Charlotte' emails, so they can see just how much work and integrity goes into every part of the process."

"YES! Yes, I love that idea," Charlotte said. "And it would stir up some interest, which will be good because the venue I want for this conference is going to be much bigger than our previous ones, so we have to sell *a lot* of tickets."

"How much bigger?" Tiffany asked, her voice going up.

"Triple," Charlotte said, tossing her hair over her shoulder and smiling proudly.

"Six thousand?" Oliver said. "You want to go from a two-thousand-seat venue to six?"

"You bet. I'd say more, but I can see you're already starting to sweat. So let's go with six for now." She hopped off the desk and unzipped her jacket, lifting her hair on top of her head. "Did someone turn the heat up? It feels hot in here." She walked over toward the wall where the thermostat was and lowered the temperature.

"Charlotte, are you sure that's such a good idea? Increasing the venue size by that much, I mean? It's a big leap," Oliver said, wrapping his blazer around himself as a blast of cool air came through the vents.

"What? You don't think I can do it? C.J. did, and she didn't have Serene as her sponsor. Oh my God, she's going to crap herself when she finds out. I can't wait to see the look on her face at the influencer lunch."

"Influencer lunch?"

"It's in December," Bella said. "It's a gathering of the most powerful female influencers in the country, like the United Nations of girlbosses. We always go, and this year Charlotte's a guest speaker."

"It's about time," Charlotte said, rolling her eyes.

"And C.J. will be there?" Harper asked, trying to keep up.

"Oh, she'll be there all right. Let's see if she's so high and mighty after this."

"Do you think we should maybe give her a heads-up?" Tiffany asked.

"Nope." Charlotte started gathering up her notebook and pens and stacking everything into a neat pile.

"Tiffany does have a point," Oliver said slowly. "From what I've heard, C.J.'s been pushing hard for a collab with Serene for a while now."

"Oh well, not my problem. She'll just have to find out with everyone else," Charlotte said. "I mean, it's not like I *stole* something from her."

"Still, I think—" Oliver tried shooting Bella a look that she did not return.

Before he could say another word, Charlotte clapped her hands together and cut him off. "*I think* that's more than enough for now. Let's get on this, shall we?"

"Sure thing," Tiffany said, her jaw tight.

"Oh, one more thing. This year's influencer lunch is going to be packed, so speakers only get one extra ticket."

"What does that mean?" Tiffany asked.

"It means that only one of you can come, but I'm going to need some time to decide who that should be," Charlotte said, waving them off.

Harper, Bella, and Tiffany quickly gathered up their things while Oliver hung back.

"She's going to need time to decide who she's taking?" Tiffany hissed, once they were out of earshot. "Are you fucking kidding me? I'm her event maestro; I should be there. It's because I said something about C.J."

"Don't be ridiculous. You heard Charlotte, it's just really packed and—"

"Save it," Tiffany said, holding up her hand and storming off.

Out of the corner of her eye, Harper saw Oliver pacing back and forth in Charlotte's office as he talked. Whatever he was saying made Charlotte throw her hands up in the air.

"I wonder what that's all about," Harper said, hoping that Bella would tell her, but Bella was already scanning messages on her phone. "I mean, it's not hard to see they're not exactly on the same page," Harper whispered.

That got Bella's attention. She pulled Harper close to her and whispered, "Shh, I'll tell you later." She said it so quietly that Harper practically had to read her lips. "I have to go deal with something else right now."

As Bella stalked off to the back of the office, Harper returned to her desk and checked the Vine. She saw all the comments that Charlotte had posted since *Nashville Starz* left, saying how great everyone had been and calling out certain people for really bringing their A game.

> OMG Community Team, you guys were rocking it today! LOVE the enthusiasm. Shout out to Halle and Debbie for wearing Green merch.

> Create Team, LOVE the Inspire conference product placement on your desks—one time exception to the no-stuff-on-desk rule! Lol. Looking sharp in all green and white today, Todd!

There were a few more *way to go*, and *you're the best* proclamations, and to her surprise, Harper found herself scouring for mentions of her name. Harper noticed there were several people who didn't get singled out, like Bella, who had taken the time to heap praise on Charlotte about how awesome she'd been and how they couldn't wait to see her on TV. The comments reeked of desperation and made Harper cringe, although Charlotte did like them with little heart emojis that were instantly liked back by whoever posted. It was an endless loop of seeking approval and then thanking Charlotte for her validation when it was received. Harper was trying to make her way through them all when she got a direct message from Bella.

> Charlotte wants to try you out for her 'Love, Charlotte' weekly email. Check out her past blasts (samples are in your email) and then write a spec one about today. Go see Aaron about what footage and pictures you can use. FYI, no one else in The Greenhouse can know it's you writing them. Connect Team only.

Standing up, she saw Bella a few desks down, listening intently to a young employee who was clearly upset about something.

"Bella said you needed to see me?" Aaron asked, appearing at Harper's side and startling her.

"What? I did? Oh yeah, I did," she said, as he started to walk off. "Where are we going?"

"My office." Aaron gave her a sly smile as he headed toward the back of the building. Harper followed him, passing Bella and the young woman, who was clearly trying not to cry, a bunch of employees who were furiously writing in their Growth Planners, and another person who was on the phone doing what sounded like a customer service call. *None of us can grow without feedback, so thank you!*

"How did you get an office?" Harper asked, pausing for a moment at a door marked STORAGE.

"By taking it." Aaron opened the door and stood aside so Harper could enter.

"This is a storage room," Harper said, taking a look around at the equipment-filled space.

"Correct," Aaron said, letting the door close behind them. He walked past Harper, disappearing around the shelves. "Bella tells me you need footage."

"She tells me that too," Harper said, waiting. It had to be at least five degrees hotter in this room than anywhere else in the building. She flexed her hands open and closed, warmth coming back to her icy fingertips. "So, can I have it?"

From behind the shelves, Aaron snorted, and Harper rounded the corner.

"Sure, it's all here," Aaron said.

Harper looked behind the shelves. Aaron was reclining in an office chair at a long, wide desk that held two giant monitors, a laptop, a couple of hard drives, and, to her surprise, a coffee cup and a half-eaten sandwich—clearly violating Charlotte's "no food or drink" rule. On the floor under the desk was an old Persian rug, and on the wall next to Aaron, he'd taped a couple of pictures: a marquis of the Grand Ole Opry, a silver Airstream on top of a mountain at sunset, a Polaroid of a beautiful dark-haired woman with black-rimmed glasses. She looked to be in her early fifties. *His mom?* Harper wondered.

"How did you . . ." Harper began, envy and awe taking her words away. Her gaze landed on a small table behind him. "And why do you have a *Nespresso machine?*"

"To make my iced coffee," Aaron said. He reached under the desk and opened a black mini fridge, revealing a door full of cold coffee in mason jars. "Want one, *Manhattan?*" he asked, stifling a laugh at Harper, who was practically drooling.

"*Yes*, I want one." She opened the jar and took a large sip. "Who are you? What is this? Are you even part of The Greenhouse?"

"I told you, I kind of have my own thing going on," he said, grabbing an extra chair for Harper and putting it next to his. He pulled up

Charlotte's website on one of the monitors, and on the other, a file with a bunch of videos. "Look, it's just an underused storage room that nobody cares about. Charlotte knows, but she never comes in—"

"Because it's too hot." She swiveled in her chair and took in the room. "Smart. I'm jealous."

"Yeah, well, stick around, and maybe you'll get your own office one day too," he said, angling the monitor toward her.

"Really?" Harper asked.

"Nah, probably not," he said, smirking.

"Nice." Harper leaned forward to look at the screen and the hundreds of videos and photographs that Aaron had apparently collected over the last week. Charlotte's followers had an insatiable appetite for content. In addition to the never-ending Instagram posts and stories, Harper had learned, she had a themed monthly newsletter that was usually geared toward some kind of group activity for the Green community—like a sugar cleanse, or a month of holistic self-care. Charlotte wrote the newsletter posts herself.

But the most personal of Charlotte's media were her weekly email blasts. *Love, Charlotte,* came off like a one-sided conversation between best friends. If the newsletter was all about selling the Green brand, the email blasts were about selling Charlotte, the "real" woman behind the brand.

"How can one person create so much content while writing books and hosting conferences and designing yoga wear?" Harper asked. No wonder her mantra was *Success doesn't sleep.*

"They can't," Aaron said as he tilted his head and considered Harper.

Harper was just about to ask him what he meant when Bella came in. "There you are. Do you have everything you need?"

"Harper was just asking how Charlotte can do all the things she does," Aaron said, leaning back in his chair and folding his arms across his chest.

"Because she's Charlotte Green!" Bella said, throwing her hands in the air. "She's amazing, and we're lucky to work for and support her. And right now, she needs our support."

"Got it," Harper said as she scrolled.

"No, I mean *right* now, as in let's go, Harper, we've got a collaboration to design and no design inspiration. Aaron, can you just send her everything you have?"

"You got it, boss," he said lazily.

As Harper rushed out of the storage-room-turned-office, she glanced back to find Aaron with a lingering smile, watching her leave. Harper's heart began to beat a little bit faster . . . and she wasn't sure if the iced coffee was to blame.

11

Thank God It's Fri-yay!!

By the time three o'clock on Friday rolled around, Harper could barely keep her eyes open. In her desperate attempt to stay awake, she'd already stolen an iced coffee from Aaron's fridge, volunteered for an errand just so she could grab an espresso, and had stripped down to a sleeveless T-shirt in the hopes that the icy cold would wake her up.

It had been a busy first week. She'd worked fourteen hours the day before and had stayed up all night to finish her presentation on designers for Charlotte. Apparently, when Charlotte said she wanted to see designers, she meant right away, in the form of a pitch deck and full creative brief. It didn't matter that Harper had never created either before and that she was used to having twelve months, not thirty-six hours, before content went public. She was quickly figuring out that time worked differently in the influencer world, where new content was generated as quickly as it was consumed. Between the daily social posts, email blasts, messages on the Vine, the intention Post-it Notes, and numerous personal errands for Charlotte, Harper could barely catch her breath. And on top of all that was the designer presentation.

Harper had wrestled with the best way to draw inspiration from designers without copying them. At first, she'd looked at fitness magazines to see what the models were wearing. Then she'd looked at athleisure wear designs online. But without the ability to draw anything herself, Harper found that the only way to get her ideas across was to cut and paste current outfits into her own document, committing the equivalent of design plagiarism. Even though some of the designers she'd found online were far from the mainstream, Harper couldn't bring herself to advise Charlotte to outright copy them. After all, Charlotte had commended her integrity and asked for *inspiration*, so what if she focused on that?

It was sometime around midnight when Harper came up with the idea of creating more of a mood board with a story. Instead of just drawing inspiration from other existing designs, she decided to take inspiration from nature. A wide-leg yoga pant was like a large palm frond, a slim pant like a tall reed of grass. The woman who wore them on her mood board was taking a journey out of her regular life into an exotic world. It was a stretch, but mixing nature images with pictures of clothing was something Harper could actually get behind, and so she had worked until sunrise and then crossed her fingers as she pressed send.

Now, as she looked across The Greenhouse into the conference room, where a small group of people were reviewing her presentation, she exhaled deeply. Two more hours and she could go home, have a glass of wine, call Poppy, and fall asleep. She didn't expect to make it past 9:00 p.m., which suited her just fine.

She turned her attention back to her email blast and reread it, making sure she sounded as close to Charlotte as she could. It was strange writing as someone else, finding their tone and working with their rhythms. So far, the hardest part had been giving herself permission to write in sentence fragments and use exclamation points with the kind of abandon that would have sounded the alarm at her old job. Charlotte wrote the same way she spoke—grammar and punctuation be damned! This would be her first email blast, an easy one, just a small announcement about

how exciting the upcoming collaboration with Serene was going to be
and what an honor it was to have them come on board as the Inspire
conference sponsor.

To: Charlotte Green <charlotte.green@greenteam.com>
From: Harper Cruz <harper.cruz@greenteam.com>
Re: Super Fab Collab

Love, Charlotte

Hey, Green Fam! Super excited about our upcoming collab with
the ever-fab and fashionable Serene. Welcoming Serene to the
Green Team has been such an honor, and we are so psyched to
have them on board.

Even though Harper wasn't writing in her own voice, it felt good to
be writing again. Wanting to impress Charlotte, Harper had taken it a
step further.

I always say that it's important to be true to yourself, so when
I was envisioning the perfect partner for our upcoming Inspire
conference, it was someone whose mission of inspiring women
was aligned with my own. I'm going to get a little vulnerable
here . . . sometimes working out is HARD—right?! After making
your family a nutritious breakfast, getting the little humans
ready for their school day, and tackling your morning emails,
sometimes the idea of adding a workout in feels impossible.
Listen, sis, you know how relatable I am and I'm here to say . . .
I get it! Which is exactly why I poured my heart into making my
upcoming collection with Serene something you'd WANT to put
on to tackle that morning sweat. Just like all of us here at The

Greenhouse, Serene knows how important self-care is—and also how important it is to look kick-ass while doing it! So check back here for exclusive sneak peeks. Nama-stay-true-to-you!

Harper pressed save and sent it to Bella to review.

"She wants to see you," Bella said, appearing suddenly at Harper's desk.

"Jesus, you scared me," Harper said, placing a hand on her chest.

"Charlotte said she wants to see you *now*," Bella insisted, her voice higher than normal. She nervously waved her phone in front of Harper. "She pinged you: Don't you have the Vine on your phone yet?"

"Of course I do," Harper said, checking her phone and seeing that a message from Charlotte had come in sixty seconds earlier. "I just hadn't seen it yet."

"You should really get a smartwatch. That way you can get notifications all the time. They're waterproof and you can sleep with them, so you'll never miss anything. Anyway, stop sitting there and go and see her!"

A smartwatch, Harper thought as she jumped up and headed to the conference room. Why would she want a smartwatch? The idea of being reachable 24/7 by anyone, let alone her boss, was a nightmare. It was important to have some boundaries, and as long as she was clear about them from the beginning, surely people would respect that. She hoped.

She opened the door to the conference room and tried to read the looks on the faces that were staring at her.

"Did you do all of this?" Charlotte asked, pointing at the deck that was open on her laptop.

"Yes," Harper said tentatively. "I've never made one before, so I didn't know if—"

"I'm not asking for excuses," Charlotte said. "I just need to know."

Harper took a deep breath and wondered if she should apologize for not asking for someone's help or for checking that she was going in the right direction, but it had been a long week and her filter wasn't working like it should, so she just told the truth. "You said you wanted something different, so I scoured the internet for the best designers I could find, which led me to look for indie brands and artist sites. I know you didn't ask for artwork but I didn't want to just copy anyone, so I included a mix of plant imagery and clothing items so you could see how nature could inform the designs and shapes. I wanted the consumer to think that if they could slip into these here," Harper said, pointing to a pair of green leggings, "then maybe they could imagine themselves there." She pointed to a picture of a woman sitting in lotus position on the beach beneath palm trees and staring out at the ocean as the sun was rising. "I just thought it was a really beautiful sentiment and, well, *serene*."

"You're right—I didn't ask for that," Charlotte said, looking at Harper carefully.

"I can take all that out if you want," Bella said, appearing behind Harper.

"I don't want," Charlotte said, getting up and moving toward Harper.

"You don't?" Bella and Harper asked at the same time.

"No. I *love* that you're thinking outside the box. This is exactly what I'm looking for. What you've given me here is a feeling. It's . . . it's . . ." she said, searching for the right word.

"Aspirational?" Tiffany offered.

"No," Charlotte said.

"Meditative?" Oliver piped up.

"No."

"Inspirational?" Harper asked, stating the obvious. It *was* what Charlotte had asked for.

"YES, inspirational. Girl, you *crushed* it!" She moved in for a high five, her hand connecting with Harper's in a loud smack. She whipped out her phone and started filming an Instagram story. "Guys, I am *freaking* out. My new Serene by Green line is going to be so incredible. I am SO excited for you guys to see the amazing designs I've come up with for you. You're going to DIE! I never thought I'd get to have this type of collab, but it just goes to show you what never giving up, following your dreams, and working *really freaking hard* looks like!" She ended with a huge smile and then stopped filming.

"Oh wow," Harper said, trying to wrap her head around how quickly Charlotte moved. "I'm so glad you liked it."

"Don't act so surprised, Harper. I knew you had it in you. I have a gift for spotting undiscovered talents that lie beneath someone's surface." She placed her hands on Harper's shoulders and looked her in the eye. "Like, you think *words*, because you worked in publishing and it's what you know, but I think *message*. I'm always seeing the big picture, since I'm able to come at it from all angles: artist, mogul, mom. I knew that if I pushed you to work beyond your narrow confines, you'd grow. And now look, it's like you've just done a crash course in branding and marketing and are totally qualified."

"Well, no, I wouldn't say that."

"Okay, that's a wrap. I have to head out a little early. We're going out of town this weekend and I want to beat the traffic," Charlotte said. She grabbed her laptop and notebooks off the conference table and put them in her tote bag.

"Oh sure, okay, I'll just let Aaron know we're doing the song now," Bella said, typing on her phone.

Charlotte headed toward the door with everyone else trailing behind her and stopped. "You know what, let Harper pick the song."

"The song?" Harper asked. She looked to Oliver, who nodded slowly and smiled.

"The Fri-yay song," he said.

"To end the workweek and kick off *the weekend*," Tiffany chimed in.

"It's a real honor," Bella said, her voice full of reverence.

"Oh wow . . . I don't know what to say," Harper said.

"You earned it." Charlotte tossed her blond hair over her shoulder. "So, pick a song."

"I don't know—what about 'I Wanna Dance with Somebody' by

Whitney Houston? It's my karaoke go-to," Harper said sheepishly. Bella quickly messaged the song request to Aaron and in seconds the sounds of Whitney Houston were vibrating through the office.

"OMG, I *love* karaoke. I bet you kill at karaoke, being half Filipino and all. Am I right?"

"Um . . ." Harper was taken aback. She looked to Bella, who acted as if she hadn't heard anything.

"I swear every Filipino I know is amazing at karaoke. Must be something in the water over there," Charlotte said, sauntering out the door.

Oliver stepped forward and put his hand on Harper's shoulder, squeezing it ever so slightly. "Good first week, Harper," he said, loud enough for everyone to hear, and then as the music picked up, he turned and whispered, "Take the win and let it go. That's just Charlotte being Charlotte."

"Sure, okay," Harper said. But one thing Harper knew for certain: anybody that tone-deaf couldn't be good at karaoke.

12

Not-So-Happy Hour

"Just one drink," Harper told Bella when she insisted they go out to celebrate her first week properly. Charlotte leaving early had incentivized everybody to head out. When Harper had mumbled something about being tired, Bella told her that it was the first Friday in months that they could leave work early enough to take advantage of the half-price margarita pitchers and three-dollar tacos at Revolucion, the Mexican restaurant down the street. She'd actually grabbed Harper by the shoulders when she said it, and Harper, taken aback by the slightly crazed look in her eye, relented.

Now, as she clinked glasses with Oliver, Tiffany, and Cynthia from accounting—the only other person in the office who seemed excited by the prospect of going out on a Friday—she was glad she had.

"Wow, that's good," Harper said, taking a sip. "Really good."

"Too good. That's why I ordered us a platter of tacos and chips and guac," Bella said as their waiter appeared and set the food down in front of them.

Bella pulled out her phone to take a picture for her Instagram story and tagged everyone, using the hashtags #teambuilding and #Fridayfeels. "Harper, you might want to take a few pictures to post too. I've seen your Insta, and it's *sad*."

"What? It's not sad. I'm just not a big social media person," Harper replied.

Oliver rolled his eyes. "None of us are 'big' on social media, but if you're working for Charlotte, you have to post more."

"Charlotte likes it when her Green Team shows how much fun it is to work for her," Bella said.

Harper pulled out her phone and snapped pictures of the drinks and the coasters. Posting them to her stories, she noticed she'd gotten a few follow requests since the night before. "Wait a minute—don't laugh, but I've gotten requests from strangers to follow me, and I don't think they're spam accounts. Who are these people?" she asked Bella.

"Wait, requests? No, your account has to be public, you work for Charlotte now. And those are probably her fans, which means they're your fans now. Her community loves to follow everyone who works for her," Bella explained.

"Just because you're not an influencer doesn't mean you're not *influential*, Harper," Tiffany said, drolly.

"Wow, I had no idea. Look out, I might crack three hundred people yet," Harper joked.

"To your first week!" Oliver said, raising his glass.

"It feels like a lot longer than a week," Harper said, raising her glass toward his and taking a sip. "Or maybe I've just crammed more into one week than normal."

She watched as the others looked at one another knowingly and smiled.

"What?" Harper asked, feeling self-conscious.

"That means you're officially on Green Time," Bella said. "Hours feel like days, days feel like weeks, weeks like months, and so on. It's like dog years. It can be disorienting at first, but you get used to it."

"So, how many years have you all worked here?" Harper asked, settling back into her chair.

"Seventy," Oliver said.

"Thirty-five," Bella said.

"Fourteen," Cynthia chimed in.

Harper laughed and did the math. "So in real years, that's ten, five, and two?"

"She's a smart one!" Cynthia said, passing the platter of tacos around.

"And you?" Harper asked Tiffany.

"Same as Bella—five. We started at the same time: me, Bella, and Mandy."

An uncomfortable silence fell over the table at the mention of Mandy's name.

"Wow. I didn't know Charlotte had been in business for so long," Harper said, with extra cheer in her voice to ease the awkwardness. She helped herself to a fish taco.

"Charlotte has been in the Charlotte business her whole life. Had to be. No one else was going to do it for her," Oliver said, a mixture of admiration and defensiveness in his voice. "She started out with a mommy blog that was all about her experiences as a new mom. She shared ideas for crafts and bake sales and homemade baby creams, that kind of stuff. But it was her hilarious videos about sneaking greens into her kids' food that really took off."

"Oh I remember those! Acting like a secret agent making smoothies and sauces—setting the whole thing to a James Bond kind of soundtrack while she did it," Cynthia said, laughing.

"Charlotte? Really?" Harper couldn't picture Charlotte not taking herself seriously.

"Oh yeah. That led to her Sneaky Greens cookbook series and appearances at farmers' markets and the . . ." Oliver hesitated for a moment, and Tiffany jumped in.

"And her viral mommy confessional," she said. When no one

elaborated, Tiffany continued, "Someone asked Charlotte at one of her events how she handled it all, and she just broke down and said she couldn't. She was a total mess."

"But it only made people love her more," Oliver said firmly, "because she was so *relatable*. And that's when I came in, because, well, she couldn't do it all, and I figured if I could be a creative director for celebrity brands, I could be one for my best friend . . . and her husband." Oliver took a sip of his drink.

"Wow, you weren't kidding when you said you've been with her a long time," Harper said.

"From the *beginning*," Oliver replied. "We met in high school and went to college together. Charlotte was my beard before I came out, and I was her date on the rare occasions I could drag her out of the library."

"Charlotte was a nerd? I thought she was a sorority girl?" Harper said.

"She was, but only technically. She joined so she could put it on her résumé later, but the truth is when she wasn't studying, she was hanging out in my dorm room and plotting her rise to power. I've been her business strategist, creative director, and chief operating officer. We all wear a lot of hats, as I know Charlotte's mentioned."

Harper chewed her food slowly. She hadn't had too many interactions with Oliver yet, but it was clear that he occupied many roles at The Greenhouse, including being Charlotte's protector. In many ways, he was the opposite of Charlotte. He was calm, cool, and measured, and Harper couldn't help but wonder, given what she'd seen in the short time she'd been there, how he stayed that way.

"Not me. I wear one hat, and it says accounting. Wow, good thing we got a table when we did. This place is hopping!" Cynthia said. She traced her finger around the salted rim of her glass and then licked it.

"Cynthia, nobody says 'hopping' anymore." Tiffany rolled her eyes.

"Sure they do—all my friends on Facebook say it," Cynthia joked, making them laugh.

Harper looked around at the hip crowd of young people that had flooded the patio during the short time they'd been there. They were all much closer in age to her, Bella, and Tiffany than they were to Cynthia and Oliver. But Cynthia was right: The patio was packed. It seemed as if everyone had gotten off work early, and Harper was suddenly grateful that Cynthia had sprinted up ahead to reserve them a table.

"You should've seen the looks I got for taking this table," said Cynthia, almost as if she could read Harper's mind. "The hostess told me I had to have my whole party here before I could get seated. I told her I had a whole party in my head, and unless she wanted me to introduce her to everyone, she should back up." Everyone laughed. With her prim and perfectly coiled braids, sensible sherbet-colored twin set, and stack of charm bracelets, Cynthia was clearly out of place—not that she seemed to care. "You know, maybe I'll get some tacos to go for the kids tonight instead of pizza. Friday night is usually pizza night," she explained, pulling out her metal straw and sticking it in her drink.

"I don't know how you do it, Cynthia. I can't even keep a plant alive working this many hours, let alone kids," Tiffany said.

"Well, I don't work as much as you do."

"Working this much is the only way I'm going to get ahead—not that it's getting me anywhere," Tiffany grumbled.

"Of course it is! It just takes time, honey," Cynthia said.

"Well, hopefully you mean real time and not Green Time, because I'm aging rapidly over here." Looking upset, Tiffany excused herself to go to the bathroom.

The whole table was quiet for a moment, and then Cynthia divvied up the remaining tacos and told Harper her story. How she'd taken a part-time job for Charlotte two years ago, when the youngest of her four kids had started school. It was supposed to be a stopgap until she found something more permanent, but she decided to stay on because it was so much fun.

"What other company has dance breaks and theme days? I'll tell you—*none*. Not one. And I'm usually hidden in the back in some office with someone nobody else wants to talk to. Everyone thinks accountants are dull, but maybe that's because our workplaces are usually so damn boring. Ever think of that?" She took another sip of her drink and licked her lips. "Damn, these are good. Sure I can't pour you one, Oliver?"

"No, just Diet Coke for me. Liam and I never know when we're going to get a surprise visit from the adoption agency," he said, picking at a taco.

"You're adopting?" Harper asked.

"Trying to, but they don't make it easy," Oliver said, forcing a smile.

"Well, I think you put yourself one step closer by getting legally married and all. These agencies can be kind of traditional." Cynthia gently patted his hand.

"I'm not sure there's anything traditional about an interracial gay couple, but if being married helps, I'm all for it," he said.

"I think this is the year," Bella said. "I've got a good feeling."

"Me too," Cynthia echoed. "And you know, you can always take a couple of mine while you're waiting. I don't mind."

"That's very generous of you," Oliver said, laughing. "But didn't you say they've scared away every babysitter you've ever had?"

"What can I say? They're *spirited*."

Harper listened as her coworkers continued chatting and let the tequila do its thing. It felt good to have her first week behind her, and she was grateful that her new coworkers had insisted she come out to celebrate. They had to be at least as wrung out as she was, if not more so, having a family of their own or, in the cases of Bella and Tiffany, working around the clock. She was suddenly overcome with gratitude. With the help of these people, she had gotten through her first week all on her own. If she hadn't been rushed off her feet, she'd have spent her time missing Poppy or her old life in New York instead of enjoying the present and this crazy opportunity she'd been given.

"And what's your story, missy? You got a kid, a husband, a wife?" Cynthia asked, dragging Harper's attention back to the present.

"You're not supposed to ask things like that," Oliver said.

"In the office maybe, but out here where it's just us I can." She turned her body toward Harper.

"No to all three," Harper said, aware that everyone at the table was suddenly paying attention.

"Okay then, what about a life?" Cynthia said.

"A *life?*"

"Yeah, a life. Hobbies, interests, friends—things you do outside The Greenhouse?"

"Well, I have all those things back in New York, of course. But I just got here." She pulled the basket of tortilla chips toward her and grabbed a handful.

"Can I give you a piece of advice?"

"Can she say no?" Oliver asked, draining his Diet Coke.

Ignoring him, Cynthia pressed on. "Get a life outside The Greenhouse—soon, and then work hard to keep it. Look, I love Charlotte, and I think the place is a real hoot, but you can't let it be your everything. Otherwise, you're going to end up like Bella here, who is about to grow an extra thumb because she's on that damn phone every minute of the day."

"I heard that," Bella said, putting the phone down. "And I have a life. I'm just waiting for Charlotte to text me that she has gotten out of town."

"Do you want her to text you what she has for dinner too?"

"Easy," Oliver said. "Don't forget that Bella is not like us old fossils. She's focused on her career and moving up, and I'd say it's working out pretty well for her so far."

Cynthia pursed her mouth and narrowed her eyes as if weighing how much to say.

"Yes, it is. But I don't think you should put all your eggs in one basket. You have to have some separation. Except you," Cynthia said, turning to Oliver. "You're like the yin to Charlotte's yang, and if you go, then the yang goes, which means . . ."

"Oh no, here we go!" Oliver laughed.

"Well, let's not get into that now, when we've got such wide-eyed young talent here. But even young talent needs a *life*," Cynthia said, shaking her finger playfully at Harper. "Speaking of which, I have to get back to mine."

"Me too," Oliver said. He took out his wallet and placed thirty dollars on the table, and then stood up to grab his blazer off the back of his chair. "That should cover it."

"Oh good, I'll catch a ride with you then," Cynthia said, adding twenty dollars and draining the last of her drink.

Oliver looked around the patio and shrugged. "I think we lost Tiffany. Tell her I said goodbye."

"Have a good weekend, ladies, and by that I mean, *have a weekend*. I promise The Greenhouse will be there Monday," said Cynthia. And with that, she and Oliver waved goodbye.

Bella watched them go and then, as soon as they were out of sight, called the waiter over for another half pitcher of margaritas and more chips and guac.

"I haven't seen the bill, but I think it's safe to say they left too much money," Harper said, slightly relieved, as she wasn't sure how much money she had left in her bank account. She wouldn't get paid for another week, and she had to be careful until she did.

"Mom and Dad always do," Bella said, reaching for the fresh pitcher the waitress had just delivered to the table.

"Mom and Dad?" Harper asked, surprised.

"It's what we call them, in a good way. They know it—although I wouldn't necessarily say it to their faces. But they're the ones who are always looking out for everyone. And as nutty as Cynthia is, she's a really good egg. I think she's the only person working at The Greenhouse who isn't worried about keeping her job. Except for Aaron, that is."

Aaron. Harper looked around the crowd on the patio, which had nearly doubled since they arrived.

"He doesn't come out with us," Bella said without looking up from the drinks she was pouring for them. "Like Cynthia, he's a big believer in keeping things separate."

Harper wouldn't have said so out loud, but she was secretly disappointed. She'd enjoyed her banter with Aaron and liked that he was an outsider like herself. "I didn't think keeping things separate was an option," she said, dipping her chip in the fresh bowl of guacamole that had appeared.

"It isn't, not for us. Not if you want to get ahead. Thankfully, I love what I do so much that I don't *want* to have a separation. If you're as lucky as we are to be a part of something so amazing, why wouldn't you want to spend all day doing it? I get why you'd want to clock out if you were crunching numbers from nine to five. But I'm already doing what I love. This isn't just a job for me. It's a movement meant to lift up ordinary women and inspire them to be their best selves. As Charlotte says, there's no clock to punch when it comes to your passion." Just then Bella's phone dinged. She grabbed it and then leaned back in her chair and exhaled. "She's just waiting for her weekend nanny to arrive, and then she's on her way out. I think we're safe to let our hair down a bit. Still too tired to hang out for the rest of the night?" she asked, tucking her feet underneath her and undoing the high ponytail she'd been wearing all day. She ran her fingers through the roots of her long black hair, massaging the spot where the elastic had been. She looked at Harper hopefully, and Harper gave in.

"I think I can stay up for a few more hours."

"Great, because I'm going to rage until at least nine o'clock and then sleep until noon. I have to catch up when I can."

She clinked glasses with Harper and leaned forward for a sip, stopping midair.

"What the hell?" she said as she stared over Harper's shoulder.

"What? What is it?" Harper asked, following her gaze. All she could see was a crowd of people leaning against the bar, hungrily eyeing the extra chairs at their table.

"What is she doing?"

"Care to narrow that question down a little bit? There are a lot of people to choose from."

Harper followed Bella's gaze to see Tiffany walking toward them . . . with Mandy trailing behind her. As Tiffany took her seat as if nothing had happened, Bella glared at her.

"Hey," Mandy said, pulling out one of the other chairs. She turned to Harper. "We haven't officially met. I'm Mandy."

"Hi, I'm—"

"My replacement," Mandy finished.

"Her name's *Harper*. What are you even doing here?" Bella asked, clearly annoyed.

"I wasn't banished; I quit. Charlotte doesn't own Nashville, even though she acts like it."

"What's going on with you two?" Bella asked angrily.

"Nothing's going on," Tiffany interrupted. "Mandy just wanted to talk to you and you're not returning any of her calls or texts, so I told her I'd help out."

"What do you want, Mandy?"

"Not to fight. Can we just talk for a minute, privately?"

"Anything you want to say to me, you can say in front of Harper and Tiffany."

Mandy took a deep breath and then exhaled loudly. "Okay. I wanted to say that just because I left The Greenhouse doesn't mean I left you. We're still friends, Bella." She leaned forward and reached for Bella's hand, only to have Bella move it out of her reach and sit back in her chair. She folded her arms in front of her chest.

"A friend doesn't hide that they're quitting and leave their coworker with all their work."

"I wasn't hiding it—I just didn't want to drag you into it. And it wasn't like I wanted to quit. I was up for a promotion and a raise that never seemed to come, just like Charlotte's *Green Zine* magazine. Remember that? I was supposed to be the editor? That thing never even saw the light of day. She makes a lot of promises, and she never follows through on any of them."

"She doesn't forget about them! There are just so many other things that she needs to be working on," Bella pushed back. "More important things."

"Oh please. I was tired of working sixteen-hour days with no reward, and when she told me that it'd be at least another year before she promoted me, I knew staying wasn't worth it. I don't know why that's so hard to understand. Tiffany gets it."

"Why am I not surprised? Tiffany will take any chance to dump on Charlotte these days."

"Excuse me?" Tiffany said, leaning forward.

"Well it's true, isn't it?"

"Just because I don't want to spend every waking hour with Charlotte doesn't mean I'm dumping on her. Speaking of which, if anyone asks, I'm out of town this weekend and back Sunday night."

"Oh, where are you going?" Harper asked, hoping to cut the tension in the air.

"Nowhere. She's making a point—she's unavailable," Bella said.

Harper wasn't sure why Tiffany needed to lie. It was the weekend, and Charlotte was away. Was there something they were supposed to be doing? She was about to ask when Bella stood up and grabbed her things.

"Bella, come on, you're overreacting," Mandy said.

"No, *you're* the one overreacting. I'm also waiting on a promotion, but you don't see me throwing a tantrum and leaving, do you? And you know why? Because I still believe that the work I'm doing matters. Come on, let's get out of here, Harper," she said, storming out.

Harper followed Bella and threw a sympathetic look over her shoulder to Tiffany and Mandy, who both looked dejected. She felt terrible about the way the night had taken a turn. But even worse, she wondered how much of what Mandy had said about Charlotte was true.

13

Tequila with a Twist

Harper and Bella walked past the crowded patios that lined the main strip of the Gulch in silence. Anyone who hadn't gotten out of work early was now waiting in line and anxiously checking their watches, no doubt hoping to get seated before the happy hour window closed. Harper didn't know where they were going, but she wasn't about to ask. Until a few moments ago, she's only ever seen one version of Bella—the sweet one that worshipped Charlotte and hung on her every word. She hadn't expected Bad Bella, with the snippy takedowns and chip on her shoulder. She had no idea *that* Bella even existed. But, she had to admit, she liked her.

"I hope you don't think badly of me. I'm not normally such a bitch," Bella said, looking sideways at Harper.

"I don't think you're a bitch—I think you're hurt," Harper said.

"It's just that we were all really close once. Charlotte called Mandy, Tiffany, and me the OG Three, because we all started at the same time at the very beginning. Mandy was—well, she was you, but she started as an intern, then an assistant, and worked her way up. Charlotte relied on her a lot, but then Mandy started questioning how Charlotte did everything, and it wasn't her place, you know? Charlotte may not always do everything right, but sometimes the ends justify the means."

"What do you mean?" Harper asked, suddenly wary.

"I mean she doesn't always say the right thing or take the safe route. She's passionate and a trailblazer, and if she were a man, nobody would ever question her modus operandi. They'd just call her a genius."

"You really believe that?"

"I do. Look at how many people admire her. She's helped so many women and taught them to believe in themselves. Surely that means something. Mandy used to think so too, but now she says that Charlotte behaves like a guru instead of a guide and emotionally manipulates her followers."

"Well, doesn't she emotionally manipulate them? I've been reading a lot of her posts, and they are very personal," Harper asked.

"Is it manipulative to connect to someone, or is it radically impactful?"

Harper hadn't been at The Greenhouse long, but she could practically see the question posted as a quote at the top of one of Charlotte's email blasts. Bella didn't wait for her to answer.

"The fact of the matter is that people are jealous of Charlotte. Take C.J., for instance. Despite all her money and *professionalism*, C.J. will never be as popular as Charlotte, which pisses her off. But that's because C.J. is practically a robot. Even the way she dresses is the opposite of Charlotte. Charlotte is all about casual comfort, looking cute and relatable. C.J. wouldn't get caught dead in anything without a designer label. They were guests at the same event once, and sure, people liked C.J., but they *loved* Charlotte. The second she was onstage, the crowd went nuts. They were crying and laughing and lining up to meet her. People like Mandy, C.J.—they're just jealous. But as Charlotte says, 'Green isn't everyone's color.'"

"Well, it's definitely yours," Harper said sincerely. "I've only been here a week, and I can see how lucky she is to have you. Tiffany was right about that."

"I'm the lucky one," Bella said. "I don't have a degree in communications. I studied early childhood education."

"Really?" Social media strategist was a long way away from teaching children.

"Yeah, I used to work at the kids' preschool. Charlotte noticed my creative spirit. She said she could tell by the things I did with the kids that I was someone who could think on my feet and outside the box. She took a chance on me and brought me in on the ground floor here in Nashville. How many people would do that?"

"Not many," Harper answered honestly. "I wouldn't think those skill sets overlapped."

Harper thought about her experiences in publishing and just how important it was to have the right school on her résumé, the right agency and publishing internships, and the right first job for the right people. But Charlotte had made it clear to Harper that she had an eye for talent and liked to take a chance on those who had it. If it wasn't for Charlotte taking risks, Harper wouldn't be in Nashville.

"Not a lot of people take a risk the way Charlotte does, but that's Charlotte for you. She's one of a kind."

"She's certainly not like any boss I've worked for before."

"Exactly! Look at you—you've only been here a week and you've already impressed Charlotte enough that she singled you out and gave you the final song of the week."

"Well, I don't know if the final song of the week is such a big deal," Harper said, laughing.

Bella stopped and looked at her. "It's a huge freaking deal, Harper. How long did it take your old boss to compliment you in front of everyone and celebrate your work? I bet it was longer than a week."

Much longer, thought Harper—it had never happened. No matter how many late hours and weekends she'd worked, she'd arrive on

Monday morning in need of a break and be expected to do it all over again.

"Mandy made a mistake by leaving," Bella said. "She doesn't realize how lucky she was to be a part of something bigger than her. Charlotte isn't doing this for herself—she's doing this for women everywhere, and we get to be a part of that."

Harper could tell that Bella meant every word, and her sincerity moved her.

"That said, I'm really glad we have the weekend off," Bella said with a laugh, then stopped suddenly at the sound of her phone ringing. She checked the display. "It's not Charlotte, thank goodness, but I have to get this. It's my mom."

"Of course." Harper took a step back to give Bella some privacy. She thought of her own parents and pulled out her phone to take a quick picture of the setting sun and texted it to them. Week one done! xx

"Everything okay?" she asked after Bella hung up. She couldn't help but notice how serious Bella looked.

"Yeah, it's just that . . . my mom has MS, and she needs me to pick up her new cane before I see her tomorrow. She lives half an hour away with my sister, Gemma, and her family. It's a lot for Gemma, so I try to help out as much as possible. I'll go over for the weekend and hang with Mom and my nieces and nephews to give my sister and brother-in-law a break."

"I'm sorry. That can't be easy."

"It's not, but I'm not the one with MS. I'm just hoping that once I get promoted, I can get a two-bedroom to share the load better and have my mom stay with me part-time."

Bella must have almost no free time, Harper realized. She made a mental note not to complain about being tired anymore. "I could never dream of owning a two-bedroom in New York City," she said, changing the subject slightly. "It's so expensive."

"L.A. too. That's where I'd really love to live one day—by the beach. But as long as I'm in a big city, and working for Charlotte, I'm good.

Who knows? Maybe she'll open an L.A. office one day and I can head it up.."

"You totally could," Harper said, meaning it. She'd been amazed at just how hard Bella worked. If anyone was tired, it was surely Bella, juggling Charlotte, The Greenhouse, and her own family.

"You know what, why don't we just grab something to go and sit by the pool at the Green Suites?" Harper asked.

"You sure you don't want to go somewhere, try a new place?"

"I'm sure. I've got the whole weekend for that." The idea of a whole weekend to herself to explore her new city—her new *home*—made her giddy. What a difference a week makes.

———

It was late by the time Harper returned to her apartment, full of pizza and tequila. She and Bella had grabbed a couple of slices and some pre-made margaritas and parked themselves on the lounge chairs next to the rooftop pool at the Green Suites. The pool could turn into a real scene on the weekends, according to Bella, but weekdays and Friday nights were generally quiet, which suited them just fine. The more Harper talked to Bella, the clearer it became that there was more to her than met the eye. Listening to how dedicated and grateful Bella was couldn't help but make Harper feel humbled. She had been so disappointed when her nascent publishing career hadn't gone the way she expected it to that she had taken each rejection so personally, and here was Bella, grateful for every one.

Harper kicked off her shoes, grabbed a glass of water, and settled onto the couch. On the coffee table Bella's WELCOME TO THE GREENHOUSE packet looked back at her. She'd been meaning to read it thoroughly but had just been too tired. Just then, she got a text from Bella. Great hanging with you tonight. Enjoy exploring the city—text me if you need anything!

Harper liked the text and then picked up the packet she'd skimmed on the first day. This time, knowing how much effort the woman behind it had put into it, she reread it *slowly*.

GROW WHERE YOU'RE PLANTED: A PERSONAL INVENTORY FOR ACHIEVING SUCCESS!

At The Greenhouse, we believe in giving you the right soil to allow you to flourish into the best version of yourself. We can't pour into our community if our own water buckets are dry! Since our fearless leader is the ultimate visionary for this Green Team, Charlotte herself will be reviewing each of your answers to create the ultimate growth guide for each of her employees.

SEED

Every thriving plant once started as a seed and that goes for our employees too! As seedlings, we believe in owning our dreams by calling out our goals. Remember, this team exists to be the water and sunlight to help you become the best YOU possible.

Do you want to be the next marketing maven? Are you counting down the days until you can grow your own little family? Is your biggest aspiration to run that big marathon you've been putting off? Please explain your deepest and biggest personal and professional goals below.

SPROUT

At The Greenhouse, we believe in planting dreams in our hearts and minds and then sowing those seeds until they are our reality. We believe in not just who we are *today* but how we can grow *tomorrow*.

Reflect on what barriers are keeping you from sprouting to the upgraded version of you. Need an accountability buddy? Try to find someone who can support you, so that you can keep your energy up to work those long hours. Write down their name so we can help *you* be accountable. Tell us how you can remain results-oriented in your personal and professional life.

BLOOM

We're the creators of our reality and we believe blooming means becoming a thriving member of the Green Team. Sometimes being a part of this garden means saying no to those pesky temptations that'll lead you astray from your goals.

Trouble with your small-minded BFF? Does your family underestimate the power of saying *YES* to change and *NO* to staying the same? Let us know how we can help keep you focused on this Greenspirational team and not the distractions outside The Greenhouse.

THORN

It's not all roses and daises and we completely understand that. Sometimes even the best gardens have a few weeds. Not to worry! Tell us in detail what your biggest insecurities and troubles are in your personal and professional life. This will allow us the space to figure out your best growth plan. Remember, the only way to grow is to share! So please feel free to leave as many details as possible.

Wow. Harper wasn't sure what to make of the assignment. On the one hand, it was great that Charlotte was willing to help her team become the best versions of themselves, but on the other, the answers she was looking for were far more revealing than what Harper would usually expect to tell a boss. A voice inside her warned her not to overshare.

But hadn't she and Bella just discussed how things moved quickly at The Greenhouse, and how different Charlotte was from other bosses—how *special*? It made sense that she'd need to know them all well if she was to help them grow. Maybe Harper just needed a bit more time to warm up. Thankfully, Bella hadn't said anything about having to get the questionnaire back to her right away, so until she did, she could just put it—and any reservations she had—aside.

She just hoped she wouldn't regret it.

14

G Stands for: Get a Life

It took Harper a moment to find her bearings when she finally opened her eyes. She'd been dreaming that she had arrived at Nashville International Airport to meet Aaron, but this time his sign read HARPER GREEN. As she got close, she noticed he had an entourage with him that seemed to include every editor and agent she had ever worked for. Her old boss Gretchen, the leader of the group, stepped forward. "I'm sorry I never appreciated you, Harper," she said tearfully. "I wish I could make it up to you. I'll be *your* assistant from now on."

Suddenly, the airport terminal turned into a green-carpeted runway, and Harper saw Charlotte approaching from the other end. In the middle of the runway was Bella, who was hauling not one but two large Towers of Power. "Over here!" she called excitedly. Harper met Charlotte in the middle of the runway, grabbed her hand, and with Bella's help, they climbed onto the tree stumps. They beamed at the audience that cheered them on and applauded as models strutted the catwalk in the Serene by Green collaboration they had put together. The runway music reached a crescendo that sounded a lot like Harper's ringtone. Blearily she woke up, realizing she had an incoming FaceTime call from Poppy.

"Shit," Harper said, squinting from the morning light as she fumbled to answer the phone. She and Poppy had scheduled a FaceTime date earlier this week and none of Poppy's three calls had woken her up. Harper had slept in an hour later than she was supposed to.

"Hello, sunshine!" Poppy sang into the camera.

"Morning." Harper sat up and leaned against her headboard, sending papers from her welcome packet—which she'd been reading in bed before falling asleep—flying.

"Wild night?" Poppy asked hopefully.

"Hardly, although it was interesting." Harper took the phone with her into the kitchen to make a cup of coffee in the little French press the previous tenant had left behind. She filled the electric kettle and plugged it in, willing it to boil faster. She'd been looking forward to this coffee and catch-up with Poppy, and felt deeply guilty she'd kept her waiting.

" 'Interesting' as in you spent some more time with your handsome new coworker?" Poppy asked hopefully. Harper had forgotten that she had told Poppy that Aaron was cute.

" 'Interesting' as in there is more to Bella than I thought, Charlotte is a god out here, and it seems I've arrived in the middle of some ex-employee and influencer feud."

"Oh, juicy," Poppy said. She turned her attention off-screen. "I want to hear all about it, but I'm afraid it's going to have to wait. We've got brunch plans with Charles's parents, and I haven't showered yet. Just wanted to make sure you were alive before we got going."

"What? I thought we had a FaceTime date," Harper said, trying not to sound too disappointed.

"We did, but you clearly needed to rest, or else you wouldn't have overslept. But no big deal—to be continued!" Poppy blew her a kiss before signing off.

Harper stared at her screen, her heart sinking a little. Seeing Poppy made her feel a little homesick for her old life. The kettle boiled, and she filled the French press and stirred the grounds. She would have to get an automatic coffee maker *and* an alarm clock this weekend. Her phone buzzed with a text from Bella.

Hey girl! Not sure if you have plans today but there's a bunch of activities on the Vine for this weekend.

How come? Harper texted back.

The twins got sick, so Charlotte came back late last night.

So we have to go?

No, it's not work. It's optional. But it's fun!

Oh, okay. Well, thanks, good to know.

She placed her phone on the counter and began rifling through the cupboard for a thermos and found not one but three, all with The Greenhouse name on them. There was also a stack of take-out menus and dozens of packets of restaurant condiments. Apparently, she wasn't the only person who had no time to cook or shop for food. Harper sipped her coffee and took a closer look at her apartment. The tenant before her might have cleared out all signs of their life, but it was equally possible they hadn't had one. She recalled Cynthia's advice. *Get a life outside The Greenhouse—soon.*

She opened the Vine on her phone and saw the list of events Bella must've organized overnight: yoga in the park, a nature hike, and a group cooking class at some place downtown. Poor Bella needed a weekend off, and it didn't seem like she was going to get one. So *this* was why Tiffany had lied about going out of town. Well, Harper didn't need to lie. She had integrity. Isn't that what Charlotte had commended her for? She scrolled through the enthusiastic replies of her coworkers and typed in Sorry to miss it, sounds like fun, and hit send. If she was going to have a life, she needed to start now.

An hour later and armed with one of those "36 Hours in Nashville" guides from the *New York Times*, Harper was in her Zipcar, ready to go full tourist. She figured if she could hold off on leasing a car, she could use the money she saved to actually buy one. It had been a long time since she'd explored a new city, and she'd forgotten how fun seeing things for the first could be. When she lived in New York, she could spot the tourists a block away, bags slung across their bodies for extra safety, toting water bottles in one hand and their smartphones displaying Google Maps in the other. Like most New Yorkers, she hated how they would stop in the middle of the sidewalk to check their phones or randomly take a selfie when she was running late for work and didn't have time to walk around their human tableaus. But this weekend she was going to trade her jaded New Yorker badge for an awestruck tourist who took pictures of everything herself.

First up was Nashville's own Parthenon, followed by a stroll through Centennial Park. Then there was the Country Music Hall of Fame, which just seemed like one of those must-do things, like visiting the Empire State Building or the Statue of Liberty. After that, there was a drive by the Grand Ole Opry and along the Honky Tonk Highway, which reminded her of Times Square, but for all things country music. Eventually, Harper parked and strolled downtown, taking herself out to dinner at a beautiful old building called the Radford that was having a pop-up food festival. She capped her night off with a Dolly Parton–inspired movie marathon at home. As much as she wished that she'd had Poppy to discover the city with, the time alone was good for her.

On Sunday, she traded her inner tourist for city resident and took herself shopping for some cute dishes and throw pillows to make the apartment feel like her own, along with a few other odds and ends. As a treat, she also bought a new pair of jeans, along with a sweater jacket that would look great and keep her warm at work. After being offline the whole weekend, she felt recharged and eager to impress Charlotte. She wasn't exactly ready to invest in a pair of cowboy boots, but she suddenly felt like she was ready to start calling Nashville home.

———

When the Greenspiration for the day came in on Monday morning, Harper was ready. *We're Better Together.* She wrote it on a Post-it Note and stuck it to the corkboard she bought over the weekend that now hung in her living room. She'd filled it with pictures from back home of her and Poppy and her family. Like everybody with a smartphone, Harper had made the internet her memory box. But she'd felt a strong urge to get the pictures offline and onto good old-fashioned paper.

Walking into work with a spring in her step and a smile on her face, Harper was confident by the number of people already there and staring at her that the new outfit she'd chosen was a winner. She tucked her freshly blown-out hair behind her ears and was just about to sit at her desk when Bella appeared beside her, grabbed her elbow, and whisked her off to the hydration station.

"Where were you?" Bella asked as they walked. "Charlotte's been looking for you."

"What?" Harper asked, whipping out her phone to see if she had any missed texts or calls. "I didn't see anything. Did I miss a meeting? Was I supposed to be here earlier?" It was barely seven thirty, and work didn't officially start for another half hour. She looked up at Bella, noticing for the first time how exhausted she appeared. No amount of concealer—and she was wearing a lot—could hide how tired Bella looked.

"If by earlier, you mean Saturday at the park or at the cooking class I arranged, then yeah, you missed something." Bella grabbed a couple shots of wheatgrass from the fridge and knocked them back.

"Wait a minute. You said those were *optional*," Harper replied, panic rising inside her. She paused as two employees walked in, took one look at her, and quickly turned around. Shit. Harper's absence at the events was why people were staring at her, not her cute outfit. "Why would you say they were optional if they weren't?"

"I said that because I had to. Charlotte's not interested in paying overtime, especially if it's for something that's supposed to be fun—"

"But it was the *weekend*," Harper said. Sweat broke out on her forehead, and she grabbed a paper towel to blot herself dry. "She can't be mad, right? I'm sure I wasn't the only one who wasn't there."

"No, neither were Cynthia, Aaron, and Oliver, but they aren't expected to be there." Bella held on to her stomach and groaned. "Ugh, I hate wheatgrass."

"And Tiffany. What about Tiffany?"

"What about Tiffany?" Tiffany asked, coming in. She reached into the fridge and pulled out a Kombucha. Harper looked at the sour expression on her face and knew the answer to her question even before she asked it.

"You didn't join in all the weekend activities either, right? You said you were going out of town." Harper was sweating now and took off her cute jacket.

"I said it but I didn't do it, which was my second fucking mistake. The first was letting Mandy post a picture of us having brunch that showed I was clearly still in town, which caused Charlotte to direct message me and call my loyalty into question." She glared at Bella. "Some fucking birthday."

"It was your *birthday*?" Bella squeaked.

"Sure was," Tiffany snapped. "And I can't think of a better way to turn twenty-nine than by taking a cooking class with the same people I work with all week instead of the friends I'm too busy to see."

"Tiff, I don't think Charlotte knew—"

"She knew. She wished me a happy birthday," Tiffany said, staring at Bella. "Then she asked me to find a better venue for the Inspire conference once we were *done with all our fun*."

"Look, I'm sorry to interrupt, but nobody told me I *had* to be there," Harper said, catching Charlotte stepping out of her office and looking her way. Their eyes locked for a moment, and Harper's legs turned to Jell-O.

"Nobody ever will because it's not supposed to be a *have to*; it's supposed to be a *get to*," Tiffany said, imitating Charlotte with an eye roll.

"Shit, well, we *have to* see her now," Bella said, checking her phone.

She popped a mint in her mouth, plastered on a smile, and walked ahead of them, leaving Tiffany and Harper practically sprinting behind her to keep up.

"Morning, Charlotte," Bella said when they arrived in her office. "Did you want me to cue the morning song?"

"In a minute." Charlotte directed her attention to Harper. "Harper, are you feeling better?"

"I, uh . . ."

"Bella told me you weren't coming to any of our activities, and I noticed that you weren't signed into the Vine all weekend. So I figured the only reason you'd stay away—the one weekend I'm in town, even though I wasn't supposed to be—was because you were sick. Why else would you want to miss all that fun, all those chances to get to know and support your Green Team?"

Harper looked to Tiffany and Bella, both staring at the floor, and then to Oliver, who was watching from his office. He leaned back just enough that he was out of Charlotte's line of sight and nodded ever so slightly.

"Yeah, I'm feeling much better, thanks. I think it was just a lot all at once, with the move and everything, but I'm feeling great now, really great," Harper said. "And excited too, really excited."

"Good, I'm so glad to hear it. Because Tiffany could use the extra help with the venue search for the conference. You can do the preliminary legwork and Tiffany can narrow it down."

"Happy to!" Harper said, a little too enthusiastically.

"Good. C.J. has decided to book a larger venue for her 'Pave It Forward' conference, *leading the way today for tomorrow's entrepreneurs*," she said, her fingers air-quoting the title. "We can't have it be bigger than the one we use for our Inspire conference."

"Pave It Forward? Is *that* what she's calling it now?" Bella scoffed as if it were the most ridiculous name in the world.

"I heard she's going to be highlighting and supporting BIPOC entrepreneurs this year," Tiffany offered.

"You heard, or you know? Because I hear a lot of things." Charlotte stood and placed her hands on her hips. "But I *see*, right here in this room, that we don't just talk about diversity at The Greenhouse; we embody it. So let's make sure we have an even bigger venue to get our message across. And speaking of message, the attendees should be diverse too. So, you know, so do what you have to do to make sure that happens." She looked directly at Tiffany and waited.

"You got it, big message, big room, big audience," Tiffany said, smiling tightly.

"Big room, big impact. That's what this is all about. It isn't about me, and honestly, it's not about any of you. It's about the hundreds of thousands of followers that look to us for inspiration, am I right? I don't do this for myself, just like you don't do this for me—"

"Oh, Charlotte, that's not true—" Bella began, but stopped when Charlotte held up her hand.

"But it should be, Bella. We do this work for women everywhere because we're inspirational warriors. And I know it isn't always easy, but good things never are. And I don't want you to think I don't appreciate that because I do. I do." She reached into her back pocket and handed a gift card to Tiffany.

"What's this?" Tiffany asked.

"A weekend at the spa, on me, for supporting everyone on your birthday."

"Charlotte, I don't know what to say . . ." Tiffany said, her cheeks flushing.

"Look, I know you put your plans aside, and I want you to know that it didn't go unnoticed."

"Thank you," Tiffany said, looking genuinely touched.

"I want you to celebrate just as soon as the conference is over, but right now, we have to stay focused. It's been a rocky few weeks what with all the changes around here, and I need my inner circle to be tighter than ever." Charlotte opened her arms wide and looked at the three women standing before her. "It might not be the original OG Three, but it's the new-and-improved G Three, am I right?"

It sounded more like a challenge than a question, and Harper could tell by the steely look in Charlotte's eyes that there was only one answer: Yes, she was right. She was *always* right.

Seeing Green Monthly Newsletter:

October

Congratulations, Green Fam! You did it! Thirty days of learning and earning the right to call yourself a graduate of the first online course in the Greenlight Inner Growth Academy. I cannot tell you how amazing it was to watch so many of you shake off the tired ways of thinking about yourselves and looking at the world. I literally watched you bloom right before my eyes. It was amazing—no, it was fucking inspiring. I learned from each and every one of you, and I want you to know that I was listening. When I read the comments some of you posted that said you felt like you had woken up from a deep sleep, I heard you, and it got me thinking—why stop now? We're just waking up! Next, we'll be walking, and do we want to stop at walking? No, we want to run! I mean, if this is how you and I feel after just one month, can you imagine what three months would be like? What would it be like to head into the holidays, the time when so many of us just give and give and give of ourselves, and feel full and emotionally empowered? Can you even allow yourself the possibility of enjoying Halloween, Thanksgiving, and Christmas this year without feeling depleted? I can. Because I know that's what I deserve. To refill the well that I am only too happy to drain for others. I drain my body, mind, and soul, not to mention my bank account—don't we all? Well, this year, before I think of anyone else, I'm going to think of myself because when I take care of me, I take care of we. So what do you say, will you join me? Sign up now, and you will get 20% off and a free Greenspiration Journal to record the incredible transformation that is occurring within you. Here's to Greenlightenment!

xo Charlotte

15

In Her Shoes, and Voice, and Head

Harper reread the monthly newsletter that Charlotte wrote and compared it to the weekly *Love, Charlotte* email blast she was assigned. She'd been working hard on getting Charlotte's voice down, finding the right tone and elevating what she was saying at the same time. It wasn't that Charlotte was a bad writer; it was that Harper wanted her to be better. Even though Harper's name wasn't on the posts, she knew that she was the one who wrote them, and now that Charlotte had entrusted Harper to take them over completely based on a handful of ideas they came up with, it mattered to her how they came across. She read the latest blast again.

To: Charlotte Green <charlotte.green@greenteam.com>
From: Harper Cruz <harper.cruz@greenteam.com>
Re: Happy Hallogreen!

Love, Charlotte

Hey, guys, Halloween is just around the corner, and you know what that means? You have an opportunity to be someone else. A chance to let your inner child shine. When was the last time you got to do that? From the moment we start talking, we're told that we're big kids—that it's time to act our age, time to grow up. We turn sixteen and suddenly we're adults, old enough to drive, then old enough to vote and drink. Everyone is always rushing us to grow up. But when we do grow, we're penalized for not being youthful anymore. All these expectations—overt societal pressures, our own internalized set of beliefs, all these people telling us what we should and shouldn't do—and no actual room to grow. Whatever happened to fun? It's still there and waiting for you to find it. Let your inner child shine this Halloween by dressing up, taking the kids trick-or-treating, and post your pics with the hashtags #GreenhouseFunhouse #personalgrowth #charlottesays #greenspiration, and we'll give two lucky followers tickets to our upcoming Inspire conference!

"You make her sound smart," Tiffany said, standing and reading over Harper's shoulder. Harper had gone outside to work at one of the courtyard tables to escape the new playlist that Charlotte was trying out for the upcoming Halloween party. Hearing "Monster Mash" on repeat was enough to make Harper feel like she was turning into Frankenstein herself.

Harper looked up and pulled her laptop closer to her. "Excuse me?"

"I'm not saying she isn't smart, because she clearly is, but she doesn't lead with that. Her whole thing is that she is just like you and me, except she *isn't*. Because you and I work sixteen-hour days, rent apartments that she *owns*, fly commercial, take public transit, and don't have staff to run random errands for us." Tiffany held up the tray of green smoothies she'd been tasked with getting for the office and rolled her eyes. "So yeah, obviously she's smart, but you might want to throw in a few *hey girls* off the top if you want people to think she wrote it." Tiffany's smile completely contradicted how bitter she sounded.

"Noted," Harper replied, closing her laptop.

"Now, where are we with the venue? I'm guessing that if you're out here writing, you've already come up with new options for me?"

"What?" Harper said, surprised. "I just sent you a bunch yesterday."

"Yes, and they're all terrible, so you'll need to send me more." She rolled her eyes and shook her head.

"Hello, ladies," Oliver called as he came outside and walked toward them. "I was hoping I'd find you two. Before I see Charlotte, tell me—how's the hunt for the Inspire venue coming along? Any luck?"

"None," Tiffany said, looking at Harper.

"I showed Tiffany half a dozen places that I thought could work. Lots of companies have used them for corporate events. They're big enough with plenty of parking and—"

"Right, because parking is the first thing people think about when buying tickets to see Charlotte," Tiffany said. She turned to look at Oliver. "This would've been so much faster if I just did it myself."

"I'm sorry I don't know Nashville as well as you, but I'm trying," Harper interrupted before Oliver could say anything. "I'll get back to researching just as soon as I finish this email blast."

"See what I mean? She can't even multitask! Meanwhile, I'm sourcing venues, planning the conference, and trying to offload ten thousand Growth Planners, like some freaking assistant."

"Tiffany, you're more than that and you know it," Oliver said calmly. "You're Charlotte's event maestro."

"Am I, though? Because last time I checked that was also supposed to come with a raise and an assistant of my own, not some newbie I have to babysit."

"Tiffany! Why don't you go inside while I talk to Harper?" Oliver said sternly.

"Gladly," she sniffed, and walked away.

Harper waited until Tiffany was out of earshot. "She hates me."

"No, she's just upset about Mandy leaving. They were good friends. Normally the two of them would be working on the conference together, but now with Mandy gone . . ."

"She's stuck with me," Harper finished.

Oliver took off his glasses. He removed a small white cloth from his blazer pocket, polished the lenses, and held them to the light.

"She's fine. Frustrated, but fine."

Harper was sure Tiffany was anything but fine. She was frustrated with Harper, and Bella, and *especially* Charlotte. More than once, she'd commented on what a waste of time looking for the perfect venue was, and that Charlotte should just make up her mind already so they could get to the more important things for the conference itself. "What did I do?"

"You made more work for her. She thought she was getting an assistant on this job, and instead, she's training you."

"Training me? I'm looking at places for her every day," Harper said, exasperated.

"I didn't say she was doing a good job of it, because clearly she isn't." Oliver placed his glasses back on his face.

So far, none of the places they had looked at or toured over the past two weeks had been the right fit. Harper had just assumed that if the venues ticked off the list of requirements that Charlotte had set forth, they would work. But so far, the places Harper had chosen had been too big, too cold, for the intimate feeling she wanted to create for her fans. The place needed to be easy to get to, with enough parking if someone was driving or close enough to a bus stop and airport if they weren't. Charlotte also wanted restaurants nearby, but not just any restaurants. They had to serve healthy food and be willing to feature a special Charlotte-created Green Meal Deal for her attendees. It needed to be a place where people could meet and talk and swap stories about how wonderful the conference was and how great Charlotte was *of course*. The list was long, and just when Harper thought she had it covered, Charlotte would come in and tour the space herself, declaring that it just didn't *feel* right. Harper was only just getting a grasp on Charlotte's voice; how was she expected to also know what her feelings were?

"I don't understand what I'm supposed to be doing differently," Harper said, discouraged. "I'd go to a conference at any of the places we've visited!"

"*Any* doesn't cut it when it comes to Charlotte. *Any* makes it sound like it's just another spot on a long list of places that someone might go. And while that might be fine for somebody like you, who's lived in one of the greatest cities in the world where there's no shortage of fabulous places to visit, it's not good enough for many of Charlotte's followers. For a lot of them, this is their *one* big event of the year."

"It's not like I'm all that fancy—I'm from Poughkeepsie," Harper said, her cheeks flushing.

"But you left to live in Manhattan, and now you're in Nashville. You're not exactly a country mouse," Oliver said. He looked around the parking lot and then back at The Greenhouse. "Do you have any idea how much these tickets cost?"

"Five hundred dollars," Harper said as Oliver raised an eyebrow at her. She obviously knew this.

Oliver nodded. "They *start* at five hundred dollars, plus transportation, which for a lot of people means airfare, a hotel room for at least one night, meals, and merchandise, not to mention childcare if they're leaving their kiddos behind without extra support. By the time they're done, it's well over a thousand. And some of the women save up for it the whole year. Do you think they want to go to an event at some corporate building with a big parking lot? No, they want something beautiful. Something they can take pictures of and post on Instagram, something special that will make them *feel* special. And believe me, there is nothing special about any of the places you've shown us." Oliver started walked toward his car and turned his head over his shoulder. "Come with me."

Harper slid her laptop into her backpack and followed him. "Where are we going?" she asked, getting into the passenger side of his silver BMW.

"You tell me. You're the one who's new here and seeing the city with fresh eyes. Surely there are places that stood out to you?"

Harper was quiet for a moment. She rolled down the window as he pulled out of the lot. "I don't know—the Parthenon, the Country Music Hall of Fame, the Grand Ole Opry. I know Charlotte wanted bigger, but I hardly think she's looking to fill those places, and we probably can't afford to rent them out either."

"Agreed. Anywhere else?"

There was one place.

———

The Radford was the site of the food festival Harper had stumbled upon. It was a gorgeous old building converted into a giant event space with a worn brick exterior and white shutters stuffed with flowers and ivy that hung down to the sidewalk. The lobby, with its black-and-white-checkered marble floor and mirrored walls, practically screamed Instagram backdrop. It had a covered rooftop deck strewn with lights, an outdoor fireplace, and a bar that would be perfect for an after-conference cocktail. It didn't have a restaurant, but Harper thought it could be fun to have a bunch of food tents like the ones she'd seen. And right next door was a hotel, making it the easiest commute ever. There was nothing corporate or cold about any of it.

"Well, what do you think?" Harper asked Oliver, brightening at the smile spreading across his face.

"What do *you* think?" Oliver asked.

Harper pulled out her phone and looked up the Radford's website. "Well, it says here that it has three separate event spaces, which would allow us to have different things happening in each place at the same time," Harper said, thinking out loud. "We could even mirror the setup in The Greenhouse, and call them Create, Connect, and Community. Plus, it photographs really well, which is important for social media; and while it's big, it still feels personal, which is really important for Charlotte's brand. Personally, I love it. I just can't believe I didn't think of it earlier."

"I think Charlotte is going to love it too," Oliver said, nodding. He walked over to Harper and looked her in the eye. "It looks like Tiffany was wrong—you're not the problem after all. Not that I believed her," he said, heading out and leaving Harper to wonder just what the hell he was talking about.

16

No Place Like Gnome

"I don't get it. What are you supposed to be?" Poppy asked, leaning toward the screen and staring at Harper. "A troll? I thought you said your costume had to be something to do with the color green."

"It *does*. I'm a gnome," Harper said, holding out her arms. She took a step back from the screen to show off her costume—a green unitard under green overall shorts—and did a little twirl.

"Seriously?"

"What?" Harper frowned. This wasn't the reaction she was hoping for. She had thought her idea was genius. It was the evening of the big Halloween party, and everyone had been allowed to go home early to get ready. Bella must've told her ten times that Charlotte wanted to be wowed. *Wowed*, that was the word she used. So far, Harper knew of at least two Green Giants, a green M&M, and a house plant. But no one, surprisingly, had mentioned going as a gnome. "It's clever. Besides, no one else is doing it."

"Wonder why? I mean, look at how sexy you are," Poppy said sarcastically. She took a sip of her red wine and raised her eyebrows.

"I'm not trying to look sexy," Harper protested.

"Mission accomplished!"

Harper and Poppy both laughed. They usually spent Halloween together, so it was nice that they were still able to carry on the tradition—virtually, at least. Every year they went to a Halloween party at a junior editor's or an assistant's apartment in Brooklyn. It was the perfect excuse to get dressed up and wear something other than the same basic Zara pantsuit they usually wore to work. It was also a great way to show a little skin, blow off some steam, and meet new people—including potential hookups. Poppy had always insisted that's what Halloween was about. As she had been with Charles forever and would never have another late-night hookup with anyone else again, she'd taken to living vicariously through Harper's slew of post-Dylan one-night stands. But there'd be none of that this year.

"I know what you're thinking, and I will stop you there. Maybe four guys work at The Greenhouse. Oliver is married and gay. There's Ryan, Charlotte's husband, some older guy in sales named Todd who definitely still lives with his mom, and Aaron, who . . ."

"Oh, I know who Aaron is. He's the *really helpful* guy who does his own thing that you never want to talk about, which is why he's the most interesting to me," Poppy said, taking a bowl of popcorn from a hand that appeared out of frame.

"Hi, Harper," Charles said, popping his head in and giving a little wave. He leaned over and kissed Poppy on the cheek. "Cool troll costume."

"Told you," Poppy said, scooping up a handful of kernels.

"What are you guys going as?" Harper asked, taking her drink and laptop with her to sit on the couch.

"You're looking at it," Poppy said, tilting the camera up to reveal Charles in sweats, reading a take-out menu.

"A tired, boring resident," Charles said.

"And his supportive girlfriend," Poppy added, returning to frame.

"Ouch," Harper said, wincing.

"It's fine. I'm happy to stay in and get takeout and watch a movie. I never really liked Halloween much anyway." Poppy kissed Charles's free hand before he walked away.

Suddenly, Harper felt foolish in her green overalls. She'd always assumed Poppy had loved Halloween—had she only gone along for Harper's sake? The thought depressed her.

"I didn't realize you didn't like Halloween. I always thought we had fun," Harper said, trying to keep her voice upbeat.

"I liked Halloween with *you*. You made it fun. But honestly, I'm glad to miss it this year. All those sad single people trying to get noticed in their costumes, working too hard to have a good time and drinking too much, acting like children instead of adults. It's kind of depressing."

"Charlotte says it's a chance for people to be someone else and connect with their inner child," Harper said.

"And your inner child wants to be a gnome?"

"Obviously," Harper said, sipping her drink.

"Well, your costume is kind of *growing* on me. *Growing, Greenhouse*, get it?"

"Groan," Harper said, rolling her eyes and smiling.

"Just promise me no weird gnome beard."

"Promise."

"And I want all the stories. I need to live vicariously through you now that I'm a hundred and thirty years old and turning off the light outside so we don't have to give out candy."

"Kids don't need candy. Adults need it," Harper said.

"Don't I know it." Poppy opened a pack of M&M's and poured it into her bowl of popcorn. In the background, Harper heard a doorbell and people excitedly greeting each other. "Hey! I'll be right there," Poppy called over her shoulder. She leaned forward and whispered, "I gotta go.

Charles's friend Andrew from work and his fiancée, Sloan, are joining us for dinner and a movie. He's nice, but she's *great*—British, super smart, insanely fashionable, and swears like a sailor. You'd love her."

"Oh, sounds like fun. I miss you, you know. Maybe next time I'm in—" Harper began, but Poppy was already blowing kisses and waving goodbye before she could finish.

Dinner and a movie: suddenly it was the only thing Harper wanted to do, and she wanted to do it with Poppy. *Sloan.* Harper checked Poppy's Instagram and was immediately met with a carousel of photos of Poppy and a super-stylish Sloan, aka @sloanslays, having dinner at some chic restaurant in Brooklyn. Since when did Poppy hang out in Brooklyn? Or get a new best friend, for that matter?

There were shots of them laughing, clinking champagne glasses, and Sloan blowing out candles on a cake. It made zero sense to be jealous of someone she'd just learned about, yet she was. She finished her glass of wine and stared out the window. What did she expect? That Poppy would wait for her to return and not make any other friends? She should be happy for her; it was all Poppy had ever been for Harper. Besides, it wasn't as if she and Poppy didn't still text all the time . . . although lately it had been harder to stay in touch, and their idea of a nightly check-in had quickly gone by the wayside. But that was because Harper had been busy helping Tiffany with the Inspire conference and Charlotte with the Serene collaboration, email blasts, and miscellaneous admin, the scope of her role as visionary support strategist ever expanding. The two months since Harper had left New York felt like six, and there was always another project, another deadline, another quick turnaround that had her sending a last-minute text to Poppy pushing their nightly chat to the next day, then the next. Never once did Poppy make Harper feel bad. She understood that Harper was still finding her feet at her new job and needed to do everything she could to make a good impression. But Poppy had a new job too, and, apparently, new friends. Harper still knew so little about either of those things.

Her phone buzzed, and she rushed to pick it up, already smiling at the text she expected to see that said Poppy was missing her too, but not to worry, they'd catch up soon. But it was from Bella.

Hey girl, ready to crush this costume party? There was a photo of Bella dressed as a bunch of grapes, sporting a green leotard decorated with green balloons.

Bella, not Poppy. Bella wasn't her first choice—none of this was—yet here she was reaching out as a friend. Poppy would be so happy to know she had a new friend. The next text that came in made her laugh out loud.

Shit! I just popped one.

Harper thought for a second and then wrote back, No use wine-ing about it! Bella sent back laughing emojis, followed by plans to meet in the lobby in five minutes.

Suddenly she heard Charlotte's voice in her head and saw the headline of her next email blast, which would include a picture of Bella in her costume. She grabbed a Post-it and jotted down *When life gives you grapes*, and then turned the camera on herself and took a snap of her outfit. Selfies were something Manhattan Harper would've made fun of, but Nashville Harper was always ready to *reach*. As Harper went to post the photo, she noticed her followers had nearly quadrupled since the last time she checked. There was something really satisfying about seeing her follower count increase with every new photo. She typed the hashtags #HalloweenFun #WorkHardPlayHarder #GreenTeamBestTeam #DreamJob.

Within just a few seconds, the photo was getting likes—and why wouldn't it? It didn't reveal that she was tired or stressed or worried about losing her best friend at all. Nobody wanted to see *that* Harper. They wanted the Harper who was always up for a good time and thrilled to be working alongside Charlotte Green. They wanted *Nashville Harper*, and she was going to give her to them.

17

Come as You Aren't

Goddesses. Harper hadn't expected to see so many of her colleagues dressed as green goddesses, which honestly sounded like a cheat, as the only green goddess she knew was a salad dressing. Still, it was easily the most flattering costume. The courtyard at The Greenhouse had been decorated with orange and green lights, clusters of jack-o'-lanterns, and not-so-spooky glittering spiderwebs that made a great backdrop for photos. There was even a little graveyard where negative feelings rather than people went to die, its tombstones reading *RIP* to self-doubt, fear, and anxiety. All the businesses and restaurants and bars on their little strip did something for Halloween, and everyone wandered from one party to another, posting pictures of their favorite costumes online. But that wasn't something Charlotte was happy about.

According to Bella, Charlotte had been the only one to host a big Halloween party when she moved to The Greenhouse office three years ago, and everyone had talked about it. There had been pictures of her in costume, just being a big kid, hanging with her team members and having fun. It had been *her thing*, not that Harper could understand how a holiday practiced by so many people around the world could be one person's thing. That was like saying you had invented Valentine's Day or that throwing a New Year's Eve party was your original idea. It wasn't possible, but that wasn't how Charlotte saw it. So, to compete with the rest of the block, she started having the party earlier and earlier to take as many pictures as possible and get them online before anyone else could. Last year she'd insisted employees bring their kids for face painting and bobbing for apples. But with the exception of Cynthia— who, along with her kids, dressed as gummy bears every year (*no sense wasting a good costume!*)—she had grossly overestimated how many of her employees had children. Bella had gathered them all into one corner of the building to make it look like more of them than there were. This year Bella had come prepared and had invited the entire classes of each of Charlotte's kids.

"That's why we're here at five o'clock," Bella said to Harper after she had given her the backstory, "so that we can get our pictures up first and so that Charlotte can go trick-or-treating with her children. Plus, it looks good for her. It shows she's a real family person and cares about her employees and their families." She grabbed Harper's arm and took a shot of the two of them to post to her social. #SquadGhouls

It was obvious to Harper how nervous Bella was. Bella's now-familiar habit of chewing her lip and nodding emphatically whenever she was defending Charlotte had kicked into high gear.

"Where is Charlotte?" Harper asked, the answer appearing before her and causing her to gasp. Making her entrance at the top of the stairs in a bright green kimono and an elaborately styled black wig was Charlotte . . . dressed as a geisha.

"Oh. My. God," Harper said, rushing in front of Charlotte to block her completely offensive costume from view. "Turn around. Turn around and go back inside."

"What are you doing?" Charlotte asked, raising her voice.

Before Harper could answer, Oliver appeared, bounding up the stairs dressed as a golfer in a green jacket holding a trophy—the winner of the iconic green Master's Cup. He took Charlotte by the arm. "You can't come out here dressed like that," he said urgently, pushing her back inside the building.

"Why? You said we needed to be a more culturally diverse company, so that's what I'm doing," Charlotte snapped.

"But you're not Asian," Harper whispered, stating the obvious. "It's offensive, like wearing blackface."

"I would *never*—" Charlotte began.

"Of course not, so you can't do this," Harper said.

"Why didn't you say anything?" Charlotte asked Bella, who had silently appeared in the middle of all this and was chewing on her bottom lip so furiously that Harper feared she might eat it.

"I thought you said you were going as a Green goddess," Bella replied, scrolling through her texts trying to find the message she was looking for. "Oh. Geisha goddess. I didn't know there was such a thing."

"Fuck, Bella. *You're* Asian. That's why I ran it by you."

"I'm sorry, I was rushing trying to get ready and—"

Charlotte snapped at Bella. "You know I have my workbook launch coming up. The last thing I need is to be dressed up as a PR nightmare."

"Here, you can wear my costume," Harper said, taking off her overalls and stripping down to her green unitard.

"You want me to go as a troll?" Charlotte gasped.

"I'm a gnome!"

"Oh, for fuck's sake, all right, but hurry up. I don't need anyone to see me like this and then threaten to cancel me," Charlotte said, walking to her office with Harper hurrying behind.

Three minutes later, Charlotte emerged, looking cuter and chicer than any gnome Harper had ever seen. One strap of her overalls was undone over the green unitard, and she'd somehow found knee socks to match her white runners. For reasons unknown, she had also given herself freckles with brown eyeliner. Harper, having borrowed Charlotte's Serene by Green T-shirt, a hoodie, leggings, and terry-cloth headband, was hoping to pass herself off as a green gym instructor. It was a stretch for both of them, but at least these costumes wouldn't cause a Halloween nightmare.

"Wow, you look great—obvi the most stylish gnome I have ever seen," Bella gushed, sucking up to Charlotte.

"We should get outside before Mandy gets here." Oliver steered Charlotte back to the entrance. "I don't want you to run into each other."

"She was supposed to get here to meet you *before* the party. That's why I sent everyone home early to get ready," Charlotte fumed.

"I know, but she texted that something came up and she was running late," Oliver said.

"Something came up, what bullshit. She's looking to cause a scene!"

"Well, she might not be the one doing that if we don't move this along," Oliver said delicately. He cast a sideways look at Bella, who looked like she might cry.

"Fine, but hurry up. I don't want to be anywhere near her or her lawyer," Charlotte said, racing out with Oliver and leaving Bella and Harper alone in the office.

Bella sat on a beanbag in the garden, accidentally popping one of her balloons. She buried her face in her hands.

Harper could tell she was crying, even though she was trying to muffle the sounds.

"I'm sorry," Bella said, wiping her eyes and trying to collect herself.

"For what?"

"Fucking up, making this mess, forcing you to give Charlotte your costume—all of it." Bella sniffled. "It's all my fault."

Harper grabbed what she hoped was a clean tissue out of the pocket of Charlotte's hoodie and passed it to Bella.

"None of this is your fault," Harper began, but the sound of footsteps made her pause. A few seconds later, Mandy walked through the main entrance.

"Hey, Bella, you okay?"

Bella stood up. She was taller than Mandy and seemed to grow more so the longer she remained quiet.

"Like you care. From what I understand, you're the only person you'll be able to talk to about any of this after you sign your NDA. Wait, do they still call it that if you sign it for *money*, or is that a legal version of blackmail?"

"Bella!" Mandy said, shocked.

"Sorry, gotta go. Not all of us can get paid to do nothing. Come on, Harper," Bella said. She walked straight ahead, forcing Mandy to quickly sidestep. Then Mandy and Harper were left standing alone. Mandy looked Harper up and down slowly. "You're dressed as Charlotte."

"I was—" Harper started and then stopped. "Yeah, I guess I am."

"As long as you can remember it's just a costume," Mandy said, as a man in a suit carrying a briefcase came in with Oliver and called her over.

"Your *lawyer* is here. Let's get this over with quickly, shall we?" Oliver said loudly, directing the two of them into his office and closing the door firmly behind them.

Harper stared at the closed door, Mandy's words of warning ringing in her ears.

Harper had never seen anyone smash a piñata as hard as Oliver. Whoever had made that papier-mâché pumpkin had used so much glue that, after countless tries, all the children—including Charlotte's, who were hell-bent on getting some candy—had given up hope and were now looking to Oliver to save the day. Oliver had been forced to use one of his golf clubs to break the thing open in an astonishing display of strength and what Harper could only assume had something to do with his meeting. After unleashing a string of profanity under his breath, the pumpkin broke open, and the kids grabbed the falling candy by the fistfuls.

"Okay, you greedy little bears, that's enough," Cynthia chided her children as they filled their small jack-o'-lanterns.

"Gather round everyone. Smile for the camera," Charlotte shouted, gathering the children for a group photo as the buses she hired for the event pulled up to take the kids home. "Smile! There you go. One more, okay? One, two, three . . ."

"Happy Hallow—Green!" Everyone cheered and then applauded madly as Aaron recorded the whole thing. The moment it was clear that he had what he needed, Charlotte called Bella over to round up the kids and get them on the buses.

"Okay, everyone, follow me," Bella called out, using Halloween loot bags to get them to line up single file so she could do a head count. Despite all the sugar the kids had ingested, they followed Bella's directions and were remarkably quiet as she did a roll call, her former life as a schoolteacher in full effect.

"Thanks again for the costume," Charlotte said, standing next to Harper. "The whole Lord of the Rings thing wouldn't have been my first choice, but it was better than the alternative."

Harper didn't bother to correct Charlotte. "You're welcome."

"I swear, you just try and do something nice and fun, and then you have to worry that someone will tear you to shreds and cancel you. Look, I get it, but what about all those great operas where people dress up. Is that not allowed anymore?"

"I think context has a lot to do with it," Harper said, treading lightly. "Someone's culture not being a costume and all. We all make mistakes, and hopefully we can correct them before they do any harm."

"Or hopefully you have enough money to make them go away."

Harper looked at Charlotte and waited. "It's funny how everything and *everyone* has a price. Pay people enough, and they'll swallow their *integrity* and stop talking shit about you," Charlotte said.

Harper had a feeling they were now talking about Mandy, but she also knew better than to say so.

"I guess that's one way to put it," Harper said. "But won't people always talk shit? I mean you can't pay *everyone* not to. Some people just want to be heard, and saying something shitty is an easy way to get noticed." Harper was thinking of those people who left one-star reviews online for books that said things like, UGH, or WHY, or MEH. Hardly a thoughtful critique of someone else's work, but in a sea of supportive feedback, they sure got noticed.

"True. That's why we just have to give them something else to talk about. Control the conversation, keep going, keep doing, offer more things, don't let anything or anyone get in your way," Charlotte said.

It sounded ominous, and Harper felt herself shiver involuntarily.

"You can't let the haters win, Harper." Charlotte waved to the kids as they took their seats on the buses. Suddenly a wave of laughter broke out, and there was Oliver wearing the now-emptied-out piñata on his head like a mask, making the kids giggle as the buses pulled away. "Look at him! He's going to make an amazing dad someday. I hope it's soon for his sake." Charlotte pulled out her phone and snapped a picture of the scene.

Harper was touched by Charlotte's sincerity. With her larger-than-life personality and habit of speaking in inspirational quotes, it was easy to forget that the tiny giant of a woman standing next to her was also a mom, and someone's real-life best friend.

"Well, that was a success!" Bella said, walking over.

"In spite of the rocky start," Charlotte added, looking at her sideways. "Make sure you get those pictures up ASAP. And be sure to read everything carefully before posting."

Bella's whole face flushed. "Of course. And again, I'm really sorry about the costume misunderstanding earlier. I'm so glad it all worked out."

"We have Harper to thank for that. *Great save*." She squeezed Harper's arm.

Harper beamed. She could get used to being in Charlotte's good graces.

"Great party as always. Have a good night everyone!" Cynthia said, waving goodbye as she walked her kids out.

"Well, shall I call it?" Oliver asked, coming toward them with Aaron.

"Yes, please. Mama needs to go home and have something stronger than pumpkin punch after today. You all have a good night." Charlotte waved goodbye and stepped into the center of the courtyard to thank everyone for coming.

"Well, ladies, if there isn't anything else, I think I'll be on my way," Oliver said, pulling bits of papier-mâché out of his hair.

"No big Halloween plans with Liam tonight?" Aaron asked.

"No, he's working late, so it looks like I get to hand out candy to all the kids by myself—again."

"I'm going to swing by and see my mom and niece and nephew, and then try and crash some of the other influencer parties. I promised Charlotte I would go and report back." Bella undid her high ponytail and shook her hair out.

"What about you, Manhattan? Have you got any plans?" Aaron asked shyly.

Oliver and Bella both turned to look at Harper, a bemused expression on their faces.

"Me? No. I mean, I bought candy, but I was just going to eat it while watching old movies," she said, her cheeks turning pink. "What about you?"

"Well," he said, then took a deep breath, "I managed to score a spot at the new talent night at the Listening Room Cafe, and I thought that if nobody had any plans . . ."

"Talent night?" Harper said, surprised. She'd no idea Aaron was a musician—what else didn't she know about him?

"Yeah, but if you're not interested . . ."

"Of course we're *interested*," Oliver said, smiling widely. "Sounds like a lot more fun than what we were going to do. Isn't that right, *Manhattan*?"

"Sure," Harper said, embarrassed. *Interested* was an understatement.

18

Can I Get a Yee-Hottie?

"These are on me," Harper said an hour later, fishing her credit card out of her wallet and handing it to the waitress delivering drinks before Oliver and Bella could say anything. They were sitting at a small wooden table marked RESERVED near the front of the stage at the Listening Room Cafe, a restaurant and live music venue. She passed the drinks around and took a sip of her margarita. She was celebrating her bonding moment with Charlotte, and even though she had no business treating anyone to anything, it felt good to share, especially since she was the only one who had come away from the Halloween party feeling like she had any reason to. Bella was still stinging from her costume debacle, and Oliver looked like he'd gone ten rounds with Mandy and her lawyer. But Aaron's shy invitation had given them something else to focus on.

Apparently an invitation was something Aaron never offered, Oliver told her, so naturally he and Bella said yes, which was how Harper found herself sitting at one of the reserved tables, looking to see where he was. The space was simple. Dark hardwood floors, exposed brick walls, and café ceiling lights that stopped just short of the room's platform stage created a cozy feeling. But it wasn't the décor that made this place so special—it was its legacy. Bella told Harper that more artists had been discovered on this stage than anywhere else, and there was an excitement in the room that the next act could be the one that took off.

"What's the occasion?" Bella asked, sipping her vodka tonic.

"No occasion, just my turn, that's all," Harper replied. "That, and we had a successful Halloween party." She smiled but was met with only stares from Bella and Oliver.

"I think we have different definitions of success," Oliver said, squeezing a lime into his mocktail and licking his fingers.

"I have to agree with Oliver. This evening was a disaster in the making. That outfit? Mandy?" Bella took a big gulp of her drink.

"Don't forget the unbreakable piñata," Oliver said, making them laugh. "Trust me, a brown man beating a paper pumpkin to death with a five iron is the last thing I need the adoption agency to see."

Harper nearly spat out her drink. "Okay, the whole party could have been a disaster, but it wasn't. We avoided it *together* and turned it around. I think that's worth celebrating."

"Someone's feeling the shine," Oliver said, smiling.

"The shine?" Harper asked.

Oliver looked at Bella and then back to Harper. "It's when Charlotte shines her light on you."

"As opposed to being in her shadow, which is when she throws you shade," Bella said with a sigh.

"Oh, come on now, Bella," Oliver reassured. "You'll have lots of opportunities to redeem yourself. You've got the big influencer lunch next month, and Charlotte wouldn't have asked you to go to such an important event if she didn't believe in you."

"I know. I just feel like such an idiot. I should've caught it. I mean, a *geisha goddess*?"

"Is that even a thing? And what does that have to do with the color green?" Harper asked.

"You're just trying to make me feel better," Bella said. She swirled her straw around in her glass and groaned.

"Look, it could've been worse. Someone could've seen Charlotte and alerted *#Canceled*," Oliver said, and shuddered.

#Canceled was a popular podcast that pitched itself as the edgier, cooler version of the print *Inc.* magazine. Both focused on business, but while *Inc.* glorified business leaders and entrepreneurs, *#Canceled* took them down. Notoriously bitchy, it was a behind-the-scenes podcast that prided itself on revealing what working inside top brands and companies was really like without actually naming names. Their choice to keep the companies they were dishing about anonymous made it all the more juicy for their listeners. Their tagline, *Telling it like it is, because they won't,* could strike fear or glee in the hearts of listeners, as it was often easy to decipher who the thinly veiled stories were about.

"Oh my God, that *would* be worse," Bella said.

"See? Look on the bright side. The party was a success for all of us. Team effort!" Harper held her glass up in a toast.

"You are getting the hang of this. Before we know it, you'll start injecting some color into your monochromatic wardrobe and drinking green juice."

"Wow. First of all, ouch. And second, I will never give up coffee. I love it too much, and it loves me," Harper said.

"Fine . . . To a team effort!" Oliver said. He raised his glass and noticed it was empty. "Wait a minute—this can't be right. Harper, I think they ripped you off. This glass was obviously only half-full, and before you say anything, that's not me being pessimistic, just honest. And thirsty." He placed his glass down and looked around for the waitress. "What kind of place did Aaron drag us to? And when is he doing his set? I'm going to fall asleep."

Harper and Bella burst out laughing.

"You're delirious," Bella said.

"Well, it's been a day. I never thought Mandy . . ." He leaned back in his chair and ran his hands over his head. "They were so close once."

"We all were," Bella said quietly.

"Never mind. It's done now," Oliver said, rallying. "And we're not going to dwell on the past. We're going to look toward the future, and that future is sitting right here at this table and just months away from the promotion she has been working so hard for."

Bella immediately brightened and reached across the table to squeeze Oliver's hand.

"Oh, and you too, Harper, even though that was a terrible Halloween costume. I mean, the whole assignment was to dress in a costume with a *g*, not troll with a *t*," Oliver said, winking. He waved his hand to get the waitress's attention and ordered them another round.

"Does this mean you'll be my boss?" Harper asked, playfully tapping Bella on the arm.

"Hardly. Although . . . *maybe*?" Bella said, a smile spreading across her face.

Harper wanted to know more about what went wrong with Mandy, but she didn't want to spoil the mood again. She'd have to find a way to ask Oliver when they were alone.

"Hey, sorry about the two-drink minimum," Aaron said, appearing at their table. He was wearing a fitted black button-down that hugged his body. Harper had never seen Aaron in anything other than loose-fitting, faded T-shirts, and she found herself trying not to stare at the suntanned patch of chest that peeked out from the undone mother-of-pearl buttons. He pulled up the chair next to her, rolled up his sleeves, and ran his hands through his hair. After a moment of silence in which Harper was aware that she wasn't the only one stunned by the sight of this newer, sexier Aaron, Oliver spoke.

"Happy to do our part. When are you going on?"

"Soon. I know it's late—or at least, it feels like it after today," he said, glancing at Bella.

"Not at all, we're just getting started." Oliver stifled a yawn, which made Aaron smile. "Okay, who am I kidding? I'm out of here the second you're done. No offense, but I'm a hundred years older than all of you, and we're supposed to paint the nursery tomorrow." Oliver said reaching for his drink the waitress delivered.

"Wait, you got a—"

"No, no, it's more of a 'if you welcome them, they will come.' It's Liam's idea. Honestly, he's been so tense that if this helps, I'll do it."

"You don't have to stay," Aaron said, fiddling with the label on his beer bottle. It was the first time Harper had seen him appear nervous.

"Excuse me? This is the first time in all the years I've known you that you've invited anyone to come watch you play. Not sure what the special occasion is, but I'm not missing it." Harper could swear Oliver was smirking at her above the rim of his glass. She was suddenly aware of just how hot the room was and just how close Aaron's leg was to hers.

"I've never been to a country western venue before," she said, hoping to distract herself. The space was now packed with people.

"Somehow, that doesn't surprise me, Manhattan. I can't imagine they have many of them in New York," Aaron said and took a sip of his beer.

"Have you ever actually been to New York?" Harper asked, turning in her chair to look at him, which meant moving her leg along his, which meant discovering it was much more muscular than she would've suspected. She was now distracted in a very different way than she'd intended.

"Actually, I have. An old friend of mine moved out there to play with the symphony." He lingered on the word a little bit as if to say, *I bet you didn't expect me to say that now, did you?*

Actually, she did. She'd done a little snooping between the Halloween party and the venue, and by the looks of Aaron's Instagram, it seemed like he was a totally different person online. His grid was filled with photos from concerts, videos of him singing covers, and no trace of The Greenhouse.

"I love the symphony," Oliver said, "but Liam says it's a bore. Still, when the baby comes, I'm going to make him—"

"Or her," Bella said wistfully.

"Or *her*, listen to classical music. Otherwise, our poor child will never know the difference between Mozart and Madonna—"

"Or Rachmaninoff and Rihanna," Aaron said, making Oliver laugh.

"Don't knock my girl RiRi," Bella said, shaking her finger at Aaron.

"Never," Aaron replied, placing his hand on his heart. "Well, I better get back there so I'm ready. I'll see you after." He gave them a nervous little wave.

Harper watched Aaron walk away. She picked up her drink, put it back down, and then gulped some water instead. Was she crazy, or had Aaron been flirting with her? He was cuter in the real world than he was at The Greenhouse, but then again, it had been so long since she had been with anyone that she could be imagining things. She turned back to Oliver and Bella, mortified to find them staring at her staring after him.

"What?" Harper asked.

"Nothing," they said simultaneously, trying not to crack up.

"I was just going to say that he cleans up nicely," Oliver said kindly. "But then I remembered I'm also the head of human resources, and that kind of thing can be taken the wrong way. You know—no office romances, no comments related to appearance. That sort of thing."

Harper was about to ask where geisha goddesses fell into the inappropriate equation until she realized Oliver wasn't kidding. "Right, well, for the record, you did say it. But don't worry, your secret's safe with me." Harper was grateful to be interrupted by the sound of applause. She turned her attention to the front of the room, where Aaron was taking the stage. He slung a guitar over his head and hugged the instrument close to his body as the lights dimmed and the room quieted. As he brushed his hair out of his eyes and leaned in close to the microphone to greet the audience, Harper had to agree—he did clean up nicely.

19

Sing to Me Like
One of Your French Girls

Harper hadn't had much luck with men. Sure, she'd dated Dylan back in high school and college, and yes, they had lived together for a year before they graduated, but this was different. Harper had never really thought of Dylan as a grown-up. He was always, in some ways to her, the boy she'd fallen hard for when they were both teens. He'd been her first everything: her first kiss, her first time, her first breakup, and her first real heartbreak. After all those firsts, it seemed cruel that Dylan was also the last guy who treated her right— if you considered "right" forgetting only *a couple* of anniversaries and only buying her flowers after that one time he got wasted at a concert in college. But it was the only romance Harper had ever known, or at least, the only one that lasted longer than a couple of dates. That was why she felt more than a little uncomfortable as she listened to Bella interrogate Aaron about the identity of the woman he had sung about in his last song. He had joined their table after his set to say goodbye to Oliver and watch the rest of the night's acts.

"Not Brooklyn?" Bella asked.

"No," Aaron said, sipping his bourbon.

"Amanda?"

"Nope."

"Jessica? It's got to be Jessica. *Soft curves that make my mind swerve?* Her body was insane," Bella said, turning to Harper and shrugging awkwardly.

"Don't ask me! I don't know who you're talking about."

"Oh, they were before your time. They all worked in sales on the Create Team. That group sees the most turnover."

"You can stop asking," Aaron said casually, "because I'm never going to tell."

Harper was glad to hear it. She didn't want to know how many more women he'd gone out with against HR policy. Not that it was any of her business—and not that she cared, exactly—but it reminded her once again how few men she had been with. Maybe Poppy had a point about her getting back out there again.

"Besides, now Harper thinks I'm some kind of slut," Aaron said, looking at her.

"The *singing* kind, obviously." Harper sipped her drink. "I see why Oliver implemented a no-dating policy at The Greenhouse. There'd be no employees left."

Bella burst out laughing as Aaron turned bright red.

"Whoa, hold up. That's not fair. I've stayed friends with all my exes, and don't forget, I've been in Nashville awhile. We don't all get to start with a clean slate. For all we know, you're leaving a trail of broken hearts back in New York."

"I'll never tell. Or write songs about it," Harper said, realizing how tipsy she was starting to feel.

"Ouch."

"I'm just kidding. All your songs were beautiful. You were amazing."

"You sound surprised," Aaron said, putting his drink down and leaning back in his chair. He tilted his head and studied Harper as Bella looked back and forth between them.

"No. It's just that it's *Nashville,* where everyone is supposedly a musician, the same way everyone in L.A. is an actor."

"Or the way that everyone in New York is a writer?"

"Or everyone in Texas is a cowboy?" Bella piped in. "No, wait, that one's true," she said, making them laugh.

"Well, I'm glad you came," Aaron continued, holding eye contact with Harper just a little too long to not mean something. He then turned to Bella. "You too, Bells. Thank you."

"Thanks for finally inviting me. Took you long enough, but now I know why."

"Why?" Harper and Aaron asked at the same time.

"Because you've been writing about me. *Six feet tall, she's the belle of the ball?* It's okay. I won't tell." She grabbed her bag and stood up. "I gotta run."

"Oh, okay." Harper stood to go too.

"No, you stay and finish your drink. I'm going to stop at a couple of those other influencer parties and schmooze for a bit. I promised Charlotte I would. I'll text you if any of them are any good." She gave a little wave and turned and left, leaving Harper and Aaron sitting alone in awkward silence.

"She's always working. I don't know how she does it," Harper said.

"Charlotte's everything to her—her boss, mentor, role model, friend, and family member. She took a chance on her, and Bella will do everything she can to prove that it was worth it."

"I get that, but I've only been here a couple of months, and it seems that The Greenhouse is her whole life," Harper said, shaking her head.

"It is. It's yours too. Face it: you've been here two months, and already you're writing Charlotte's email blasts, helping to organize events, and hanging out with her inner circle."

"Inner circle—that sounds so cliquey." Harper shuddered.

"I know. But it matters. It sends a message that Charlotte believes in you. And when she does, you believe in yourself more, and other people start to take notice."

Harper studied Aaron for a moment. She hadn't expected this from him.

"And here I thought that you with your separate office and separate life looked down on all of this."

"Nah. Charlotte took a chance on me too. It's because of the job she gave me that I can do this. She believed in me before I believed in myself. I'd been kicking around Nashville a long time before I met Charlotte. I was broke, and a friend who owns a production agency had talked me into filming one of her conferences when his videographer bailed. I didn't know what I was doing. I had taken some filmmaking courses in college, but nothing serious. Just enough to make videos of my band at the time. But I needed the money, so I said yes. And she took a liking to me, and as they say, *the rest is history*."

I'm sure she took a liking to you, thought Harper. Of all the people at The Greenhouse, Aaron was the one person she'd seen Charlotte truly relax around. Not even Oliver had that effect on her, but there was something so easygoing about Aaron, something that so clearly said he didn't really give a shit—but in the best way—that she could only imagine what a relief that must be to Charlotte, who cared so much about everything all the damn time.

"I have to admit that it does feel good to be liked by her," Harper said.

"It's more than that, though. She sees people. She turns weaknesses into strengths and rewards them. To other people, I was a guy dabbling in everything and mastering nothing, but to Charlotte, I was experiencing life, someone who was willing to try anything. And she thought that meant I had potential, to become someone she could rely on. I don't know about you, but I haven't met a lot of people so committed to building up others. It's why we're all willing to look the other way on the other stuff."

"What other stuff?" Harper asked.

"You know, Charlotte being Charlotte," Aaron said, stretching his arms in the air and exposing just the tiniest bit of tanned abs as he did. It wasn't much, but it was enough to make Harper forget to ask for more details and agree to let Aaron walk her home.

After a lightning round of Two Truths and a Lie as they strolled, Harper was floating. Aaron was funnier than she expected, regaling her with anecdotes about some of the places they passed. It was clear that he loved Nashville the same way she loved New York, and that he also felt a little nervous, just like she did. They were walking along the sidewalk when a costume-clad teenager came speeding toward them on a skateboard. Reacting quickly, Aaron pulled Harper out of the way. As his hand lingered on her waist, she could feel his hip pressing up behind her, and she held her breath, her whole body suddenly wide awake. For a moment, neither of them moved. "Saved your life," Aaron whispered, and let her go.

Harper laughed nervously. "Who knew Nashville was so dangerous?"

"It's not all cute cowboys and charming influencers," Aaron said, his hand brushing close to hers as they walked.

"No, it's heroic musicians too," Harper joked.

They slowed their pace as they arrived at the Green Suites, and they rode the elevator up to Harper's apartment in silence.

"Well, this is me," she said as they reached her front door.

"So it is."

They stood for a moment staring at each other.

"Thanks for coming to my set." Aaron took a tiny step forward and leaned his hand against the doorframe.

"Thanks for being really talented. It would have been so awkward otherwise."

"Well, I wouldn't want things to be awkward," he said, smiling wryly.

Harper's cheeks burned and she closed the gap between them, only to jump back quickly at the sound of a text message notification sounding loudly in her purse. She'd forgotten she turned the sound back on after the performance in case Charlotte needed anything. Harper reached inside her purse and looked at the display.

"Everything okay?" Aaron asked.

"Yeah. It's Bella. She says the other parties were lame and she's calling it a night."

The mood broken, Aaron took a step back and nodded. "Sounds like a good idea. I should probably do the same."

"Yeah, me too," Harper muttered, stuffing her phone back in her purse and wishing she had never checked it. She took out her keys and opened the door. "Well, good night."

"Night, Manhattan. Sleep tight." Aaron gave her one last lingering look before heading down the hall.

Harper shut the door behind her and leaned against it, sleep the last thing on her mind.

———

The next morning Harper awoke to the memory of her time with Aaron and felt her whole body smile. She couldn't remember the last time she'd had such a great night. Aaron was funny, and sexy, and full of surprises. Like Bella, he was grateful that Charlotte had taken a chance on him. Maybe Harper could let herself be seen differently too. She didn't have to be the woman who moved to New York, couldn't get ahead in publishing, and had to take a job in Nashville with an influencer she had never heard of. She could be the woman who moved from New York to Nashville to forge her own path because she was tired of the old way of doing things and knew a great opportunity when she saw it. She wasn't running away; she was running toward something new and better. Her phone dinged, announcing Charlotte's intention for the day on the Vine. *We can, so we must . . .* This time Harper didn't wait to see what others wrote and immediately typed back *choose success!* To Harper's surprise, Charlotte replied. *YES*, and then *failure is a choice*.

Harper watched as the other answers came in: *We can, so we must do better; be better; try harder; care more . . .*

They were all true, but Charlotte wasn't giving any of them the thumbs-up that Harper had received. That one little validation had simultaneously buoyed Harper and stoked her competitive streak. She refreshed her feed, checking to see if anyone else had gotten an all-caps response from Charlotte, and was secretly pleased to see that they hadn't. She knew it was childish and more than a little petty, but after being overlooked despite the long hours she was putting in, it felt good to be recognized. In fact, it felt so good that it was enough to motivate Harper to finally fill out the questionnaire she'd gotten in her welcome packet. Charlotte's shine warmed Harper more than she wanted to admit, and, basking in its glow, she had no plans to let it dim.

Seeing Green Monthly Newsletter:

November

This month is all about giving thanks. While some people feel like it's too controversial to celebrate Thanksgiving because of the whole colonization of other people thing, I like to focus on the giving thanks part of it. So this November, let me start by saying Thanks for Giving—your time, your love, and your support to this little dream of mine to create a community of like-minded soul sisters who refuse to be colonized by anyone or anything other than ourselves. We've shown that we're women who won't be bossed around or held back, women who know that when they put their mind to it, they can do anything. (Ditto for all our kick-ass male and non-gender-conforming supporters!) I truly believe that, because that's what you've shown me. Remember when all of this was just little ol' me and my blog, sharing the joys and challenges of being a mom and how hard it was to find time to connect to that part of myself that had existed before my children came along? That woman who had her own dreams and desires? I do. Remember how you reached out to me and shared your stories and let me know that my sharing helped you share? I do. Remember the first time we met? How excited we were? You better believe I do. I'll never forget it. In fact, I'll never forget any of the wonderful moments that we've shared because I make sure to write them all down on my daily Gratitude Cards. And that got me thinking—why not make this something we can all have? After all, we did this together! These beautiful hand-designed cards are the perfect way for you to record all the things you're grateful for. They're my way of saying thanks to you, and they're free for the first five hundred people who buy a limited-edition Serene by Green athleisure set that will premiere this weekend, just in time for Thanksgiving. Here's to giving thanks—here's to us!

xo Charlotte

20

New Levels, New Devils

It was officially Sprint Season at The Greenhouse, which meant that for the next three weeks everyone needed to work as hard as they could to get presales happening for the Inspire conference. It was only four months away—which, in Charlotte's world, was a blink of an eye.

Sprint Season. Harper knew the two things didn't go together. A sprint was a short burst of energy, whereas a season indicated a longer period of time, a chance for things to grow and mature and evolve. It required patience, and patience wasn't something Charlotte had. So when Charlotte uttered the phrase for the third time inside of a minute, Harper just bit her tongue and stuffed the last salad roll that the housekeeper, Annette, had put down hours earlier for their working dinner and brain squeeze.

"When I say we need to squeeze it to find it, I mean we gotta *squeeze* it," Charlotte said, clenching her fists dramatically. "That's how I came up with the idea of including men and non-gender-conforming followers in the last newsletter. I thought, you know what, I am woman hear me roar—*everyone*. The more warriors we've got on board with us, the more seats we fill for the conference, and the more we all win our self-enlightenment war. So come on, don't storm, *squeeze!*"

A brainstorm was a whirlwind of ideas building on top of each other, whereas a *brain squeeze* was generating ideas and building them out until you felt like you had nothing left in the tank—but kept going. Charlotte claimed that some of her best ideas came when she was absolutely sure she had nothing left to give, which was why Oliver, Bella, Tiffany, and Harper had been made to stay so late.

As Harper chewed on the now-hard salad roll, she tried to ignore the sight of Ryan appearing in his robe. He'd been hovering all night. He wandered over to the kitchen table where Harper, Oliver, Tiffany, and Bella had camped out with their laptops and notebooks.

"Babe, what are you doing?" Charlotte asked. "I thought you'd gone to bed."

"I did, but I need a snack," he said, sidling over to the cupboard and taking out a box of crackers.

"It's kind of late for that, isn't it?" Charlotte said, wincing at the sound of Ryan stuffing crackers in his mouth and crunching.

"No, but it *is* kind of late to be working," he answered, chewing loudly. "I thought you were having a working dinner."

Harper could feel everyone hold their breath. It was hard to tell by the look on Charlotte's face how she was going to respond.

"We were," Charlotte said, looking at Ryan as if to say *What's your point?*

"Well, dinner was hours ago—the kids have gone to bed; Annette's gone home."

"I know. I'm the one who came home to feed them and get them to bed, so Annette could leave and you could *rest*," she said through clenched teeth.

Harper felt like a kid witnessing their parents fighting and fidgeted with her napkin. She snuck a look at Oliver and Bella, who were both suddenly very busy with their phones.

"Ladies, come here for a second. I want to show you something," Oliver said, pulling them down to his end of the table, as far away from Charlotte and Ryan as they could get without leaving the room. He stood up and beckoned for them to gather around his laptop at the kitchen island, pointing exaggeratedly at the screen as if to say, *Don't mind us; we aren't paying any attention to you.*

Charlotte and Ryan stared at each other in silence.

"I just thought that you could use some rest too," Ryan said, frowning.

"Aw, that's sweet. Thanks for your concern, hon, but I'll decide when we're done," Charlotte replied. Although it was clear by the tone of her voice that what she was really saying was *Piss off.*

She turned back to her laptop and started typing.

"I'm only trying to help," he said, softening his tone. He reached over and tucked a loose strand of hair behind her ear. "The conference isn't for months, babe. You still have lots of time to roll out your marketing plan and push your athleisure wear. You know, maybe you could even do a pop-up in the next couple of months to stir up interest," he said. "Just an idea."

"Oh well, if we're throwing ideas around, then please, pull up a seat," Charlotte said, pointing to an empty chair.

"No, I didn't mean—"

"No? Because the way you keep popping in when I'm working almost makes me think you miss it."

"I miss having a wife. *That's* what I miss," he said, a little too loudly. "It would be nice if you actually came to bed when I was still awake for once. You know, maybe practice all that shit you preach about keeping romance alive." He threw his hands in the air and walked out, leaving Charlotte sitting with her mouth open in shock.

It was a full minute until Oliver finally broke the silence.

"He's still adjusting," Oliver said gently. "Once he gets his *Mister Class* up and running and has his own thing to focus on, he won't be so touchy."

"Yes, he will. He's used to getting everything he wants without having to lift a finger. Fancy boarding schools, legacy acceptance to an Ivy League university, being made the CEO of his daddy's company the day he graduates. It all worked out just fine until he realized his wife's *little business* wasn't so little after all, and that she wasn't going to get bored and quit like he does. He's never had to work for anything, so he has no idea how much work it takes to keep it going." Charlotte walked over to the marble wet bar at the end of the kitchen and pulled out a bottle of tequila, five crystal glasses, and a lime. She brought them over and then rolled the lime back and forth on the counter to soften it before cutting wedges for each of them.

"Not like us," she said, pouring each of them a shot. "We know how hard we need to work to be successful, and because we know, we do." She raised her glass and downed her shot.

"I'm good, thanks," Tiffany called over. "It's really late. Maybe we should call it a night."

Charlotte shrugged at Tiffany. "Suit yourself."

"You know, calling it isn't a bad idea," Oliver said gently, placing his hand on Charlotte's. "We'll be fresher in the morning."

Charlotte was quiet for a moment. "You're right," she said, giving Oliver's hand a little squeeze. "Okay, get a good night's sleep, everyone! We'll get back at it rested and refreshed tomorrow."

Tiffany was already halfway to the door when Bella tentatively stood up. "I really think it's going to be our best conference yet."

"No doubt," Charlotte answered as Bella and Oliver gathered their things and started to head out.

Harper started to pack up too, but Charlotte looked so tired and deflated that she couldn't bring herself to go with them. "Go ahead without me—I'm going to stay and help clean up. I'll get an Uber back," Harper said.

Oliver rolled his eyes, but he and Bella walked out all the same.

Harper joined Charlotte at the bar, where she was making herself another drink. Without looking up, she poured one for Harper too, then carried the glasses out to the lounge chairs that faced the pool.

"You don't have to worry about me," Charlotte said as Harper accompanied her.

"I'm not. I just thought you might want some company."

Charlotte passed Harper her drink, stretched her legs out in front of her, and covered her toes with the folded monogrammed towel at the edge of her chair. "Because of Ryan? Please, that was nothing. I've dealt with much worse, believe me. You never know how fragile a man's ego is until he's next to a successful woman. And Ryan was a big part of my success, but my followers can only relate to him so much. He's not a regular person, no matter how much he pretends to be. Regular people can't start one business after another without having to worry about it succeeding. First it was a juice bar, then a fitness gym, and now this *Mister Class*. I thought that The Greenhouse would be enough for him, but once people stopped patting him on the back for *helping* me get to where I am and started patting me on the back for *staying* there, it wasn't as rewarding for him." She took a big sip of her drink and exhaled. "But you know what *is* rewarding? This." She nodded toward her giant house. "Sometimes I come out here just to admire it. This is a long way from the house my parents took a second mortgage out on to help put me through school."

Harper sat up straighter and stared at Charlotte.

"But I thought—"

"I know what you thought. Doesn't mean I didn't still work two jobs, but it does make the story less interesting to say I also got a little help, just like you did."

Harper looked down at herself through the pool's reflection and thought about her own life. Not many people knew about how much Poppy and her family had helped her financially back in New York.

Maybe Charlotte and I aren't all that different after all. Maybe she really does get it.

She sighed and folded her hands behind her head. "Anyway, my parents wouldn't want me to share that kind of thing. They like keeping their business private, which was probably why I went the other way as soon as I could. Just knowing that now it's my money and my hustle that pays for all of this—that's rewarding. And I'll be damned if anyone is going to take it away from me."

"I didn't know that anyone was trying to," Harper said, turning on her side to face Charlotte.

"Oh, they're always trying, believe me. I need someone with fresh eyes who can see things for what they are and not just tell me what I want to hear. I don't need another Mandy-like surprise. We have too much to do for the conference. But new levels bring new devils, so if you hear anyone complaining or suspect anything is off at The Greenhouse, you come to *me*."

"Have you talked to Bella or Tiffany about this?" After all, they had been with Charlotte the longest. If anything was off they'd know, so why was she asking Harper instead?

"No. I'd rather Tiffany didn't know that I'm concerned. She's been a bit touchy lately. As for Bella, she wouldn't want to upset me even if she did know something. Besides, she tends to see things with rose-colored glasses, which is great for our brand but not always great for our business. Look at Mandy. She and Bella and Tiffany were close. Surely she would've said something to one of them about leaving, but I didn't hear it. Instead, I got blindsided with some bullshit workplace misconduct lawsuit."

Harper couldn't believe that Charlotte was talking to her about all of this. It felt very fast to be pulled into her confidence, but then again, she *was* on Green Time.

"I don't know what happened," said Harper slowly, "but I do know that Bella was really angry and upset when she saw Mandy at the

Halloween party." She couldn't imagine that Bella was capable of anything other than total loyalty to Charlotte.

Charlotte considered this for a moment. "I suppose it's *possible* she didn't know. She tends to believe the best of people, which is why we love her. But you're smarter—"

"Oh, I don't know about that."

"Harper, it's just us—you don't have to do fake modesty with me. Save that for our followers. I didn't need to read your questionnaire to know you have aspirations greater than just being my visionary support strategist. But I did learn that coming from a humble background you have a complicated relationship with money and fame, although I'm guessing you'd be fine with both."

Harper turned bright red in the darkness. "Well, it's just that—"

"No need to explain or apologize. I get it, believe me. But what I'm trying to say is that you are smarter than Bella, and you're savvier too. You can be objective, which, as much as I appreciate her loyalty, Bella can't be. Oliver thinks I'm being paranoid, but I know that where there's one weed, there's another. And if someone knows who it is and isn't telling me then that makes them just as guilty, now doesn't it?"

Charlotte swung her feet around to the side of her chair and sat up to face Harper. Her eyes were gleaming in the dark. "I need to know that I can rely on you. Can I?"

"Of course," Harper said. And she wasn't exactly sure why, but she meant it. Harper couldn't remember the last time someone in power had spoken to her like a . . . what? Friend, colleague? *Confidante*. That was it. Charlotte didn't just believe in Harper; she trusted her. Charlotte had taken a chance on her when it felt like no one else would—why *wouldn't* she be there for her?

"And this is just between you and me. Got it?" she said, grabbing Harper's hands.

"Got it," Harper said, not looking away until Charlotte let go of her hands and lay back in her chair.

Harper did the same. It really was incredible that Charlotte had built all this on her own—not just her house, but her career and her company. If it had been possible for Charlotte, then who's to say it wasn't possible for Harper as well? She stretched her legs out in front of her and took a sip of her drink. But she didn't need the tequila. Just the very idea that she too could have all this one day was intoxicating enough.

21

Check Your Gr-attitude

"I'm grateful for my husband and for this wonderful job I get to do, all thanks to my friend of over twenty years who made it happen," Oliver said, holding the gratitude gourd as he spoke. It was the final day before the Thanksgiving holiday, and per tradition, Charlotte had gathered everyone to pass the gourd around and share what they were grateful for.

Bella took the gourd from Oliver. "I'm grateful that I get to spend time with my mom this holiday. She's had a rough couple of months."

"Well, that explains things," Charlotte whispered under her breath, just loud enough that Harper, who was standing next to her, caught it. Harper didn't think Charlotte was being fair. Sure, Bella had been a little off her game lately—leaving work an hour after everyone else instead of two, and making her deadlines on time instead of ridiculously early—but she was still doing her job. If anything, Bella just seemed more human than superhuman these days.

Bella started to pass the gourd to Cynthia and then pulled it back. "Oh, and of course, I'm grateful for all of you. Especially you, Charlotte. It's such a privilege learning from you and being part of the work we do here. I'm so excited for everything you've got coming up and just know you're going to kill it at the influencer lunch this year."

Charlotte placed her hand on her heart. "Aw, thanks, Bells. You *know* I am—and you'll be right by my side when I do." She winked at Bella, who beamed as she passed Cynthia the gourd.

Harper immediately looked at Tiffany, whose face was hard as stone.

"I'm grateful for elastic waistbands because, after this weekend, I'm going to need them!" Cynthia said, making everyone laugh.

By the time the gourd reached Harper, she knew exactly what she was going to say—she'd pulled it from Charlotte's Greenspiration journal. She hadn't told anyone, but she'd been taking the course along with Charlotte's followers.

Harper cradled the bright orange gourd and took a deep breath. "I'm grateful that every failure I've ever had led me to this moment. If I hadn't experienced those, I couldn't experience this." Charlotte grinned, taking the gourd.

"As for me," Charlotte said as she walked into the center of the circle, turning slowly and making eye contact with everyone, "I'm grateful for all of you. Gratitude, like everything, is a choice. There's a reason the word *attitude* is in there, because your *attitude* affects how you see the world around you, and it affects how the world responds to you. If you think you're a failure, you'll be a failure. If you think small, small is all you'll ever know. But if you are grateful for every challenge and obstacle that comes your way and embrace them with everything you have, then you and your world will grow in ways you never could've imagined."

Harper scanned the faces of her colleagues in an effort to gauge if anyone seemed disgruntled, the way Charlotte had asked her to. Although Tiffany still looked a little pissed, everybody else looked like students after exam week who were excited to go on spring break. The past few weeks had indeed been a sprint to the Inspire conference between finalizing the venue, researching potential guests, and designing the Serene by Green ad campaign.

And just this week they'd finalized the Serene by Green athleisure line items. Harper was thrilled that Serene had loved her ideas and run with them. She had no idea there could be so many variations on a pair of leggings or that leggings themselves could be so polarizing. In the end, the collection had two bottoms: black leggings with a strip of bright green that ran down the outside of the leg and a pair of seafoam-green drawstring joggers. There was also a cropped hoodie and a simple T-shirt that said NAMA-STAY GREEN. The finished products looked amazing, although even Harper, who was used to overpaying for workout wear in New York, had sticker shock. Even more surprising was the target sales sheet Serene had sent over, outlining how their financial commitment to the conference was directly related to the number of units sold.

Oliver, always composed, looked like he was going to be sick when he saw the numbers for the first time. How they were going to get women who saved up for months for their conference to come up with a few extra hundred dollars for the collection was beyond him. But Charlotte was undeterred. She was taking things to the next level, which meant next-level risk and next-level reward. It was also too late to do anything about it, as there was a signed contract in place. Harper shifted her attention back to Charlotte, who was now standing still and looking serious.

"Now, a lot of us will be seeing family over the holiday, and as wonderful as that is, it can also be challenging. Not everyone out there gets what we do in here. Trust me, I know—I have in-laws too." She rolled her eyes, making people laugh. "But even though family is important, your *chosen* family is just as important. What you do here and what *we* do here is important. Every day we work hard to lift *people* up and inspire them to be their best selves, and that's something that isn't always easy to explain, am I right?"

There were murmurs of acknowledgment and agreement.

"What are some of the things that your family says about your job? Go on, tell me. We should hear it in here before we hear it out there."

A young woman who worked as an assistant on the Community Team and often spent a lot of time just staring at Charlotte spoke up. "My dad always asks if I still do advertising for that blogger."

"*Blogger?* Okay, so he's a little behind the times, but . . . what else?" Charlotte asked.

"My mom tells people I'm a party planner," stammered another woman who worked in product ideation.

"My parents think I belong to a cult!"

Everyone laughed nervously at that one.

"Okay, what else? There's gotta be more," she said, waiting.

By the looks on some people's faces, Harper could tell that there *was* more, but people seemed too anxious to say anything else.

"What about . . ." Charlotte offered, "you should work somewhere that has better hours? Ever heard that one?"

A ripple of agreement went around the circle as people nodded their heads yes.

"Or it's not even your company—why do you care so much?"

People were agreeing out loud now, surprise and relief on their faces that Charlotte was the one to say these things.

Charlotte smiled and nodded, waiting until the room had settled down. "They're not wrong. You do work crazy hours, and yes, I ask a lot of you. All of that is true. But anyone who says those things is wrong about the way they view what it is we do. Your efforts are not small and insignificant; they are big and meaningful. You don't just work for me— you work *with* me. This is *your* company as much as it is mine. We are in this together, and together we're changing the world. We're reaching out to people and waking them up!" People began clapping. "We're helping them find their inner warrior! That's a powerful thing. Powerful people can be intimidating and not always understood. Our families—they don't always get it. And that's okay. The last thing I want you to do is spend your holiday wasting your energy trying to convince them that what you do matters. You know it matters. *I* know it matters. And one day, if they are willing to grow and evolve, they'll know it matters too. So go home, enjoy them for who they are, eat all the pie, and stay connected on the Vine. And if you need a reminder, at any time, of just how valuable you are, reach out to Bella, and she'll be sure to tell you." She smiled at Bella, who looked surprised but quickly recovered and nodded. They ended the meeting with three claps.

"Aaron, cue the music!" Charlotte yelled.

Aaron started blasting "We Are Family," and an impromptu dance party began that Charlotte immediately started recording. Watching her coworkers dancing their hearts out made Harper want to dance, too. What other kind of company, what other kind of *boss*, was this real and raw with her team?

Genuinely inspired, Harper jumped into the center of the carpet and started dancing next to Charlotte, who bopped along to the music and nodded approvingly. It was one thing to buy into Charlotte's beliefs— it was another thing entirely to *feel* them, and Harper was feeling them in a big way.

"Hey everyone, I'm with the incredible Green Team, and we're FIRED UP about Thanksgiving. Wherever you are, whoever you are, I'm challenging you to stop what you're doing and join us in a Green Team dance party. I don't care if you're at the grocery store or in an office; take a moment and be GRATEFUL that our bodies can move, shake, and dance it out!" Harper cheered into the camera on Charlotte's phone.

Charlotte let out a whoop then lifted her phone above her head to get a shot of everyone dancing. Once the song ended, The Greenhouse started emptying out, everyone eager to start their long weekend. Harper made sure she was the last to leave.

———

Harper surprised herself by checking the Vine the minute she landed at LaGuardia Airport. It wasn't that she expected to find some crisis; it was that she wanted to see what her colleagues at The Greenhouse had posted while she was in the air. There were lots of selfies of her coworkers loading up the trunks of their cars, a whole thread about suitcases, who could pack light and who couldn't. Then there were photos of everyone's travel meals, polls about the best and worst Thanksgiving foods, and a list of the most dreaded questions people were expecting from their families. The mood on the Vine was lively and fun, and Harper couldn't help refreshing her feed in the hopes that there would be more updates. Normally she would've used the train ride from the airport to her parents' to catch up on her neglected *New Yorker* magazines or to make a sizable dent in the latest hardcover from her to-be-read pile, but Harper hadn't read anything other than Charlotte's books since landing in Nashville. There just hadn't been time, a fact that was sure to disappoint her father, who loved to read and compare notes with Harper in their unofficial book club for two.

Except for herself and a handful of other employees, everyone was in Tennessee and had already arrived at their family's homes for the weekend. Harper watched the cute videos of her colleagues being greeted by family dogs and laughed at the sight of faces being licked and tails wagging at double speed. She made sure that she liked each one that she watched, so engrossed by the lives of her colleagues that she didn't even notice the glorious fall colors of the trees that carpeted the Hudson Valley.

This year, Harper's mother had invited all her sisters from San Francisco to stay for the long weekend—one widowed, one divorced, one with a husband that had moved back to the Philippines—all of whom had married daughters who would thankfully be spending the holiday with their in-laws. It wasn't that Harper didn't love her family, but they were just so different from her. For starters, most of her cousins were parents who brought their kids with them everywhere they went, so every occasion felt larger and noisier and longer than it needed to be. For some reason, they were unable to get together like normal families, arriving for dinner and leaving shortly after dessert.

Even though Harper's mom tried to do what she thought other families did, her mom's family was Filipino. And just as Charlotte had Green Time, the Cruz family had Filipino Time. Everyone liked to get together early and hang out, but they wouldn't actually eat until the last person arrived, hours later, indulging in a never-ending array of dishes. Their get-togethers always involved a huge group chat and endless correspondence until the event started. There would be a theme, dress code, and itinerary with time marked off for things like charades and poker. Each person was assigned a task like being in charge of appetizers, making a signature cocktail, or putting together party favors because apparently, no occasion should be without a gift that no one really needed.

Harper had found it so much fun when she was younger, but the list of things assigned to her had become longer and longer over the years. Her cousins felt that she had much more time than they did because she didn't have kids. But she had a career. A career that her cousins and aunties, fully immersed in the world of babies and birthday parties and extracurricular activities, thought of as a poor substitute for marriage and motherhood.

For a brief moment, Harper had been relieved that her mother had chosen this year to host Thanksgiving, when her cousins all had other plans, until she realized that she would be the sole focus of her aunties' attention. But then she'd gotten the text on the train announcing that cousin Christian, recently jilted by his fiancée, would be joining them, and her relief returned. The only thing worse to her aunties than a single woman approaching thirty was a mama's boy with a broken heart.

22

Happy Holidaze

"Christian, I'm so sorry to hear about Janice—you must be devastated," Harper said. She was sitting in the living room catching up with her cousin and aunties. The little wood and stone house that was down the driveway from the Inn smelled of woodsmoke and chicken adobo. With her aunties Maria, Gloria, and Bianca in town, Harper knew there was going to be even more traditional Filipino foods added to the Thanksgiving menu than usual, and she was here for it.

"I feel like I can't breathe." Christian wept. "Like, I've had the life sucked out of my body, and now I'm just a zombie stuck between heaven and hell—"

"Purgatory," Harper interrupted.

Unlike Harper's mom, Eva, who had always been independent, Harper's three aunts operated like their own planetary system. They constantly circled each other and were almost always together. The baby of the family, Eva had moved away from the West Coast after high school—a decision that Maria, Gloria, and Bianca thought was absurd, but one that her mother had often credited for keeping her sane.

Harper's aunts were *extra*. Extra chatty, extra loud, extra judgmental, and often extra meddlesome. Maria was the second youngest. A divorced mother of two girls, she was already a grandmother, or, as she liked to call herself, a hot Lola, Filipino for grandmother. Then there was Christian's mother, Gloria, a no-nonsense woman who had been putting others before herself her whole life. After her husband moved back to the Philippines, and her daughter started a family of her own, her son became her whole life, which worked out quite well for him, if not for the women he dated. And then there was the oldest sister, Bianca, a widow. Harper's mom used to joke that her brother-in-law's death was a choice, as it was the only way to get away from his critical wife.

"No, I'm not in purgatory. I'm stuck in that other place. You know, the one where people wander aimlessly after they die?" Christian said.

"Purgatory," Harper repeated, as she looked at her aunts, who crossed themselves.

"No, no, no—LIMBO!" Christian said, the word coming to him. "I feel like I'm stuck in limbo, and not the dancing kind, the . . ."

"Yeah, I get it," Harper said, not needing to get into it.

"I can't move on, and I can't forget her," he said, starting to cry. His mother grabbed him a Kleenex from the box on the coffee table while her other aunties made shushing noises and patted his arms and back.

"She didn't deserve you. She was impossible to please!" Gloria said.

"I'm sure it will take some time to get over," Harper said, standing up. The only patch of Christian that her aunties didn't cover was the top of his head, which she awkwardly patted.

"That's just it. I don't want to get over it. I want her to come back." He started to cry even louder, causing Harper's aunts to give her the stink eye. Harper took that as her cue to slink off to find her mother, who, just as she suspected, was baking in the kitchen and hiding from her sisters.

"Let me get a better look at you," her mom said.

Harper smiled and adjusted her new outfit, a Target replica of Charlotte's usual cashmere wrap and dangly boho necklaces.

"You look great," Eva said. She brushed Harper's hair off her face and tucked a loose strand behind her ear. Harper appreciated that, unlike her aunts, her mom would never say that she looked too skinny or tired. It had always driven her mother nuts how freely her sisters commented on other people and their business, and she had decided she wasn't going to do that to Harper.

"I'm good. Tired, but good. I'm working a lot, but I like it."

"And Nashville?" her mom asked, pouring them each a cup of coffee and heating up some milk on the stove, the way that Harper liked. "Is it really full of cowboys and country music stars?"

"Yes, and influencers," Harper said, washing her hands at the sink and drying them on one of her mom's many brightly patterned tea towels. "I didn't know there were so many in Nashville."

"I didn't know what an influencer was until you started working for one," her mother said, putting the coffee on the table and a selection of cookies on a plate. From where Harper sat near the window, she had a view of her parents' property. Outside she could see her dad chopping wood next to an already enormous pile of stacked logs.

"Are we expecting a freak blizzard or something?" Harper asked.

"No, it's just . . . you know your dad. The decibel level can only go so high before he can't take it anymore." She cast a glance toward the aunties trying to soothe Christian in the other room. Eva pushed the cookies toward Harper, took one for herself, and dipped the end in her coffee before biting off a big chunk.

Harper did the same and closed her eyes. "Is it awful that I'm kind of grateful to Janice for dumping him so that the heat is off me?"

"Yes," Eva said with a twinkle in her eye, "but not nearly as awful as Christian leaving out the fact that the reason Janice broke up with him was because he was caught on Hinge."

"What?!" Harper said a little too loudly. She heard the noise level drop in the other room, which let her know that her aunties were eavesdropping. She leaned forward and whispered, "Why was he on Hinge?"

"You know Christian," Eva whispered back, "he's not the brightest, but he is the cheapest. He told her he had three matches he hadn't met up with just sitting in his in-box, and he thought he owed it to himself to do so before he canceled his premium subscription because, you know, he'd already paid for it."

That did it—the two of them burst out laughing, Harper regretting it immediately when Christian wailed, "Laughter. I'll never laugh again."

"Harper!" Bianca reprimanded from the other room.

Harper cringed. "I'm going out to see Dad." She picked up one of the fleece jackets that always hung by the back door, slipped on an old pair of her rubber boots, and left.

"Hey, Harper!" her dad exclaimed when he saw her. "Now that you're here, let's grab your mom and make a run for it!" He put down his ax and wiped the sweat from his brow. He gave Harper a huge hug and lifted her off the ground.

"Oh, come on, it can't be that bad. Didn't they all just get here?" Harper asked, looking back at the house.

"Didn't you just get here? And you're already outside!" he said, putting her down.

"I'm just here to help you prepare for the next ice age," Harper joked, indicating the huge stack of wood.

"I just needed some air. I love your aunties and Christian, but Christian's—"

"Fiancée dumped him," Harper said, finishing her dad's sentence. She laughed, not so much at the joke but at the fact that her parents shared the same sense of humor.

"If that was me, my mother would've smacked me upside the head and said it served me right. Instead, they're all clucking around him and feeding him like he's some giant baby. But then again—"

"He *is* a giant baby," they said together.

"Well, I'm glad you're here. I don't think I could get through this weekend otherwise."

"I'm surprised you guys invited everyone to stay at the Inn. I would've thought that it was going to be busy this weekend, what with Thanksgiving and the fall colors and all that. Isn't this usually peak tourist season?"

"We are making the most of it, just not in the way you think," her dad said, packing the wood into a wheelbarrow and avoiding her gaze.

"What do you mean?"

"Well, your mom and I think this might be the last Thanksgiving we have at the Inn. So we thought, why not make the most of it and have everyone over?"

"What are you talking about?" Harper asked, unable to hide her surprise. "You guys said that things were tight, but you didn't say they were closing-the-Inn tight."

"We didn't want to upset you, make you think you had to stay and help when you had a new job waiting for you."

Harper's whole body flushed with shame, first for not knowing how dire things really were and then because the idea of staying had never really been one she'd considered. She just stupidly thought things would work out because they always had. If business was slow, her mom would host more weddings, offer discounted catering packages, or sell her famous cookies at the local farmers' market, while her dad would organize more hiking tours, clean the Inn himself, and spend extra time crunching numbers to see where they could save a few dollars. Even when things were tight, her parents always found a way. But apparently, they hadn't found a way this time.

"Oh, Dad, I'm so sorry. There must be something we can do."

Her dad wiped his hands on his pants and placed them on her shoulders. "There is: We can enjoy it as much as we can until we sell it at the end of August. Your mom and I want to pack in as many weddings and events as possible next summer." He paused and gave Harper a small smile. "Oh, and you can help me clear out the attic. There's a lot of junk but also some things that may be worth keeping—like that big box of all your old journals. I put that in your room. You might want to take a look, since there's some good stuff in there—not that I was peeking."

He was putting on a brave face by trying to make light of things. The fact that he was doing it for Harper only made her feel worse.

"But what will you do after this?"

"I don't know—retire, travel? We'll have to see how much it goes for and whether we need to sell the house too."

The idea of Harper's parents needing to sell the family home made her heart sink. That possibility hadn't even occurred to her.

"There's a lot that needs to be fixed and updated, and we always thought we'd have more time. But between having to repave the driveway after last year's bad storm, and then having to replace the burst pipes in the Inn, it's been one thing after another—and there's only so much money to go around. But who knows? I hear that it's trendy to rehab old, I mean, *authentic*, places. Maybe we'll get lucky and there'll be a bidding war," he said wryly. "Then we can really enjoy our retirement."

"Maybe we could sell it this weekend with Christian in it?" she joked.

"I'm not *paying* someone to take it," her dad said, wrapping his arm around her shoulder. "Now, come on, don't let this spoil the weekend. Christian's already had so much taken from him, so let's not ruin his Thanksgiving too." Cracking up, they both headed for home.

———————

Later that night, Harper felt her throat tighten as she entered her bedroom. Although she'd hardly spent more than a few nights in a row in it since moving to New York, the idea that it would always be there for her was comforting. She thought of all the times she'd sat at the small window bench writing in the countless journals her parents had gifted her over the years—journals that now sat in a big cardboard box on the floor, untouched. Harper crossed the room to the little bench, sat down, and sighed.

She'd had her first sleepover here, her first kiss, and had even gotten to second base when her parents had gone out of town. (She had wisely saved losing her virginity for Dylan's house, just in case her father caught them and happened to have his ax nearby.) Harper smiled at the memory, just one of many that her room held.

She unpacked her small suitcase into her antique wooden dresser that she and her mom must've painted a half dozen times over the years, each color visible under the small piece that had peeled back on the inside of the top drawer. Slipping her feet into the old Uggs that she always kept in the closet to wear as slippers, she took a deep breath and exhaled slowly. Nothing was decided, she told herself. A lot could happen between now and the summer, but if her parents were really going to have to sell the Inn, she should listen to her father and make the most of what would be her last Thanksgiving here. She should be grateful for this time they had together. She picked up her phone to take a picture of the view out her window to post in the Vine chat when she saw the comments come in.

> OMG

> CAN YOU BELIEVE IT?

> WTF?

> NO!!!

> ???

Harper quickly scrolled up in the comments to see what everyone was saying. And there, at the end of all the dog videos and pictures of families gathering, was a comment from Tiffany.

> What I'm most thankful for this Thanksgiving is that I never have to work for Charlotte again.

Next to it was a five-second Boomerang of her spilling a pot of tea into a teacup and raising her eyebrow.

"Shit!" Harper yelled so loudly that her mother came running upstairs.

"What's wrong?" her mom asked, opening Harper's door. "Did you hurt yourself?"

"No, I'm okay, but Tiffany quit, which means Charlotte is going to lose it. It was bad enough she suspected there was still a bad weed in the garden, and what's worse was that no one knew. I didn't see it, Bella certainly didn't see it, but Tiffany's already out there on Insta threatening to spill the tea!" Harper said, throwing her hands in the air. She stared at her mother, who stared back at her as if she had been speaking gibberish, and then sat on the end of the bed with her head in her hands.

Her mom sat next to her and gently placed her hand on her back.

"I don't understand most of that, but I gather that somebody important quit, and your boss is going to be angry. Am I right?"

"Worse," Harper said, scrolling through her phone to see if anyone else, namely Charlotte, had posted anything. So far, it was just her coworkers. Not even Bella or Oliver had commented yet, which Harper took as a sign to wait. She was refreshing her feed when her mom slipped the phone from her hands and placed it on the bed.

"Honey, there's nothing you can do about it on a Wednesday night, so come join us. It's Thanksgiving weekend! I promise you no one is going to be working anyway," her mother said confidently. Harper nodded and followed her mom downstairs, knowing full well that her mother's promise was about to be broken.

23

Turkey with a Side of Judgment

There wasn't enough wine in the world to get through her first family dinner of the holiday weekend. As annoying as Harper usually found her extended family's need to go from one activity to another, not doing anything because Christian wasn't up for it was even harder.

"You know, maybe it's for the best that you broke up," Bianca said to Christian as Gloria spooned some more sweet potatoes onto her son's plate.

"How can you say that?" Christian asked, the subject of his breakup becoming the topic of conversation once again. At least it was keeping the heat off Harper.

"Well, for one thing, she was too focused on her career," Bianca said, aggressively cutting a piece of chicken with her knife. She said *career* like it was a dirty word.

"No, she just really loves her job, and she's good at it too. She was the spa's employee of the month three months in a row," Christian said proudly.

"Yes, but she's not a *manager*, like you, and you never have to work late, do you?" Bianca asked pointedly.

"True! You are always home in time for dinner." Gloria patted her son affectionately on the shoulder.

"Why does she need to work so hard anyway, if she's going to have a family?" Maria chimed in.

Harper stared at her mother, who just shook her head, signaling that it wasn't worth getting into.

But Harper was having a hard time staying quiet. There were so many things wrong with this conversation that she didn't know where to begin. For starters, Janice wasn't just some employee—she was an executive in charge of franchising for Body Beautiful, one of the country's largest spa and massage chains. Harper also knew that it was Janice's job that made the most money and had the best benefits, whereas Christian's management position at his brother-in-law's bodybuilding gym was more of a favor than anything else. Not to mention that the dinner he was always home in time for was at his mother's house.

"Maybe having her own career is important to her?" Harper asked, unable to take it anymore. "Maybe she finds it fulfilling and is thinking that Christian can stay home and raise the kids."

At this her aunts gasped, and her mother quickly stood up with a bottle of wine.

"Refill anyone?" Eva asked, topping off glasses.

"Not for me," Christian said, polishing off his plate of food and pushing his chair back from the table. "I think I'm going to go to my room."

"What about dessert?" Gloria asked, her hand going to her chest.

"I'm too upset. I'm just going to take some time to myself. Thanks for dinner," he said, slinking away.

Christian's timing to excuse himself right after he finished and before the cleanup began was not lost on Harper. She bit her tongue and stared at her plate, ignoring her aunts looking at her like it was her fault that he'd left. For a moment the only sound was her dad's clinking cutlery, and then Maria spoke.

"So, Harper, I'm guessing you didn't move to Nashville for love, am I right?" she asked, her lips pursed tight.

Harper translated in her head. *Because unlike heartbroken Christian, all you care about is your career.*

"No, I moved for a job, and it's going great! It's a huge change, and even though I miss New York and never planned to leave, it's a good opportunity, and I'm learning a lot. My boss, Charlotte Green, sees a lot of potential in me, and she's kind of a big deal."

"What did you say her name was again?" Bianca asked, sipping her wine.

Translation: *It can't be that big of a deal; I don't know who she is.*

"Charlotte Green," Harper repeated.

"Charlotte Green, the blogger?" Gloria asked.

"She's an *influencer*," Maria answered, clearly approving of Harper's boss by the way she smiled at Harper. "She started out as a blogger, but now she's a major businesswoman and author. She wrote all those self-help books and has all those cute journals. I just love her."

From the look on Bianca's face it was clear she had no idea who her sister was talking about.

"You *know*, she does those big Oprah-like conferences, where she stands onstage, jumps up and down, and gives a talk—"

"If she's Oprah famous, I'd know who you were talking about," Bianca said, shaking her head.

"You *do* know. She's the one Janice showed us on Instagram—the *tiny* one?" Maria held her hand three feet above the floor to indicate that Charlotte was very short. *Although not quite that short*, Harper thought. The fact that Janice, enemy number one of the Cruz family, was a fan didn't bode well for her.

"You know," Maria continued, "she says that thing, 'there's a warrior woman inside of you,' and 'you've got this,' 'greenlight,' 'you grow, girl'? She's the one with the green Vans and the long blond hair."

"Oh . . ." Bianca said, finally realizing who Maria was referring to. "The nice white lady who is always talking about her feelings and selling things."

Translation: *What does she have to complain about?*

A collective sound of recognition went around the table, followed by the clucking of tongues, which Harper knew signaled both approval and disapproval all at once. *The nice white lady* probably wasn't the description Charlotte was hoping for, but it was interesting how Harper's aunts saw her. Feeling protective of Charlotte, Harper pressed on.

"She's really great, actually. Her books and courses are amazing— she's very inspirational. People all over the world really love her."

"You can't really love someone you don't know," Bianca piped up. "People love the *idea* of her."

The fact that Harper's aunts were willing to look past Christian's numerous flaws while being so critical of Janice, then her, and now a woman they didn't even know, set Harper off.

"They love the fact that she's honest about who she *is*. She connects to them, and is always trying to grow and better herself. That's a lot more than some people can say."

She picked up what was left of her wine and finished it.

"What's that supposed to mean?" Gloria asked, turning in her seat to face her straight on.

"Well, maybe if, for example, Christian was honest about what he wanted and who he was, he wouldn't be in this mess. I mean, you don't step out on your fiancée because you have a few Hinge matches left on your account. You step out because you want to see what else is out there. Maybe everyone should stop being so mad at Janice for calling him out and be mad at Christian for screwing things up."

"Harper!"

Harper's mother had tossed her napkin on the table and was staring at her in shock. "There's no need to pile on Christian. He's not even here to defend himself."

"Well, they're piling on Charlotte and me, and she's not here to defend herself!"

Eva tilted her head to one side and looked at Harper. "Honey, no one's piling on you. Meddling, sure," she said, giving her sisters the hairy eyeball, "but not more than usual."

Her aunts seemed to agree on both points.

"And Charlotte's your *boss*, Harper. That's different from a friend."

"She's more than that, actually," Harper said, knowing it was true the moment she said it. "She's like . . ." She stopped short of saying family. As true as it felt, she didn't want to make things any more awkward than they were already. So she just said, "She's like an older sister and mentor all rolled into one. Thousands of people applied for the job I have, and she personally chose me. I owe her." Harper was surprised to hear how emotional she sounded.

She saw the look of concern on her mom's face. "You don't owe her anything. You work for her. She didn't take pity on you—she *hired* you. The only thing you owe her is to be a good employee, and you owe it to yourself to not take it all so seriously. It's just a job. It's not your life."

Harper's aunts pursed their mouths and nodded in that *I told you so* way that always drove her nuts. But they were all wrong. This job *was* Harper's life. And she was proud of it.

"Now, now, why don't we all just take a deep breath," Harper's father piped up for the first time that evening. Everyone turned to look at him in surprise, as if having forgotten that he was even there. He looked at Harper and winked.

Harper exhaled deeply. "I think I'm just tired," she lied. "It's been a long day and an intense few months, and I just need a good night's sleep." She smiled for her mother's sake and, to make peace with her aunties, said, "I'll go check on Christian, take him some dessert before I call it a night."

As Harper excused herself and walked out of the room, she pretended not to hear her aunts start talking about her. Charlotte had been right to warn her Green Team—family just didn't understand. And in that moment, Harper was more grateful than ever for her work family always having her back.

———

For the rest of the night, Harper stayed in her room. She felt like a child, in part because she was acting like one, and also because nobody seemed to understand that she was capable of knowing what was best for her. What was clearly best for her right now was finding out what the hell was going on at The Greenhouse.

"Did Tiffany tell you she was leaving?" Harper whispered to Bella. She'd called her the moment she went upstairs, hiding under the covers in case anyone came in to check on her.

"No. Believe me, if I knew she was quitting, I would've said something to Charlotte, or at the very least to you. I couldn't keep something like that to myself, nor would I want to. Tiffany's totally screwed up the rollout for the conference *and* the launch of the clothing line, and what makes me so mad is that she did it on a holiday week—on purpose. You should see her Instagram feed. It's all these videos of her celebrating and saying things like, 'Oh, the secrets I could tell.' "

"Like what?" Harper asked. "What secrets does she even have?"

"Oh, you know—just things about Charlotte being Charlotte."

It was the third time she had heard someone use that expression. "Wait, what does that mean, exactly?"

"Nothing. It's just sometimes she can come off as politically incorrect or kind of pushy, but those of us who really know her know that's not what she means."

Harper was quiet for a moment. "Do you mean like her geisha costume and her mandatory 'optional' weekend activities?"

"Right. Clearly, she was just being fun in both cases, but Tiffany didn't always see it that way." For a moment Bella was quiet. "She did tell me that not getting to go to the influencer lunch was the last straw, but she's had a lot of *last straws* recently. I thought she'd get over it."

"Is it really that big a deal?" Harper asked.

"Harper, it's huge. It's a who's who of the influencer world. There's tons of media and a boatload of swag, and Charlotte's a keynote speaker this year. And I'll be right there, at her table."

It was obvious to Harper how much this meant to Bella, but before she could ask more, Bella cut her off. "I gotta go. My mom needs me."

The second she hung up, Harper checked Tiffany's Instagram and read her most recent story.

> Guess which big-time influencer acts like she's all woke and
> supportive but is actually a clueless Karen and big-time bully?

She had pasted a little sticker where you could answer the question and send it to her.

Oh, shit, Harper thought, reading Tiffany's post. It looked like "Charlotte being Charlotte" wasn't quite as harmless as Bella thought.

24

No Room at the Table for Traitors

Charlotte had been rage-texting on the Vine all night, and she was still going strong the next morning. Harper read the latest tirade and winced.

> Who knew Tiffany was leaving? I find it hard to believe she
> didn't say a word to anybody, considering how freely she's
> shooting her mouth off. But I find it even harder to believe
> that anyone would withhold something like this from me.
> I was right here, willing to listen, as I ALWAYS AM! But I
> can't know if someone is unhappy if they don't talk to me.
> I'm a lot of things—kind, passionate, hardworking, loving,
> and yes, I hold the bar high, but only as high as I myself am
> willing to jump. But one thing I am NOT is a mind reader,
> so if ANYONE else is unhappy, or has something they want
> to share so that I am not BLINDSIDED again, now is the
> FUCKING TIME!!

When no one answered after a full minute, Charlotte continued posting.

> So no one knew? Really? What am I supposed to do with that? And while we're at it, what am I supposed to do with ten thousand Growth Planners? Tiffany was supposed to be doing a promo with them. But I guess she was lying about that too. I suppose I'm going to have to figure that out all by myself as usual, and sell all these fucking tracksuits that I worked so goddamn hard on while we're at it because apparently nobody is willing to help me.

There was another long pause of thirty seconds, and then:

> I think the thing that really upsets me is that somebody must've known this was coming, which means that the real betrayal of my trust and goodwill didn't come from Tiffany but from someone else, someone inside, someone who is STILL betraying me by not coming forward now. Whoever you are, you're a traitor, and we don't tolerate traitors at The Greenhouse. I've said it once and I'll say it again—we pick the WEEDS out of this garden! To everyone else, the only way we are going to get through this is by sticking together. Watch your backs, and have a great Thanksgiving!

"Damn," Harper said out loud, half expecting her phone to implode. She had just placed the final fork on the table, her total lack of culinary skills relegating her to the impossible-to-screw-up task of setting the table for Thanksgiving dinner that night. Everyone was here at the Inn, getting a start on the day. Her mom had decided to host dinner in the main dining room and was using the larger kitchen to prepare. This way they could spread out, and if things went late—as they were prone to do, judging by the afternoon's schedule—Harper and her dad could sneak back to the house and get some rest.

The first thing on the holiday agenda was the family hike of the Hudson Valley Rail Trail, which was really more of a walk-stop-take-pictures kind of thing. Then there was the great snack off, where everyone made hors d'oeuvres that were judged in a blind taste test while sipping on this year's signature cocktail, a peartini crafted by Maria. The winner of the best snack got a pass on dish duty, which made the contest a highly competitive affair among the four sisters, where everyone voted for themselves and tried to guilt the others into voting for them. Then there was dinner, followed by dessert, a game of charades where the rules were flexible at best, and finally, a high-stakes poker game that went into the wee hours of the morning. Usually only the aunts made it to that one.

"What's going on?" Christian asked, strolling into the dining room and noticing Harper glued to her phone. Apparently Christian was also lacking in the culinary skills department.

"Shit's hit the fan at work," Harper said, staring at her screen.

"You work for that influencer, right? The one Janice likes?"

"Yeah," Harper said, not looking up.

"Do you think that maybe you could get her to autograph one of her books for me to give to Janice?"

Harper looked at Christian. "I thought you had broken up."

"We have, but I thought I would try and win her back." He stuck his hands in his pockets, looking sheepish.

It's going to take a lot more than a book, Harper thought.

"My mom told me what you said last night, and it sounded just like something your boss would say. You're right. I got cold feet and wanted to make sure I wasn't missing anything, and I wasn't. But I am now, and I'd do anything to get Janice back."

Harper was touched in spite of her previous rant, and also flattered that her advice sounded like something Charlotte would say. Immediately she thought of how much Charlotte would love this story and how she needed to retell it when she got back to The Greenhouse.

"Sure, I can send you a book when I'm back in Nashville. Charlotte's going to be getting ready for the launch of her *Green with Envy* guided workbook and doing a ton of events—maybe you could even come to one with Janice?"

"Well, I have to get her to talk to me first," Christian said.

"Okay, well, why don't you give her Charlotte's brand-new Growth Planner in the meantime? I brought an extra one, because mine's almost full." Harper thought for a minute. "Or better yet, why don't you write down all the ways you want to grow for her and then give it to her?"

"Really? You think that could work?"

"I think it's a start. If you want things to be different, you're the only one who can change them." She paused for a moment, considering the situation. "You know, we could always film you reading the list of things about Janice that you're grateful for and then post it on our site, maybe have Charlotte give you some advice. Janice would definitely notice that."

"I don't know. That's kind of personal," Christian said, shifting in his spot.

"That's the whole point. It's a public apology *and* declaration of how much you love her."

"I'll think about it."

"Harper, can you come here for a minute?" Eva asked, appearing in the doorway.

Harper followed her mom through the kitchen to the back door and away from her aunts, who were busy prepping food and singing along to a Top 40 Spotify playlist that sounded like it belonged to a teenager.

"What is it?" Harper asked, concerned by the look on her mother's face.

Her mom wiped her hands on her apron and leaned in close

so that no one could hear her. "Harper, I couldn't help but overhear your conversation with Christian—do you really think that's a good idea?"

"What? You were the one who told me that I need to be nicer to him," Harper said, checking her phone again as it pinged. The Vine was alive and well this morning, and everyone was writing to tell Charlotte how upset they were at Tiffany and how much they appreciated Charlotte. It was all very gushy and sincere, and Harper had been thinking all morning about what she could write that would stand out from everyone else.

"Yes," Eva continued, "but it feels kind of exploitive, doesn't it? Putting him on display like that?"

"No one is putting him on display; it was just a suggestion. Besides, there's nothing wrong with being honest and sharing what you're going through. Charlotte does it all the time. Sometimes you just have to be an *open book*," Harper said, borrowing a line from her early days at The Greenhouse.

"But that's her *business*. This is his *life*."

"It's more than just business, Mom; it's who she really is. She really cares about her followers, and she actually practices what she preaches. She does it to help people's lives—people just like Christian. I don't know why everyone needs to attack her."

"No one's attacking her, honey," her mother said, taken aback.

"Well, it feels like it. First me, then her, then me for working with her."

"Harper—"

"I don't get it. I thought you'd be happy for me."

"I am happy for you," her mother replied, taking a step toward her and touching her arm. "I don't understand why you're getting so upset. You just started there. Maybe keep an open mind and don't rush to conclusions. Give it some time, okay?"

Time. That was what was bothering her mother. Harper felt her shoulders relax and exhaled. It wasn't her mom's fault; she didn't understand that time worked differently at The Greenhouse, and Harper didn't really feel like getting into it right now. So instead, she agreed.

"Okay," she said as she squeezed her mom's hand and smiled reassuringly. She knew that her mom was just looking out for her, but she also knew that the only people who could really understand what her new life was like were busy chatting away on the phone she held in the palm of her other hand, and it would be four more days until she saw any of them.

Her phone dinged again, and her mother glared at her. "I have to check this—it's work."

"It's Thanksgiving!" her mother said.

"Mom, it could be an emergency."

Hearing the word *emergency*, her aunts rushed over. "What kind of emergency?" Bianca asked.

"A work emergency," Harper said.

"If it's a work emergency, then it's not your problem," Gloria said.

"Well, it is my problem because the person who just quit left a lot of work behind, and that means more work for all of us."

"No, it means they hire someone else," Maria chimed in.

"It's not so easy," Harper answered.

"Sure it is. If your boss is so great, lots of people will want to work with her!"

"It's a holiday," her mother added gently. "There is nothing you can do. Please, Harper."

Harper nodded, but then hurried out of the room to read the latest from Charlotte.

> Hey everyone, just wanted to say thanks for all your messages,
> it really means a lot. Sometimes it's hard to see the garden
> through the weeds. But after taking some time with my
> beautiful family to process what happened, I realized that

they are where my focus should be, and I want you to do the same. Enjoy every moment of this time you have with your families, and when you come back, come back more fired up than ever! Peace. xo

Harper slid the phone into her back pocket. If Charlotte could do it, so could she.

25

Must Love Frowns

Manhattan. There's no place like it, which was why Harper had planned to spend the day after Thanksgiving in the city with Poppy. What she hadn't planned on was her aunties coming with her to do some Black Friday shopping.

She looked out the train window as the scene changed from the countryside to the city. Harper couldn't wait to get to Central Park before brunch at The Plaza—Poppy's idea and treat.

"I heard that Taylor Swift sang at the Macy's Thanksgiving Day Parade yesterday," Maria said. "Maybe we'll see her while we're out shopping!" She was sitting next to Harper, scanning through *People* and dog-earring the corners of the pages she would return to later. Even though it was a magazine and not a book, Harper still winced at the sight of those pages being maimed.

"You sure you don't want to join us for a little sightseeing?" Maria asked Harper, turning to face her.

"I can't, I'm sorry. I haven't seen Poppy since I left, and this is the only time we can meet up."

What a pity, her aunt's face seemed to say as she turned back to her reading.

"Who's Poppy?" Bianca asked.

Harper pulled up a picture on her phone to show them.

"Oh, Poppy . . ." they said in unison, nodding.

"With the legs," Maria added.

Harper looked at her aunts. "So it's Charlotte with the hair, Poppy with the legs, and Harper with the . . . ?"

By the way her aunts stared back at her, Harper knew there was something. She watched as they exchanged looks between them as if deciding who was going to tell her. Finally, her oldest aunt spoke.

"Harper, with the frown," Bianca said, leaning forward and pointing to the pinched spot between her eyebrows. "You know, it wouldn't hurt you to smile more. Men like a woman who smiles." She demonstrated this by smiling at a young man sitting across the aisle from Harper, who seemed taken aback but smiled warily in return. "See?"

"I smile plenty," Harper replied, mouthing a silent *Sorry* to the man the second her aunt looked away.

Her aunts muttered their disagreement, making Harper frown even more.

"We're only trying to help," Gloria said, unwrapping a candy and sucking on it loudly. "You're not getting any younger, and you don't want to miss the window for marriage. Besides, frowning gives you wrinkles." She raised her eyebrows at Harper in that all-knowing way of hers that made Harper crazy because she actually knew very little about Harper's life.

"There's no window," Harper said. "And besides, lots of women my age aren't married or thinking about kids. We're focused on our careers. Look at Poppy! She smiles all the time, and she isn't married."

"Doesn't she have a boyfriend?" Maria asked, folding her arms across her body and narrowing her eyes at Harper.

"Yes, but he knows that her career is her priority, just like mine is. That's the only window I worry about closing."

Maria reached over and patted her arm. "You know," she said to her sisters with a sad smile, "maybe she's right. I mean, a career can't cuddle you or keep you warm at night, but who wants those things?" She rolled her eyes.

"True," Gloria said, now crunching her candy loudly. "And she could always get a cat if she needs company; they don't need much."

A single frowning cat lady—Harper's imaginary future was getting better by the second. Wait until she told Legs about this.

––––––––––

Harper got out at Seventy-Seventh Street just so she could walk through Central Park to The Plaza. It was only twenty extra blocks, and as excited as she was to see Poppy, she wanted some time to herself. She inhaled and exhaled deeply, her shoes crunching along the fallen leaves that blanketed the paved pathway, and rubbed the crease between her brows. *Harper, with the frown.* It wasn't entirely untrue, but Harper thought there were a lot of other ways her aunts could've described her. What about hardworking Harper or Harper with the career? Neither of those had anything to do with her appearance, which was why her aunts had not mentioned them, and even though she found their obsession with how people looked irritating, the nickname still stung. But unfortunately, they were also partly right. The line between her eyebrows was now there whether she was frowning or not, a reminder that she was aging—just like everyone else.

She shook it off and told herself that she was just on a different path than her aunties' children and that it was all how you looked at it. She could think of herself as a sad single woman nearing thirty, or she could think of herself as an ambitious, jet-setting single.

Once she arrived at The Plaza, Harper pulled out her phone to take a selfie with the hotel in the background, the wording of the post already forming in her head. *Brunch at The Plaza, #thankful #grateful #nyc #ladieswhobrunch.* It could've been a postcard, she thought, running it through a quick filter and posting it for her two thousand followers. Bella had been right—working for Charlotte meant that her follower count was steadily growing, and she had to admit the regular comments and likes were a real ego boost.

Of course, Harper had been *inside* The Plaza before. She'd often stopped in at the end of one of her walks in the park to use the bathroom and marvel at the opulent interiors: ornately patterned carpets, intricately crafted walls with gilded mirrors, and tables decorated with mercury glass vases full of varying blooms in a singular color palette, today's being different shades of burnt orange. It was luxury with a capital L: a fairy tale for most, and for a privileged few, home. But she had never had a meal there beyond a celebratory drink for getting her first job—a big treat that meant a dinner of pizza slices on the way home—but now that she was earning big money, she was excited to see what all the hype was about.

"Hey, you!" Poppy said, walking toward her in a sweater dress and suede boots that made Harper immediately think, *Legs*. She wrapped Harper in a hug and squeezed her tight. "You survived the train ride with your aunts. You have to tell me everything. Are they as judgmental as ever?"

"Worse. Apparently I frown all the time and am going to die alone because I'm too focused on my career."

"Oh, they've taken it up a notch," Poppy said, laughing.

"Well, you know, the *window* is closing. Wow, you look great," Harper said, taking a step back to admire Poppy's outfit. Poppy always had great taste in clothes, but this was a whole other level. The dress, the scarf, and the boots were all very on-trend. "It's cold out. Didn't you bring a coat?"

"I left it in my room," Poppy said, her smile wide. She looked so happy she was practically glowing.

"Your *room*?"

Poppy hooked her arm around Harper's and led her toward the restaurant, where they already had a table.

"Poppy, what's going on?" Harper asked as she slid into the velvet-lined booth. Poppy sat next to her so that the two of them could look out at the grand dining room with its high backlit glass ceiling and marble columns flanked by potted palms.

Before Poppy could answer, a waiter came over and placed a circular silver stand with three trays of goodies—scones, tea sandwiches, and pretty little pastries—down on the table. Harper had always wanted to have high tea at The Plaza, but the $95 price tag—$125 if you added champagne—had always stopped her.

"Poppy?" Harper asked as two glasses of champagne appeared before them.

"We're celebrating!" Poppy said, holding up her glass to toast Harper. "To your new job!" She clinked glasses, and that's when Harper saw the large emerald-cut diamond that sat on a single platinum band on Poppy's left hand.

"And to your *engagement*?!" Harper shrieked, loud enough that people turned to stare. "Wait, when did this happen?"

"Last night! Right here—well, not exactly here. There," Poppy said, pointing out the window toward Central Park.

"No, he didn't," Harper said, knowing exactly where this story was going but not quite believing it could be true.

"He did. We were walking through the park after our run like we always do, and he stopped to rest on a bench—"

"And it had your names on it," Harper finished. The Central Park bench proposal was something that Poppy and Harper had alternately pined for and mocked depending on where they were in their romantic lives. Shortly after meeting, the two friends had stayed up late one night, and it was sometime during their second bottle of wine that they both tentatively admitted that, in addition to being ambitious, independent feminists, they were die-hard hopeless romantics.

Lovers of serious literature, they had also read every meet-cute, friends-to-enemies, friends-to-lovers book they could get their hands on, and had watched every top rom-com that had ever been made.

This meant that they also had a secret list of places and things they considered the most romantic ever. Engraving a small $10,000 plaque on a Central Park bench as a way to pop the question was at the top of the list. For Harper, it had been the height of fantasy, making daydreaming about it so fun. And even though she knew that both Poppy and Charles came from money and that Charles was *also* on his way to being a well-paid surgeon, she'd still never expected that to be a reality for either of them. But now, sitting next to Poppy, she felt a little silly for not realizing sooner that the only one for whom it would ever be out of reach was herself.

"It did," Poppy said, beaming. "It was the corniest and the cheesiest and the sappiest."

"And the *best*," Harper added. She waited for Poppy to set her glass down and then took her hand to admire her engagement ring. "Wow, it's gorgeous. Huge, and slightly blinding, but gorgeous."

"It was his grandmother's—the stone, that is. He had it reset in something simpler." The ring took up the whole width of her finger. "It's big, I know, but I love it." She took a scone and some jam and passed the plate to Harper. "I wanted you to be the first to know. After my parents, of course. Charles asked my dad at the driving range, so they knew it was happening."

"Well, I'm honored," Harper said, "and I've just spent a ton of time looking at venues for conferences in Nashville, so it's safe to say that if you wanted to get married there, I could help you out. If you don't want to make everyone go there just for me, then I hope you can wait until I'm back at Christmas to go looking at places. I think I still have that list we made after watching *Bride Wars*."

Poppy took a bite of her scone and smiled. "No need to wait until Christmas! We've found a place."

"You have? Wait, when? You just got engaged."

"I know, but I told Sloan—you remember Sloan, my super-stylish friend who goes out with Charles's friend Andrew from work—"

Harper remembered, all right. "Of course," she said, trying to sound casual.

"Well, I told her how I had always wanted to get married at the Boathouse, but it's impossible to get in for years. Apparently, her law firm has a standing date booked there every summer for a fundraiser, and she offered to give it up for us. Isn't that great? I mean, it's crazy because it'll be Labor Day weekend, less than a year away, but it's not like we need to wait. And you should be back by then, so it's actually kind of perfect."

Harper reached for a cucumber sandwich and put the whole thing in her mouth to stop herself from saying, *Sloan? I thought I was the first person you told.* This was Poppy's day, and she didn't want to ruin it by being petty and childish, which was why she was now reaching for another sandwich.

Poppy furrowed her brow as she looked at Harper. "You okay? You seem kind of . . . *hungry.*"

"I am. I rushed out of the house this morning without eating anything," she said, taking a sip of her drink.

"You're upset."

"I'm not." Harper avoided eye contact.

"I know we always said we'd find a place together, but I just couldn't pass this up."

"Of course not! Don't be crazy; I'm thrilled for you. And let me guess: Where we are now is where you're going to have your engagement party?"

Poppy looked at Harper sheepishly. "Do you think that's too predictable?"

Central Park bench proposal, engagement party at The Plaza, reception at the Boathouse—the only thing left on their dream wedding plan was a honeymoon in Fiji, which Harper had no doubt was already in the works. It was all very Upper East Side socialite, which Harper had to admit made it perfect for Poppy and Charles.

"I think it's incredible," she said honestly, "and you deserve it. I should thank you for not making me have to do any more research or work because I honestly don't know when I would find the time."

"The only thing you have to do is be a guest, and . . ." Poppy reached into her purse and pulled out a little blue-and-white Tiffany box. Harper held it in her hand and admired it.

"Open it," Poppy said, smiling.

"Wait, am *I* now getting proposed to?"

Harper opened the box and pulled out a beautiful Tiffany bracelet that was engraved with the words *Maid of Honor*.

"Harper, you're my best friend, and I can't have my most important day without you by my side. Will you be my maid of honor?"

"Of course!" Harper said, slipping on the bracelet and hugging Poppy.

"I know you're busy with your new job, so if you want to say no, I'll understand."

"Poppy, I could never be too busy for this," Harper said, although her heart was already beating faster at the idea of having to take on one extra thing.

"Great, because I was hoping we could get started and talk about the engagement party, which is on Christmas Eve *Eve*. Which is weird, I know, but Charles says it's the only time that he knows everyone will be off, and it's the anniversary of our first date, so I had to say yes."

"Of course."

They were silent for a moment. There were so many things Harper wanted to talk about—Charlotte, The Greenhouse, Tiffany's sudden departure, Harper's rising star at work—but that wasn't what this brunch was about. It was about Poppy and Charles and their future.

"I'm sorry, I haven't even asked you about work. How's it going?" Poppy asked, taking a pastry off the tray. It was like she'd read Harper's mind.

"Oh, it's fine. I'm still finding my feet."

"Sounds like you're doing more than that from what you've told me—you're killing it. Now tell me more about Charlotte. She seems like a real trip," Poppy said.

Harper could tell that Poppy was just trying to be fun and support-ive, but she didn't want to reduce her experiences at The Greenhouse to a sound-bite just so they could get back to talking about the wedding.

"There's not much to tell, just work stuff. Let's talk more about your wedding."

"Really? Are you sure?"

"Positive," Harper said.

"Okay, well, no arguments from me!" Poppy said twiddling the fingers on her left hand with a smile. "I'll grab some of the menus they offer for event catering and we can go over them. I'll be right back!" And with that, Poppy was heading to the maître d'. The second she was gone, Harper snuck a look at her phone.

Wishing you all a Happy Thanksgiving week. Signing off. See you Monday! The picture Charlotte sent featured her, Ryan, and the kids all in coordinating outfits by the pool. Harper scanned the photo for signs of trouble but saw nothing but big smiles.

She texted Bella. Everything okay?

Looks like it. I texted her, but she's really offline. You ok?

Yeah. You?

Yeah.

Happy Thanksgiving, Harper added.

Happy Trollsgiving, Bella replied, sending a picture of Harper and Bella in their Halloween costumes.

Have a grape time with your family! Harper typed, smiling at the line of laugh-cry emojis Bella sent back.

Harper tucked her phone in her pocket as Poppy slid back into the booth with a folder.

"Okay, so we have options," she said, opening the folder and showing it to Harper.

Harper heard about the people Poppy wanted to invite and the ones she'd have to, the band vs. DJ debate, and where she and Charles were going to register. And then there was the question of where they would actually live once they were husband and wife. Harper could see it all—the apartment that Poppy's parents would give her as a wedding gift, the year they'd take to renovate it, the country home they'd get in Connecticut to spend weekends at and eventually move to full-time once they had kids. She wondered how long Poppy would stay at the publishing house, which she didn't even mention, or if she'd continue there once she became a mother. She didn't really have to work, but she would need to even less once she married Charles. Somehow being in the same city in the same apartment pursuing the same career had allowed Harper to trick herself into believing that they were more similar than they were different, but now she wasn't so sure.

As she listened to Poppy talk about the engagement party and the new friends of Charles's that she wanted Harper to meet, Harper felt herself missing her own new friends and wishing she was back in Nashville. Her New York life as she knew it before leaving felt further away from her than ever.

26

It Pays to Be Sick

Harper watched Charlotte's Instagram story on the plane ride back to Nashville. Makeup-free, in her pajamas with her hair piled on top of her head, Charlotte sat on her bedroom chaise and talked directly to the camera.

"Hey everyone, I hope you had a great Thanksgiving. I know I've been kind of quiet on social the last forty-eight hours, so I didn't want you to worry. But the truth is, I'm doing this Instagram story at four in the morning because, well, I've been having a really hard time, and you've always been there for me, so I don't want to hide my pain anymore. As you may have heard, someone who used to work for me—who I thought was a friend—has been threatening to say really nasty things about me, and while I think that everyone has a right to speak freely, I also think that the truth matters. So I wanted to tell you some of the things I think they are going to say, because I have nothing to hide. They're going to tell you that I'm a bad employer and work my staff too hard."

Charlotte sighed, closed her eyes, and shook her head. "They're right. Not that I'm a terrible employer, but I do work my staff hard.

The important thing, though—what this person *won't* say—is that I only work my staff as hard as I'm willing to work myself. That's because I know that in order for women to make it in this world, we have to work twice as hard as men. It's just expected that we can do more. It's expected that we can do it *all*. And if I'm accused of believing that *my* people, my chosen family that make up The Greenhouse, *are* capable of doing it all because they're all so damn special and talented? Then yeah, I'm guilty. I'm guilty of believing in my team's potential. This person is also saying that I don't give credit where credit is due, and well, we all know that's not true. I'd be nowhere without my Green family. I'd be nowhere without my supportive and loving husband, nowhere without my amazing children, nowhere without *you*. None of us gets ahead by ourselves. Although some of us clearly only think of ourselves and not all the wonderful people they've worked with all these years, people whose jobs they endanger when they come after me—when they come after *you* for believing in me and what we do here." She took a deep breath and bit her bottom lip as tears streaked down her face. "I'm sorry, I don't mean to cry; it's just so painful when someone you cared about turns on you out of jealousy. I should've known, but I ignored the signs because I *believe* in people. But like I always say, when someone shows you who they really are, believe them." Charlotte nodded slowly.

"Now, I wasn't going to say anything, because I didn't want to ruin your Thanksgiving with your families. I wasn't about to let this ruin Thanksgiving with mine, but all the stress and negativity made me really sick." She coughed and took a sip of water. "I actually had to check myself into the hospital overnight so they could monitor me." Charlotte moved the camera down to show the mountain of tissues on her bed. "I'm home now, but to say I felt betrayed and heartbroken would be an understatement. No warning, no reason, no 'thanks for all your mentoring, the great opportunity, raises, special trips, and spa days.' And to do it so maliciously, on this week of all weeks, a holiday week where our community is celebrating hashtag gratitude and hashtag giving thanks.

Not to mention that our big Inspire conference is only months away. It's all *so* devastating. But you guys know that I don't back down from a challenge even if it means I don't sleep, and believe me, I'm not. There's just so much to do." She sniffled and sighed. "And because I am so grateful for all of you and the support you've given me, making this conference the best yet for all of you means everything to me. And we're so lucky to have Serene on board. I worked my butt off on those designs for our collection, and it was worth it." Charlotte took a deep breath and wiped away a tear. "But when you play with the big guys, they want big results. And, friends . . . I'm sorry, I just need a second to get myself together . . . oh, this is so hard, I'm so embarrassed . . . but I promised I'd always be honest with you . . . I have to tell you that *sales are down*. And the only reason I can think of is that the person who left didn't tell you how important it was to register early for the conference. Those presale tickets send a message to our sponsor that they backed the right woman and the right company, that we are as big and strong and supportive a community as I told them we were. Now, I know you'll all eventually buy your tickets because you'd never let me down, but I need you to do so now so we can still have a conference. And if my Green VIPs can buy two tickets, that's even better. Anyway, there it is, the whole truth." She placed her hand on her heart and nodded sincerely. "Thanks for having my back like I've had yours all these years. It means everything. I may be down for the count right now, but you know I'll be back up and fighting with everything I've got as soon as I'm better to make next year's conference the most *inspiring* ever."

Harper must've played the reel ten times to make sure she hadn't missed anything. She'd never seen Charlotte look so bad. She'd immediately texted Bella, who was taking a couple of extra days to be with her mom after she had a rough few days.

Have you heard anything?

Nothing, Bella replied.

It seemed no one had been able to get a hold of Charlotte since her last message on the Vine, and speculation about how she was doing was running wild. *She's got the flu, she has mono, she's suffering from burnout, she's back in the hospital.* Nobody seemed to know the real story. Not even Oliver was picking up his phone.

The moment Harper had dropped her things off at her apartment, she'd gone straight to the drugstore to gather supplies. She got lozenges, Kleenex, tea, and a bottle of orange and echinacea immunity boost, and she'd brought a package of her mother's famous cookies from home to add to the care package. She planned to drop it all off at Charlotte's on her way to The Greenhouse. She wouldn't stay long—just long enough to show her support. After seeing how upset and abandoned Charlotte felt, she wanted Charlotte to know she was there for her. She was showing up and keeping her word, just like Charlotte had asked.

Harper stood on the steps of the Green residence and rang the doorbell, once, then twice, but no one came. She crept in front of the living room windows and peered in, hoping to see someone, but the house was empty. Then, from the backyard, she heard what sounded like yelling, and walked around to see what all the noise was about.

"Do it again, Maddie! But this time smile!" Charlotte called out. "You too, Henry and Jagger!"

"Did you get that one, Mom? See how high I went?" Maddie asked.

"I did! That was amazing, sweetie! Now let's get one of you all holding hands, Wyatt and Willow too."

Harper rounded the corner to find Charlotte fresh-faced and full of energy, taking pictures of the kids holding hands and bouncing on a giant trampoline.

"Harper!" Charlotte called out. "You're just in time; you can get one of the kids and me." She casually passed her the phone and then hopped onto the trampoline to jump with her children. "Okay, everyone, on the count of three, jump and smile, hands in the air! One . . . two . . ."

Harper took as many photos as she could before they landed and then stared, dumbstruck, as Charlotte handed the kids off to Annette.

"All right, kiddos, have a great day at school," she said, kissing each of them on the top of the head, "and remember . . ."

"I am strong, I am smart, I am unstoppable!" they yelled in unison.

"That's right!" she said, and they headed off. Once they were gone, she turned to face Harper. "How was your Thanksgiving?" she asked, taking back her phone. She checked the photos and began cropping and tweaking them as Harper struggled to find her voice.

"Um, uh, I . . ."

"Harper, you okay?" Charlotte asked, looking up.

"I thought you were *sick*, like, really sick. I was worried about you, so I brought you all this stuff to help you get better," Harper said, taking the grocery bag off her shoulder and handing it to Charlotte.

Charlotte slowly took the bag from Harper and examined its contents.

"Thank you, that's so thoughtful. But I'm fine. However, I will work from home today, just to be careful. Optics and all that. I don't need anyone gossiping that I was faking it," she said, tearing open the pack of citrus-flavored lozenges Harper had bought. She popped one into her mouth. "I love these; they're like candy. Want one?"

Harper stared at Charlotte, confused. "I don't understand. You said you were sick."

"I was. Sick to my stomach that someone I trusted quit without warning, sick that they came after me and tried to ruin my reputation. Sick and tired of having to solve every problem myself. I've been talking about our need to get ticket sales up for *weeks* now, which Tiffany was supposed to do, but sales are finally climbing thanks to *my* Instagram story." Charlotte placed her hand on Harper's back and walked them inside the house.

"I totally get that. But it's just that, on your Instagram story this morning, it seemed like you were . . ."

"Physically sick, and you believed me. Good, that's good."

Harper didn't know what to say. She hadn't thought that Charlotte was faking it for one second. Had Oliver? Maybe that's why he hadn't been answering her calls.

Charlotte wandered into her kitchen, pulled bottles of green juice out of the fridge for each of them, and motioned for Harper to sit at the counter.

"Look, I did what I had to do. It's not like I haven't been as sick as I said I was. I've gone to the hospital for dehydration and exhaustion—I just haven't told anyone about it. So in that way, I wasn't lying because it *has* happened before; it's just the timing that's different. And more importantly, it's what had to be done. If people believe Tiffany and turn on me, then those tickets don't sell, and we lose our sponsorship. And if we lose our sponsorship, then we can't afford the conference, which means we'll be left footing the whole bill, and to pay for that, there'll have to be cuts, which means people are going to have to be let go. So you tell me, is a little reframing of events worth it to save your colleagues' jobs?"

She cracked open her bottle and drank the whole thing at once, staring at Harper as she did.

Harper sipped her drink and took a moment to wrap her head around Charlotte's logic, which was hard to argue with, as twisted as it was. Of course saving jobs was important. And it wasn't like any harm had been done; Charlotte's fans were going to buy the tickets anyway. She'd just encouraged them to do it on her timing.

"Of course it's worth it."

A smile crept across Charlotte's face. "I'm glad to hear you say it because your job would've been one of the first to go. Nothing personal, of course, just a matter of seniority. Although you've shown more promise in the short amount of time you've been here than some of the others . . ."

Harper put her drink down and hesitated. "Uh, thanks."

"You're not like the others, Harper, you know that? You could have a real future at The Greenhouse. But I need to know: Have you made up your mind yet?" Charlotte leaned forward.

"Excuse me?" Harper asked, taken aback. "Made up my mind about what?"

"Let's be honest, you've gone back and forth about working for me. Not that it's shown in your work, but I can tell. You've been in, but I need my people to be *all* in. And I get it—this isn't New York City, and it's not where you thought you'd be. But we've already covered that you're ambitious and have integrity and a strong moral compass, judging by how upset you looked when you realized I wasn't sick. But no amount of praise from me will make a difference if you aren't in the whole way. And I can't afford to water any more weeds. I'm too tired and it's too stressful, so before I invest any more time in you, tell me: Are you *all in*, Harper?"

It was an honest question, and if Charlotte had asked it a few months earlier, Harper might've had a different answer. But if her trip back home had shown her anything, it was that everyone was moving on. Soon Poppy would be married and most likely starting a family, and her parents would sell the Inn and go who knew where. Everyone wished Harper well, but the only one extending a life raft to her was the tiny powerhouse of a woman who stood before her, who was more real and honest than Harper had ever seen her. There was only one answer. "Yes, I'm all in," Harper said, a sense of relief flooding her the moment she said it.

"Good," Charlotte said, taking Harper by the shoulders and putting her face close to hers. "Because I want you to come to this industry lunch with me." She grabbed an invitation from a stack of papers on the counter and handed it to Harper. "You'll want to do your research. It's a who's who of influencers, and yours truly is going to be profiled."

"Wait, isn't Bella going with you?"

"Not anymore," Charlotte replied. "Her mom's sick, and she needs to spend time with her."

"Right, but I know that she was really looking forward to this," Harper said.

"And I was really looking forward to a successful launch of my workbook, but so far all I've heard is crickets. I'm going to have to set up my own fucking signings. I don't know what's going on. She obviously can't handle multitasking right now. This way, she can focus on her mom, and that's more important, don't you think?"

"Of course, but . . ."

"Good, because I need you to tell her. She'll be too upset if it comes from me."

"Oh, I don't—"

"You better get to the office. Let everyone know that I appreciate all the good wishes and that I'm on the mend!" Charlotte said, leaving Harper standing in her kitchen staring at the invitation, the feeling of relief she felt only moments ago suddenly replaced with dread.

The idea of being the one to tell Bella that she was taking her place at the influencer lunch made her feel ill. Charlotte may not actually be sick, but Harper certainly was.

27

Paging Harper

It was still cold, of course, but the fact that it was ten degrees warmer in Nashville than it was in New York this time of year meant that Harper could sit outside at her favorite coffee shop, the Frothy Monkey. She'd stumbled upon the place one morning after arriving at The Greenhouse before it was open. In need of caffeine and a strong Wi-Fi signal, Harper had wandered down a few blocks and been lured by the smells of beans roasting. Now, sitting beneath a patio heater, she tore off a chunk of her chocolate chip cookie and then decided to take a picture of it to send to her mom as things between them were still a little strained since Thanksgiving.

Not as good as yours, Harper texted along with a little heart. She knew her mom was still hurt that Harper had been so distracted by her phone during Thanksgiving. But Charlotte was in a crisis and Harper needed to know what was going on. Hopefully her mother would eventually understand.

Harper put down her phone and yawned loudly. She was getting out of the Green Suites earlier and earlier in the hopes that she wouldn't run into Bella on the way to work. She'd only been back a week, and she wanted to avoid having to tell Bella about the influencer lunch for as long as possible. If Harper timed it right, she could get to The Greenhouse just as Bella was heading out with Charlotte to do her local workbook signings—a week of events that Charlotte had hastily organized.

Harper had seen the photos for the workbook launch splashed all over Instagram, and she could tell from her years of publishing experience that these events were not well attended. If the room had been full, there would have been wide shots of the crowd instead of pictures of getting the room ready and a handful of readers clustered together in the front row. The pictures posted on Charlotte's Instagram tended to favor Charlotte reading aloud or signing, not the audience. Harper saw the stern look on Charlotte's face when she returned to the office, how Bella trailed after her, her whole body covered in worry as she overdid it with compliments about how great Charlotte had been and how happy the bookstores were that she could come by.

It wouldn't take a genius to figure out that the sales weren't going well, and it only took one email to find out that numbers for the *Green with Envy Workbook: A Guided Journal for Turning Jealousies and Marital Discord into Hot Date Nights* were in the low hundreds. Hundreds: not thousands, or tens of thousands, as Charlotte had predicted. A little digging with Poppy—who asked her publicity team about it—revealed that Bella had sent the press release late, which meant that nobody had enough lead time to feature it. Harper was also hearing that people had expected that Ryan would be promoting the workbook with Charlotte, doing book signings and talks about all the ways they kept their love life alive. It was, after all, a workbook for a healthy marriage, but Ryan was too focused on his *Mister Class* and too bitter about Charlotte's success to join her.

Harper's phone buzzed. It was Bella, asking if she had time for a little book brainstorming and catching up.

> It seems like we've barely seen each other since we got back!

> I know, crazy, right? I've been trying to get some writing done before work.

> Oh . . . that explains it. What do you say we do a Wine + Whine Wednesday?

Wine + Whine Wednesday was the new tradition that Harper and Bella had started after the Halloween party. They would spend Wednesday nights sharing a bottle of wine while venting about the happenings at The Greenhouse and gushing over the latest pop culture scandals.

> And let's listen to the latest #Canceled podcast. I need a BREAK.

> Sounds good!

> Great! Off to visit bookstores with Charlotte. Later!

They exchanged thumbs-ups and happy faces and Harper felt her stomach sink. She hated the idea of upsetting Bella.

"So *this* is where you've been hiding," Aaron said, standing before Harper with a cup of coffee in his hand. He was wearing a beat-up leather jacket over a dark brown crew neck with little flecks of gray that matched his eyes.

"Who said I'm hiding?" Harper replied, quickly shutting her laptop that had the pictures of all the influencers that were attending the luncheon. "I'm just getting some work done before going into the office, that's all. What are you doing here?"

"Feeding my slow-roasted, overpriced coffee bean addiction."

Aaron cocked his head and narrowed his eyes at Harper. Slowly, a smile spread across his face as he sat down next to her.

"You okay?"

"Me? Oh yeah, I'm fine, totally fine."

"Alrighty then. So my next question is: What's going on? And don't lie again," he said, placing his hand on her leg for a second, "because you're clearly no good at it."

Harper felt a little jolt go through her body when Aaron touched her. She stared into his blue eyes, wondering if he had felt it too, and then remembered that he had asked her a question.

"I just like it here, and the coffee here is really good."

"And . . ."

"And I can work here without any distractions." She picked up her cup and took a sip.

"Are you calling me a distraction?" Aaron asked, raising his eyebrow.

"*No.* Well, okay, *yes*, but you're not the only one."

"*Really?*" he said, sounding intrigued.

"No, wait, I didn't mean it like that, I . . ." she said, getting all flustered. She opened her laptop and turned it to face him. "I have to go to this influencer lunch, which means I have to research everyone else who's going, and I didn't want anyone at work to know."

Aaron looked at the screen and then back at Harper, puzzled.

"Wait, isn't Bella supposed to go to that? She's been talking about it all month."

"Yeah, exactly. You want to tell her?" Harper said, slumping back against her chair.

"But how did you—"

"Charlotte says that Bella's got enough on her plate with the conference and the workbook launch, so now she can focus on her mom."

Aaron exhaled deeply and ran his hands through his hair. "She's pissed," he said, taking a sip of his coffee.

"Well, she will be when I tell her, which is why I'm hiding out here."

"No, not Bella. Charlotte." Aaron put his hand on her shoulder, and she softened.

"Because of the book sales?" Harper asked, not wanting to move for fear of Aaron taking his hand away.

"No, because of Tiffany and Mandy. Charlotte's convinced that Bella knew about them leaving and didn't say anything."

"She is?" Harper sat up straight.

"Yeah. They all used to be close, and then Mandy left, and now Tiffany, and that just leaves Bella. The way Charlotte sees it, either she knew something or she's going to leave too."

"That's crazy. Bella worships Charlotte and she's up for a promotion—she's not going anywhere," Harper said, disbelieving that anyone could question Bella's loyalty. "Wait, how do *you* know all this?"

"Charlotte talks to me; she always has. I guess it's because I just listen and don't say anything," he said, shrugging.

"You don't say *anything*? Not even if you know that something isn't true or right?"

"Not really. I don't know what's true, so I don't want to get involved. I like to stay neutral. You know, like Switzerland."

"Uh-huh," Harper said, trying to grasp how anyone could work so closely with Charlotte and not have an opinion one way or the other.

"It's not a secret; it's not like I'm *hiding* it or anything," he said pointedly.

"Right," Harper said, closing her laptop and gathering her things. "But what if you could help her?" Harper asked.

"Are you asking me that, or are you asking yourself that? Because there isn't much I can do." He gave her arm a quick squeeze and then stood to go.

Maybe there isn't, Harper thought as he walked away. But there *was* something she could do, and she hoped it would help.

28

Team Harper

It was sometime after they'd finished whining about how they never had time to go to the gym anymore, and how rude it was that no one had made a *Real Housewives of Nashville* yet, that they finished their bottle of wine. With another successful Wine + Whine Wednesday in the books, Harper finally felt ready to tell Bella about the influencer lunch. She was feeling good about the fact that she'd come up with a save-the-day marketing plan for Charlotte's workbook that included a promotional giveaway, an interview with two podcasters that she'd worked with before, and a five-minute appearance with a local day-time talk-show host who had a book that Poppy was currently editing. Harper had called in that last favor, promising that Charlotte would feature the host's book on her Instagram when it came out. Hopefully Bella would be so grateful for the help she wouldn't be mad about the lunch.

"I don't know how to thank you for all of this," Bella said from her spot on Harper's couch. She reached for her glass of white wine and took a big sip. "I mean, this is way more than I expected, and I think it could work. Charlotte's going to freak out, but in a good way, not the Jesus-Christ-Do-I-Have-to-Do-Everything-Myself way."

"I'm happy to help. I would've pitched in sooner if I knew you needed it."

"I didn't think I did," Bella said, finishing her wine. "I thought I could do it all, but I think I've been more distracted about my mom's health than I wanted to admit."

Harper saw her opening and went for it. "How could you not be? Your mom's health is obviously more important than any workbook launch, and let's face it, you have so much on your plate even without that going on. I've honestly never worked with anyone who does as much as you."

"Thank you for saying that," Bella said. "I think sometimes I forget how much we do at The Greenhouse and just figure it's normal, you know?"

"Right, but it isn't. I mean, normally, you'd have a whole team of people to do what you do, and then on top of The Greenhouse already being a lean operation, Mandy and Tiffany left, and I'm just getting started, so . . ."

"Oh no, you've been such a big help," Bella said, placing her hand on Harper's. "As upsetting as Mandy's leaving was, I'm really glad you're here."

Harper tried to smile, but inside, her heart was starting to beat faster. She squeezed Bella's hand and swallowed hard. If she could make it seem like the lunch wasn't such a big deal, maybe Bella would see it that way too.

"That's all I'm really trying to do. Help. I think that's what Charlotte is trying to do too—make sure she's got everything covered. It's why she's spreading the work around." She saw a flicker of fear in Bella's eyes and stood up to clear their glasses.

"Spreading what work around?"

"Oh, you know, events and things like that. For instance, you're handling the workbook signings, and I'm going to the influencer lunch." She kept her back to Bella as she loaded the dishwasher, hoping not to have to see the look on Bella's face, but the silence that followed stretched on long enough that she was forced to turn around. She watched as Bella slowly stood up from the couch and walked over.

"What are you talking about? Since when are you going to the influencer lunch?"

"Charlotte told me when you were away with your mom. She didn't want you to have to worry about one more thing," she said, grabbing the giant brownie that she'd gotten for dessert out of the fridge and putting it down on the kitchen island. She avoided eye contact with Bella as she stabbed her fork in and took a huge bite. "I thought we could share."

"I was with my mom over a week ago," Bella said, her mouth a tight line.

"Or weeks, if you're on Green Time." Harper laughed uncomfortably.

"Which is even worse if you think about it. You knew all this time, and you didn't tell me?" Bella crossed her arms in front of her.

"I thought Charlotte would change her mind," Harper said. "She asked me to go with her right after Thanksgiving when she was really angry, and I just assumed she'd cool down."

"Really angry at *me*?"

"No, not you—at Tiffany, and whoever it was that knew Tiffany was leaving but didn't say anything."

"I don't believe this. You just started. You don't know a thing about the influencers who are going," Bella said, raising her voice.

"Well, it's been a few months, which again, on Green Time . . ." Harper stopped at the sight of Bella's nostrils flaring. "I know I don't know anyone, but I've been researching everybody for days, and I think I'm up to speed," Harper said, her cheeks flushing.

"Right, you were researching because you were *so sure* that Charlotte would change her mind about you going," Bella said, shaking her head. She marched into the living room and began stuffing her laptop and notebooks into her bag. "So that's what tonight was really about, the gossip and wine—you feeling guilty. That's why you helped me with all the workbook stuff."

Harper exhaled deeply and walked over to Bella. "I wanted to help. Things haven't been going well with the launch. I didn't want Charlotte to find out you sent the press release late and get angry at you."

Bella grabbed her bag, swung it over her shoulder, and faced Harper, her eyes wide and angry. "You *know*? Have you been checking up on me?"

"No, it's not like that. I mean yes, I checked, but only because I wanted to help. Don't worry, I didn't say anything to Charlotte," Harper said. She stepped forward to reassure Bella, but Bella stepped back.

"Don't worry? So you just went digging on your own. Wow. For what? To have dirt on me? Something to hold over me?" Her cheeks were red, and there were tears in her eyes.

"Of course not—I wanted to help. I was trying to save your job!"

Bella's mouth dropped open, but no words came out. After a moment she spoke. "I didn't know my job was in danger," she whispered. "I guess because nobody told me."

"Bella, come on, we're a team," Harper said, immediately regretting her words.

"*Team?*" Bella stormed past Harper and out of the apartment. "Yeah. Team *Harper*," she hissed, and she let the door slam behind her.

29

Ladies Who Lunch

> Hey all, just a reminder that the influencer lunch is today!
> Harper will be posting from the event, and we'll need
> everyone to like, share, and comment—you know the
> drill. Also, let's make sure we have those Growth Planners
> wrapped and ready to go.

Sitting outside The Greenhouse, Harper read Charlotte's comment on the Vine, and then, for the umpteenth time, read the email invitation for the lunch. She practically knew it by heart. It was the first time the annual lunch was being held in Nashville, and Charlotte had made it clear how important it was that everything went perfectly. She'd gone through the roof when Harper told her that she was speaking third instead of first and demanded she fix it. So Harper had called the organizer of the luncheon and insisted the only fair thing was to put everyone in alphabetical order—not that she gave that reason to Charlotte.

Harper liked being able to fix things, and she really liked the praise she got when she was able to do so. Instead of worrying about things that Charlotte might find wrong, she found herself looking for problems that she could preemptively remedy, just to be the focus of her attention. Admittedly this hadn't made her more popular with her coworkers, but she justified this by telling herself that she was just doing all she could to make sure things at The Greenhouse were the best they could be. It's what Charlotte was always preaching anyway. *One more time*, she told herself, reading the invitation again.

Welcome to the annual Influential Ladies Who Lunch!

This year in Nashville!

Join us as we celebrate our very own north stars, the women who guide us in business, beauty, fashion, and self-empowerment! This year's lineup brings together the best and the brightest for a meeting of the minds, bodies, and spirits. We'll be delving into the importance of supporting one another, the benefits of a shared alignment of interests, and the responsibility that comes with power and popularity. If there's one thing we know, it's that it's a wide world out there (literally, it's the internet), and there is room for all of us. And together, we can continue to be an influential force for good and lift up people everywhere!

Featured Speakers

<u>Charlotte Green</u>

This Greenspirational empowered thinker and motivational speaker is focused on helping women unleash the warrior within. Charlotte brings her wisdom and popularity as a bestselling self-help author and Greenlightenment expert. She'll be speaking about creating community, how to be a kick-ass boss, and the importance of inspiring one another.

Corrine James

A graduate of the Harvard School of Business with a specialty in data analytics, C.J. made her money on Wall Street. A self-proclaimed factual influencer, she will discuss how numbers don't lie and how feelings can't be trusted. A serial entrepreneur, C.J. encourages women to take their emotions out of their decisions when it comes to business. As her famous saying goes, "feelings are for bedrooms, not boardrooms."

Evie Landon

Former Coca-Cola CEO and mompreneur Evie Landon knows her beverages and also how much sugar our kids are drinking, which is why she created WaterWorks, a BPA-free, lightweight, biodegradable water bottle with a built-in carbonator and time-released natural flavor capsule that already has a wait-list of ten thousand. She'll be speaking on meaningful monetization.

Chloé Minou

Self-Care with Coco CEO Chloé Minou has built a million-dollar industry reminding women of the importance of making time and taking time to care for themselves. Her organic, fair-trade, vegan skincare line, Coco Knows, recently landed her on the Fortune 500. Chloé will provide actionable steps for following her company's motto: "Make yourself your first customer and you'll never go wrong."

All set? Charlotte asked on the Vine.

Yup! We're gonna kick ass and take names! Harper typed, her face breaking into a smile when she saw Charlotte write back, You know it!

Immediately a flurry of likes came in, and Harper checked to see who they were from. The usual Vine keeners were commenting right away, then the people who had been there longer. Oliver sometimes commented, not that he had to, and Cynthia never did, not that anyone expected her to, and the same went for Aaron. But the comment Harper was hoping to see was one from Bella. It had been a week since their argument, and Harper was surprised that they had barely spoken even though they lived in the same building and worked opposite each other. Whenever the two of them found themselves alone, Harper would somehow get pulled away by Charlotte. And whenever Harper texted Bella, she only got short, polite replies. Then Bella canceled their weekly Wine +Whine Wednesday, claiming that she wasn't feeling well, which was why Harper was now sitting outside The Greenhouse in the courtyard a full hour before it opened. She was determined to speak to Bella before the influencer lunch so they could get past this.

"She's not coming in this morning," Aaron said, wheeling his equipment to a stop in front of Harper.

"Who's not?" Harper asked.

"Bella."

"Shit. How did you know it was her I was waiting for?"

"Because you two are always together, and yet this whole week you've both been working hard to not be in the same place at the same time. It's kind of obvious."

"What is?" Harper said, collecting her things. She stood and met Aaron's gaze.

"That you're both hurt and waiting for the other to apologize." He smiled.

"I've got nothing to apologize for. It wasn't my idea to be at the influencer lunch; it was Charlotte's. I was only trying to be good at my job and help Bella with hers. The last time I checked that isn't a crime."

"No, it's not, but it might make you less popular, at least for a little while," Aaron said gently. "See it from her point of view. Hotshot New York City girl with a fancy education starts work and in a matter of months is where it took her years to get to. And you didn't even want it at first."

Hotshot. Was that how Aaron saw her?

"I want it now," she said, blushing.

"I know you do," Aaron said, placing his hand on her shoulder. "And there's nothing wrong with that, but it will take Bella some time to come around. Just be patient."

"Easier said than done. I tried that at my old job and it didn't exactly get me anywhere."

Aaron studied her a moment. "So you're trying to make up for lost time."

"No, I'm just not waiting anymore." Harper could feel her body heat up as Aaron continued to stare into her eyes.

"Some things are worth waiting for," he said, his voice low.

Harper found it impossible to look away. "I hope so," she whispered.

"I know so," he said, giving her shoulder a squeeze.

"And sometimes you just have to go for it," she said, making him blush now.

Aaron let go of her shoulder and cleared his throat. "Well, speaking of going, we better get going to that luncheon." He extended his arm for Harper to lead the way.

Harper started to walk and then stopped and turned to him. "Aaron— thank you."

"You're welcome, *Manhattan.* I got you," he said, his eyes twinkling.

Oh yes you do, thought Harper, her heart pounding. *You* definitely *do*.

30

Sour Grapes

The site of the influencer lunch was a stunning vineyard just outside Nashville. Set on one hundred acres with a tasting room, picnic areas, and a converted barn that served as a venue for intimate concerts and weddings, it had been photographed from every angle, backdropped by one glorious sunset after another, and showcased on countless Instagram accounts. Still, no matter how many beautiful images there already were of people walking among the grapes, holding glasses of rosé up to the sunlight, or sitting on picnic blankets to stare across the land that stretched farther than the eye could see, Charlotte had Aaron film her doing those very same things before the event officially started.

The three of them had arrived early, with Charlotte insisting that Harper place a Growth Planner on the seat of every guest attending. She'd gotten the idea that morning. She would have everyone fill out the first line, stating how they wanted to grow and then go around the room and have everyone read it before she gave her speech. The exercise wasn't in the schedule, but it would catch everyone by surprise and force them to say something nice before she started. She wanted to set the tone and send a message to everyone else, especially C.J., that she was good and in a good place, even though C.J. now had one of her former employees working for her. The announcement that Tiffany had been named C.J.'s new director of communications had come out the day before, and Charlotte had lost it.

"Okay, maybe let's get one more shot of the vineyard behind me," Charlotte said, sitting sideways at a picnic table, journal open, pen in one hand, chin resting on the other, as if she were deep in thought. "Harper, we can tease these out all day."

"Of course," Harper said, pulling out her phone and taking a few pictures. She must've had hundreds already, but Harper knew that one could never have enough content. She'd put what she didn't post today on Charlotte's Instagram story and share in an email blast, the newsletter, the calendar they were working on, and the year-in-review holiday card. She had to admit that she wanted to take a photo for her own Instagram too, but didn't want to rub it in Bella's face. So she snapped a quick selfie and refrained from posting. *Just for the memories.* She then turned her attention to the idea that she'd been burning to share with Charlotte since they arrived.

"I was wondering if you wanted to add something to the top of your speech, maybe something about how you were writing in your journal this morning and then got 'an idea,' " Harper said, using air quotes, "to have everyone take a moment to write in theirs?"

"You mean make it *look* spontaneous?" Charlotte said.

"Exactly."

Charlotte stood up and moved slowly to another spot. "I love it. And then C.J.'s right after me, and she's so goddamn stiff, it'll make me look even better." She high-fived Harper and smiled. "Harper, do you know how long I've been waiting to be a featured guest at this luncheon? Every year I go and kiss everyone's ass, and finally, now that it's in Nashville, I get to be a speaker. And at the influencer lunch right before we have our biggest conference yet. This is what I'm talking about when I say 'Don't give up, get up!' "

Harper recognized the line from the speech she helped write—and was happy to hear that it had stayed in. Ever since their conversation after Thanksgiving, she had been able to write in Charlotte's voice so clearly that she no longer had to wait for Charlotte to approve her email blasts, which were reaching a wider audience and gaining more attention than ever.

"You're going to crush it," Harper said, taking one last shot. She tucked her phone into the pocket of the new sweater blazer she had gotten at Charlotte's favorite store.

"You know we are." Charlotte pumped her fist in the air before heading to the lunch site at the far end of the property.

We. Harper heard it, and judging by the look on his face as he turned his camera on her, so had Aaron.

"*Influence*: the capacity to have an effect on the character, development, or behavior of someone or something, or the effect itself. That's how the dictionary defines it," Charlotte said, standing onstage. She'd spoken about community and the best way to be a kick-ass boss and was now coming to the end of her speech. She gave a little knowing smile as she scanned the room and then leaned into the podium and spoke earnestly. "But you should know that I personally, I believe it's more than that. I believe it's about *initiating, igniting, and inspiring* each and every person to be the best they can be." She paused for effect and then stepped out from behind the podium and walked across the stage, her voice growing stronger and louder with each point she made. "*I believe* that it's our job, no . . . our *duty*, to *show* folks they deserve more than what they've settled for. It's our duty to *offer* them the transformative tools they need, our duty to *give* them the *greenlight* to invest in themselves, so that they can be a part of this incredible movement! A movement intended to lift *all* people up!" She paused as everyone in the tent, riveted, murmured in agreement. "And where does that start? It starts with *us*. I didn't get into this line of work by choice, I was *called* to it—by a deep desire and genuine belief that the work we are doing matters. Because *you* matter. *We* matter. *This*," Charlotte said loudly, gesturing to the room, "*matters*. And when we do the work, when we put in the time, when we invest in ourselves, we can all be warriors, and then, together, we can continue to inspire and *influence* one another. Together we can change the world!" Charlotte preached, pumping both her fists into the air, and sending the room to its feet in a frenzy of applause and cheers.

Harper felt chills as she saw how moved the guests were by Charlotte's—and Harper's—words. If a room full of two hundred people could feel this electric, what would a room of ten thousand feel like? Harper wanted to know.

As Charlotte walked off the stage, women flocked to her, leaving no doubt about who had already won the afternoon. The room was buzzing and as Charlotte mingled, it was agreed that Harper would head back to The Greenhouse with Aaron after he got some more B-roll footage. Harper had just ducked outside the tent to post some more photos on Instagram when she heard C.J. on the other side of the thin wall.

"You got to hand it to her. First with those fucking notebooks, then with that speech. She can preach, that's for sure. Too bad she doesn't have an actual product to market."

"What about her books? People love those." Harper recognized the other voice as belonging to Evie Landon, the self-proclaimed mompreneur.

"Please, have you read those books?" C.J. scoffed.

"No, have you?" Evie asked.

"I don't think *Charlotte's* even read them. She sure as shit didn't write them, according to Tiffany. She plagiarized whole sections of the book from some little-known self-help writer who lives in New Zealand."

"No, that's not possible. Something like that would have gone public a long time ago. Someone would have to know!"

"Someone *does* know, not that she'll ever be able to say anything about it now. She signed an NDA."

"I don't believe it; that's disgruntled employee gossip. She wrote those books with her husband," Evie said.

"*Husband.* We'll see how long that lasts. You don't see him around anymore, do you?"

"I heard he's trying to get some kind of master class off the ground," Evie said.

"Spare me. He goes from one project to another, and each one is a bigger flop than the last. He's failed at everything he's tried since leaving The Greenhouse. I guess that's what happens when Daddy hands you the role of CEO for his branding company right out of college and you ditch it to help wifey, who ends up stealing your spotlight. The guy's an empty Brooks Brothers suit."

"Wow. If I didn't know better, I'd say this is personal."

"Hardly. This is business. I have a *business*, not a *platform* or *personal brand*." Harper could hear C.J. start to move away and tried to follow her.

"Ouch. I have a *business*," Evie said. "Chloé has a business."

"Chloé has a hobby her boyfriend is funding. She'll be onto something—or someone—new by next year, mark my words."

"What about Charlotte?"

C.J. walked out of the tent and straight into Harper. For a moment, she looked taken aback, and then seemed to place who Harper was and smiled. "Charlotte? Oh, she'll either explode or implode. Only time will tell."

Harper glared at C.J. as she walked off with Evie and immediately scanned the crowd to ensure that Charlotte wasn't in earshot. Seeing Charlotte surrounded by a group of women taking selfies, she breathed a sigh of relief and grabbed the largest glass of Riesling off one of the trays that was being walked around. Bella hadn't been kidding about

C.J.—she really *was* ruthless. She reached for her phone to text her, but then remembered they were in a fight and stopped. It was then that she became aware of a woman watching her. She'd noticed her sitting off to the side during Charlotte's speech, furiously scribbling notes in a black Moleskine journal with a small tape recorder perched on her knee. While the other guests seemed enraptured by the women taking the stage to speak, this woman's face held a bemused fascination, not unlike someone watching animals at the zoo.

"Harper," she said, extending her free hand while holding a glass of wine in the other. "We haven't met. I'm Tasha. I'm writing a feature on female influencers for *Inc.* magazine."

"Nice to meet you."

"Tell me, what were those two on about?" she asked, looking in the direction of C.J. and Evie.

"You'd have to ask them," Harper said, trying to shrug it off.

"I plan on it, but I was hoping to ask you a few questions first," Tasha said. "Mind if we take a walk? I have a feeling I've inadvertently bombed enough selfies for one day." She ducked out of the frame of a group of women wearing prairie dresses and wide-brimmed felt hats who leaned in close to one another and flashed a peace sign.

"Sure," Harper said.

They walked until they reached a picnic table that faced the vineyards and sat side by side, taking in the view.

"Okay, now I get all the Instagram photos," Tasha said.

"It really is beautiful," Harper agreed.

"It's a long way from New York City." At the look of surprise on Harper's face, Tasha continued, "It's just research. Honestly, I wasn't familiar with any of these women or their companies, so I had to get up to speed. Much like yourself, I gather. Pretty big change from being a writer and then working in publishing."

Being a writer. It had been a long time since anyone had called Harper a writer, and it threw her.

"*Aspiring* writer might be more like it. A bunch of freelance articles and a manuscript that sits in a drawer? Not sure that counts," Harper said self-consciously.

"Well, I hope it does, because you've basically just described the first half of my career." Tasha laughed and Harper felt herself relax. "But now you're working as a— What's your official title again?"

"Visionary support strategist," Harper said. "And yeah, it is. But something tells me you already knew that."

"You're right. I was fishing."

"For what?"

"An honest answer. I've talked to all these women and all their assistants, support strategists, consultants, community managers, brand ambassadors, or whatever else you want to call the people behind them. All of them give me the same canned answers. 'It's so great to work for so and so, it's so inspiring, she's the best boss I know, we're like a family.' It's like listening to a bunch of robots, and I thought being new and not being from here, you might have a different perspective."

Harper took another sip of her wine and noticed for the first time that her glass was almost empty. That was the problem with a good Riesling—it was sweet and delicious and went down fast.

"Can I top you off?" a waiter passing the two of them asked.

"I really shouldn't," Harper said, realizing that she hadn't had anything but green juice all day. She'd been too busy during the luncheon to actually eat anything.

"Me either," said Tasha, "but we all know the best part of these events is the free drinks, so I'm going to."

She held out her glass and Harper did the same, and the waiter refilled both.

"You know, most people would think that a profile where an employee is quoted saying really good stuff about their boss is a good thing—for both of you," Tasha said.

Harper considered what Tasha was saying. She had a point. With Tiffany leaving and shooting her mouth off, it was even more of a reason for Harper to tell Tasha just how great Charlotte was. So with the Riesling flowing and her glass never empty, Harper answered all of Tasha's questions . . . even some she hadn't thought for a moment to ask.

31

Keep Calm and Write On

It was early evening when Harper finally made it back to the Green Suites, more than a little tipsy and grateful that it had been Aaron who had driven her home and put up with her favorite Taylor Swift playlist. The event had been a huge success. People had bought tickets for the conference, there was a lot of traffic on their site, and the conversation with Tasha—from what she could remember of it—had gone well.

By all accounts, Harper should've been flying, but she had no one to share it with. She tried calling Poppy, but she was out on a double date with Charles. She called her parents, but they were busy working. The truth was, the only person she really wanted to talk to about her day was Bella, so she stood in the hallway outside her apartment balancing two boxes, one with a small Hawaiian pizza and another with two of Bella's favorite cupcakes, hoping her friend would give her another chance. She leaned her ear against the door, the sounds of a television in the background, and knocked. As she heard Bella walk to the door, she exhaled and ran through what she wanted to say. How it wasn't her idea to go to the luncheon, how she'd wished that Bella had gone instead . . .

But then the sounds paused, and Bella's footsteps retreated. Was she really pretending not to be home? Harper felt the hot sting of tears in her eyes and knocked again. Silence. Humiliated, she backed away and walked down the hall to the elevator as fast as she could, taking the food with her.

Back in her apartment, Harper sat on her couch, took a big bite out of the red velvet cupcake she'd bought, and stared at the blinking cursor on the blank page on her laptop. Bella might not talk to Harper at work or answer any of her calls or texts, but she was sure to read the latest email blast that Harper wrote for Charlotte. It was the only way she could think of to make her feelings known. Whether it would work or not, she didn't know, but it was worth a try.

To: Charlotte Green <charlotte.green@greenteam.com>
From: Harper Cruz <harper.cruz@greenteam.com>
Re: Green with Generosity

Love, Charlotte

 Hey everyone, just wanted to tell you that today was a big day for your girl. Not only did I get invited to the Influential Ladies Who Lunch, but I was the first to speak and got a standing ovation! There were so many people who came up to me afterward to tell me how they connected with my talk on building community and what it takes to be a kick-ass boss lady and meaningful mentor. So many women said they wished they had a woman like me in their lives when they were starting out in business, and I know how they feel—I wish I had someone like me too. But there was something else I saw, and I feel weird writing about it because I don't want to sound ungrateful. Girl, you know how grateful I am. I am all about the gratitude, but I think it's important to mention this other thing because it exists. And that thing is . . . envy. I saw it in the eyes of some of the women who told me they wished they had a job that they loved as much as I love mine that also paid the bills, that they wish they could've built an entire business and brand on their own terms instead of taking the safe route. They said I was lucky to be able to publish books without a literary agent, to make my own money, and be my own boss. They were praising me while also envying me, and here's the thing: I get it. I know what it feels like to want something so badly that you have trouble celebrating someone else's success. I know how tempting it is to believe someone's victories are the result of luck instead of hard freaking work. This is why I said to every single woman I met that my success is your success, because my success means that if it is possible for me to have everything I've ever wanted, it is possible for all of you too. When one of us does well, we all do well, and we create more opportunities for one another to shine. Dimming someone's light doesn't make yours any brighter. There's enough success to go around! So the next time someone you know does well, don't let it make you Green with Envy—let it make you Green with Generosity.

After pressing send and falling asleep, Harper woke the next morning with a start. Her phone had just lit up with a text message. It was from Tasha.

> Great talking to you, loved your last email. I'll be in touch.

> Charlotte deserves all the credit.

> Charlotte, sure 😊 Talk soon.

———————

"And now," Charlotte said, as the morning song ended and everyone threw their hands up and cheered, "there's something I'd like to say." She called Bella over to help her get up on the Tower of Power and then shooed her away. Harper felt her stomach drop at the way Bella backed away and kept her eyes averted from everyone else. "A lot of you wrote in the chat this morning that you were really moved by the latest email blast. And I wanted you to know that you are not alone; it's already one of our most-read pieces. It's so popular that we're going to get T-shirts made up that say 'Green with Generosity' on them."

Harper beamed and stepped forward ever so slightly, getting ready to be thanked.

"Now, if you know one thing about me, it's that I believe in giving credit where credit is due . . ."

Harper beamed and shook her head slightly, already preparing to indicate that she wasn't expecting anything and didn't need the attention.

"So, please join me in thanking one another, because as I wrote, my success is your success, and thanks to you, this next conference is on its way to being the most successful yet." Charlotte rubbed her hands together and smiled widely. "Now for something fun! Oliver and I have created a special Eventbrite where customers can put in codes you give them so we can track your sales. The first person to sell two hundred tickets before lunch gets Monday off. So reach out to all the people on your list and call them directly, offer a discount if you need to, and re-member to mention the Growth Planners. Okay, let's do this, everyone!" She applauded everyone in the room, and they applauded her back and returned to their desks, fired up and ready to win.

"Um, Charlotte?" Harper said, catching up to her.

"Harper!" Charlotte said, putting her hand on her back and whisking her into her office. "Did you have fun at the event yesterday? Tasha called me and told me you two had a great conversation."

"We did," Harper said, a little nervously. "She wanted to know what it was really like to work for you, and I told her it was the best, *obviously*."

"Obvi," Charlotte echoed. She sat at her desk and opened her laptop. "Well, you made a really great impression on her. No surprise, I'm the one who picked you out of *all* the people who applied and gave you a chance, so I should know."

"Right, of course," Harper said, taken aback.

"Is there something you need?" Charlotte was already busying herself with her notebook.

"I just wanted to say I'm so glad you liked the email blast and that it's getting so much traction."

"Oh yeah, it's terrific. Didn't I just say that out there?" she asked, tilting her head to one side. "It's one of the most popular posts we've done all year. You're really getting the hang of taking everything I say in real life and organizing it."

Organizing. The choice of word bothered Harper, but she wasn't sure how to explain it. I didn't *organize* it; I *wrote* it for you.

Harper's face must've shown how she was feeling because Charlotte said, "Harper, have a seat." She leaned across the desk and took Harper's hands in her own. "Here's the thing. You're killing it. I know it, you know it, *they* know it," she said, pointing to where Harper's colleagues worked. "And while you know how much I believe in celebrating success—well, of course you do; you just wrote a whole email about it—I want to be sensitive to the fact that there are *other* people who need a little credit. Hence the contest. I want to give them a chance to shine too, you know. We're a *team* here." Harper's face flushed. In a matter of minutes she'd gone from proud and convinced that she was Charlotte's favorite employee to ashamed that she had expected to be singled out. "Now if there isn't anything else, I think you should really focus on selling those tickets. Remember, the first to get to two hundred wins!"

Harper returned to her desk in a bit of a daze and turned on her laptop. The Vine chat was buzzing with people updating their stats, and the race to two hundred ticket sales was on. Harper replayed the conversation over and over in her head, the comment about Tasha calling standing out. Had she said something she didn't need to? Was Charlotte upset that Tasha had taken a liking to her? It didn't make sense and yet that was how it felt, like Charlotte needed to put Harper in her place.

"It's not you," Bella said, lowering her laptop screen so she could see Harper. They were the first words she'd said to her since their fight.

"It's not?" Harper asked, swallowing the lump in her throat.

"At some point, everyone close to her gets the sandwich."

"The sandwich?" Harper asked, leaning forward.

"Compliment-insult-compliment. She builds you up, then knocks you down in case you start to think too highly of yourself, then builds you up again so you keep trying."

Harper would never have expected this coming from Bella. "Wow, that's awful." She looked at Bella, expecting her to agree, but Bella just shrugged.

"Think of it like she really believes in you and knows you can do more. It's worse if she says nothing. You're lucky she cares."

Harper wanted to keep talking, but Bella slipped back behind her computer and put in her earbuds. If what Bella was saying was true, Charlotte's approach was a really shitty way to motivate someone. But as much as she hated to admit it, it was probably effective. Harper had run relay in high school, and it wasn't really different from what she was going through now. Her coach would always alternate between yelling and praising, reminding her team that they needed to be outstanding on their own, but that they were also nothing without each other. It was the only way to win, and now that Harper knew what winning felt like, she didn't want to stop.

She grabbed her laptop and phone and walked slowly around the room to see what other people were doing. Some of her colleagues were at the photocopy machine making flyers about the conference to drop off at local businesses; and she heard a couple of women, who apparently had been in the same sorority as Charlotte coordinating an email blast to their fellow sorority sisters; another was on the phone asking her mom to buy the tickets as gifts for her company's team-building event. All of them were great ideas. She needed a great idea too, something that would motivate people and appeal to their emotions.

Harper circled the room thinking: What would make her appeal different? She thought back to all those editorial meetings at the publishing house that she had sat in on and the one question that all the senior editors would ask: *What makes this book different from all the others like it?* Harper was asking that very question right now, and then it hit her.

She picked up the pace, practically sprinting to the back of The Greenhouse, where Aaron was reviewing footage of the influencer lunch in his office.

"Hey, you busy?" she asked.

"Kind of. Why, what's up?" he said, leaning back in his chair.

"I was hoping you could help me with this challenge, to sell two hundred tickets before noon."

"You're asking the wrong guy. I don't know a thing about selling."

"Of course you do. All those videos, that's exactly what they're about—selling." Harper pulled up a chair to sit next to him.

"That's cynical," he said. "I prefer to think of them as storytelling."

She smiled. "Then help me tell the story of a power couple who is really just like you and me, who've gone through ups and downs and who, through it all, have still managed to grow and change and support each other."

"And let me guess, this couple is Charlotte and Ryan?"

"Yes, and every person who buys two tickets will be eligible to win a dinner date with them, as well as two copies of their book."

Aaron looked at Harper sideways. "Have you run this by Charlotte?"

"No, but it's going to work."

"What makes you so sure?"

"Because we're going to tell a love story, and love stories are always inspiring."

"Are they now?" Aaron asked, leaning toward her and making her stomach flip.

"You know they are. You write about them all the time, and you could even put some of your music behind it."

"You realize you're asking me to make you a film?"

"It's not a film. It's just sixty seconds, and I'm going to narrate it. I just need some help cutting it together." When he didn't answer, she continued, "Please. I'll owe you one."

"If I say yes, you can't tell Charlotte I helped."

"I promise. It will be our secret."

"Oh, I like the sound of that," Aaron said slyly.

"I'm serious," Harper said, trying to stay focused on the job at hand.

"But you'll have to stick to your word about owing me. I'm thinking dinner," he contemplated, his face serious.

"Okay."

"And dancing," he added, pulling up Charlotte's Facebook account on his screen.

"You dance?" Harper laughed.

"You want me to help you or not?"

"Dancing it is," Harper said, thinking this was a win-win situation. Help with the ticket competition *and* a night out with Aaron? She wasn't sure if it was a date, but she'd take it. As Aaron put together a little montage of their love story, Harper wrote.

> Some people think the Inspire conference is about empowerment and finding the warrior woman within. But it's also about connection. Connecting to who and what really matters in our lives. For some people, it's their first chance to be part of a like-minded community. For others, it's a second chance—to reconnect to a long-lost passion, friendship, or

relationship. Connection takes work. But it's the best kind of
work, because it comes from a place deep within us, a place
of love. And who better to show us how inspiring that kind of
work can be than Charlotte and Ryan, whose love and desire
to connect with each other and all of you is what led to the
very first Inspire conference? For every two tickets purchased
with the code LOVE INSPIRES before 12:00 PM EDT today,
you'll be eligible for a double date with our favorite couple,
as well as two copies of their bestselling book.

The making of the video didn't take nearly as long as Harper thought
it would. It helped that there were a million photos of Charlotte and Ryan
online and a bunch more behind-the-scenes pictures that Aaron hadn't
yet shared on The Greenhouse socials. Cobbled together with a snippet
of one of Aaron's songs, the video told the story of Charlotte and Ryan's
journey from students to Green powerhouses.

"It looks fantastic," Harper said, watching the video set to music. It
was moving and romantic and Harper's voice-over was timed just right.
"Damn, you're good."

"You've no idea," Aaron replied, making Harper turn beet red.

"Okay, I better get back to my desk and get this up and running.
Thank you." She gave Aaron a quick hug, surprising them both, and
dashed off.

Sitting back at her desk, Harper created a LOVE INSPIRES link and
then made the video public on the website and her IG story, tagging Charlotte and The Greenhouse. She tried to quell her nerves about not getting
Charlotte's permission. She knew that the ends-justifying-the-means
argument only went so far and that she probably should've checked with
Charlotte first, but she was hoping that she would be successful enough
in winning the contest that she could always beg forgiveness later if she
had to. It wasn't a perfect strategy, but she didn't have time to make it
perfect; what she needed was to get back in Charlotte's good graces.

She followed the directions posted on the Vine on how to check the back end of Eventbrite to see how many tickets she and her colleagues had sold. She was discouraged that her sales were still in the single digits half an hour later. Everyone was glued to their screens, an equal number of furrowed brows and hopeful smiles. Behind the walls of her glass office, Charlotte and Oliver were watching too. With only an hour left to go, it looked like Bella and the woman who was having her mother buy tickets for all her employees were in the lead. If it couldn't be her, Harper hoped that Bella would win.

She was ready to admit defeat when she heard someone say, "Whose code is LOVE INSPIRES?"

Harper looked at her screen, and her seven tickets had become thirty, then fifty, seventy, one hundred and ten, one hundred and thirty-five. Every time Harper refreshed her feed, there were another twenty or so tickets sold, and then it was over two hundred, three hundred, four hundred.

Bella, who had been watching the video, stood up and came over to Harper. "You should've checked with Charlotte first. A double date? She and Ryan aren't exactly cozy these days."

"She'll get over it," Harper said, sounding more confident than she felt. "The important thing is to sell tickets."

Bella seemed surprised to hear her say it. "You sound like Charlotte."

Good, thought Harper.

"Holy shit!"

Harper swiveled in her chair to look at her screen and gasped, the ticket count climbing faster than she could refresh. As soon as the clock hit noon, she checked her final count—she'd sold over five hundred tickets. She started pacing near her desk and did the math—she'd made the company over two hundred fifty thousand dollars.

Everyone in the office turned toward her, their faces a mixture of awe and envy. Harper was waiting for someone to say something when Charlotte walked out of her office and straight to where Harper was standing.

"LOVE INSPIRES?"

"That's me," Harper answered nervously as Aaron walked out of his office toward her desk.

"And you didn't think to ask me, before making a video of me and Ryan, if it was okay to shill us out on a double date?"

"I did, but decided not to," Harper said, laying it on the line. "I didn't want to lose any time. Plus, I wanted it to feel spontaneous and genuine. I hoped that it would resonate with people and it did. I mean, who *wouldn't* jump at the chance to share a meal with you and Ryan?"

"I see," Charlotte said slowly, her face breaking into a huge smile. She turned to address the room. "Great job, everyone, thank you!" She then shifted her focus to Harper and lifted her arm for a high five. "But we have a clear winner! Let's give it up for Harper and Aaron." She then led the room in a call-and-response chant.

"I say 'Go!' You say—"

"Green!"

"Go!"

"Green!"

"Go!"

"Green—"

"Team!" they all yelled along with Charlotte. As everyone pumped their fists in the air, Charlotte turned to Harper and whispered, "See? Now everyone feels good about themselves, *and* you won." She winked as she walked off, leaving Harper feeling victorious and schooled all at once.

As the round of cheering came to an end and the normal Greenhouse buzz filled the room, Harper caught a glimpse of her and Aaron in the reflection of Oliver's office glass. *Love does inspire*, Harper thought. And thanks to Charlotte, it also rewarded.

Seeing Green Monthly Newsletter:

December

Well, here it is! The final month of the year, the last chance to do all those things you meant to do, see all those people you meant to see, and keep all those promises you didn't mean to break. One month of holiday celebrations before you gather around the Christmas tree (or menorah! I don't discriminate, obvi!) and open those presents and take pictures you'll post of you and your loved ones in your super-cute matching pajamas. It's the time of year when all those great holiday cards with updates go out, featuring picture-perfect families, making us think, *Why isn't my family like that?* Well, I'm here to tell you that no family is perfect, no house is that clean (promise!), and even though it may look like everyone else has it all together, you have to trust that not everyone does—not even me. But that doesn't mean we can't aim for perfection! It doesn't mean that we should settle. So instead of waiting for the new year to make your resolutions, why not get a jump-start on everything you want to improve on now? Personally, I love having flaws because it means that I am still evolving and that there is always room to grow. This year, being the overachiever that I am (nothing wrong with that!), I'm going to do a 14-day Clean Green Cleanse so I can enjoy my Christmas (or Kwanzaa!) treats without any worries I would normally have. This December, give yourself the gift of good health and join me in going Green and Clean for just $49.99. You'll get our customized menu, a daily motivational message, access to our library of workout videos, and the ability to talk to any of our team members whenever you need it. Wishing you all a Green Holiday!

xo Charlotte

32

Something Blue

"Can we do caviar *and* shrimp, or is that too extravagant since we're having oysters too?" Poppy asked over FaceTime while Harper packed.

"I think it's perfect," Harper said, as she folded clothes for her trip back home. She'd thought it was perfect the last time they'd talked about it. It seemed on the rare occasions that they talked, it was about what Poppy should serve, wear, and say at her engagement party.

"Oysters and champagne—that's classic, right? Okay, yeah, I'll do that instead of the shrimp cocktail." Poppy circled something in her notebook, then paused. "No, you know what? I'll do both. I can do both, so I should do both. After all, you only get engaged once!"

God willing, Harper thought. She hardly recognized Poppy since she'd gotten engaged. It wasn't that she begrudged her best friend any of the excitement she was feeling. It was just that, with everything she had to contend with at work, she was having difficulty caring about what type of shellfish guests would be served.

"Unless you think that's too over-the-top?" Poppy asked, looking at Harper.

"At The Plaza? No such thing. I think it's perfect."

Over-the-top was Harper's credit card bill. She'd already spent a small fortune on a new dress after Poppy had decided to make the engagement party a black-tie affair and had opened a registry at ABC Carpet & Home, the extravagant home store that Poppy's family frequented. Charlotte had kept Harper so busy on the day the registry opened that Harper had missed the chance to buy the least-expensive option of monogrammed napkins and candlestick holders and had gotten the only quasi-affordable thing that wouldn't completely break the bank: a blown-glass decanter.

Harper stacked a small pile of clothes on one side of the couch. She wouldn't go home for Christmas for a few more days, but if she'd learned one thing from working at The Greenhouse, it was to make the most of her free time when she had it. Who knew what last-minute task Charlotte was getting ready to throw her way? After Charlotte launched her Clean Green Cleanse, Harper had been put in charge of hiring a diverse group of fitness instructors in a matter of days. *Just make sure we have one of everything. I want everyone to look different. Remember, Harper, everyone has a seat at our table . . . or in this case, workout bench.* Then she had to organize the film shoots with Aaron. *I offered videos, so we better have some!* On top of all that, Harper was also organizing the Christmas party with Bella. *Fuck, better call it a holiday party. I can't come across as insensitive!* She was ready for a real break.

Thankfully, Christmas this year was going to be a small affair with just her parents—the aunties were staying in California with their children—so she was looking forward to eating, cross-country skiing, and watching *Miracle on 34th Street* without running family commentary. Even so, things with Harper and her mother were still tense. Every time they talked, her mom harped on how she worked too much and was always distracted when they spoke. To which Harper always replied that she worked as much as she needed to and that she wasn't distracted, she was *busy*.

Like all of Harper's interactions outside of work, her communications with her parents and Poppy had been reduced to a series of infrequent text exchanges sent at times when the other couldn't respond immediately—most of which was Harper's fault. The reality was that she didn't have time to get into big conversations with anyone, let alone big text exchanges. She was so busy working that it was just easier to wait until she could see them in person. Still, she promised herself that she'd answer anytime Poppy sent a text ahead of her call that read *Wedding Business*. She was her maid of honor, after all.

"Don't forget to pack your cowboy hat for the engagement party," Poppy teased, reminding Harper to stay focused on the task at hand.

"I've packed three, actually: one for me, one for you, and one for Charles. It was going to be a surprise, but happy engagement!"

Poppy laughed. "I was wondering if maybe you wanted to pack a cowboy too? I'd make an exception to the no-plus-one rule for my maid of honor, you know."

Harper crossed her legs on the couch and pulled the laptop closer. "When would I have time to meet a cowboy?"

"What about Aaron?" Poppy asked, fiddling with the metal straw in her drink. "I guess I was kind of hoping it wasn't all work that's been keeping you so busy."

"Poppy, you'd be the first person I'd tell."

"Really?"

"Well, after Sloan, that is," Harper teased.

"Ouch!" Poppy joked. "She's a new friend, like Bella, but she's no replacement for you."

Harper felt a mix of relief and regret all at once. "I'm glad to hear it. And I'm glad that you have a new friend. It's important. I miss having friends around." The reality of just how lonely she'd been now that she had a minute to catch her breath hit her. "Things aren't that good with Bella and me right now."

"What's going on?"

"Let's just say it turns out that there's as much competition as there is community at The Greenhouse, and every win I get with Charlotte is a loss with someone else. But I guess that's just the price of success."

"Wow, that's dark."

"I'm serious! Take a look at Charlotte—she's incredibly popular and super successful, and yet her fellow Instagrammers would like nothing more than to see her fall flat on her face."

"How come?"

"They're *jealous*. They know she's winning, and they can't stand it. Because no one wants to see a self-made mogul like Charlotte climb her way to the top of Forbes' most successful entrepreneurs. Even her husband is jealous of her."

"That's sad," Poppy said.

"It's life. I guess that's why they say it's lonely at the top. Let's face it, if everyone is out to get you, you've got to be doing something right." Harper grabbed her bottomless cup of coffee. She'd been working so much lately that she'd taken to hiding coffee in her water bottle at work, hoping that no one would call her out on it. It wasn't exactly part of Charlotte's clean green regimen, but then again, neither were the triple nonfat matchas Harper had gotten for her this week.

Poppy put her drink down and looked at Harper, her face serious. "You don't really think that, do you? I mean, it's possible to get ahead and not leave a trail of haters in your wake."

"Maybe. If you're connected and have an all-expense-paid trip to the top on a path that someone else has carved for you, then yeah, it's possible."

An awkward silence fell between them, the realization that Harper could've been talking about Poppy hitting them both.

"Well . . ." Poppy said slowly, "maybe the reason her colleagues aren't rooting for her has less to do with her success and more with her as a person."

Harper exhaled sharply and shook her head. "Would you say that about a man? That he has to be likable?"

"I'm not being sexist about women in general—I'm saying it about Charlotte."

"Who you don't even know," Harper snapped, the irritation in her voice unmistakable. Harper waited for Poppy to say that Harper didn't really know Charlotte either. After all, she'd heard it a hundred times from her mother and aunts, so she didn't need to hear it again.

"No, you're right, I don't," Poppy said quietly.

Harper hadn't expected that, but she appreciated it. "I should probably go. I still have to shower."

"Right, of course. See you soon—can't wait," Poppy said, trying to sound cheerful.

"Me either," Harper replied, although, by the looks on both their faces, neither of them quite meant it.

33

Gin-gle All the Way

"Well, well, she owns a *dress*," Oliver said as Harper walked in. He was standing at the bar of the Valedictorian, wearing a beautiful silver suit, glittery silver loafers, and a light green silk T-shirt that matched his eyes. He looked perfectly at home in the swanky boutique hotel in downtown Nashville. Harper was sure that Charlotte had chosen the holiday party venue for its dark green velvet booths and palm leaf wallpaper, its color scheme in keeping with The Greenhouse's own. With its marble floors and gold bamboo mirrors, it had a real Hollywood Regency vibe, an old-world glamor that Harper's dress—the same one she'd bought for Poppy's engagement party—was perfectly attired for. Oliver sipped his gin martini and raised his eyebrows in approval at her outfit.

"This isn't just a dress. It's a *designer* dress," Harper teased, turning around once. "At least that's what the sign said in the clearance section of Nordstrom's. I got it for an engagement party."

"You're engaged?" Aaron asked, joining the conversation.

"Why, hello there," Oliver said as he checked out Aaron, making both him and Harper laugh. Harper was gobsmacked by how good Aaron looked. He was wearing a modern slim suit over a simple gray T-shirt. His hair, still slightly damp from showering, was brushed back from his forehead and tucked behind his ears. "Clearly, that sale at Nordstrom was a good one. And here I am in this old thing. Next time someone tell me," Oliver teased.

"You look fabulous," Harper said, "and no, I'm not engaged. My best friend, Poppy, is. She's having her engagement party on Christmas Eve Eve. But no sense in making a good dress wait." She picked the menu of customized drinks off the bar—all starting with *g*, naturally—and ordered a gimlet.

"You know that's not a thing, Christmas Eve Eve," Oliver said, smirking.

"I know, but I'm not going to be the one who tells her," Harper replied, taking her drink from the bartender. "The first rule of being a maid of honor? *The bride is always right.*"

"I'm always the maid of honor," Bella said, startling them all as she appeared behind them. She looked incredible in a long-sleeved black sequined dress that stopped mid-thigh and showed off her toned legs. Oliver let out a low whistle, and she swatted him playfully.

"Being a maid of honor is such a big job. All those events and parties, the bachelorette party and shopping for the wedding dress, helping out with the rehearsal dinner and the post-wedding brunch? You're essentially on call until the bride and groom go on their honeymoon. It's like another full-time job."

"Right," Harper said, suddenly wishing she had more time to help Poppy. "Well, thankfully, my friend has it all under control."

"For now, but don't count on it. I've seen even the most level-headed people turn into total bridezillas. All the stress can really get in the way."

Oliver was quiet for a moment and then looked at each of them. "Do you mean the kind of stress that gets in the way of friendships? Because I've seen that happen," he said.

Harper and Bella looked at each other awkwardly.

"Maybe," they said at the same time, making each other smile.

"Well, here's to a holiday without bridezillas, or friendzillas, or mother-in-lawzillas," Oliver said, raising his glass. "Now that we've cleared that up," he said, turning to the bartender, "it's time for another round. Four glasses of gampagne, please."

"Champagne?" Bella said, taking her glass once it was poured and looking at Oliver questioningly.

"It's not champagne, it's *gampagne*, with a *g*, and we're drinking it because we're celebrating," he said.

"We *are*?" Harper asked.

"Yes. Liam and I have been matched with a baby, and we're going to be parents!" Oliver said, his whole face breaking into a smile.

"Oh my God, that's incredible," Bella said. "I'm so happy for you!"

"Congratulations," Harper said.

"Amazing," Aaron chimed in, slapping Oliver on the arm.

"Thank you. We've been waiting so long that I can't believe it's finally happening."

"Liam must be so excited," Bella said.

"Excited and terrified. He told his job that he was going to need paternity leave and they let him go."

"What?!" they all said.

"They can't do that," Harper said.

"Actually, they can, and they did. There's no union of interior designers, so we're kind of screwed."

"What are you going to do?"

"Well, Charlotte's offered me a raise so Liam can stay home with the baby for the time being. And she's agreed to let me take my paid paternity leave, but we're so busy right now that I'm not going to be able to take more than a few weeks. All of it means that I'll be working more. Helping Ryan with his show and getting that off the ground was part of the deal." He forced a smile and took a large drink.

Harper, Aaron, and Bella stood in silence for a moment, and Harper knew what they were all thinking—how could Oliver work any more than he already did? But now wasn't the time to spoil the good news.

"This is the best news ever," Bella said brightly.

"Well, let's see if you still think so after you hear Charlotte's good news."

"Oh?" Bella asked, leaning in.

"Well, I'm not supposed to say anything but . . . the votes are in for employee of the year, and it looks like you're the winner!" He squeezed Bella's hand. "Charlotte's going to make the announcement tonight."

"Oh, Bella, that's amazing!" Harper said, hugging her. She was thrilled and relieved. Now Bella could lay to rest any of her suspicions that Harper's success was impeding her own.

"I think we're going to need more *gampagne*, please!" Harper called out to the bartender, making Bella laugh.

"I think we're going to need some food too," Aaron said, eyeing Harper's empty glass.

"I think I'm going to need to sit down before I faint," Bella said, her face glowing with joy.

Harper and Bella grabbed the last vacant booth as Aaron went to get some footage and Oliver was whisked off by a group of adoring and ambitious young employees that Harper knew were vying for the role of event maestro, recently vacated by Tiffany. On the makeshift dance floor Cynthia was getting down and dirty, egged on by a small group of tech employees with some impressive moves of their own. It was clear by the volume of the party, how busy the bartenders were, and how quickly the trays of hors d'oeuvres were being emptied that everyone from The Greenhouse needed to blow off some steam.

"Go, Cynthia! Go, Cynthia!" Bella cheered.

Cynthia danced over to their table, beaming. "Don't think you two are going to get away without joining me for one last dance."

"Last dance?" Harper asked, surprised.

"Oh yeah, the hubs got a promotion so we're moving to Arizona!" she said, leaning on the table to catch her breath.

A look of shock covered Bella's face, and she choked on her gampagne.

"Does Charlotte know?" Bella asked.

"Oh, she will, I just emailed her my resignation. We leave in two weeks!" A song by Lizzo came on, and Cynthia threw her hands in the air and returned to the dance floor.

"Wow, and just like that she's gone. Can you imagine?" Harper said, with a mixture of awe and disbelief.

"That's Cynthia for you. She always said this was *just a job*."

Harper and Bella were quiet for a moment, and then Harper spotted a waiter passing by with a full tray of sushi. "Oh, excuse me, we'll take that." She placed the tray between her and Bella and popped an avocado roll in her mouth.

"Nicely done," Bella said, filling a napkin with California rolls. They ate in silence for a moment and then started to speak at the same time. They laughed.

"You go first," Harper said, refilling their glasses with the bottle of gampagne she'd gotten at the bar.

"I just wanted to say that I'm sorry I took out my insecurities about Charlotte on you. I've really been struggling to find the time to give to work *and* my mom, who needs me right now."

"I'm so sorry. It must be so hard to have all of that on you," Harper said, reaching for Bella's hand.

"Thanks. The truth is, I could've juggled it all a year ago, but things haven't been the same since Mandy left, and Tiffany leaving made it even worse. I've been so wrung out and I think everything has just made me really paranoid. I know that it was Charlotte's idea to have you at the lunch, but it still hurt. I'm really sorry." Bella gripped Harper's hand harder and gave it a little squeeze.

"No, I'm sorry. I should've said something right away instead of waiting. We could've dealt with it and moved on, but instead, I made it all weird by avoiding you and keeping it a secret. You should've gone to that luncheon, not me. But if it's any consolation, I didn't even get to eat lunch, and I got the worst hangover from the wine."

"Small consolation, but I'll take it," Bella said, smiling.

"Friends?" Harper asked tentatively.

"Of course. Friend-friends, not just Green-friends."

"Cheers to that!" Harper clinked her glass with Bella's and took a long sip, relief washing over her. She looked around the room. Conspicuously absent were Charlotte and Ryan.

"She should've been here by now. I know she and Ryan like to make an entrance, but this is late even for them," Bella said, checking her messages.

"I'm sure everything's fine."

"Yeah, you're probably right. I'm having such a hard time reading her lately, and that's not like me. One minute she's telling me she couldn't do anything without me, the next I'm getting the cold shoulder because she's convinced that I knew that Mandy and Tiffany were leaving."

"I know, but you heard Oliver. You're *employee of the year,* so obviously she's moved past that. You weathered the Charlotte Tsunami, and there are clear skies ahead. Don't worry," Harper said, her own phone lighting up. To her surprise, it was Tasha.

"Hello?" Harper said, getting up to take the call in the lobby where she could hear.

"Oh, hi, I didn't think you were going to pick up, so I was going to leave a message. Are you at a concert?"

"No, I'm at our holiday party. It's really loud," Harper said.

"Right. Well, I won't keep you, but I wanted to let you know Charlotte is quickly becoming the star of this article, so I was just hoping that we could meet up again. Could you give me a tour of The Greenhouse?"

"Wow, that's great. Do you want me to arrange a meeting so you can talk to Charlotte?" Harper asked.

"No worries, I'll set that up. I'd love to talk to you some more, though. My editor really loved the whole 'new girl with fresh eyes' angle. It lets more people in, and readers can relate to what you say because you're not just some brainwashed groupie."

It made a lot of sense, so Harper agreed. She liked Tasha, and she was happy to hear that she wanted to learn more about Charlotte. Maybe the article could just be about Charlotte, and she could skip the other women altogether. If Harper could pull that off, she could be promoted to event maestro, and then Bella could have the director of communications job and they wouldn't be forced into competing. It was worth a shot.

Harper was hanging up when the music cranked up to ear-splitting levels, and she turned to see Charlotte and Ryan making their entrance to Beyoncé's "Crazy in Love." Ryan was dressed in a dark green velvet suit to match Charlotte, who was stunning in her green sequined jumpsuit and platform heels, her blond hair blown out and waved perfectly around her face. They were holding hands and waving to everyone, but something was off—Harper thought that their tight smiles seemed almost angry. She glanced over at Bella to see if she noticed it too, and judging by the look on her face, she did.

"Charlotte, you look amazing," Harper said when she reached their table.

"You really do," Bella agreed.

"Do me a favor and make sure he doesn't have too much to drink, will you?" Charlotte asked, nodding at Ryan, who was already at the bar. "I need to find Oliver." With that, she rushed off.

"Shit, my mom's calling," Bella said, checking her phone.

"Go take it. I'll watch him." Harper moved toward Ryan, who already had two gimlets in front of him and was in the process of downing one.

"Oh, you ordered me a drink. You shouldn't have," Harper said when she reached him, trying to sound playful.

"Let me guess. *Mom* told you to keep an eye on me," Ryan mocked.

"No, she wanted me to see if you would like any food or—*water?*" Harper asked, nodding to the bartender, who filled a glass with water and placed it in front of Ryan.

"Oh, for fuck's sake. I don't need a babysitter. It's a party, aren't I supposed to have fun?" he said loudly.

"Is he bothering you, miss?" the bartender asked, leaning forward with a raised brow.

"Excuse me?" Ryan interrupted. "Do you know who I am? I'm paying for this fucking party."

"No, sir, Charlotte Green is paying for this party, and if you want to stay, I suggest you simmer down."

"He's fine. I've got it, thank you." Harper pulled Ryan away from the bar and out into the lobby, where they would be out of sight of the employees.

"Did you hear that? *Charlotte Green is paying.* There wouldn't be a Charlotte Green without me, now would there?" Ryan said, spilling his drink a little as he stumbled. He fished in his pocket, pulled out a cigarette, and lit it.

"Excuse me, sir!" the doorman exclaimed, coming toward them.

"I'm sorry. We're going outside," Harper said, and pushed Ryan through the revolving doors and out into the cold night air. "You can't smoke in there. And that's not because of Charlotte—that's the law."

She watched for a few seconds as he fumbled to light his cigarette and, unable to watch him struggle any longer, took the lighter from him and pressed down hard to emit a bright blue flame. Ryan leaned in and steadied his hand on Harper's as he finally lit his cigarette. He took a drag and waited a beat before stepping back and blowing smoke in the air.

"I didn't think you'd still be here," he said, narrowing his eyes at Harper.

"It's only nine o'clock," she said.

"I didn't think you'd still be *here*, working for Charlotte," he said, slurring.

"Why not?" Harper asked, waiting for the usual list that people gave her.

"You're too much like her."

That one Harper hadn't expected.

"Excuse me?"

"You're ambitious and driven and have something to prove. It reminds me of a young Charlotte, before she became, well . . . Charlotte. Plus, I hear the way she talks about you. And I've read the stuff you've been writing for her. You're impressive."

Harper felt her cheeks burn. "I'm just doing my job."

He sucked on his cigarette and smirked. "Just as long as it's your job that you're doing because, believe me, the second Charlotte thinks you're trying to do *her* job and crowding in on *her spotlight*, you're in trouble. Trust me, I'd know," he said a little too loudly. "She makes you think she really believes in you while you're working for her, but the second you try and step out on your own, you're out."

"I'm sure that's not true."

"Oh really? You've seen the way she dismisses me like I'm some lowly intern she had to let go instead of her husband. Always making comments about me not working. Well, you know what, I *am* working. I have a *Mister Class*!"

Harper was aware of a few people stopping to stare at them on their way into the hotel and faked a laugh as if Ryan had just said something hilarious. The last thing she needed was for people to start talking.

"Excuse me, oh my gosh, are you Harper Cruz?" a young woman standing with her friends asked.

"Yes," Harper said, trying to place where she had seen them before. "Have we met?"

"No, but we follow you on Insta. You're Harper, Charlotte Green's support strategist."

"Yeah, I am," Harper said, taken aback.

"Do you mind if we get a picture of you?" the young woman asked, not waiting for an answer as she and her friends whipped out their phones to take selfies with Harper.

"Hang on," one of the girls said, walking up to Ryan, who was happy to be noticed. He slicked back his hair and smiled. "Would you mind taking one of us all together?" She handed him her phone.

Harper saw the look on Ryan's face that said he was about to explode and grabbed the phone. "You know, better yet, why don't we get all of you a picture with *Charlotte*? She's just inside. Tell the host I sent you," Harper said, rushing them off—and not a moment too soon.

"What the fuck was that?" Ryan smashed his glass on the ground. "Do I look like some assistant?"

"Ryan!" Harper shouted, stepping away from the broken glass in shock as a security guard ran outside.

"Sir, you're going to have to leave." The security guard took him by the arm.

"Get your hands off me!" Ryan said, losing his balance. Harper looked around, aware that people were starting to stare.

"Sir, please, let me get him an Uber. I promise, he'll go right now," she said. The guard paused for a moment, considering, then sighed.

"Two minutes, and if he's still here, I'm calling the cops."

Harper pulled Ryan away from the building and ordered an Uber that was a minute out. "You have to go home," she said to Ryan sternly.

"I don't have to do anything," he sneered at her.

"Yeah, you do, because any minute those girls are going to come back out and take pictures and post them and there goes your *Mister Class*."

"This is bullshit. You know that, right? It's my money that paid for her to start all this. She wouldn't be here without me, which means you wouldn't be here without me either!" Ryan yelled.

It was such an ugly display that Harper was relieved to see the Uber pull up. She opened the door and practically pushed Ryan in before sending him off.

————

"I'm so sorry, I didn't know what else to do," Harper said, her brow furrowed, after Charlotte had finished posing with the trio of young women under an archway of green, white, and gold balloons that had been set up for perfect Instagram shots. Behind her, the party was in full swing, with the rest of her colleagues none the wiser about what had happened outside just a few minutes before.

"It sounds like you did the right thing," Oliver said, jumping in. He and Bella had rushed over when it was clear that something was wrong. "Where is he now?"

"In an Uber on his way home."

Charlotte closed her eyes and exhaled deeply. When she opened them again she turned to Bella. "This is all your fault. I asked you to watch him."

"I'm so sorry, but—"

"Charlotte, this isn't Bella's fault," Harper interrupted. "He was being really rude, and the bartender even threatened to throw him out." She glanced at Bella, who looked like she was going to burst into tears.

"So why didn't he?" Charlotte asked, looking Harper straight in the eye, her face hard.

"Because I took him outside—"

"So you avoided a scene here *and* outside while you, Bella, were doing . . . what?" Charlotte asked, her hands on her hips. Harper cringed as she heard Justin Timberlake's "Cry Me a River" play. *Not now*, she thought.

"I was talking to my mom," Bella said quietly. "She called, and I had to get it. I would never have left Ryan if I didn't think Harper could handle it."

Charlotte sat down at the bar, ordered a drink, and collected herself while they all waited. "Right, of course you wouldn't. I understand that."

Oliver's whole body sighed, and Bella exhaled loudly.

"Thank you, Charlotte," Bella said. "Thank you so much."

"Of course, Bells, I mean, I'm not a monster. I understand how much your family means to you. My family means a lot to me too. I've spent a lot of time building *this* Greenhouse family. Some people would say too

much time. Some husbands would say more time than I've spent with
my own family."

"Please, no one would say that if you were a man," Harper said,
hoping to change the subject.

"No, you're right, they wouldn't." Charlotte seemed to be considering
something as she took a sip of her drink. "Alrighty, let's give these Green
Awards out before I have another emergency to dodge," she said, hopping
off her barstool and walking ahead. She raised her hands to cut the music
and held up her bright green envelope that contained the name of the
employee of the year inside.

Charlotte walked onto the little stage at the far end of the room where
the DJ was set up and took the microphone.

"Everyone having an amazing time?" she asked, turning the microphone toward the cheering crowd. They apparently weren't cheering loud
enough. "I *said*, is everyone having an *amazing* time?!"

"YES!" everyone yelled.

"Great! And we'll get back to having an amazing time in just a minute.
But first, it's that time when we give out the award for employee of the
year. Now, this girl has stood by my side from the second she stepped
foot as a little seedling into The Greenhouse. She's shown intelligence,
initiative, and, if I'm honest, even reminds me a little of me."

Bella beamed. She fixed her hair and breathed in deeply. Harper
could feel the excitement coming off her and gave her arm a little squeeze.

"Now remember, ladies," Oliver whispered under his breath behind
them, "act surprised."

But he needn't have worried. Because when Charlotte opened the
envelope, she proudly exclaimed, "Everyone, please put your hands
together to congratulate . . . *Harper*!"

34

Cookie-tastrophe

Harper pulled her phone close to her face. It could be 5:00 a.m. or 10:00 a.m.—she had no idea. It was the first day of the holiday break and the one time she hadn't set her alarm. Wiping the sleep from her eyes, Harper rolled over in bed and opened the Vine to scroll through the holiday wishes coming in from everyone heading out of town two days before Christmas. Harper skimmed to see if there was anything new from Bella, which there wasn't. Bella had gone silent since the holiday party, but Harper kept hoping she'd give some indication that she was okay.

Harper's brief reconciliation with Bella had been torpedoed by Charlotte's last-minute decision to present Harper with the Employee of the Year award. It didn't matter how many times Harper tried to convince Bella that there was no way she could've known, let alone orchestrated the events of that night in her favor—Bella wouldn't listen. In the end, it was Oliver who talked Bella into taking a few extra days off to allow her to focus on her mom and give Charlotte a chance to cool down. Maybe a little distance would do both of them some good, even if it meant that

Oliver and Harper would be busier than ever and have to work right up until the moment the office closed. Once again, Harper was relieved that she had packed early, as there hadn't been a moment to spare.

She dropped the phone onto the bed and buried her face in her pillow as light streamed through the windows she had never bothered to get curtains for. What was the point in having curtains when she got up before the sun rose most days anyway? Tonight she would be back in New York, and, as it was less than a week—only five days—Harper planned on doing the unthinkable and actually unplugging from work. What was even more unthinkable was that Charlotte had suggested the idea to everyone, which, if Harper was honest, was probably the only reason she would be able to do it.

She heard the welcoming sound of her coffee machine beep three times and hopped out of bed and into the kitchen for her first of many cups. The programmable machine and her milk frother had been two of the best investments that Harper had made since moving to Nashville, easing the pain of the wake-ups that happened earlier and earlier and that couldn't be relieved by the French press. Harper downed the first half of her cup and then immediately refilled it to the top. Her flight wasn't until that afternoon, which meant that she still had time to do a little last-minute shopping for stocking stuffers at the airport.

After a quick shower and one final check that she had everything on her packing list, she was ready. She was just heading out when her phone rang. It was Charlotte.

"Harper, where are you?" Charlotte shouted into the phone.

"In my apartment. Why?"

"Oh, thank God, I need you to come over ASAP. It's an emergency."

"Is everything okay?"

"No, everything is *not* okay. Everything is terrible—that's why it's an emergency. Now can you help me or not?!"

A half hour later, Harper was walking into Charlotte's house.

"Who does this?" Charlotte railed. "What nanny just up and leaves before the holidays? She wanted Christmas off, so I gave her Christmas off. She can't just spring needing more time off on me days before the holiday! I get that she's got a family, but I have a family too, and my family pays for her to take care of her family, so you'd think she'd be a little more accommodating."

Harper walked through the house, which looked like a bomb had gone off. There were kids' toys and books strewn everywhere, and all the pillows had been taken off the couch to make a fort where Charlotte's young children were currently sprawled out watching a movie at full volume. The kitchen sink was full of dishes from that morning, and the island was covered in baking supplies.

"She just quit?"

"Yes! Well, no, I fired her. But what choice did I have? She works for me, not the other way around. Although now she works for no one, and she better not expect a letter of reference because she sure as shit isn't going to get one." Charlotte threw her hands up in the air. Still in her pajamas, Charlotte looked like she'd just rolled out of bed, her face makeup-free and her frizzy hair flying everywhere.

"Where's Ryan?" Harper asked.

"On a golf trip with Jameson, since he's spending the holidays with his mom, *again*. You'd think Ryan would insist he spend it with his brothers and sisters, since he only sees them a few times a year, but noooooooooo, we wouldn't want to upset *Jameson*," she muttered as she paced back and forth. "You know he blames me for breaking his parents up and for having to split his time between us? Why would he even think that? Annabelle, that's why. Well, let me tell you, it takes two to tango. You can't put the blame on me, *I was single*. Those two can hold a grudge, I'll give them that. Gold star for grudge holding."

"When's Ryan coming back?" Harper asked gently.

"He won't be back until late, which means that I have no one to watch the kids while I bake. We're supposed to deliver one hundred cookies to the children's hospital tomorrow, and there's no way I will be able to do that now. Oliver's gone, Bella's taking care of her mother, so it's just me. It's always just me." Charlotte burst into tears.

Harper stood glued to the spot, unsure whether she should comfort Charlotte or pretend that her outburst hadn't happened so she wouldn't embarrass her. For a moment, it looked like Charlotte had regained her composure. She wiped her face on her sleeve, took a deep breath, and stood up straight. But no sooner had she done so than her five kids started yelling about who got to pick the next movie, and Charlotte crumbled under the sound of their shrieking, ran out of the kitchen and up the stairs, leaving Harper alone.

What was she supposed to do? She stood in front of the TV.

"You're in the way! We can't see anything," Maddie shouted, wrestling the remote control from Henry.

"Give it back to me!" Henry yelled, lunging toward his sister.

"Stop fighting," Jagger said, throwing his hands up in the air and startling the twins, who were busy playing with their stuffed toys.

"Wow, okay, everyone, calm down," Harper said, taking the remote control from Maddie and holding it up in the air. "Now listen, your mom . . . has a bad headache, so you need to stop fighting."

"Tell that to her and my dad. They're the ones always fighting." Henry narrowed his eyes at Harper while Maddie scowled.

Harper felt herself soften at the sight of their angry little faces. No wonder they were acting out—they were scared. "Oh, you shouldn't worry about that; parents fight sometimes. Mine did, and they've been married thirty years."

"Thirty years! They must be old," Jagger said.

"Well, I wouldn't call them old, just older." Harper smiled. "Nothing wrong with being old. It's a good thing! It means you've done a lot of living."

"Mom says it means that people don't care about you anymore," Henry said, hugging one of the couch pillows closer to his body.

"Yeah, they only care about what's new and hot." Maddie snuck a look at Willow and Wyatt who had gone back to playing happily with their stuffed animals.

Harper sat down on the carpet and crossed her legs to face Maddie, Henry, and Jagger. "Hey, your mom doesn't really mean that. Being older also means that you're wiser. Think of all the things that you know and that you've done that Willow and Wyatt haven't even tried yet." She leaned in closer and whispered, "It kind of gives you three an advantage, doesn't it?" She winked at them, relieved when she saw them smile. She checked her watch—she still had a few of hours before she had to leave for the airport. "Now, what do you say? Do you want to help me tidy up, and then we can bake those cookies your mom needs for tomorrow? That could be fun, right?"

Henry and Maddie looked at each other and then at Harper. "I don't know," Henry said.

"What's in it for us?" Maddie asked.

"Your mom will be so surprised!"

"And?" Maddie said.

"You'll be setting a great example for Willow and Wyatt." She had a feeling she knew where this was going.

"And?" Maddie said again, rubbing her thumb and fingers together.

"And I'll give you ten bucks each," Harper said.

"Deal!" Maddie, Henry, and Jagger answered.

It would seem to Harper that she had overestimated the children's capacity for chores and underestimated Charlotte's for wallowing. After a few hours of cleaning, organizing, and getting the kids dressed, she heated up a frozen pizza for lunch and turned on a movie, the one with the longest running time being the winner. She was exhausted, and there was no way she'd be able to bake cookies before she had to leave for the airport. As the kids stared at the screen, she tiptoed up the stairs and knocked on Charlotte's door, opening it when no one answered.

"Charlotte?" she whispered into the darkened bedroom. "I'm going to have to get going, or else I'm going to miss my flight."

She waited but got no reply. "Charlotte?" she said, creeping across the white shag carpeting to the bed, where Charlotte lay with a pillow under her knees and a quilted eye mask on, an essential oil diffuser spritzing the air with the calming scent of lavender.

She didn't know whether to stand or sit on the bed. She had never been in her boss's bedroom before, and so she ended up half crouching, half leaning over her, waiting for a response. She shook Charlotte's arm gently to wake her.

"What time is it?" Charlotte murmured.

"It's just after noon. The house is clean and the kids have eaten, but I really have to go to the airport now. I'm cutting it close."

"And the cookies?" Charlotte said, turning toward her, lifting her eye mask.

"I'm sorry, I don't have time to bake them," she said sadly, feeling as if she had let Charlotte down.

"Of course not. Thanks for everything." Charlotte squeezed her hand. "It's nice to know there is one woman who has my back."

"Oh, there are lots of women who have your back," Harper said, looking at Charlotte's hand in hers.

"No, there really aren't. You'll see. One day when you're as successful as I am, you'll see how easily they can turn on you. They're just waiting for me to fail, and it looks like they're going to get their wish. The lawsuit with Mandy, the list of expectations from Serene—even Ryan wants me to fail, all so he can prove that I can't do it without him. Do you know that he's been threatening a divorce?"

"That's terrible," Harper said.

"Terrible for my *brand*, which is why he's doing it. He's not upset that I'm not a better *wife*. He's upset that I'm a better *business*. It wasn't supposed to be this way. As far as he was concerned, this was supposed to be a hobby, a way to keep me busy so I'd stay home with the kids and stay out of the way. But I'm good at this. I'm better than all those other influencers put together, and that's the problem." She sat up, leaned back against the bed's tufted headboard, and pulled her knees to her chest. "You think they'd just let me have it. They don't need it like I do. C.J. with her collection of companies that she's backed, Evie with her millions, and Chloé with her sugar daddy. It's not the same. *I* built all of this through hard work and hustle, not Ivy League connections, and if it all goes away, I'll have nothing to show for it."

You'll have your kids, Harper thought, but before she could say it, Charlotte beat her to it. "I know, I'll have my kids, and I adore them, but I don't want to *just* be a mom to them; I want to be an *inspiration*. I want to show them they can have it all if they can give it their all. I don't want them to see me as a failure."

It was a lot to take in, and the fact that Charlotte trusted Harper enough to share this with her—and believed that Harper could be as successful as she was someday—made her feel special in a way that nothing and no one else she had worked for ever had. Maybe Ryan was right: maybe she and Charlotte really were alike after all. *What would Charlotte do if she were in my shoes?* Harper thought, and the answer came to her the moment she asked the question.

"Well, you're not going to fail," Harper said firmly. Because if Charlotte failed, Harper failed, and Harper was employee of the year, so there was no way she was going to fail. She'd push her flight by a day, she'd get her mom's special polvoron cookie recipe, and she'd wait to leave until Ryan got home. And tomorrow, when Charlotte was feeling like herself, she'd know that it was Harper who had saved the day.

35

Non Voyage!

Wishing you a Green Holiday and an inspiring New Year,
from our family to yours!
xoxo, Charlotte, Ryan, Maddie, Henry, Jagger,
Willow, Wyatt, and Jameson

Harper stared at the holiday card set out for her on Charlotte's kitchen island. It was one of those professional vacation shots taken by a resort photographer. Dressed in various shades of white and beige on a bright green golf course with the ocean behind them, the family nestled together lovingly and smiled wide for the camera. On the other side, there was a handwritten note:

> OMG! The cookies are delicious! The kids at the hospital are going to love them. Help yourself to coffee and whatever else you want to eat. If I don't talk to you before you leave, have a wonderful holiday!
>
> xo Charlotte

Harper reread the note for the third time, making sure she hadn't missed anything. But no matter how many times she read it, there was no true thank-you, no declaration of undying gratitude or statement about how Harper was the best, nothing that would indicate that just hours before—and it really *was* only hours before—Harper had been baking and wrapping cookies before falling asleep in her clothes in the guest room. Harper had *saved the day*.

She parsed out the words again. Like a middle schooler obsessing over a yearbook message from her secret crush, she was trying to find hidden meaning in Charlotte's choice of words. *OMG!* (that was good, she'd even used an exclamation mark!), *delicious!* (delicious was great; she could have said good or yummy!), *help yourself...* (which was really saying make yourself at home—like family, because you're like family), *If I don't talk to you . . .* (because I obviously have no plans to, or else I would've woken you up or left you a text message or a voice mail, but I didn't, so that means that I won't), but *have a wonderful holiday* (another exclamation mark!).

Harper's eyes rested on the little *xo* at the bottom of the note. It was Charlotte's signature sign-off, the one she did for everyone, and her stomach fell. She had been expecting so much more. There had to be more. And then she realized no one else at The Greenhouse had gotten one of these cards, and what's more, Charlotte had written it by hand. A handwritten note was so much more meaningful and personal than just a text. But that didn't stop Harper from grabbing her phone the second she heard it beep in the hopes that it was a notification was from Charlotte. Instead, it was from the airline:

Weather warning. Please allow extra time for departure. And it was then that she looked out the window and saw it—snow, rapidly falling from the sky.

"Is there any way you can go faster?" Harper asked, checking her watch from the back seat of her Uber. She had already pushed her flight to the last one available and if she missed this one, she was in trouble. By the time she left Charlotte's, half the roads were closed due to weather, and she managed to get the only Uber driver who refused to go a single mile above the speed limit.

"Sure, I could go faster, but the roads are really slippery, and it's not like I have snow tires. Not that I've ever really needed them, but with all this global warming, who's to say what we need nowadays."

Harper could say what was needed—less talking and more speeding, that's what. If she was in NYC, her taxi would be flying down the streets, avoiding bicyclists and buses and narrowly missing hot dog carts on the sidewalk with every hectic turn. She refreshed the airline's app and was relieved to see that her flight had been delayed by an hour, which would give her more than enough time to get to the airport and still get to her parents' place around four. She'd have just enough time for a quick hello, shower, and outfit change and still make it to Poppy's engagement party by seven thirty. It was tight but doable.

After what seemed like an eternity, Harper arrived at the airport along with half of Nashville. Unable to find a curbside spot to stop, Harper insisted her driver let her out in the middle of the road, even though it was against the law, even though he was sure he would get a ticket, and if he got a ticket, she was paying for it. And in her effort to get her suitcase out of the trunk as quickly as possible, she ended up losing a wheel. Dragging it across three lanes of traffic and into the airport, she jostled her way through the crowd gaping at the screens for updates on their flights at the American Airlines kiosk, checked herself in and went through security, and headed to her departure gate, only to find it completely full. People stood in line, ready to board, their faces tired and angry, even though boarding hadn't been announced and the screen behind the frazzled-looking attendants flashed DELAYED. Surely all these people couldn't be here for the same flight. She worked her way up to the counter and waited for two attendants to finish their conversation and acknowledge her.

"I just don't see it happening, not with all these delays," one said to the other.

"There's no way all these people are getting out of here."

"What does Delta say?"

"Delta canceled their flights for the day, United Airlines too. They're not even prepared to reschedule. We're the only ones still flying out."

"Not without a plane we're not."

"We still don't have one?"

"Not large enough for all these folks."

"Well, don't call it yet. I don't want a riot. I'm still hopeful we can get one or two more flights out in the next hour or so, but after that, I hear that LaGuardia's not going to let anyone else land."

"Are you serious?" Harper asked, making them turn to face her.

"Oh, you heard all that, did you, hon?" the first attendant asked, her face full of sympathy.

"Unfortunately, yes," Harper said, panic rising in her. "Please tell me that I'm going to be able to get out today. My best friend's engagement party is tonight."

The attendant took Harper's boarding pass and entered her information into the computer.

"Let's see, when were you supposed to leave?" She frowned and then looked at Harper. "Huh, that's too bad; it looks like you rescheduled. If you'd left earlier, you'd be fine."

Harper's cheeks burned. "I couldn't leave, I had a work . . . emergency."

"Well, I hope your boss appreciates you, because nobody is going anywhere unless this weather turns around. And even if it does let up, I can't make any guarantees. We're the only ones with flights still departing, and we're overbooked."

"You're *overbooked*?"

"Afraid so," she said, sliding the boarding pass back to Harper.

"But I *have* a seat," Harper cried.

"Well, actually, it looks like you're booked to go standby."

"What? No, that's a mistake!" Harper said, worrying that in her rush she had booked the wrong flight. "I need to get home by Christmas."

"Well, you might want to make other arrangements," the attendant said, sighing heavily. "With all our other flights booked and everyone else canceling theirs, I doubt you'd even get a seat."

"No, please, I really need to get home," Harper said, her voice rising.

"I know, honey, I know. Hang on," she said, answering her phone. Judging by the way her face fell, Harper guessed that it wasn't good news. She hung up the phone and leaned in close to Harper and whispered, "If I were you, I would start driving. They just canceled the rest of our flights. It'll take you a whole day by car, but you should be fine as long as they don't declare a state of emergency."

———————

Thirty minutes later, a state of emergency was declared. Worse than the call to her parents, who were understandably disappointed but still hopeful Harper would get on a flight by Christmas, was the one to Poppy. She was beyond angry.

"So you're telling me that you're going to miss my engagement party because your boss needed a daylong nap and someone to bake her fucking cookies?"

It wasn't like Poppy to swear, but she was more than making up for it now.

"I know, I know, I'm sorry. I wouldn't have stayed if it wasn't so serious. She was really distraught," Harper said, holding the phone closer to her ear and wincing as Poppy continued to yell.

"Like your maid of honor not coming to your *fucking* engagement party kind of distraught? The only thing I asked of you is to just show up. You didn't even have to do anything except be there."

"Poppy, I'm sorry! I thought I could just take another flight and be back in time—I didn't know it was going to storm. Believe me, I wanted nothing more than to celebrate with you and Charles tonight."

There was a long silence on the other end of the line, and for a moment, Harper thought the call had dropped. But then Poppy spoke, her voice cold and hard. "I really wish that were true, Harper, but the truth is you do want something more than that, and I hope she gives it to you." Poppy hung up.

Harper was shaking as she made her way through the terminal, tears streaming down her face. She'd expected Poppy to be disappointed, but she had thought that because of the snowstorm, she would be more understanding. The last thing she'd expected was for Poppy to blame Harper for missing the party. To make things worse, Harper knew that Poppy was right, at least in part—she had made a choice, and that choice had been Charlotte.

She pulled out her phone and checked The Greenhouse Instagram to see several reels of Charlotte and her family visiting kids in the hospital and handing out cookies. She scrolled through the comments about how wonderful and selfless Charlotte was, how supportive her husband and kids were, and how unbelievable it was that she had found time, on top of everything else, to bake for these kids. Next to all the comments, Charlotte had clicked the little heart indicating that she liked the message, but not once did she reply or comment to reveal that it was Harper who had been selfless and generous and done all the baking. She could understand not mentioning it the first time somebody commented, but the other comments were logged over a series of hours, and surely it would have crossed Charlotte's mind at some point to say something about Harper. The only thing even remotely close was a response Charlotte had written to someone who complimented her on how delicious the cookies looked. *Thanks, babes, one of my favorite fam holiday recipes! xo*

She stumbled out to the curb, her whole body deflating at the sight of the long line for a taxi. If only she had leased a damn car. It would be at least an hour before she could get a cab—not that it mattered. It's not like she was in a rush to be anywhere anymore. She joined the hordes of angry and disappointed travelers, their faces tired and stressed as they called the people they were supposed to fly out to see to tell them they wouldn't be coming. Every now and then, someone would give a weather update. *It's supposed to stop in an hour, they're saying it's the worst in history, tomorrow's weather calls for clear skies*, and people would look back at their little screens in the hope that their flights would resume, but no such luck. You didn't need a weather app to tell you that, by the way cars were slipping and sliding and unable to get out of the airport, nobody was going anywhere.

As soon as people accepted this, the frenzy to get a room at the airport hotel kicked in. It was this latest development, the idea of spending Christmas Eve Eve ordering a microwaved burger and emptying the minibar in a sad hotel room, instead of being with Poppy and Charles eating oysters and drinking champagne at The Plaza, that made Harper burst into tears. Poppy was right to be mad at her. If it wasn't for Poppy, she wouldn't have had a roof over her head while living in Manhattan. Poppy had done so much for her, and she'd let her down. The crying started softly and gradually gained volume and strength, causing a ripple effect that no surrounding baby or toddler was capable of resisting.

"I'm so sorry," Harper said, as parents stared at her in disbelief, their own children now wailing. "I didn't mean to . . . It's my best friend's engagement party tonight at The Plaza," she tried to explain feebly, only to be met with unsympathetic stares until she finally excused herself and got out of line.

"Harper!" she heard a voice yell. She turned around to see Aaron coming toward her. "What are you doing here?" he asked, taking in her tear-stained face.

"Making babies cry and being an awful friend," she said, wiping her nose on her sleeve.

"No, I mean," he said, trying not to laugh, "why are you still in Nashville? I thought you were leaving yesterday?"

"Me too," Harper said, crying even harder as Aaron wrapped his arm around her.

"It's okay," he said, pulling her close, making her dissolve into a puddle of tears.

"It's really not," she muttered into his shoulder. But if she was going to be stuck anywhere, she thought, closing her eyes and inhaling his scent, this was a nice place to be.

36

To Bee or Not to Be

As Harper stepped up into Aaron's car and he started the engine, she promised herself she would never make fun of another pickup truck again. High off the ground with big fat tires, it traveled through the snowstorm with ease. Harper warmed her hands on the heating vent that blasted hot air.

"Wait, you know why I was at the airport, but why were you there?"

Aaron was quiet for a moment as he changed lanes and then looked sideways at Harper as if deciding whether to tell her.

"What?" Harper asked, wiping her nose self-consciously.

"I was dropping Charlotte and her family off," he said. "They're flying with Ryan's family to spend Christmas in the Bahamas."

"Not in this they aren't," Harper said, feeling slightly better to know that Charlotte's plans were going to be messed up too.

"Actually, yeah, they are. They were the last private plane out."

There were so many things in that sentence that upset Harper that she didn't know where to start. She sighed heavily, leaned back against her seat, and closed her eyes. "I should've asked them to drop me off in New York City."

"I'm sorry. If it makes you feel any better, at least you *had* holiday plans that got canceled. I have no plans for the holidays, which is actually even sadder."

Harper turned her head toward him. "Except something tells me that was intentional and that you like spending the holidays on your own."

Aaron shrugged and smiled. "Well, kind of. It's a long story."

"Well, if you care to share it, I'm not going anywhere," she said, not wanting to pry but kind of wanting to pry.

"Well, maybe I'll tell you over dinner. You still owe me dinner, by the way, although you might be getting off easy since I don't think a lot's going to be open in this weather."

"Shit," Harper said. "I don't have anything in my fridge."

"Do you ever?" Aaron asked. "I doubt you cook a lot."

"Well, that's just rude."

"No, I just mean working as much as you do, it's got to be a lot of takeout."

"It is," Harper admitted. "And coffee and peanut butter. I always have coffee in my freezer and peanut butter in my fridge."

"Yeah, well, at least I know you're not a psychopath," Aaron said, making her laugh. "I'll tell you what—why don't we go back to my place and I can see what I can rustle up for us to eat? Unless you have other plans you were hoping to miss."

"Um, no, I'm thinking my friend's engagement party and Christmas Eve lunch at my parents' is good for now. I'll have to let you know about Christmas Day and the rest of it. It really depends on this weather and how upset I want people to be with me even if I can get on a flight."

"Sounds good. My place it is, then." Harper looked away so he couldn't see her blush.

There was a small part of Harper that wished Aaron lived in a boring boxy condo or some tiny dingy apartment—anything that could pierce his cool-guy image that Harper hated to admit he lived up to. It would also put a damper on the stirrings she was feeling in her long-neglected and left-for-dead libido. Instead, she found herself standing in his stereo-typical yet ridiculously gorgeous loft in a converted garment factory, with exposed brick walls that boasted an assortment of guitars and worn hardwood floors that were covered in old Persian rugs. There were even café lights dangling alongside the exposed pipes in the kitchen, and Harper was willing to bet there would be some retro Americana quilt on his bed . . . not that she was thinking about his bed. *Don't think about his bed*, she thought to herself.

"Wow, this place is ridiculous," she said, taking off her coat and hanging it on the rack by the door.

"Ridiculous?" Aaron asked, stepping out of his boots.

"As in amazing. I mean, it looks like it's out of a movie or something."

"A music video," Aaron replied.

"What?"

"Not a movie, a music video. I shot a music video in here for one of my songs, and a friend of mine art-directed the whole thing. I liked the way it looked so much that I just left everything the way it is. He's letting me keep everything until he needs any of it again."

"A music video—that's a big jump from open mic night," she said, looking at his guitars.

"Well, don't get too excited. That was a year ago. I haven't actually done anything with it yet." He filled a kettle with water and put it on the stove, then grabbed a couple of mugs from the cupboard and loaded up a French press with coffee.

"Why haven't you done anything with it yet?" Harper asked, but Aaron just shrugged.

"I got busy, and then, well . . . I've got a good thing going at The Greenhouse, and I'm not sure I want to mess that up," he said, bringing their mugs over and setting them down on the coffee table. He walked over to an old dresser that doubled as a bar and offered up a bottle of Baileys. "Some holiday cheer?"

"Yes, please. Double cheer if you don't mind; it's been a rough day." She sat on one side of the couch as Aaron sat on the other. "Wait a second, I thought the whole point of your job was that it allowed you to do other things."

"It is," he said, pouring the liqueur into their cups, "but what if it doesn't work out? Do you know how many people come here hoping to make it in music and fail?"

"Do you know how many people go to New York to be writers and fail?" she asked, clinking her mug against his.

Aaron sat back against the armrest and pulled his legs up so he was facing her. "Is that what you wanted to be, a writer?"

"Yeah, but a writer doesn't get health care or dental or other benefits, so I figured a job reading all day was the next best thing." She sipped her coffee, which was warm, sweet, and boozy. "But that didn't go as planned, so here I am."

"Well, you're still a good writer," he said, nudging her foot with his. "I read all the 'Love, Charlotte' email blasts."

"You *have* to read those emails."

"Actually, I don't. But I do now that you're writing them. You're a great writer."

"Some of my finest work," Harper joked.

"I'm serious. I know you have to write in her voice, but you bring something more to it. And just because you work for Charlotte doesn't mean you can't still find time to write on your own," he said.

Harper smirked and gently kicked his foot. "Touché." She yawned. "Sorry, I haven't been sleeping much, and yesterday at Charlotte's kind of knocked me on my ass."

Aaron leaned forward, took Harper's mug from her, and placed it on the table. He reached behind where she was sitting, grabbed a blanket, and draped it on her.

"Why don't you take a nap, and I'll see what I can make us for dinner?"

"Are you sure? Shouldn't I help?" Harper asked, pulling the blanket around her and snuggling into a throw cushion. She started to insist that she pitch in, but she wasn't sure how many words actually came out of her mouth before she fell fast asleep.

———

It was dark when Harper woke up, the sky outside black except for the swirls of snow that were illuminated under the streetlights. "What time is it?" she asked, sitting up and rubbing her neck.

"Six o'clock," Aaron called over the low hum of music playing from a speaker he kept on the kitchen counter.

"Oh my God, you made dinner." Harper inhaled the scent of ginger and garlic that suddenly made her realize just how hungry she was. "I'm so sorry; you should've woken me up."

"It's fine! You were tired, and now that I know you can sleep on the couch I won't feel so guilty about not giving you my bed." He started rinsing a handful of basil under the tap.

To the confused expression on Harper's face, he continued, "The state of emergency still hasn't been lifted and there's an extreme weather warning, and no one is going out in that. I can try to take you back to your apartment tomorrow, but it looks like you're going to have to crash here tonight."

"Good thing I brought my suitcase with me," Harper said, walking over to her bag and pulling out her toiletry case. "Speaking of which, which way is your bathroom?"

"That way," he said, and pointed down the hall.

Harper washed her face and brushed her teeth, applied some

moisturizer and deodorant, and generally tried to make herself a little more presentable. She didn't want it to be too obvious, but if she was going to spend the night at Aaron's, she wanted to look less puffy-eyed and cuter than she currently did. She let her hair down and put a little gloss on her lips and cheeks. It was a far cry from how she expected to look tonight, the expensive dress she'd bought for the engagement party folded in her suitcase and the new makeup she'd purchased unopened in her little cosmetics bag. She sighed, trying not to let herself become emotional at the thought of what she was missing right now. "You can't bawl in front of him again—get it together," she whispered to her reflection, and walked out.

The food was warm and savory, and it was all Harper could do to not scarf it down. She cradled the brown ceramic bowl with one hand and, with her chopsticks in the other, scooped up a mouthful of soba noodles and shrimp in peanut sauce. "Tell me why I need to take you to dinner if you can cook like this?"

"Because I only know how to make two dishes, and this is one of them."

They were sitting on barstools, eating at the kitchen counter and drinking red wine. "What's the other one?" Harper asked.

"French toast."

"Ah, I see," Harper said, a smile creeping across her face, "one meal for the night before and one for the morning after. No wonder you write a lot of songs."

Aaron blushed and took a sip of wine. "It's not like that, exactly."

"Sure, sure. You should know that just because I'm sleeping on the couch doesn't mean I'm *not* expecting French toast for breakfast," she said, taking a drink of her own wine.

Aaron looked at Harper over his glass, his face growing serious. "I'm really sorry that you're missing your best friend's engagement party. That's got to suck."

"It does," she said quietly.

"But I'm really glad you're here," he said, his voice even softer.

"Me too. Don't get me wrong, The Greenhouse is great, but it can also be kind of—lonely, you know what I mean?" The moment she said it, she knew it was how she had been feeling, although she hadn't been able to put it into words until now.

"I know exactly what you mean. I'd be lying if I didn't say I hadn't been thinking of this for a while now."

"And all it took was a natural disaster to make it happen," Harper whispered.

"It was fate," Aaron said tenderly, his voice gentle and low.

Harper stared at Aaron, her whole body aching to be touched. As if reading her mind, Aaron put his hand on hers, and for what felt like an eternity—in Green Time or any other time—they were quiet, each waiting to see what would happen next. First, her fingers entwined with his, then there was his hand on her knee, which moved to her thigh as she moved closer to him. She placed her hand on his chest as he wrapped his arm around her back and pressed her body against his. Standing, she moved between his legs, her mouth finally on his. Tongues exploring, they folded into each other, abandoning any thoughts about anyone sleeping on any couch—or sleeping at all for that matter—stumbling and groping and consuming all the way into the bedroom.

———

"Why a bee?" Harper asked, looking at the little tattoo above Aaron's heart as they lay in bed together. She was still catching her breath. Sure, it had been a long time since she had had sex, but it had been even longer since she'd had sex like *that*. Her whole body buzzed and whirred, laughter and tears threatening to come out at the same time if she didn't focus her thoughts on something, and that thing right now was the little bee tattoo above Aaron's left nipple.

"What?" Aaron said. He followed her gaze. "Oh, that's a reminder to *bee kind*."

There was something about the way he threw away the answer that struck Harper. She leaned forward, brushed the hair out of his face, and looked in his eyes. She hadn't known Aaron for long, but he didn't strike her as a *bee kind* type of guy. "What's it really for?" she asked, kissing the tip of his nose gently.

Aaron sat up on his side and faced her, his free hand tracing a line from her shoulder to her hip.

"My mom," he said quietly. "She passed away five years ago, around this time, and I got it to remember her. Her name was Beatrice, but her friends all called her Bee."

Harper recalled the photo she had seen the day she first went into Aaron's office.

"I'm sorry," Harper said, reaching for his hand. "And your dad?"

"Never knew him. It was just the two of us, and then after she got sick, it was just me."

"That must've been hard," Harper said.

"I lost my way for a while after she died. I was drunk a lot and couldn't play a thing. Just too fucked-up and sad all the time. But then I started working at The Greenhouse, and I met all these great people, and eventually, my music came back."

Harper lifted his fingers to her lips and kissed them gently. "I'm really glad."

"Well, I have to give Charlotte credit. If she hadn't taken a chance on me, I'm not sure where I'd be. After she hired me she gave me all her books, enrolled me in her courses for free, and sold me her old truck for practically nothing when I was too broke to afford a car. She even wrote my landlord a letter of reference for this place, after I'd destroyed my credit. She changed my life."

So that's what he had meant when he said he was often willing to look the other way—because of all she'd done for him. Harper looked at his hand in hers and worked up the courage to ask the question she'd wanted to, ever since it first came up.

"Hey, can I ask you something?"

"Sure . . ." Aaron said warily.

"Did Charlotte *really* write her books?" Harper asked. "At the luncheon, I overheard C.J. say that Charlotte plagiarized some writer in New Zealand, and she insinuated that Tiffany knew about it."

Aaron was quiet for a moment, then spoke. "You know C.J. hates her, right? She'll do basically anything to tear Charlotte down."

"I had no idea. Still, the designs for Serene, the emails, the books, the videos—Charlotte Green is the self-made mogul that *does it all* and yet . . ."

"And yet she doesn't. Did you really think she did? She's one person. How would that even be possible? Do you think Katy Perry writes every song herself, Martha Stewart makes every recipe on her show, or that Madonna wrote all her own children's books? No. They're brands that have other people working for them, just like Charlotte—except people also expect her to be just a regular person like they are. Well, you don't get to have it both ways," he said, his voice oddly tense. He unlocked their fingers and lay on his back.

"Whoa. You can't blame me for asking. There's been a lot of talk lately, and people are asking *me* things, and I just wanted to know if any of it's true."

Harper rolled onto her back too and stared at the ceiling. As Aaron lay there silently, Harper worried that she had ruined everything.

"I guess I'm just extra sensitive because of what happened with Mandy and Tiffany," he said finally. "I feel for Charlotte. She's given everything to The Greenhouse, and she's been really good to me." He rolled back onto his side and tucked a strand of Harper's hair behind her ear. "And even though she's not always perfect, her heart's always in the right place, you know? You have to give her that."

Harper nodded, but didn't say anything.

"And . . ." he continued with a small smile, "she introduced me to this really sexy woman"—he gently kissed her stomach—"who is super smart and ambitious," he went on, kissing her breasts, "and who I'm *very* glad . . ." he said, reaching her neck and whispering in her ear, "got stuck in Nashville tonight." Harper smiled and wrapped her arms tightly around him, putting any more talk of Charlotte to bed.

Seeing Green Monthly Newsletter:

January

New Year, New You! Isn't that what they always say? But what if it was the same you, only better? Still you, only smarter? The real you finally emerging? Life is a journey, and personally, I don't want to start every year from scratch. I want to build on what was before, and I want to take all those things I learned and use them to make me stronger. Every hurt, every betrayal, every disappointment—I'm going to shine those babies up and wear them like medals of honor, proof that I'm still standing strong. This year, my inner warrior is ready to take it all on! But like I always say, we can't do it alone. We need community, there's strength in numbers, and I want our numbers to be the best yet!

When I started the Green Revolution, it was just you, me, and a handful of our friends. Then a few friends told a few more friends, and we became a group. This is where people always like to "cut to" where they are now. But no, I won't "cut to." I won't erase or forget each and every person that got us to two million followers because *we* did this, and I know we can do it again. Will you join me in making this year at The Greenhouse the best yet? For a limited time only, I'm offering a special Greenlight Your Life package that includes a signed copy of my internationally bestselling *Greenspirations: Daily Doses of Wisdom for Warrior Women* (and men too!), a limited-edition Serene by Green athleisure suit, and a special VIP pass for all of you who have already bought a ticket to the Inspire conference! Don't have your ticket yet? Don't worry! Buy it today and you'll still be eligible for the current early-bird price. Together we're going to make it the best year yet!

xo Charlotte

37

New Office, Who Dis?

"Harper!" Charlotte called out the moment she saw her at work. Harper hadn't expected to see Charlotte. After returning to The Greenhouse the week between Christmas and New Year's, Charlotte was supposed to go to a spa in Utah for a three-day, post–New Year's Eve retreat to recharge.

"Welcome back!" Harper said as everyone filed into work and settled at their desks.

"Well, it's not like I actually left. I mean, I'm always here, even if I'm not *physically* here," Charlotte said. "I realized I couldn't bear to start my new year anywhere other than The Greenhouse." Tanned and practically glowing, she placed her hand on Harper's shoulder and looked at her meaningfully.

"Right, I meant welcome back *physically*," she said.

"Of course. That doesn't mean that I don't appreciate that *you've* been physically here during the holiday break and that you missed some things with your family . . ."

"Things" being Poppy's engagement party and Christmas with my parents, thought Harper. Not only had all flights been canceled until after

Christmas—at which point she had to be back at work anyway—but the weather-related state of emergency meant she hadn't been able to drive, so she had spent the holiday alone in her apartment watching reruns of *Friends* while eating instant ramen.

"And the cookies, which were delicious. I've been asked to go on *Baking with America* and show everyone how to make them. So I'm going to need that recipe."

"Oh my God, my mom is going to be thrilled."

"Right, what's her name again?"

"Eva. You know, my mom would always say that a cookie is more than just a sweet treat; it's a four-ingredient love letter."

"I love that. You know, hang on, we should film this for our social." She circled her finger in the air to signal that she was rolling camera and then realized that Bella wasn't there and called Aaron, who came over immediately. She cleared her throat and started again.

"Harper, you know I'm always saying that everyone here is like my family. Well, I mean it. And this Christmas, when you volunteered to stay here and keep working instead of being with your *own* family, I knew that you meant it too. And this is my way of saying thanks. I know you've only been here four months, but like we always say, four months is like four years when you're running on Green Time!" She passed Harper a little green box.

"Wow, I don't know what to say," Harper said. She didn't actually volunteer to stay, but now was obviously not the time to bring that up. She opened the box and pulled out a key chain with the letter G on it and a small key.

"It's a key to your new office!" Charlotte said, squealing with delight at the look of surprise on Harper's face.

"Oh my God, are you serious? I get an office?"

"Of course! As my new director of communications, you're going to need it." She angled herself toward the camera and placed her hands on either side of Harper's arms. "I knew when I took a chance on hiring you, out of all those other people dying to work here, that you were going to go the extra mile—heck, you went a couple thousand of them, moving from New York to Nashville, and I wanted to reward you for it."

Harper looked at Charlotte, recognizing that expression of hers that said she expected a compliment in return, and quickly answered. "Charlotte, I can't thank you enough. You're such an inspiration to work for and truly the most generous boss I know. I'm so lucky you took a chance on me."

Charlotte folded her hands over her heart and tilted her head to one side, gracefully receiving Harper's praise, holding the moment until Aaron took his cue to stop filming.

Harper couldn't believe it. Director of communications was supposed to be Bella's job—she'd been working toward it for years. Bella was going to freak when she found out that Harper had gotten it after just a few months. Maybe Harper could suggest Bella for Tiffany's old position of event maestro? She was just about to bring up the idea when she caught sight of Tasha standing at the front of the room with Oliver. *Shit.* In the chaos of the holiday, she'd forgotten she'd invited Tasha to the office today.

"Tasha!" Harper called out, waving.

Charlotte looked in Tasha's direction, a look of surprise on her face that Harper wasn't sure was genuine. "I arranged to show Tasha around today," Harper offered. Charlotte beamed.

The four of them walked toward each other, meeting in the middle of the Green Garden. "Congratulations on your promotion," Tasha said. "Was it a surprise, or did you know it was coming?"

"Total surprise," Harper said, still processing it. "But I'm so grateful."

"Well, I'm just glad I happened to catch it, and *you*," Tasha said. Something about how she said it made Harper think there was something else she wanted to say.

"Me too," Charlotte chimed in. "What good luck! I wasn't even supposed to be here today. I've been in Utah with my husband working on our next book. In fact, he's still there working on it."

"Really? What's it about?" Tasha asked.

"Change and growth. How important it is to honor that in each other, even if it isn't what you expected."

"Sound like you're speaking from experience," Tasha said.

"What do you mean?" Oliver interjected.

"Well, there have been so many changes at The Greenhouse lately, I'm sure it's been a challenge keeping up."

Charlotte stepped forward and looked Tasha in the eye. "Like I always say, 'I alone cannot change the world, but I can cast a stone across the waters to create many ripples.' "

Harper recognized the quote immediately as belonging to Mother Teresa and could tell by the way Tasha's eyes grew wide with surprise that she did too.

"Wait, isn't that—"

"A quote from Mother Teresa, an original warrior woman if there ever was one! Yup, we all love that saying," Harper said quickly. "Personally, I also really love this quote by Charlotte: 'Change is just another opportunity to grow.' So inspiring."

"Inspiration. It's all around us." Charlotte flashed a wide smile and turned to Tasha. "And on that note, Oliver, what do you say we let Tasha pick the song of the day to get us started? Let's show her what going *Green* is really all about!"

———

Tasha saw it all—the dance party, the sharing circle (people shared their New Year's resolutions and how they were going to keep them), and the cheer that marked the end of the morning ritual and sent everyone back to their desks.

"Is it really like this every day?" Tasha asked Harper when they were alone at the hydration station.

"It really is," she said, grabbing each of them a green juice from the fridge.

"Interesting." Tasha took a drink.

"What is it? I feel like there's been something you've wanted to say since you got here."

"No, it's just . . . you hear a lot of different things. How driven she is, how demanding she can be, and yet, this feels like summer camp on steroids with a dash of cult thrown in."

Harper had to laugh. "I can't argue with you. It's exactly what I thought when I started here. But now, I've drunk the Kool-Aid, and I like it! And I mean, there are worse things than having fun at work and being close to your colleagues. I know it can seem a bit strange, but unlike a cult, Charlotte isn't doing all of this to make herself more powerful. She's doing it to empower others."

Tasha studied Harper for a moment. "Okay, fair enough. But does she always film everything? I mean, what other boss would film your promotion and then blast it out on social media immediately?"

"What other job would give me a promotion after four months? This isn't just a job; it's a movement." Harper recalled the conversation she had with Aaron about Charlotte as they lay in bed, about not being able to have it both ways. "And Charlotte Green isn't just my boss—she's a brand. Everyone wants to know everything about her and her life behind the scenes. But if she shows us something that we don't expect, we say it's too much. We all want her to be our inspiration—not a person with flaws—but we also expect her to be just a regular person like we are."

"You're saying we want it both ways."

"I'm saying we want it *all* ways. And maybe that says more about us than it does about Charlotte."

It was clear by the look on her face that Tasha was impressed by Harper's answer. "I think it does, I think it says *a lot*. Maybe more than you realize." She paused. "Congratulations on your promotion, by the way. It's obvious you deserve it." She waved goodbye and walked away to find Charlotte.

As good as it was to hear those words from Tasha, it would be better if *Bella* felt the same way. Maybe then Harper would feel like celebrating.

38

How the Polvoron Crumbles

It wasn't even 7:00 a.m. when Harper, wired on coffee and running on fumes, was adding up the latest ticket numbers for the Inspire conference while waiting for Charlotte's *Baking with America* segment to be posted on the Vine. She was excited for Charlotte to share her mother's cookie recipe with the country, and also hoping that her mom would get a shout-out. Harper looked at the ticket total again—3,500. Any other year, Oliver told her, Charlotte would have been thrilled by that number. They were already almost double what she had done the year before, but having tripled the size of her venue, half the seats were still empty, and she was on them all the time to get sales up. Oliver had reasoned that the worst-case scenario was that they would have to offer free space to additional vendors to fill out the place. But Charlotte wasn't interested in hearing anything but ways to sell more tickets, even threatening that if she couldn't reach her goal of ten thousand attendees, she'd cancel altogether.

All of January and February had been a blur as Harper had practically lived in her little office at The Greenhouse. The news of Harper's promotion had gotten her a lot of attention. It had been blasted on social media, celebrated with trademark enthusiasm on the Vine (with the exception of Bella, who was still icing her out), and gushed about on Harper's own Instagram account with emoji-laden glee. She'd posted a pic of her new desk with a single white orchid that Oliver had gifted her with the caption *Upgraded*, and carefully concealed the fact that the space wasn't so much an office as it was another storage closet at the end of the hallway where all The Greenhouse merchandise was kept. And the key that Charlotte had made a big display of giving her wasn't a key to the door, but rather a key to the filing cabinet inside. At least the door had glass panes, which Harper told herself was kind of like a window, although it was one that looked out onto The Greenhouse. So far, the tiny office, new title, and increased workload were the only "perks" of the new job.

Harper, who had originally thought that any attention she received was the result of Charlotte, could no longer deny that her growing fan club of followers was eager to see what she herself was eating, drinking, and doing every day now that she was pretty much a fixture in Charlotte's IG stories and reels. Although it was flattering, it was also time-consuming, as Harper felt a responsibility to engage with her followers if they were going to pay her this much attention. But the thing that seemed to get the most attention was Harper's side-by-side photos of Charlotte's Post-it Note morning inspirations and her own evening reflections on how that inspiration had gone. Posted on the sliding glass doors to her balcony, they had the same backdrop every time: Nashville in the morning and then at night. It was an easy solution to Bella and Charlotte's insistence that she post something every day, but the favorable response had totally taken her by surprise, so she'd kept it up.

She grabbed her phone to check her follower count when she was notified of a new update on the Vine and sat down to read.

OMG, Charlotte, you were amazing

Loved your segment!

So fun!

Those cookies looked super YUMMY!

And that story about your nanny? So moving.

WEEPING!

Soooooo sweet.

Harper clicked the link to the *Baking with America* segment, her mouth falling open as she watched. Everything everyone had posted on the Vine about Charlotte's appearance was true. Charlotte *was* amazing, the cookies *did* look yummy, and the story about her Filipino nanny sitting with her after she'd had a hard day was *moving*. But it wasn't true. Harper rewound to the part where Charlotte talked directly to the camera, tugging at the heartstrings of millions of viewers at home.

"When I was a little girl, my nanny, Eva, would put a little plate of fresh baked polvorons in front of me and tell me that a cookie was more than just a sweet treat—it was a four-ingredient love letter." She placed her hand on her heart and turned to Ginny, the show's host. "She used to tell me that even if you don't know what to say to someone, you can always show them you care with a cookie."

"Oh my gosh, *love that.*"

"It's what I think of every year when I stand in my kitchen. I'm not just making cookies for all those children at the hospital—I'm baking them a love letter."

"That's beautiful. Really, I don't know where you find the time."

"You can always find time for things that matter," Charlotte said sincerely.

Harper couldn't believe her ears. The only people who knew that this wasn't true were Harper, her mother, and, Harper had to assume, Oliver, because he was currently rushing into her office.

"What the fuck was that, Oliver?" Harper said the moment she saw him.

"Shhh . . . keep your voice down," he said, closing the door behind him and taking a seat next to Harper. "I know, I know, you have every right to be surprised."

"*Surprised* isn't the word I was thinking of," Harper said, pointing to the screen.

"I know. Just think how great the segment was. Charlotte's even going to call it Eva's recipe and post it on our site."

"That's because it *is* Eva's recipe. Oliver, it's one thing to pretend that she made the cookies herself—or even that it was her recipe—but that was *my* story, about *my* mother. My *mother*, Eva, *not* some fictional *nanny*. Is that what she thinks all Filipino women are—hired help?"

Oliver ran his hand over his face and sighed heavily. "Harper, you're her director of communications now, which means you're in charge of her messaging. You crafted a message for her that connected with millions of people, and she made it her own. Instead of giving a shout-out to just your mom, she gave a shout-out to the entire Filipino community. You gave her something personal, and she made it *universal*."

"That sounds like spin," Harper said.

"Listen, you need to let it go. You and I don't have that kind of reach, but Charlotte does, and the response has already been phenomenal."

"Has she ever taken any of your experiences and made them her own?" Harper asked.

"She can't exactly pretend to be brown and gay. But if you're asking me if I've ever felt like she's used my identity to her advantage? Then yes, I have. But I'd rather be working here than not, and I know her heart is in the right place. It's just—"

"Charlotte being Charlotte," Harper said, drily.

"Exactly," Oliver said, as if that explained everything.

The problem was that for Harper, it only raised more questions. What else had Charlotte gotten away with in the name of personality and the greater good? If borrowing really meant stealing, did being inspired really mean copying? Was *making something your own* really just another way of saying appropriating? Harper knew that it was only a cookie recipe, but she couldn't help but wonder why Charlotte couldn't have just as easily said *an employee of mine's mom is Filipino, and she makes these delicious cookies and I'm so excited to share the recipe with you all*. And did she make Eva a nanny in her story *because* she was Filipino?

An uneasy feeling of doubt swelled within Harper that she tried to push down. Charlotte must've had her reasons for doing what she did, Harper told herself, and she was sure that once she heard them, she'd feel better. She'd talk to Charlotte once she got back to the office. But until then, it wasn't fair to give her anything but the benefit of the doubt. After all, the cookies had been delivered to kids in the hospital and put a smile on their faces, and now it was doing the same thing for people across America. Wasn't that really the most important thing?

"You know," Oliver said, bringing her back to the present, "she got *Breakfast with America* to post how people can donate to the hospital at the end of the segment, so let's just focus on that. Big picture." He stood to go.

"Big picture," Harper replied, just as his phone dinged.

Oliver stared at the screen, glued to the spot. "Oh, shit! This isn't good," he said, showing Harper the notification. *Not good* was an understatement.

Harper had listened to the #*Canceled* podcast many times, riveted by the insider stories of anonymous employees who had a bone to pick with their boss or their job. But it was a whole other thing to be the target of their takedown. Their latest episode featured a former employee of a top influencer. Titled "Welcome to the Meanhouse," it wasn't hard to figure out who the influencer—described as a tiny terror with a frat-boy-turned-bad-boy husband—was. The podcast was full of salacious gossip, calling out long working hours, low pay, and abusive behavior, while hinting that not only was this boss not the warrior they claimed to be, but a *Charlatan*. Harper and Oliver listened to know how bad the damage was, fast-forwarding through the parts that felt like they were ripped from some trashy supermarket tabloid.

This major influencer pretends that her marriage is a bed of roses when really the bloom has been off for a very long time. The truth is that this boss lady and her jealous loose-lipped husband don't even sleep in the same room. She's terrified that if anyone finds out it will be bad for her bottom line. And that's the only bottom that this woman has ever cared about because, trust me, she is definitely a top.

Harper gasped out loud and looked up at Oliver, her eyes wide and mouth agape.

"Oh. My. God," he said, burying his face in his hands.

But it's not just her marriage that's a lie; it's her whole brand. Having made her fortune from being just like you and me, I can tell you that the only thing she really has in common with her followers is that they both worship her. A raging narcissist with a penchant for drama, this influencer preys on the neediness of her staff, building them up and knocking them down and regularly taking credit for their talent by giving herself credit for hiring them. But apparently that's not all she takes credit for. It would seem her liberal use of the term inspiration *more closely resembles plagiarism. After all, who would pay five hundred dollars for a ticket to a conference called Plagiarize?! Her insatiable ego and pathologically mandated sunny outlook mean that the only rain that can ever fall on her parade are the love showers she has her employees give her—a list of glowing comments read out loud until she is fully sated. For all her talk about empowering women, the only woman she is interested in empowering is herself.*

"Is this for real?!" Harper asked, her head spinning.

"I'm afraid so. And we haven't even gotten to the end yet," Oliver said, sweating.

Harper skipped past the parts about the ritualized workday, the forced-fun dance parties, and the mercurial mood that swung from love-bombing to shunning—the time stamps all helpfully noted in the podcast description—right to the wrap-up.

I'm sure that many listeners will think "Boo-hoo, there are worse jobs," and they are right. Influencing is a business, bad bosses are nothing new, followers are really buyers, and buyers have always had to beware. But it's one thing to be influenced and another to be lied to. This woman talks a good game about inclusivity, making sure that her key staff all do a good job of projecting the right image while she routinely mines the ideas and creations of lesser-known artists and claims them as her own. I suppose that's why for all the colors in the rainbow, there's only one thing that she really cares about—green, the color of money.

"Holy shit!" Harper said, her hand covering her mouth. "This is terrible!"

"Well, at least I know you weren't the source."

"Me?"

"Well, the work you do in this office, baking all those cookies, missing Poppy's engagement party and Christmas with your family? No way would you have done all that if you had been hiding this."

"Oliver!" Harper said, shocked that he could even think that she could be behind something like this.

"Relax, it's obvious that you're just as shocked as I am, so I'm glad I have at least one person I can cross off my list. But Harper, this is bad. This is really bad, as in bring-the-whole-thing-down kind of bad. Get canceled kind of bad. If this doesn't get handled the right way, everyone could lose their jobs, and I can't afford that, especially now." He looked like he might cry. Oliver closed his eyes and inhaled deeply, exhaling slowly in an effort to calm himself. Knowing how much he was shouldering with his adoption and sole breadwinner status, Harper softened.

"Oliver," she said, reaching across the desk and placing her hand on his. "I promise you that I had no part in this, nor do I know anyone who did. What about Mandy or Tiffany?"

"Mandy signed an NDA, so that doesn't make sense. And Tiffany can be a bitch, but this seems a bridge too far, even for her."

"Is it, though? At the influencer lunch a few months back, I overheard C.J. saying that Tiffany told her that Charlotte plagiarized whole parts of her book. I mean, that tracks with the podcast," Harper said, leaning back in her chair.

Oliver practically jumped out of his chair. "*A few months back?* What are you talking about? Why didn't you say anything?"

"I did! I mentioned it to Aaron."

"Jesus, Harper, you don't mention things like that to your work crush; you mention it to *me*," Oliver said, throwing his hands in the air. "How am I supposed to get ahead of stuff like this if I don't know about it?!"

Harper turned bright red and her eyes filled with tears that she quickly blinked back. "I'm sorry. It didn't seem like that big a deal—it was just gossip—so I didn't think to mention it."

Oliver shook his head in disbelief. "Well, maybe you should have. Because someone's going to get blamed for this, and if you're the only one who saw it coming and didn't think to say anything, that someone might be *you*."

The second Oliver left her office Harper burst into tears. If Oliver was this freaked out, she could only imagine how upset Charlotte was going to be. She thought about calling Poppy but then thought better of it. Poppy was still mad at Harper *and* Charlotte; the last thing she'd want to listen to was any more work drama. And she was too embarrassed to call her mother. What would she even say?

Her notifications were coming in fast and furious. Comments about the podcast were all over social media. Some of Charlotte's followers had already started rallying around her, even though she hadn't said anything about it yet. When Harper searched Charlotte's name on Instagram, she saw the posts her fans had made with the hashtag #teamgreen, #canceledbs, #hatersgonnahate. They demanded that *#Canceled* stop hiding the identity of the person they'd spoken to, #callout, #canceled. Others, though, were saying that if the podcast was telling the truth, then they wanted nothing to do with Charlotte anymore. It took only a few minutes before the hashtags #calloutcharlotte turned into #cancelcharlotte. Polls titled "Team Green vs. Team Mean" popped up on people's Instagram stories, asking people to vote on whether they believed the podcast was about Charlotte or someone else. Harper checked the pages of some of Charlotte's most ardent followers to see the comments.

> Team Green all the way, there's no way this is Charlotte

> I don't want to think so either, but it's obvious that the person is calling out Charlotte

> And we haven't seen Ryan in ages

> I always thought they were too good to be true

The comments went on and on, with everyone chiming in with their opinion. Harper checked her direct messages, which were full of people asking her what she thought, but before she could answer any of them, her phone dinged with a text from Tasha. Any idea who the source is?

"Fuck," Harper said out loud.

There was a little tap on her door, and Harper looked up to see Bella. "Bad time?" Bella asked, holding up her phone.

39

Damage Out-of-Control

The listening circle was Bella's idea. Within minutes of arriving, she and Harper had resolved to put aside whatever disappointment and conflict they had between them for the time being. Bella reasoned that she could always stay mad at Harper later, but if they didn't work together now, there wouldn't be a job for either of them to be mad about. No sooner had they pitched the idea to Oliver than Charlotte's comment on the Vine came through. There would be no song of the day and no Greenspiration—just an all-staff meeting the moment she arrived.

By the time Charlotte walked into The Greenhouse dressed in her Serene by Green athleisure outfit for some fun promotional videos that she was scheduled to shoot, Harper and Bella had gathered everyone into the circle while Aaron stood off to one side, filming.

"What the hell is this?" Charlotte asked Harper at the sight of everyone gathered. She took off her coat and bag and dropped them on the nearest desk. "And why are you holding my crystal?"

"It's a listening circle," Harper said, stepping forward. "We thought that in light of the terrible podcast that came out this morning—which is either obviously not about you or full of lies—that it would be best to get ahead of things and show everybody what an amazing and inspiring boss you really are. We thought we could film all of us passing the crystal around, giving whoever has it the chance to speak while you're listening."

Charlotte narrowed her eyes and looked around the circle until she landed on Bella's face. "I see," she said, and then looked back at Harper. "And tell me, was this your idea?"

"No, it was Bella's. She deserves full credit."

"Don't tell me who deserves what. I'll decide that," Charlotte snapped.

"I just meant—"

"I know what you meant. I've read your questionnaire—you want everyone to like you, you're afraid of conflict, you're the good student and the good daughter," Charlotte said dismissively. "But sometimes being good gets you nowhere. As you've mentioned before."

Harper couldn't believe that Charlotte would reveal details of her questionnaire so casually.

"But I'm not afraid of conflict," Charlotte continued, "especially if it means protecting everything I've worked so hard for." She slowly walked toward Bella, and the phrase *tiny terror* rang through Harper's head. Even though she was almost a foot shorter than Bella, she still seemed to tower over her.

"I've been wondering all morning who would say such terrible things about me and not even have the guts to come forward about who they are," she said. "At first, I thought it had to be Tiffany or Mandy, but then I wondered—what if it wasn't a former employee at all? What if it was someone who is *still* working here that feels like they'd been wronged? Someone who believes that they deserve better, someone who was over-looked for a promotion they really wanted? Someone . . . who was the last member of the OG Three." Charlotte tapped her finger on Bella's clavicle.

"Charlotte," Oliver warned, walking over and placing his hand on her shoulder.

"I swear it wasn't me," Bella said, stammering.

"First Mandy, then Tiffany, and now you. I guess it's true what they say: bad things always come in threes."

"Everyone back to your desks; we've got work to do," Oliver ordered. As everyone in the room scattered, Charlotte and Bella remained glued to their spots. "After everything I did for you, Bella, I didn't think that you would repay me like this," Charlotte practically spat, "and all because you were upset that I passed you over for employee of the year and a promotion. Which, given how poorly you handled my workbook launch and the incident with Ryan, you clearly didn't deserve."

"Charlotte, *please* . . ." Bella said, trying not to cry.

"You're fired, and this meeting is done." She started to walk away when Oliver stopped her.

"You can't fire her," Oliver said. "It will be bad PR."

"Are you kidding me?" Charlotte said, whipping around to face him.

"Take a look around—everyone is watching, and you don't actually know who spoke to *#Canceled*. Think about it."

Harper could practically see the wheels turning in Charlotte's head.

Charlotte walked over to the Tower of Power, placed it in the center of the room, and stood on it. "Listen up, everybody. I think I speak for all of us when I say how upsetting that podcast was, and the idea that someone could do that to me—do that to *us*—is just something I won't stand for. I want all of you to know how much you mean to me, and I hope you can see that I will go to the fucking mat for anyone who tries to shit on who we are and what we do here. I've got your back. Thank you for having mine." There was an unmistakable moment of hesitation where applause would normally have started. Harper caught the look of surprise on Charlotte's face that her speech hadn't immediately caused the outpouring of support that it normally would have. Instead, people were looking at Bella, their faces full of shock and sympathy. After a minute, Oliver started applauding loudly until everyone joined in, and Aaron turned on "Lean on Me" for them to sway to.

Charlotte shimmied on the stump and then stepped down with

Oliver's help. With a huge fake smile, she walked over to Bella and whispered menacingly.

"You can stay for now, but hear me when I say someone is going down for talking shit about me. Do you have any idea how bad this is?"

Harper stepped in and touched Charlotte's arm. "Tasha's profile is going to be out any day now, and once it is, no one will think twice about this."

"You better be right," she said.

"We'll make sure of it," Bella added. "Thank you for believing in me, Charlotte."

Charlotte took a look around the room, at the employees staring at her, and then opened her arms wide and embraced Bella in a show display of Greenhouse solidarity. Harper instinctively pulled out her phone to capture the moment, careful not to show the fearful look in Bella's eyes. The whole thing made Harper feel sick, but she knew it had to be done. She immediately posted the photo with hashtags #greenhouse #nicehouse #mentorshipinaction #dreamboss #sharingcircle #wearefamily #haters gonnahate, and then waited to see what would happen.

I was just wondering when the piece is going to come out? Harper texted Tasha. She was sitting in her pretend office, pretending not to be completely freaked out by the out-of-control Instagram stories that Charlotte was posting in an attempt to clear her name and prove that she was none of the things the article said she was. But comparing herself to Mother Teresa and her followers to lepers didn't exactly do her plight any favors. Especially not when her next video was an actual challenge to the person who had contributed to the podcast to meet her outside The Greenhouse and settle this like adults—unless that person wasn't an adult, but some sad fucking loser who never had any friends in high school and still lived in their parents' basement.

To make matters worse, Charlotte had been wearing her Serene by

Green athleisure outfit when she said it, and the company had reached out with concern about the *optics*. Eventually, after taking the videos down, Oliver had to hide Charlotte's phone so she couldn't do any more damage, which was why, through her glass door, Harper could see her stalking the office looking for it.

Tasha finally texted her back. The article comes out tomorrow morning. Just a few last-minute changes. Harper didn't know what that meant, but she knew it wasn't good.

For the first time since Harper had started work at The Greenhouse, time seemed to move slowly. Charlotte's inability to incessantly document all the comings and goings at The Greenhouse, along with every thought that entered her head, meant that there was a lot more free time for her to watch the clock and do laps around the office. Eventually, she'd decided that the only thing to do was go to the spa.

For everyone else, every minute was put toward damage control. Bella furiously sent out a blast to everyone on their mailing list, asking all of Charlotte's followers to share some of their best experiences of meeting her at the Inspire conferences, using the hashtag #greenspiration #standbyCharlotte, and #teamgreen, while Oliver did damage control with Serene's publicity and marketing department. If that wasn't enough, Harper overheard Oliver telling Ryan on the phone that this was definitely *not* the time to do a show on how all these accusations were hurting the launch of his *Mister Class*.

Having written half a dozen possible responses in anticipation of Tasha's hopefully vindicating article that Charlotte would be able to post the moment it came out, Harper took a break to see Aaron. With Harper working late every day and weekend on the conference and Aaron working on the video presentations, it had been weeks since their snowstorm sleepover, their interactions reduced to short texts that left Harper worrying that getting the French toast breakfast meant that there would be no more sleepovers, snowstorm-related or otherwise.

"Hey," Harper said, poking her head into Aaron's office.

"Hey," Aaron answered, looking up from his screen. "What's up?"

It wasn't the greeting Harper had expected, but she tried not to show it. "Oh, you know, just managing a giant PR crisis even though I've never done that before, and hoping that Charlotte doesn't blow it all up before the profile comes out."

"Right," Aaron said, looking back to his screen.

"Is everything okay?"

"What makes you so sure the *#Canceled* podcast is even about Charlotte?"

Harper did a double take. "Are you being serious?"

He pushed his chair back from his desk and swiveled it to face her. "Yeah, I mean, there are *a lot* of other influencers. It could be about anyone. Why is everyone jumping to conclusions?"

Harper leaned against the doorframe and paused for a moment before answering. This was the same way Aaron had reacted when Charlotte came up after they'd slept together, and she wanted to tread carefully.

"*Meanhouse? Charlatan?* It's kind of obvious."

"The only thing that's obvious about any of that is you wanting to be where Charlotte is," he said.

"Excuse me?" Harper said, her whole face going red. "I've been working my ass off for her."

"And for *yourself.* You could at least have Charlotte's back—like Bella does."

"Where's this coming from?" Harper asked, stung. "I've always had Charlotte's back."

"I just think the timing is interesting. Charlotte wrecks your holiday, and right after you sleep with me you ask if she really writes her own books."

"What are you saying?" Harper asked, the room starting to spin.

"You're smart, you figure it out." Aaron clenched his jaw.

Harper couldn't believe it. After everything she had done *for*

Charlotte—not to mention the connection she *thought* she had with Aaron—he would think that *she* was the one who had gone behind her back?

"You're right," she began, feeling hurt and angry. "I am smart. Smart enough to know when someone finds it easier to project their shit onto others instead of taking a good look in the mirror. After all, if Charlotte is perfect, then why would you ever need to leave and do something for yourself and your own career? You can just stay here forever, hiding away in this back room you pretend is an office. At least I try to get ahead and take risks. You don't even try."

Aaron looked like he'd been slapped in the face. He opened his mouth to speak but then changed his mind and turned back to his screen. "You know what, forget it. This is why I don't like to mix work and play. It never works out."

Harper's eyes burned with tears, and she quickly blinked them back. "Well, for the record, I wasn't *playing,* but at least now I can stop wasting my time."

———————

It was a shitty thing to say, but Harper couldn't believe Aaron would turn on her like he did. She replayed the conversation over and over, and by the time she crawled into bed that night, her mind was buzzing and her eyes were burning from staring at her phone all day. Thousands of followers had come through for Charlotte. Their comments and posts of support far outweighed the dozens of negative ones on both Charlotte's and #*Canceled*'s Instagram pages. As awful as it was to read people gleefully trashing her boss, it was far more heartening to see how many others had been touched by her. Harper had even managed to spin the controversy into an opportunity, booking Charlotte on some popular morning shows to talk about the pressures of making it as a woman at the top. At least Charlotte was trending—even if it wasn't in the way she wanted.

All that she could do now, as she lay her head down, was push her fight with Aaron from her mind and sleep the few hours left before sunrise. Tomorrow was a new day, and she chose to believe that it would be better. *Surely it couldn't be worse*, she thought as she drifted off to sleep.

Famous last words.

40

Revolving Glass Door

Girl, are you tired of all the phony backstabbers, mean-girl competitiveness, and endless strivers? People who are gunning for your job when they should be doing everything they can to support you? Do you wish you could work for a wicked-smart boss lady who will generously mentor you and give you her hard-earned wisdom that she didn't learn from some snotty East Coast college but got from hustling in the real world? Well, if you want to be with a diverse community of like-minded badass babes who are interested in working for the greater good and not just their own good, then this is the job for you. Although "job" isn't really the right word, it's more of a calling, an answer to the warrior woman that lives inside of you, who knows that there is no "I" in team, but that Together Everyone Achieves More, and understands not only what a gift having a real leader is but how empowering it can be to help them. If this sounds like something you're looking for, then this director of communications job is for you! What are you waiting for? Join us at The Greenhouse!

Harper felt the whole room spin. Sitting up in bed as the light streamed through the window and across her face, she read the ad that Poppy had sent her, along with a message that asked, Everything okay? Having forgotten to take the notification off the job search that she had created for Harper back in the summer, Poppy had gotten the alert early that morning and wondered what was going on.

She wasn't the only one. Whether it was fear or fatigue, or a combination of both, Harper's whole body started shaking, and she thought she was going to be sick. Something was wrong. Something was terribly wrong. She checked her phone, mortified to see that today of all days, she'd slept in. But what was worse was that no one had called to yell at her and demand to know where she was. Was there a message about taking the morning off that she had missed? She quickly texted Bella, Sorry, I slept in, never happens, be there soon! But after a few minutes, she still had no reply.

Heart pounding, she checked the Vine, but her access was denied. She jumped out of bed and started pacing, her whole body wide awake with panic, and called Oliver, but it went straight to voice mail.

"What the actual fuck?" Harper shouted. The only person left to try was Aaron, but she didn't want to call him, so she texted instead.

Please tell me what's going on

There was a long pause, and then he replied with the link to Tasha's *Inc.* article. The headline read "The Women Behind the Influential Women We Love," and on the first page was a picture of Harper.

Harper's legs wobbled. She fell back onto her bed and began to read.

Tasha had done a brief profile of all the women who had been at the influencer lunch, along with a small write-up of what a typical day at their offices was like. But less interested in the influencers and their practiced smiles and pithy sound-bites, she'd focused the article on their right-hand people instead. People who, as far as she could tell, did as much work, maybe even more, than the influencers themselves. She highlighted the strategic efficiency of Tiffany, who she predicted would move from one top influencer to the next as she built her own brand. And then there were Lulu and DeeDee, Evie's and Chloé's assistants, who she described as interchangeably sycophantic in their hero worship and canned replies. Still, they had learned how to take advantage of the interns who burned out and left with letters of reference instead of paychecks, so they could move forward in their own careers without damaging the bottom line. But the main focus of the article? Harper.

Tasha described Harper as an outsider in the influencer world, much like Charlotte had once been and still liked to pretend she was—even though her lifestyle of private planes, spa retreats, and a net worth of fifteen million dollars proved otherwise. Through Tasha's lens, The Greenhouse wasn't so much a community as it was a cult. The fun activities weren't about boosting morale but about creating a distraction from the ridiculous amount of work people were expected to do, with gift certificates and prizes handed out as a poor substitute for the lack of overtime and benefits they would be entitled to at other companies. In her opinion, all the other assistants seemed to understand this except for unjaded Harper, whom she described as having drunk the Kool-Aid: "This isn't just a job, it's a movement. And Charlotte isn't just a person; she's a brand." Tasha had something to say about that.

> But what happens when the brands we buy into turn out to be made in factories with poor working conditions, or, as recent accusations assert, are built on the sweat equity and inspiration of others who don't get recognized for their contributions? Where company mottos and words of wisdom belong to someone else? If left unchecked, these shortcuts that are routinely excused and explained as quirky little characteristics will only fester and multiply until their injustices become too much to bear. And when that happens, these false idols that we worship with clicks and likes and reposts will turn on the very people who lifted them up and espoused their greatness in the

first place—the assistants who serve as rungs on the ladder of success.

But it's important to remember that not every woman becomes a Charlotte, but every woman starts out as a Harper: honest, hardworking, and believing that not only do their contributions matter but are valued. If only they were given the credit they were due, they'd stay that way. But then again, if they knew their worth, they might not just move on from the job they have, but into a spotlight of their own.

Harper dropped her head in her hands. How could Tasha do this? She thought they were . . . what—*friends*? The photograph, the focus on Harper, the inference that Harper could one day move out of her boss's shadow and cause her light to dim as a result—did she have any idea how bad this would look? Her phone rang, and she grabbed it, surprised to see it was her mom.

"Poppy called me. She told me about the job listing and the article."

Harper hadn't even told Poppy about the article, but she'd found it anyway—she must've been looking out for Harper even after their fight.

"Honey, are you okay?" her mom asked.

The second she heard her mother's voice, Harper burst into tears. No, she was definitely not okay.

41

It Was the Best of Times, It Was the Worst of Times

As Harper stood inside The Greenhouse, she thought of the summer when her parents decided to send her away to sleepover camp at the age of twelve. Neither of them had the opportunity to go to camp when they were growing up, and, as Harper was an only child, they wanted her to have the chance to be around other kids her age. Harper had been nervous about going but also excited. Her friends had told her that it was the best time of their lives, and after that one summer, Harper understood why. The friendships she'd made in those two short months were the greatest she'd ever had, the adventures she took were the boldest, her romantic crushes the most intense. It was like she'd taken the experiences of a whole year and crammed them into a couple of months, and on the last day she'd stood in the parking lot sobbing as she hugged her new best friends goodbye. At the time, she had no idea how she'd survive a whole school year before seeing them again, so she'd gotten her mother to arrange a sleepover just before Christmas. But instead of the enthusiastic reunion she'd envisioned, their get-together had been strained and awkward, the friendships they had forged with one another only able to exist in a certain time and place. As Harper entered The Greenhouse that evening after everyone else had left for the day, she could already feel that her time and place in Nashville with these people was slipping away.

"Thanks for coming in," Oliver said as they walked past the empty workstations to his office.

"I would've come in sooner, but you told me to stay home," Harper replied, sitting across from him.

"I wanted to give Charlotte some time to cool off," Oliver said. He leaned forward and folded his hands under his chin. Up close, Harper could see he had bags under his bloodshot eyes, and she wondered if he was getting any sleep at all. "I know you didn't mean it."

"Mean what?" Harper asked.

"To steal her thunder. It wasn't what she was expecting, especially after the *#Canceled*'s podcast came out. She was expecting something that would put her back in the public's good graces."

"She does realize that I can't control what a reporter is going to write about?"

"Of course, and she doesn't want you to think that your leaving has anything to do with the article. The job just isn't a good fit."

There it was. Harper leaned back in her chair and crossed her arms. "My leaving?"

"Yes." Oliver sighed. "Because you got another opportunity back in New York and Charlotte was so excited for you that she insisted that you take it—"

"Like the generous, appreciative, supportive boss she is." She tilted her head to one side and looked at Oliver. "You must be getting pretty good at this by now."

"It wasn't my decision—"

"But you didn't exactly fight it," Harper replied, knowing by the look on his face that she was right. "Oliver, this is bullshit. Everything I said to Tasha about Charlotte was positive. I've done nothing wrong."

"I know," he said quietly.

"So then why is she firing me? *Not a good fit.* Come on, you both know how hard I've worked and how much I've done for this place. Besides, I thought we were friends," Harper said, her voice cracking.

"We are," he insisted.

"Then please, just be honest with me. Why not defend me? Why not try to change her mind?"

Oliver sighed and leaned back in his chair. "She's jealous. She thinks you're stealing her spotlight and is worried that you're a real threat."

"Me? A threat? She confided in *me*, she told *me* to keep an eye out for any other weeds and report back to her if I suspected anyone of being disloyal. I don't understand. I did everything she asked. I did everything right," Harper said, hating herself for starting to cry.

"No, you did it better. And she can't have that," Oliver said gently. "She's afraid, Harper. She doesn't know who she can trust anymore. You have to understand that."

Harper couldn't believe what she was hearing.

"At the end of the day, it's still *her* company, and the decision is hers. I'm sorry. But I tried to get you a good deal, and I hope you'll take it."

"What kind of deal?" she asked, collecting herself.

"If you stick with that story, she'll ignore the clause in your contract that says if you leave before the year is up, you have to pay back your wages."

Harper's mind rewound to the rush she'd been in taking the job— she must've missed the fine print.

"And also no comments, no posts, no more interviews of any kind about Charlotte and The Greenhouse." He slid a piece of paper tucked inside a manila folder toward her.

"A nondisclosure agreement?" Harper asked, disbelieving. "You're kidding, right?"

"I'm not. She's having everyone sign one from now on. But she's also willing to pay out the rest of your year. It's a good deal, and I fought for it, so please think about it."

Harper *was* thinking about it. She didn't have the money to pay back her wages, and an additional six month's salary could go a long way to helping her—and her parents, if she took her mother up on her offer to move back home until she got back on her feet. But that only reminded her of how unfair all of this was.

"And then what? I'm just supposed to disappear, and no one here ever speaks to me again?" Harper asked, choking up.

"Not if we want to keep our jobs."

"I don't believe this." Oliver, Aaron, Bella—they were all just expected to pretend that the last six months hadn't happened. "And you're okay with it?"

"Of course not. But I'm starting a family, and I'm the sole bread-winner. I have to believe that Charlotte will come around. It wasn't always like this—*she* wasn't always like this."

"And what if she doesn't come around?"

"Well, if that happens, then she's going to need someone to be here when it all blows up," Oliver said, smiling sadly, and Harper got the feeling that wasn't so much a case of *if* but *when*.

"Fine, tell Charlotte I'll take it. But she'll have to wait for my sig-nature. This time, I'm going to read the fine print." She took the folder from Oliver and stood to go.

"Thank you. I'm so sorry; I wish it didn't have to be this way," Oliver said, coming around to face her.

Harper knew he meant it, but it was little consolation. "You know what they say—wishing isn't enough. You have to actually *do something* if you want things to be different." She walked out into The Greenhouse, stopping at her desk one last time. She opened her drawer, but of course it was empty—no personal belongings, no trace of her existence. It was like she was never even there.

42

In Her Own Words

She can take away your job, but she can't take away
your voice—unless you let her. Don't let her. I wish I hadn't.

Harper read the little Post-it Note she'd found in the bookcase while cleaning out her apartment. It was the same handwriting that had been on the first Post-it she'd discovered on her mirror when she arrived in Nashville, the one wishing her good luck. She'd tucked it into the journal her dad had given her for Christmas, the one she'd never filled out, and now wished more than ever that she had.

She thought about the NDA she'd told Oliver she would sign, and yet, reading the Post-it Note gave Harper pause. *I wish I hadn't.* Harper wished for a lot of things—that she'd never left New York, that she'd swallowed her pride and stayed with her parents while she worked things out, that she had spoken up the first time she heard an offensive comment from Charlotte so her silence wasn't just assumed the second and third time she heard one. She wished she had listened to her family when they tried to warn her about The Greenhouse, that she'd said no to taking Bella's place at the luncheon, and that she'd challenged Aaron's insistence that sometimes it was better to just look the other way and let Charlotte be Charlotte. *But wishing isn't enough. You have to actually do something if you want things to be different.*

Harper took the NDA out of her bag, gave it one last look, and then ripped it up. Staring down at the pile of ripped paper on the floor, she knew there was something she wanted to say. She opened her laptop. She'd been locked out of the Vine, her work email, and Charlotte's Instagram. But there was still one place she could reach the people she hoped would hear her before Charlotte told them not to listen. She opened her Instagram and wrote one final, honest, heartfelt post—not in anyone's voice but her own.

> Hey, you're going to hear a lot of things and read a lot
> of things in the next few days, and I won't be on social to
> answer any of them. But know this: I came to this job having
> no idea what to expect, and if I'm honest, I thought it all
> sounded a bit bonkers. I went from working in publishing
> to being a visionary support strategist, which is about
> as made-up a title as it sounds. One minute I'm running
> errands; the next, I'm organizing a conference and directing
> communications. And as stressful and exhausting as the past
> six months have been, they've also taught me that I really
> can do anything I set my mind to. But most of all, I learned
> that we should never believe in someone else more than we
> believe in ourselves. The answers you're looking for aren't
> here because the only one who has them is you. If you really
> want to be inspired, INSPIRE YOURSELF. All titles are made
> up. Go ahead and make yourself the chief visionary director
> of your own life.

No sooner had she posted than the comments started pouring in.

> Good luck, Harper!

> We'll miss you

> Stay strong! #teamharper

> @#teamharper Did you see the latest Instagram video of Charlotte accusing Harper of biting the hand that feeds her?

> She was raging

> She acted as if she owned her, so rude

> I heard she fired Harper for stealing her thunder!

> Egomaniac much?

> I've never seen her so mad!

> Charlotte was jealous

> And a liar . . . Do you know she never even had a Filipino nanny?

> WTF?

> Harper's mom is Filipino AND named Eva!

> OMG!

Charlotte fired Mandy too and had her sign an NDA

No!

Yes!

Why an NDA? What's Charlotte hiding—Ryan?

LOL

Seriously, where is he?

I heard he never came back from their couples' retreat

I heard he coupled up with someone else!

Once a cheater, always a cheater

What?!

He left his first wife for Charlotte

No!

Yes!

What goes around comes around

Serves them right!

Harper stared at the conversations happening under her post with shock and awe. #TeamHarper. That was something she hadn't expected to see, and if Charlotte hadn't gone online raging, maybe she wouldn't have. For a moment, she was tempted to see if there was a workaround to being blocked so she could check Charlotte's video, to see what she was saying about her. She could always respond with a video of her own, and then . . . she stopped herself. Charlotte would always be the aggrieved party in her mind—the one betrayed, the victim in her story. There was no winning with her. Harper scrolled to the top of her screen to delete her Instagram account and paused to take one last look. She'd written hundreds of posts, all of them documenting her time at The Greenhouse. As Harper reread them it dawned on her—she had filled in her journal after all—one digital entry at a time.

There was no way Harper was going to miss her flight this time. That morning, she'd slipped an envelope under Bella's door with the keys to her apartment and a letter. There was so much she wanted to say to her in person, but she didn't want to make things any harder for her with Charlotte than they were already, so she poured it all out in a note instead, signing it Friend-Friends, and telling Bella she was welcome to talk or visit her in New York anytime she wanted.

Before heading for the airport, she decided to buy herself a shiny new release at the local bookstore—it was going to take a while to retrain her brain to stop checking her phone, so she might as well start now— and stop at the Frothy Monkey one last time. Sitting with a coffee in front of her, she ran her hand over the cover of her new book, smiling at the fact that, after all this time, a book could still give her comfort. How had she forgotten that? She opened the first page and started to read when she heard a familiar voice.

"Were you just going to leave without saying goodbye?"

She looked up and saw Aaron standing on the other side of her table.

"No need to do it twice," Harper said, thinking of the fight they'd had back at The Greenhouse.

"Yeah, there is, especially if you were a total ass and fucked it up the first time." Aaron leaned forward and gripped the back of the chair, looking down at the table. "I came here hoping to find you before you left so I could say I'm sorry. I know you didn't help that stupid podcast and I know you weren't out to steal anyone's job, but the truth is it was a lot easier for me to try to convince myself that you were doing something wrong instead of someone I've been working for and, if I'm honest, turning a blind eye to all these years. I never thought she would go this far. Taking it out on Bella, firing you—she's really changed."

Harper could see how hard it was for Aaron to admit all of this, and she was touched that he was being so honest. "We all change; it's just *how* that matters. Maybe it's okay for you to change too. I'm sorry about what I said, by the way," she said, giving him a sad smile. "You obviously take risks, or you wouldn't be here. Listen, I know how hard it was for you to find your way after your mom passed, but you did it. *You* did that. So whether you decide to stay at The Greenhouse or go somewhere else or pursue music full-time, I know you'll be great at it."

"I'm not good with goodbyes, especially when I don't want someone to go," he said, exhaling loudly.

"This is hard for me too. I'm the one leaving everything and everyone behind."

"I really am sorry," he said.

Harper could see he meant it. She didn't want to leave angry—it would only make moving on so much harder—so she said, "I'm not. Now I get to have an achy breaky song written about me."

"Oh, do you now?" he said, a smile creeping across his face.

"Yeah, you know, *so long Manhattan, bye-bye Big Apple, I hardly knew ya, New York*," Harper riffed.

"Wow, okay. Maybe leave the songwriting to me," he said.

They were quiet for a moment, and then Harper stood and grabbed her things.

"I've got to go. I'm not going to miss this flight, no matter how good your Thai noodle dish is," she teased.

Aaron stepped forward and hugged her tightly. Harper could feel his heart beating against his chest, and she kissed him on the cheek. "Just remember," she whispered, "change, like goodbyes, is always hard. But not taking chances is *harder*." And with that, she turned and walked away before he could see her cry.

43

New Beginnings

It was the sound of birds that woke Harper up. Not her alarm, or her phone, or her coffee machine beeping in the darkness, but the small family of birds that had taken up residence in the large maple tree outside her bedroom window. Somehow, they hadn't gotten the memo that they were supposed to leave for warmer climates, choosing instead to stay together, close to the birdfeeder that Harper's dad kept full year-round. They were tough, beautiful, and stubborn, and their presence reassured Harper that she was going to be okay.

"You're up," her mom said, peering into her bedroom with two cups of coffee. "We were starting to wonder if you were going to sleep the whole day."

"What time is it?" Harper sat up in bed and checked her phone. "Noon? I can't remember the last time I slept so late. That's midnight if you're on Green Time."

"But you're not on Green Time—you're on Harper Time now," her mom said, passing her a mug and sitting on the edge of the bed. "And you should stay on that time for as long as you need to—"

"Or at least for a few more minutes. Then your mom could use some help making a couple hundred polvoron for the bridal shower," her dad said, appearing in the doorway.

Harper had a feeling that her parents had been checking in on her all morning, and it made her smile.

"What bridal shower? Christian's?" Harper asked.

"No, although they are dating again. Janice is putting him through his paces, but they seem happy," her mom said.

Harper was glad to hear it. "I'd be happy to help. I've got to earn my keep around here while I figure out what to do next."

"Maybe this will help," Harper's dad suggested as he pulled a little Moleskine notebook out of his back pocket. "You can write down your thoughts."

"Oh, I've been writing them," Harper said, holding up her phone. "They're all in here."

"Nothing like good old-fashioned paper, Harper," he said, tossing her the little notebook.

"Thanks, both of you. I honestly don't know what I'd do without you." Harper reached for her mom's hand and gave it a squeeze.

"Don't thank us yet. Poppy wants five hundred polvoron. We need to get started." Eva kissed Harper on the head and stood up.

"Poppy?" Harper asked. And then she remembered: Poppy's shower was tomorrow. It was just like her to find a way to show her support without making a big deal of it. Harper was touched. This time there was no way she would miss her friend's celebration.

"Yup, she's having one hundred guests and wants five for each one," her dad explained.

"Wow, that's a lot of work," Harper said, drinking her coffee quickly.

"It's a lot of money too. I told her she only had to cover the cost of the ingredients, but she insisted on paying what she called 'Park Avenue prices.' " Eva smiled and shook her head as she headed out.

"Now, if only we could do a couple of those a week," her dad said, following close behind.

Maybe you can, thought Harper.

––––––––––

Baking with Eva, the TikTok channel that Harper and her mom launched together, didn't exactly have the same budget or audience as *Baking with America*, but it certainly had more charm. Harper's mom was a natural, and her dad, cast in the role of sous chef and amiable sidekick, was adorable. It took countless polvorons and more than a few media-training sessions to get the first video right, but the results were worth it. And just as Harper hoped, her former followers met her first post-Greenhouse Instagram appearance—a collaborative post with a request to follow her mom—with enthusiasm and love. So far, the only downside had been the abundance of cookies that Harper still managed to find irresistible. At the rate she was going she was going to be one-third butter by summer.

It was a small sacrifice to pay for the extra money that started to trickle in for her parents, enough to let them start on the long list of repairs that needed to be done. And there was talk of adding more Filipino recipes to the breakfast menu at the Inn and upgrading the kitchen. Harper was hoping that if they got enough followers, she could get a sponsor to donate new appliances, and maybe even get kids from the local high school to help with orders on the weekend so her mom could expand her business.

Baking with Eva didn't just bring money in and bring Harper and her parents closer together—it also made use of the many skills Harper had learned at The Greenhouse. Working with Charlotte had taught her how to turn inspiration into innovation, tackle new challenges, pivot when needed, market products, and engage with her audience. It also taught her that nobody really got where they were going alone, and that the friendships she made were worth keeping. And so, as soon as she and her parents found their feet, Harper sent a box of polvorons—a four-ingredient love letter—to Bella, Oliver, and Aaron.

In the midst of *Baking with Eva*, Harper started working on a project of her own. Every day, armed with a thermos of hot coffee and a dictation app, Harper went on a walk and talked out her time at The Greenhouse. She had so many feelings to work through—disappointment, anger, embarrassment, *shame*. How could she have let herself get so carried away? How could she have neglected her parents and Poppy? How could she have let herself believe she was anything other than a pawn, easily replaceable and quickly forgotten?

It was on one of her walks when she was feeling particularly blue, having just made another trip around the sun, that her phone dinged with a group text from Bella, Aaron, and Oliver to wish her a happy birthday. Harper couldn't believe that they would remember; she herself had spent the whole morning trying to forget.

Thanks, you guys.

Celebrating? Bella asked.

Wallowing, Harper replied.

Don't! It'll give you wrinkles, Oliver chimed in.

Harper laughed out loud at that one.

You get a fresh start! Bella texted.

Blank page, Manhattan. Blank page, Aaron added, along with a heart emoji, making Harper smile.

As she stared at her phone, she realized that they were right. Her life was a blank page. Her story was still being written . . . there was still plenty of time to get it right.

21

Eighteen Months Later

"Nervous?" Poppy asked, stepping into Harper's bedroom.

"Very, although it's a good kind of nervous, you know?" Harper said, putting down the card that had come with the beautiful flower arrangement from Oliver, Liam, and baby Camilla. She checked herself in the mirror, adjusted the strap on her dress, and exhaled deeply. Her childhood bedroom had seen a lot of firsts and today marked another. She looked out the window at the perfect fall day, recalling a different Labor Day two years earlier, and shook her head at how much had happened since then.

"You look beautiful," Poppy said, walking toward her slowly, her hands automatically cradling her belly that seemed like it would pop any second.

"What about Aaron? How does he look?"

"Nervous. I heard your dad ask him if he knew anything about making cider. Something about teaming up with a local brewery to use all the apples you have on the property, and getting Aaron to play music at tasting nights?"

Harper laughed out loud. "Yeah, he's been working on his cider collaboration for a year now, and it's actually coming along. Poor Aaron. He may have gotten more than he bargained for."

"I gotta hand it to you, I had my doubts about a long-distance romance, but it looks like you're living your own rom-com now!" Poppy said excitedly, briefly losing her balance.

"Are you sure you should still be wearing high heels?" Harper asked, steadying her friend.

"Not you too." Poppy rolled her eyes. "Charles is convinced I'm going to slip and fall and hurt the babies, but I've assured him that it's impossible for me to slip when I can barely move. If I'm going to look like an egg on a stick, I'm going to look good doing it."

"I wasn't sure you were going to make it," Harper said, gently placing her hand on Poppy's stomach.

"I wouldn't miss it," Poppy replied. "I won't let you be upstaged by a couple of twins. They can wait a few more days. Oh wait, one second—I told Bella I'd get some behind-the-scenes shots. She'll kill me if I forget." She stood back and snapped a few photos on her phone and hit send. A moment later, Bella entered the room.

"Seriously? You think I can use these?" she said affectionately to Poppy, waving her phone. She moved Harper's toiletry bag off the dresser and placed the flower arrangement from Oliver there instead. "Much better. Now, let's try this again, ladies, shall we?" she said, directing Harper to look out the window, read a card, smell the flowers. She snapped away. "Okay, that should do!"

Thankfully Bella had decided to leave The Greenhouse just before it imploded, accepting an offer to work at an event planning firm in California and taking her mother with her. It was a huge move but she was more than ready, and after a few months of working as hard as she did for Charlotte—but this time getting credit for it—she had already been promoted. She had offered to plan Harper's big day for free in exchange for testimonials, pictures, and a place to stay, and Harper had only too happily agreed. Bella's timely departure distanced her from what was one of the most epic online meltdowns Harper had ever seen. After not meeting her goal of selling ten thousand tickets for the Inspire conference, Charlotte had lashed out at her fans and canceled it with no refunds, which caused them to turn around and cancel *her* as well. It was around this same time that Ryan finally launched his *Mister Class* with his kickoff episode, catastrophically titled "A Room of His Own," where he stayed on the air for a full twenty-four hours espousing the plight of men everywhere who felt overshadowed by their wives' successes. This sadly boosted his brand, albeit temporarily, by trending with the hashtag #hardoutthereforawhiteguy, rivaled in popularity only by Charlotte's own hashtag, #ungratefulgreen.

Like a sandcastle built too close to the water, it had been stunning to see how quickly The Greenhouse had collapsed. Oliver, ever loyal, had stayed right until the bitter end. Much to his relief and everyone who cared about him, Oliver's husband had found work quickly, allowing Oliver to be a stay-at-home dad. Harper was happy to hear that he had even decided against joining Charlotte on her recent Rise From the Ashes Tour, where, in true Charlotte fashion, she apologized and monetized in equal measure to pave the way for her comeback story.

Now, as they made their way out to the back garden, Harper stopped to look at all her guests seated and waiting. She'd kept things simple with the decorations, the valley resplendent in all its natural glory, and the huge planters of flowers that her parents had dotted the newly landscaped garden with were still in bloom. Harper had convinced her parents that they needed to make sure the outside of the Inn had lots of Instagram-friendly backdrops if they wanted to keep attracting bachelorette parties and weddings.

"I can't believe how much better the Inn looks," Poppy said.

"It's getting there."

Harper and her parents had spent a whole year tackling the first of many planned improvements that had already paid off and managed to keep the Inn afloat. It was still month to month, but with Harper's help,

Baking with Eva now had three hundred thousand Instagram followers and a growing mail-order business that helped make each month a little bit better than the last. Eva's growing list of brand partnerships didn't hurt either.

Now Harper was helping her parents build a brand and audience for the Inn. It wasn't easy, but it was rewarding. And working with them to protect what they had created filled Harper with pride. With Bella's expertise, Harper had organized a roster of local makers that could attract new customers, and the plan was to scale up as the Inn got busier. And Poppy had helped Harper host two author events that she hoped would grow into a proper literary festival and writers' retreat one day.

Looking at everything now, Harper was glad she'd taken her parents up on their offer to move back home, and she had to blink back tears at the enormous sense of pride she felt.

"Okay, let's get on with it before everyone thinks you've gotten cold feet," Bella said, leaving to take her seat.

Harper took a moment to collect herself.

"You've got this," Poppy said with a smile.

"You know, if you're half as good a mother as you are an editor and friend, those twins will be the luckiest kids on the planet," Harper said. She gave Poppy a hug and then turned and walked down the aisle to the sound of applause. Harper took her place at the front of the garden and thanked everyone for coming, her eyes stopping at the sight of Aaron blowing her a kiss. Taking a deep breath to calm her nerves, she took a book from a huge stack, her name shining back at her from the bright green cover, and began reading aloud from her novel, *Under the Influence.*

-the end-

Acknowledgments

Holy smokes, we did it.

You might have thought there was a typo in that last sentence. But going from idea to bookshelf, the creation of a novel truly takes a village. In the process, writing these acknowledgments seemed especially daunting, mostly because I feel so fortunate to have so many people in my life that I didn't want to forget anyone. As a debut author, I browsed the bookshelves of my favorite authors for a source of inspiration on how to put these pages together.

What I found, are most authors:

A. Are super cool and have a brief one-paragraph tribute with mostly names and a few choice words

B. Give longer shoutouts and call out their favorite coffee shops

C. Have sentimental tributes that are quite lengthy

Being a new author and feeling a little bit like I get to go rogue with these pages, I will be doing the latter. This feels like my grown-up yearbook, so here we go.

This book would not be possible without my extraordinary literary agent, Mollie Glick. You believed not only in me, but in this story, and I am forever indebted to you. To know I am on your roster of clients from Matthew McConaughey to Natalie Portman, I still pinch myself because my street cred is not nearly cool enough to share you as an agent with them. Thank you times a million.

To my wonderfully brilliant editor, Molly Gregory, who since the first phone call has blown me away with her passion and vision for *Under the Influence*. My deepest gratitude to the rest of the Simon & Schuster team who have cared for this book. From teaching me that oysters aren't in season during the winter and reminding me that a character is still standing—your attention to detail has brought this book to a place it could never have gone without you.

Gina Sorell, you are the Yoda to my Luke Skywalker, the Jiminy Cricket to my Pinocchio, the Dumbledore to my Harry Potter, and my author Mr. Miyagi. This book wouldn't be this book without you.

To my incredible manager, Jennie Church-Cooper, holy crap . . . we did it. Thank you for enduring all my middle-of-the-night text messages, for not caring that our group chat had a bunch of emojis in it, lengthy phone calls, and being there for me every moment I panicked during this process. Sincerely, thank you.

Megan Dailey, you are my greatest confidant, my soulmate in a million ways, and the truest friend I have been honored to have for two decades. My biggest wish for everyone reading this is that you are lucky enough to have a Megan in your life. You were the first person I told this *"crazy idea about a book I want to write."* You were my first phone call about my book deal. Plus, you endured the pain of reading all the versions of this novel, and let me bore you with the early sucky Microsoft

Word chapters. Megan, there are no words for all the ways I want to tell you thank you. So, I will keep it simple: my life wouldn't be my life without you in it.

To my partner in crime and the Miranda to my Carrie, Ally Beaulieu. You have had a front-row seat to this journey. From late-night runs for celebratory ice cream at Van Leeuwens, fancy champagne at bars we can't afford, and the millions of minutes clocked of me ranting about this book's journey. When I think about my life's biggest moments, you are next to me through every one.

My life would be incredibly less bright without CC Calbonero. Somehow it feels like we've lived a thousand lives in one and I am so grateful that you've been by my side through every one of them. Doing life together has brought so much joy into my world. Also, I'm much closer to having a six-pack because of the laughs we've shared. This book is better, and I am better because of you.

Thank you to my incredible friends who somehow always answer my unannounced last-minute calls, Dominique Castellanos, Brad Chandler, Amber Herron, Lindsay Honnaker, Lo McConnell, Austin Gandy, and Madison Tucker. Thank you for locking elbows with me and being the best cheerleaders I could ask for.

I basically had the song "Firework" by Katy Perry playing on repeat while working on this book, along with every Taylor Swift album. Certainly, neither of you will read this section of the book, but if somehow you do . . . Hi, I love you!

Cooper, the best quarantine buddy, *the goodest boy*, and the one who always licks my tears away. If you are not a dog person, then you will think I am crazy. If you are, you understand the depths of companionship a pup can have in your life. Cooper, thank you for being the most loyal pet and staying up with me during the long nights.

A huge, slightly tearful thank you to my parents. My mother is the blueprint for what being a strong woman looks like. There wasn't a day in my life that I doubted what a woman was capable of because of you. Most young kids think their dad is a superhero, but how lucky am I to know my mom is superwoman.

To my late father, I hope you are proud that our last name is on a bookshelf. My favorite memories are the ones in the library—checking out too many books and having Mom get mad at us when we had to pay the late fees. I know in another world you are reading this novel, dog-earring the pages, and probably calling me upset about the chapters with Aaron. Thank you for giving me your love for books. I still see you down every book aisle, and our memories will forever be held in the pages of this book.

Thank you to Angela and Kevin Olivero for being there, always. Thank you for the endless meals you've supplied me (I probably still owe you a Venmo or two), thank you for making your guest room my second home, and thank you for being my two rocks I can always turn to. Your support during this process has meant the world to me.

A from-the-bottom-of-my-heart thank you to my brother, Jeremy Crooks, who reminds me through his dedication every day to never give up on your passion. An extra special thank you to the rest of my family, the greatest built-in best friends a girl could ask for. You guys make the good days great and the bad days better. To my grandma Evangelina, who sadly passed away during the creation of this novel. You moved to the US from the Philippines at such a young age, and I am honored to have been given the opportunities I have today because of you. I can because you did.

To New York City, my home. A place comprised of so many main character stories. The backdrop where all of my wildest dreams came true. I can't imagine a better setting to inspire me, energize me, and ultimately rebuild my life. I loved you in a New York minute, thank you.

Bringing up the anchor is the one person I thought might never exist. Brett Conti, I don't know what I did right in the world to deserve you, but I do know that I'll never stop thanking the universe for it. You have been there for me unconditionally since the day you asked me for coffee at that Italian coffee shop in the West Village (and, oh man, I am so glad I said yes). Thank you for talking me up to anyone who would listen, for waking me up every morning with a smile, and for reminding me who I am when I have doubts. Your love and support fuels me on the hard days. Thank you for turning all the love stories into *real-life stories*. You will always be the last sentence of every book or story I ever tell, this one's for you. I love you.